SOME GOLDEN HARBOR

BAEN BOOKS by DAVID DRAKE

SOME GOLDEN HARBOR

DAVID DRAKE

SOME GOLDEN HARBOR

A Baen Books Original

Baen Publishing Enterprises
P.O. Box 1403
Riverdale, NY 10471
www.baen.com

ISBN 10: 1-4165-2080-5
ISBN 13: 978-1-4165-2080-1

Cover art by Stephen Hickman

First printing, September 2006

Distributed by Simon & Schuster
1230 Avenue of the Americas
New York, NY 10020

Library of Congress Cataloging-in-Publication Data:

Drake, David.
  Some golden harbor / David Drake.
      p. cm.
  "A Baen Books original"—T.p. verso.
  ISBN-13: 978-1-4165-2080-1
  ISBN-10: 1-4165-2080-5
  1. Leary, Daniel (Fictitious character)—Fiction. 2. Mundy, Adele
(Fictitious character)—Fiction. 3. Space warfare—Fiction. I. Title.

  PS3554.R196S66 2006
  813'.54—dc22

                                    2006015234

Printed in the United States of America

10 9 8 7 6 5 4 3 2 1

DEDICATION

To Barry Malzberg
A friend of many years,
with whom I live in the Land of Science Fiction

ACKNOWLEDGMENTS

Dan Breen, my first reader, continues to catch clerical errors that I'd missed at least twice. Not infrequently he'll also ask a question like, "How did she get from there to here?," which is even more valuable.

Oh, *boy*, did I kill computers this time. The score was four or five, all for different reasons and all within a period of weeks. The prize was when I decided to change my pattern and bought a brand new Compaq, which gave splendid service before dying on Day Five (yes, taking with it my day's work; but that was my fault). Compaq instantly sent a new hard drive, which solved the problem. (And I redid the work. Hey, nobody's shooting at me.)

Keeping me going with expertise, parts, and labor were Mark Van Name, my wife Jo, and most particularly my son Jonathan. And I should mention that in the course of my frustration, Allyn Vogel taught me to disconnect the Insert key, which has been a thorn in my side ever since I had to switch to the Windows operating system. My life would be much darker without family and friends.

Dorothy Day checked continuity for me during the writing, and my webmaster Karen Zimmerman dug up bits of desired information. (For example, finding the lyrics to *Morgenrot*, which I then translated in a rough-and-ready fashion for a throwaway scene.) Both of them also archived my texts as I completed them. (See above. This was a *really* good book to archive in distant parts of the country.)

Dorothy and Evan Ladouceur then went over the completed manuscript for mistakes that'd survived my first two passes. (And believe me, I caught my share of stupid errors.)

Besides picking up replacement keyboards (yes, two of them) and the like and feeding me superbly, my wife Jo provides someone to whom I can burble about the plot problem I'm facing or the neat thing I've just learned. This is enormously helpful.

Even though *Some Golden Harbor* is a solo novel, it would be significantly less good if I didn't have a support structure which you literally couldn't buy. This is a blessing whose full extent can be appreciated only by those few who are similarly fortunate.

—Dave Drake
david-drake.com

AUTHOR'S NOTE

I've based the setting of *Some Golden Harbor* on political and military events taking place during the early fifth century BC in Southern Italy (Aricia, Cumae, and the Etruscan federation). All right, that's a little obscure even for me, but I found the discussion of Aristodemus of Cumae in an aside by Dionysius of Halicarnassus to be an extremely clear account of the rise and eventual fall of an ancient tyrant.

There's more real information here than in the lengthy, tendentious, and generally rhetorical disquisitions on Coriolanus (a near contemporary, by the way). I suspect that's because Aristodemus is unimportant except as a footnote to Roman history, whereas Gaius Marcius Coriolanus provided one of the basic myths of Rome. The real Coriolanus and the real events involving him are buried under a structure of invention, but nobody had a reason to do that in regard to Aristodemus.

While the basic politico-military situation comes from ancient history, I took most of the business on Dunbar's World from the South during the American Civil War and the Republicans during the Spanish Civil War. I've enormously simplified what went on in both cases.

Every time I really dig into a period I learn that what a secondary history gave two lines to was an incredibly complex business that could've as easily gone the other way. I'm pleased when I meet people who know any history at all, but I do wish that people who've read only secondary sources (or worse, have watched a TV show on the subject) would keep in mind that there's a lot beneath the surface of any major historical event. I want to scream every time I hear someone say something along the lines of, "What *really* caused the Roman Civil War was—"

No, it didn't. Nothing that complicated has a single, simple causation. When somebody frames his statement in those terms (those doing so have invariably been male in my experience), he proves that he doesn't know enough to discuss the subject.

The scattered human societies I postulate for this series would have many systems of weights and measures. Rather than try to duplicate that reality and thereby confuse readers without advancing my story, I've simply put Cinnabar on the English system while the Alliance is metric. I don't believe either system will be in use two millennia from now, but regardless: my business is storytelling, not prediction.

—Dave Drake

And some are wilder comrades, sworn to seek
If any golden harbor be for men
In seas of Death and sunless gulfs of Doubt.

—Alfred, Lord Tennyson
Prefatory Sonnet to "The Nineteenth Century"

CHAPTER 1

Xenos on Cinnabar

"This way, mistress," said the hostess of Pleasaunce Style, dipping slightly at the knees before turning to lead Adele Mundy into the restaurant. "Your luncheon companion is waiting. Ah . . .?"

She turned, a look of question if not concern on her perfectly formed face. "Your companion requested a table in the Sky Room where you'll be seen by all. You were aware of that, mistress?"

The hostess was slender and had been tall even before she'd teased her brunette hair up on stiffeners of mauve feathers that matched her dress. The coiffeur formed a curtained cage in which an insect the size of Adele's thumb sat and shrieked. That would've been irritating enough by itself, but all the waitresses were wearing similar hairdos. The insects sang in stridently different keys.

"I didn't know that," Adele said, trying not to sound snappish, "but it doesn't matter."

"Of course, mistress," the hostess said and resumed her smooth progress into the restaurant.

Adele supposed the question had been a criticism of her suit, light gray with a thin black stripe. Though as expensive as the clothing of the other diners, it was conservatively cut. The hostess might've preferred rags—which could've been a cutting-edge fashion statement—to Adele's muted respectability.

1

Adele smiled thinly, wondering if she might be able to convince the hostess that she was really a trend-setter; that in the past several weeks her severe garments had become the rage on Bryce and Pleasaunce, respectively the intellectual and political centers of the Alliance of Free Stars. She very possibly could—she could ape a Bryce accent flawlessly—but it'd be a pointless thing to do.

Given that life generally appeared to be pointless, though . . . She'd see whether the idea continued to appeal to her after she'd met with Maurice Claverhouse.

The hostess led Adele up a sweeping staircase to the mezzanine hanging over the middle of the regular dining area. People on the main floor followed them with their eyes. Under other circumstances that would've irritated her, but this meeting was work. Adele was a signals officer in the Republic of Cinnabar Navy and an agent for Mistress Bernis Sand, the Republic's spymaster. Both appointments had put her in situations more uncomfortable than lunching in a trendy restaurant.

"Watch your step," the hostess warned, gesturing toward the flared landing at the top of the stairs. It joined the mezzanine proper on a thin curved line: the Sky Room must rotate. Though the floor had a cloudy presence when viewed from below, it was clear when Adele looked down.

There were only six tables in the Sky Room, arranged to put the diners on display. A reservation here obviously required more than money, making Adele wonder again why Claverhouse had chosen this venue for their meeting. Several of those present were dressed in fashions as extreme as those of the servers, though they didn't have insects in their hair.

Adele permitted herself a minuscule grin. Not deliberately, at any rate, and in this company the likelihood of lice was slight compared with the sort of places in which poverty had forced Adele to eat and sleep for many years.

The Mundys of Chatsworth had been among the wealthiest and most powerful nobles on Cinnabar, but their property'd been confiscated when they were executed for treason during the Three Circles Conspiracy seventeen standard years ago. Adele, then sixteen, had survived because she was on Bryce to continue her education in the Academic Collections there. The director, Mistress Boileau, had acted as Adele's protector as well as mentor, but she herself wasn't wealthy.

Adele kept a straight face as she glanced past the man at the adjacent table wearing diaphanous garments trimmed with what seemed to be random patches of fur. If it hadn't been for the Three Circles Conspiracy, Adele Mundy would've had a circle of acquaintances who'd keep her abreast of current fashions like those. She'd continue to manage to live with her ignorance, however.

The hostess stopped beside a table whose present occupant, a man in what looked at first glance like a uniform in gold braid and puce, rose to greet her. "Little Adele," he said. "Still the studious little girl, I see."

"Good day, Maurice," Adele said. *What was proper etiquette in greeting a man who'd been old when you last met him as a child?* "I'm still studious, yes. And probably as girlish as I ever was."

Which meant not girlish at all, as people generally defined such things. Adele'd been quiet and serious from as far back as she could remember. Her best friends had always been books and the knowledge books brought her. Her little sister Agatha, though, had liked dolls and people and games. When Agatha was ten years old, two soldiers had identified her as a Mundy and therefore a traitor; and they'd cut her head off with their knives.

The hostess drew a chair out for her. Adele found such displays of empty subservience irritating, but objecting would simply delay matters and might offend the man from whom she hoped to glean current information about the situation on Dunbar's World.

Why *had* Claverhouse picked a place like this to meet, though? Adele didn't care, but she'd have thought he'd have been more comfortable in Chatsworth Minor, now her townhouse and a familiar resort for Claverhouse in the days when her father, Lucius Mundy, led the Popular Party.

The old man sat back heavily. The years had weighed on him. He wasn't overweight in the usual sense, but flesh seemed to hang in soft masses from the rack of his bones. He wheezed slightly as he said, "Little Adele. I was more surprised than I can say to hear from you as soon as I arrived back on Cinnabar after all these years. I hadn't realized that you—"

He paused, meeting Adele's eyes; his breath caught again and his hand tightened on his glass. He'd been waiting long enough—though Adele was precisely on time—to have gotten a drink layered in liqueurs of differing colors.

"—survived. If you don't mind an old man saying so."

Why don't the layers mix? As the question popped into her mind, Adele reached reflexively for the personal data unit she carried in a pocket specially sewn into the right thigh of every pair of trousers she owned. The little unit probably held the answer. Even if it didn't, she'd coupled it to every major database here in Xenos—including those whose access was supposedly restricted.

Some people said that knowledge was power. To Adele Mundy, knowledge was life itself.

But the knowledge she'd come to gather had nothing to do with drink preparation, so she managed to restrain her hand. Smiling to herself, she said, "I was off-planet during the Proscriptions. Your assumption would've been correct for the other members of the family, however."

Maybe the smile was the wrong expression under the circumstances. Claverhouse looked stricken and gulped down half the contents of his tall glass.

Adele grimaced, wishing she were better at social interactions. She never seemed to say or do the right thing. *For pity's sake,* he'd *brought the subject up!*

"I was surprised to see the name of an old acquaintance—"

Should she have said "friend"?

"—when I was checking records of recent arrivals from Dunbar's World, Maurice," she said, plowing ahead because she couldn't think of any better way to proceed. "I've been assigned to assist Commander Leary—I'm an RCN officer myself, warrant officer that is—in his mission to Dunbar's World, so I need information on the present situation there. The invasion by Pellegrino, that is."

"You said as much when you asked for a meeting," Claverhouse said heavily. "Among the other surprises that gave me was was learning that Lucius' elder daughter had joined the Navy."

"Navy" was the civilian term for what anyone in the service called the RCN. Adele didn't correct him—the old man *was* a civilian, after all—but her smile was a touch stiffer than it might otherwise have been. Claverhouse had reminded her how much she'd had to change because the world into which she'd been born had changed.

The odd thing was, the thing that Adele would never have believed at the moment she learned that the heads of her parents and most of their friends were displayed on the Speaker's Rock in the center of Xenos, was that the change was largely for the better. Better by the terms in which she judged things now. The RCN had become more of a family than her blood relatives would ever have been, and she had a remarkably close friend in Daniel Leary.

Even though his father, Speaker Leary, was the man whose proscriptions had ended the Three Circles Conspiracy and most of the Mundy family.

"Would mistress like a drink before her meal?" asked a waitress. This one's fine blond hair gave Adele a better view of the caged bug. It had six legs, large, clear wings, and a thoroughly unpleasant voice.

Daniel would be interested: he liked both natural history and pretty young blondes. As well as pretty young brunettes, pretty young redheads, and any other variety of pretty young woman.

"Yes," said Adele, taking the wine list and indicating the first offering under the heading WHITE WINES. She didn't care, not even a little bit, but she'd long since learned that saying, "I don't care," to a waiter would only create more delay. "A glass of that. Thank you."

"And another Volcano for me," said Claverhouse. An amber half inch remained of his drink; he finished it and shoved the glass toward the waitress.

His eyes remained on Adele. When the blonde and her insect took themselves away, he said, "Do you suppose that they really do dress like that on Pleasaunce? Or is it an elaborate joke?"

Adele shrugged. "In my experience," she said, "the people who really care about fashion don't have a sense of humor. Yes, I think a certain class of people on Pleasaunce goes about with bugs in its hair... or did recently, at any rate. I suppose there's some delay in information since war's become open again."

The Republic of Cinnabar and the Alliance of Free Stars were the major groupings that'd appeared since the thousand-year Hiatus from star travel. There was always rivalry and often war, but even during war there was a degree of social and artistic intercourse. There was nothing surprising about a restaurant in Xenos, the capital of the Republic, naming and modeling itself on the style of the chief planet of the Alliance; nor was it surprising that Adele Mundy had studied for a decade on Bryce while the RCN battled Alliance squadrons across the whole human galaxy.

"Sometimes it's difficult to keep a sense of humor," Claverhouse said, his eyes unfocused. He cleared his throat and went on more purposefully, "You said, 'the Pellegrinian invasion of Dunbar's World' but that's not precisely what happened. Pellegrino isn't within Ganpat's Reach the way Dunbar's World and Bennaria are; it's just

outside. Pellegrino's a significant trade hub, but the Reach itself—
and certainly Dunbar's World—was a backwater where an exile
could carry on a business without attracting attention."

He smiled at a memory, looking suddenly younger. "Miroslav
Krychek had been an Alliance colonel," he went on. "He killed one of
Guarantor Porra's favorites in a duel and arrived on Dunbar's World
at almost the same time I did following the Proscriptions. I had a
considerable amount of cash from liquidating assets that weren't on
Cinnabar proper, and Miroslav had two hundred armed retainers.
We went into partnership."

The waitress brought the drinks with a chirping flourish. The
bugs seemed to make the sound with their legs instead of their
mouths. Adele firmly believed that there was no useless knowledge,
so she'd gotten something out of the experience . . . but she certainly
wished that Claverhouse had come to Chatsworth Minor instead.

"And then the Pellegrinians invaded," Adele prompted, since her
host appeared to be concentrating on the fresh drink. She couldn't
imagine how Claverhouse had gotten to his present age if he drank
like this as a regular thing; perhaps the shock of being driven from
his home again had overwhelmed him.

"Not exactly," said Claverhouse, looking at her shrewdly. "You
really are interested in Dunbar's World, aren't you?"

"Yes, of course," Adele said, holding her temper with some
difficulty. *If he isn't drunk, is he senile?* "I'm accompanying
Commander Leary to help our ally Bennaria oppose the invasion of
their ally, Dunbar's World."

"In the middle of war with the Alliance, the Navy is sending one
of its most successful young officers off to the back side of
nowhere?" Claverhouse said. "You see, I've done some checking
myself. And I'm afraid I don't find your story convincing, Mistress
Mundy."

Adele felt her face stiffen. She carried a pistol in her left tunic
pocket, its weight as familiar and comforting to her as that of the
personal data unit. She'd killed with it in the past, killed more times
than she could count. An old man who'd called her a liar would be a
slight additional burden to her soul.

Then instead she smiled. "Maurice," she said, "I wouldn't have
thought I had to tell you that Cinnabar politics can be harsh.
Commander Leary was thought, perhaps with justification, to be a
favorite of Admiral Anston, the former Chief of the Navy Board.

Anston retired after a heart attack shortly before Commander Leary returned to Cinnabar in a captured prize. The new Chief, Admiral Vocaine, is most definitely *not* a partisan of Commander Leary. One might surmise that this mission to 'the back side of nowhere' was a Godsend to both men."

Adele paused and licked her lips; they'd gone dry with the rush of adrenaline that had urged her hand toward her pistol. "I tell you that," she continued, "on my honor as a Mundy. I hope you won't question my word, Maurice."

Claverhouse set his drink back on the table and met her eyes. "No, of course not," he said. "My apologies, dear girl. My sincere apologies. As for Dunbar's World—"

Skre-e-ell! "Would you care to hear the specials on today's luncheon menu?"

Claverhouse gave the waitress a look of cold fury and said, "No, we would not. Bill me for two soups and salads and eat them yourself while leaving us alone."

He glanced at Adele. "Unless you, my dear . . .?"

"No, quite right," said Adele.

"Then be gone, " Claverhouse snapped to the waitress. "And take your vermin with you!"

He cleared his throat and went on, "Yes, Dunbar's World. Chancellor Arruns, the leader of Pellegrino, has a son named Nataniel. Nataniel Arruns is an active, ambitious young man. He's not ideally suited to living quietly at home and waiting to rule Pellegrino when his father dies in the normal course of events. Nataniel has gone to Dunbar's World with ten thousand mercenaries to conquer a base for himself."

"So it's not a Pellegrinian invasion after all?" Adele said, frowning. Mistress Sand hadn't been able to provide much information, but that much at least had seemed certain.

"Technically, no," said Claverhouse. He smiled coldly. "But those mercenaries were until a month or so ago members of the Defense Forces of Pellegrino, and I have suspicions as to where their pay is coming from even now. The fact that it's not legally war between states is useful for all concerned, however. It'd wreck Pellegrino's economy if vessels trading to Ganpat's Reach couldn't stop there as they ordinarily do."

"Ah," said Adele, nodding. This was a legal fiction which, like so many other things that looked like lies, made normal human interactions possible. That was much of the reason that Adele was uncomfortable with human interactions.

She brought out her data unit now—properly, because they'd gotten onto the business of the meeting and she didn't have to worry that she'd offend Claverhouse. What the staff of Pleasaunce Style thought of her was another matter, but she *really* didn't worry about that.

"Ten thousand troops is a large force to transport even a relatively short interstellar distance . . .," she said as the unit's holographic display bloomed in pearly readiness. Daniel had told her Pellegrino was from three to five days from Dunbar's World as a civilian vessel would make the voyage. "But Dunbar's World has a population of half a million according to my information. Is that correct?"

"Close enough," Claverhouse said. "There's no army, there wasn't, I mean, but if everybody'd been behind the govern. . ."

His voice trailed off as he stared at Adele. "What in God's name are you doing?" he demanded. "Are those chopsticks?"

Adele grimaced in embarrassment; another person might have forced a smile instead. "These are the wands I use to control my personal data unit," she said. "With practice they're much faster and more accurate than a virtual keyboard. I, ah, prefer them."

Claverhouse shook his head in wonder. "I always thought you were a clever little girl," he said. In a different tone he added, "So much has changed. So very much."

Adele shrugged. "I suppose times always change," she said. She smiled faintly. "Sometimes they even change for the better."

Her amusement was not at the thought itself but because the thought'd come into the mind of Adele Mundy. A few years ago—before she met Daniel and became part of the RCN—it would've been beyond her conception; and that was the best evidence of change for the better that there could be.

"Do they?" said Claverhouse. "Well, perhaps you're right. But you want to hear about Dunbar's World."

Adele nodded crisply, then smiled again—this time at the serious way she'd responded to what Claverhouse had meant as a mild joke. Fashion-conscious people weren't the only ones who had difficulty finding humor in their specialties.

"The planet has one temperate continent," Claverhouse said. "Most people live there, three-quarters of them at least and probably more. But there's islands, more than anybody's counted so far as I know, with villages and individual farms. The islanders're pretty much ignored by the national government, but they have to trade with merchants on the mainland, especially in Port Dunbar on the west coast."

"The capital," Adele said. She wasn't looking at her display, but it helped her concentrate to have the unit live and the wands in her hands.

"Until the invasion, yes," Claverhouse said. "The islanders have no reason to love the folk in Port Dunbar. Some are helping Arruns, and even those who aren't probably don't think they'd be any worse off under him than under the mainland government. Arruns landed on Mandelfarne Island, a dozen miles off the coast from Port Dunbar, then attacked across the strait. He gets food from the islanders, and I've heard that military supplies still come from Pellegrino."

"The Pellegrinians haven't captured Port Dunbar, though?" Adele said. "Some of the reports said they had."

The only information on what was happening in Ganpat's Reach had arrived with an ambassador from Bennaria, whose sun circled a common point with the sun of Dunbar's World. The two planets had close relations, and Bennaria was technically allied to Cinnabar—the Senate had declared it a Friend of the Republic.

The Bennarian ambassador had asked Cinnabar for aid against the threat to the region. Ordinarily—particularly in the middle of all-out war with the Alliance—the Senate would've responded with polite regrets. Because the Manco family drew much of its wealth from Bennaria and Senator Manco was a member of the Republic's current administration, the Senate had instead directed the Navy Board to provide all help possible during the present emergency.

The Navy Board was responding by sending an advisory mission. Rather than a retired admiral to head the mission or perhaps a senior captain with a drinking problem, Admiral Vocaine had picked Commander Leary, an officer with a brilliant record despite his youth.

"Arruns very nearly did capture Port Dunbar," Claverhouse said. "He took the northern suburbs and made the harbor too dangerous to use, but then he bogged down. It's all street fighting now, that and Arruns shelling the city. The government's moved to Sinclos in the middle of the continent."

Claverhouse drank, but this time he was simply wetting his lips after talking rather than trying to gulp himself into oblivion. His voice had strengthened; Adele saw signs of the man she'd met in her former life, one of her father's closest associates.

"Ollarville on the east coast is a starport too," Claverhouse continued. "There's always been rivalry between the regions, and the war's made it worse. I don't know that Dunbar's World can survive as a single state no matter how the fighting comes out."

He shrugged and smiled with bitter humor. "Not that it matters to me, of course," he said. "I'll stay on Cinnabar till I die. I didn't particularly want to come back, but thanks to the Edict of Reconciliation I could. Poor Miroslav can't go home so long as Porra lives; he's on Bennaria now. My share of what we salted away will keep me for the rest of my life, but he's got a household of two hundred to care for."

"Perhaps Colonel Krychek can resume business on Dunbar's World after the war," Adele said. "Even if Pellegrinians win, there's no reason they should object to third-planet traders, is there?"

Claverhouse laughed until he started to cough; he bent over the table to catch himself. Straightening, he sipped from his drink and met Adele's gaze.

"There's a problem for Miroslav and me, yes," he said, speaking with a hint of challenge. "We met our suppliers on uninhabited worlds, moons often enough, and traded them food and liquor for their merchandize. Then we sold the merchandize to landowners on Dunbar's World."

"You dealt with pirates," said Adele, her eyes on Claverhouse but her fingers cascading images across the data unit display. Piracy was common outside the center of the human-settled galaxy, and Ganpat's Reach was well on the fringes.

"Very likely we did, yes," Claverhouse agreed coolly. "We didn't touch Bennarian goods, not when we could tell, but most of our stock probably came from Pellegrino."

He drank again and continued, "Our freighter, the *Mazeppa*, was well armed, and Miroslav's retainers were well able to convince our suppliers that it wouldn't be worth the effort to try robbing us instead of trading. Mind, we were honest businessmen. We dealt fairly on both ends of our transactions. But when Arruns arrived, well—the firm of Claverhouse and Krychek closed, and the principals got off-planet very quickly."

"I see," said Adele. "Will Bennarian support be enough to drive Arruns back to Pellegrino? I'd think that the Bennarian fleet operating so close to home would be able to intervene."

"I've never known the Bennarian fleet to put more than one ship in orbit at a time," Claverhouse said, curling his lip. "And I don't imagine there's much enthusiasm for open war among members of the Council. They're the heads of the wealthy families, and all their trade passes through Pellegrino, remember."

"I see," Adele repeated, and of course she did. The leaders of Bennaria didn't like what was happening on Dunbar's World, but neither were they willing to pay the cost of stopping it. If an RCN squadron set things right, everything would be fine; and were it not that the present war stretched RCN resources rather beyond their limits, that might well have happened.

Except—because Adele saw things from a wider perspective than parochial bumpkins in Ganpat's Reach did—RCN intervention would probably have been followed by a commissioner from the Bureau of External Affairs in Xenos; who'd in turn be followed by a senatorial advisor to oversee the activities of the Bennarian government. Cinnabar would have to make assessments, of course, to pay for administrative costs and for a proportion of the expenses of the RCN which defended Bennarian interests so ably.

And the Bennarians would pay and obey. If they didn't, the RCN would be back.

Adele looked up from her display. She'd been running estimates of Bennarian trade and the potential income to the Republic from tribute based on that trade. It was an empty exercise now since the RCN *wasn't* sending a squadron, but Adele couldn't help following a chain of causation when it suggested itself.

Claverhouse was glaring at her. "Maurice?" she said in puzzlement.

"Aren't you going to lecture me about trading with pirates?" he said. "Tell me that it was unworthy of a Cinnabar noble?"

Adele smiled faintly. "I'm not your conscience, Maurice," she said. "And the Proscriptions would've taught me what Cinnabar nobles were capable of, even if I knew nothing else about our Republic's history."

Often in the dark hours after midnight, Adele was visited by people she'd killed. In dreams she saw their faces clearly. When it'd happened—when she'd shot them—they'd been blurs without sex or personality, aiming points in the shattered swirl of a firefight.

Adele felt her smile broaden, though her lips were as hard as glass. *She* should object to the way someone else made his living?

Adele stood, sliding her personal data unit back into its pocket. "Thank you," she said. "This has been very helpful."

The glass of wine stood to the side where she'd set it out of the way of her data unit. She raised it and drank; she hadn't been doing much of the talking, but her thoughts had dried her mouth.

"I thought you intended to kill me," Claverhouse said into his own empty glass. "I thought that was why you wanted to meet me."

Adele stared at him. His face was suddenly that of a corpse.

"What?" she said. Then, "*Why?*"

"They caught me while I was on my way off-planet," Claverhouse said, raising his stricken eyes to her. "Not the Militia—a squad of Speaker Leary's private goons."

He means the Three Circles Conspiracy, not whatever just happened on Dunbar's World. . . .

Claverhouse licked his lips. "I made a deal," he whispered. "I gave them names, dates; everything I knew. And afterwards they let me go."

Adele set her glass down. She hadn't finished the wine. She said nothing.

"I checked on you, little Adele," Claverhouse said. "I know you're a spy. You knew what I'd done; and *I* knew that a Mundy of Chatsworth wouldn't let the Edict of Reconciliation or any other law stand in her way."

"No, I don't suppose I would," Adele said carefully. She'd thought about the implied question before answering it, because she *did* think things through before she acted. And then she acted, regardless of potential consequences.

She quirked a smile. At least she now knew why Maurice had chosen the most public venue in Xenos for their meeting. It wouldn't have stopped her, of course.

"Do you recall my little sister Agatha?" Adele said. "Yes? Did you personally cut her head off, Maurice?"

"What?" said Claverhouse. His hand twitched, knocking over his empty glass. "What do you mean? Are you joking?"

"Yes, I suppose I am," Adele said. "That would take a different sort of man, wouldn't it, Maurice? Well, since you didn't, I think I'll leave you to your own ghosts. Thank you again for the information."

She turned, reminding herself that the stairs down from the Sky Room would have moved . . . and so they had, but the room had made a full rotation and the stairs were in almost the same place they'd been when she'd come up them.

That seemed to be generally true of life, Adele had found. If you took the long view.

"Please come in, Commander," said Madam Dorst, holding the door for Daniel. She wasn't fat, but she'd become a good deal plumper than she'd been the day she'd bought the dress she was in. Her hair was drawn back with a black fillet, mourning for her son.

"Oh, Commander Leary, Timothy would be so proud!" said the younger woman, Midshipman Dorst's twin sister Miranda. "We're honored that you've taken time to visit us."

Her dress was simpler than her mother's and probably hand-made; she'd sewn a black ribbon around the right cuff. Like her brother, Miranda was tall and fair; not a stunning beauty, but a girl who drew a man's eyes at least once.

Daniel wore his first-class uniform, his Whites, with his medal ribbons. Full medals would've made a much more striking display, particularly because Daniel had a number of gaudy foreign awards, but he wasn't here to show off. Midshipman Dorst had been brave, as was to be expected in an RCN officer. He'd been competent at shiphandling and astrogation, though without the exceptional skills that Midshipman Vesey, his colleague and fiancée, had demonstrated.

But beyond that, Dorst had shown a unerring instinct in battle. He'd brought his cutter so close to enemy vessels that his salvos were instantly disabling. Despite his lack of brilliance, Dorst would've gone far in the RCN if he'd survived; but it wasn't likely that an officer who put defeating the enemy ahead of every other consideration would survive, and Dorst had not.

Dorst's attitude had brought his widowed mother and his sister a personal visit from his commanding officer, though, since Daniel *had* survived against the odds.

"Thank you, Madam Dorst," Daniel said, bowing with his saucer hat in his hand. "Mistress Dorst. Your Timothy was a valued officer, both to me and to the RCN. I felt I needed to express my condolences in person."

"Oh, Commander," Madam Dorst said. "Oh, Timothy would be so—"

She put her hands to her face and turned away, sniffling uncontrollably toward the mirror across the entrance hall. She fumbled for a handkerchief in her sleeve.

"Please come into the sitting room, Commander," Miranda said, taking Daniel's right hand in her left and guiding him away while the older woman settled herself. "We have tea waiting."

Softly she added, "Timothy idolized you, you know. That's the only word for it. He hoped . . . he hoped that someday he. . . ."

"Midshipman Dorst had my full confidence," Daniel said forcefully, hoping to forestall tears. "Passed Lieutenant Dorst, I should say. I was very lucky to've had his support during several commands."

Daniel had a great deal of experience with women starting to weep. The only thing he knew to do about it was to put his arms around them and hold them, feeling uncomfortable. That wasn't appropriate here, and besides there were two women.

The room beyond was dim. Curtains draped the windows on the side wall, and there was more furniture of plush and dark wood than that was really comfortable in the available space. Lace doilies protected the backs and arms of the chairs. The sixth-floor apartment held the remnants of a much larger establishment, and while this building was respectable, it was hanging on to that status by its fingernails.

In the center of the room was a low oval table with a top of richly figured wood. A tea service waited there on a matching porcelain tray; a knitted cozy with a design of fish covered the pot of hot water.

"What an attractive cozy!" Daniel said with false enthusiasm. He bent closer to the service, largely as an excuse to look away from Miranda. "I grew up in Bantry on the west coast. The pattern here takes me back to my childhood."

"Please do sit, Commander," said Madam Dorst from the doorway, apparently recovered. "Take the maroon chair, please; that's the one Timothy used when he was home. And my dear husband before him."

Daniel seated himself with care; his Whites were closely tailored. He'd been taken aback by the degree of grief the two women were displaying. Unless something had gone badly wrong at Navy Office, they'd have been informed of Dorst's death at least three months before, and it'd been a quick, clean end. The cutter Dorst commanded had been hit squarely by a pair of 20-cm plasma bolts fired at close range. He and his crew had vaporized before they knew they were in danger.

Mind, you always said something of the sort to the families. It did no good to tell civilians that their beloved offspring had died coughing his lungs out or had drifted away from the vessel into a bubble universe in which she'd be the only thing human until she screamed herself to death. But in this case, it'd really been true.

The women sat in the brown chairs to either side of Daniel. As Madam Dorst filled the pot with hot water, she said, "What ship have they given you now, Commander? Surely it'll be an important one after you've accomplished so much with your little corvette as a lieutenant."

"Now, Mother," Miranda said, lifting a plate of little cakes. "Don't embarrass our guest. He may be off on a secret mission that he can't talk about. Commander Leary, will you have a macaroon?"

"Thank you, mistress," Daniel said, pinching one of the squishy little cakes between thumb and forefinger. "There's nothing mysterious about my present assignment, and in fact I don't have a ship to command. I'm off to Ganpat's Reach as an advisor. A Cinnabar ally's gotten into difficulties and the Navy Office found it easier to spare a very junior commander than a cruiser squadron."

It was obvious that Dorst'd been talking about him. Very likely the boy had also talked about Adele and the work she did for her civilian mistress. That was unfortunate, but it was bound to happen with a small, tightly knit company like the crew serving with Daniel.

"See, Mother?" Miranda said with a pretty smile. "We mustn't ask him about that or he'll be required to lie. Commander, what will you have in your tea? Mother, it should be ready to pour."

"A little milk," said Daniel, feeling extremely awkward. "Just a little milk, please."

He wasn't beyond letting a pretty girl make him out to be a dashing hero; indeed, if she were pretty enough, he wasn't beyond encouraging her. Daniel Leary was twenty-four years old, and no one who'd known him any length of time doubted that young women were matters of great delight and concern to him. Here though, he was paying his respects to the family of a slain shipmate. It didn't seem right to trade on the situation.

"In all truth, Mistress Dorst," Daniel said, providing more detail than he normally would've done with civilians, "I don't have many friends in the Navy Office at present. This business arose just in time to get me out of the way, to Admiral Vocaine's benefit and mine as well. I was worried that I'd be assigned to command a guardship or a logistics base in a quiet sector."

"Oh, that can't be, Commander!" Madam Dorst said, glancing in horrified amazement from the cup she was turning right side up on its saucer. "Why, Timothy told us that everybody at the highest levels of the RCN was full of your praises. The *very* highest levels!"

"I'm sure Timothy believed that, madam," Daniel said, taking a tiny sip of the tea to wet his lips. "But you'll appreciate that his knowledge of the inner workings of the Navy Office was. . ."

He shrugged and gave Madam Dorst a lopsided smile.

"Not extensive," he concluded.

"Please call me Miranda, Commander Leary," the younger woman said with a soft smile. "I won't presume to call you Daniel—which Timothy never did. But—"

"Daniel, of course," Daniel said. "Ah, Miranda. I'm not your superior officer."

When looking in her direction as he spoke, he noticed a data console sitting between flower vases on the table across from the doorway. It was a tiny folding unit, quite new. The rack of chips beside it included several whose coded striping was familiar to him even from six feet away: Foote's *History of the Republic of Cinnabar Navy*; *The Navy List* in its most recent update; and *General Regulations and Ordinances Governing the RCN*, also updated.

"My goodness!" Daniel said. "Are those Dorst's?" He cleared his throat in embarrassment. "Timothy's, that is. I hadn't taken him for so studious a—"

He broke off as the obvious answer struck him. "Ah," he said. "Perhaps Midshipman Vesey left these books while she was on deployment?"

"The books are mine, Daniel," Miranda said, her voice calm but her back suddenly a little straighter in apparent reproach. "I felt I should become familiar with the RCN since Timothy had decided to make it his career."

"And as for Elspeth Vesey," Madam Dorst said with unexpected sharpness, "*she* hasn't so much as called on us since she's been in Xenos. I suppose she's just gone on with her life as though Timothy's death meant nothing to her."

"She always felt she was too good for Timothy, *I* think," Miranda said with equal venom. "Quite full of herself because she did so well in classes. Well, classwork isn't everything."

Daniel placed his cup on the saucer he held on his right knee. "I really think you're mistaken about Midshipman Vesey," he said. He was trying to imagine the quiet, self-effacing Vesey as being full of herself; it was like trying to visualize Daniel Leary wearing priestly vestments. "She was completely devoted to, ah, Timothy. And him to her, if I'm any judge."

"Then why," said Madam Dorst crisply, "has she not come to see us, Commander? Why?"

Daniel looked at the older woman, groping for the right words. He needed to explain what he felt was the truth, but he was squeamish about intruding into Vesey's privacy.

"Madam," he said at last, "I was afraid that the salvo which killed your Timothy had effectively destroyed Vesey as well. In a way, I think it did: she's just as efficient an officer as she was before—a *very* efficient officer, one whom I'm glad to have with me on the coming mission, just as I'd be glad to have Timothy if the fortunes of war had spared him."

The women watched him closely. Their expressions were politely reserved, but Daniel had the impression of a pair or cats eyeing a bird.

"She's efficient, as I say," he continued, "but she's no longer really alive. For the time being—and I hope that it's only for the time being—she's stepped away from everything except her duties. From what you say, that includes people whom I'm sure she loves and respects a great deal."

"Well," said Madam Dorst with her lips pursed. "I'll certainly consider your opinion, Commander."

"I'm shocked that they haven't found you a command, Daniel," said Miranda, thankfully changing the subject . . . albeit back to another awkward one. "The Alliance outnumbers us badly, and while I know that one of our spacers is worth two of Guarantor Porra's brutes—"

Daniel sipped. He'd be the last to object to pride in Cinnabar and the RCN, but spacers were spacers and he'd met Alliance officers who were every bit as skilled as anybody who came out of the RCN Academy.

"—it's still unthinkable that the RCN would waste its finest officer!"

"Miranda, thank you," Daniel said, lowering his cup to his knee again, "but the RCN has many fine officers, thank the Gods. And I'm not being wasted, I'm being sent to help an ally. It's a very responsible position and one that may be of more importance to the Republic than anything I could do if in command of a destroyer."

Or even in command of the cruiser *Milton*, as the captured *Scheer* had been renamed in RCN service. Ordinarily a heavy cruiser would be commanded by a captain, not a mere commander, but Daniel'd had his hopes. Not only was the *Milton* foreign built, she was of an oddball design intended for convoy escort and commerce raiding. A commander with the support of Admiral Anston, the Chief of the Navy Board, might very possibly hope to command the *Milton* when she came out of the shipyard where she was being repaired.

Miranda'd said she was shocked that Daniel wasn't offered a ship when he brought the damaged *Milton* back for repair. That was nothing to how Daniel himself had felt when he learned in Cinnabar orbit that his prize crew—spacers who'd been with him in some cases from before he had a ship of his own—were being transferred straight to a receiving ship instead of being paid off to enjoy a well-earned leave in Xenos.

The response to Daniel's protest had brought him a worse shock: Admiral Anston had retired after a heart attack. His replacement as Chief of the Navy Board was Admiral Vocaine, and one of the latter's first decisions had been to stop all leave. Spacers were kept under guard until they were transferred to an outbound ship.

It seemed to Daniel that treating people like so many pieces of hardware was unlikely to bring out the best of them in service, but the new Chief wasn't interested in Daniel's opinion. His petition had been heard—and ignored—by a junior clerk in the personnel division.

Daniel'd initially been so angry about what was happening to his crew—and many thousands of other spacers, of course, but *his* crew was his responsibility—that he hadn't thought of what the change in the Navy Office meant for him personally. When his sputtering fury had turned to resignation, he'd realized that he was going to pay heavily for having had—or being thought to have—Anston for a supporter.

"Well, I still think it's a pity," said Miranda. "Another macaroon, Daniel?"

"Oh, no thank you," Daniel said, smiling. He patted his cummerbund. "We were undercrewed on the voyage back to Cinnabar so everybody with rigging experience, myself included, got plenty of exercise. I lost three pounds, and I intend to keep it off."

He could've said more, but bragging about his astrogation would've been just as out of place here as hitting on the bereaved. He'd had a crew of seventy-five to manage a cruiser with a normal complement of four hundred. That would've been bad enough, but battle had scoured the masts and yards from the *Milton's* stern portion besides.

Despite the short crew and the jury rig, the *Milton* had made the run from Nikitin to Cinnabar in seventeen days, a week sooner than a vessel in normal commercial service. It wasn't a record run on paper, but it was as nice a piece of sailing as Daniel'd ever managed.

"How will you get to Ganpat's Reach, Commander?" said Madam Dorst over the rim of her teacup. The porcelain was so thin that her tea with lemon was an amber shadow through the wall of the cup. Like the room's furniture, the service must date back to a more prosperous period in the family's fortunes.

"Yes, that's a three-week voyage, isn't it?" said Miranda. She'd obviously been studying the *Sailing Directions* to have been able to pull that—accurate—datum up from memory. "And there's no direct trade, or almost none."

"I've been studying the route," Daniel said. "The Navy Office is chartering a vessel for the mission, a former corvette now in private hands. We have the full support of Senator Manco, of course."

What the mission really had was Adele Mundy, whose skill with information resources went beyond even the high standard to be expected of a librarian. The RCN was indeed chartering the *Princess Cecile* from its owner, Bergen and Associates ... Daniel's own company, left him by his uncle, with Speaker Leary as a silent partner. The contract and funding request were on record as having been approved by every necessary office in Navy House and the Exchequer.

If some months down the road the officials concerned didn't recall granting those approvals, they were still unlikely to call attention to the business. The very best they could expect was questions about the oversight of their department.

And it wasn't really corruption: the charter was on fair terms and the only practical way Daniel could see to accomplish the task he'd been set. It would've taken months to go through normal approval channels; however, the request probably *wouldn't* have gone through. As Daniel'd told the women, Admiral Anston's fair-haired boy didn't have any friends in Navy House now.

He finished his tea, smiled, and added, "I believe it should be possible to shave a little time off the usual voyage with a tight ship and a good crew. I'm actually hoping to make the run in fifteen days. Unless we get to Bennaria quickly, we might as well stay in Xenos."

"Can you find a good crew in these days, Daniel?" said Miranda with a frown. "Can you find any kind of crew, in fact? I know the situation wasn't as serious when you and Timothy lifted four months ago, but now the RCN is having to strip merchant ships to minimum crews. Even so we're short of spacers."

She was a *very* handsome girl, more so than Daniel'd thought at first glance, and she understood the situation better than he'd have expected her brother to. Dorst was a fine officer, a splendid officer, but no one would've called him quick on the uptake.

"As a matter of fact, my, ah, staff is working on that problem," Daniel said. "I hope to have a solution by midmorning tomorrow."

"My staff" again meant Adele using her ability to enter databases and modify the information in them. Her other employer had outfitted her with the very finest tools for the purpose, and she saw nothing wrong with using them in aid of the present mission. It was, after all, a task which the Senate had ordered the RCN to carry out and whose execution the Navy Office in turn had assigned to Commander Daniel Leary.

Daniel smiled at a thought: Admiral Vocaine would be angry if—and probably when—he learned what'd happened. But he wouldn't complain either.

The older woman directed the teapot toward Daniel's empty cup. He quickly set his hand over it.

"No, no—no more tea for me, please, Madame," he said. "I really have to be getting on."

He set the cup back on the tray carefully and rose. "Ah?" he added. "If I might ask a personal question?"

"Of course, Daniel," Miranda said. She flushed, and it struck him that she might've misunderstood his purpose. "Of *course* you may."

"Your, ah, Timothy was owed a considerable sum in prize money from the Alliance convoy we captured in the Bromley System," he said. "And the escort as well, a heavy cruiser that was bought into service. Has this money been paid you yet?"

"To tell the truth, Commander," Madam Dorst said, "no one will even tell us if there *is* money owed. Clerks keep sending us to different offices."

"We've been approached by some, well, brokers I suppose you'd call them," Miranda said, standing and lacing her fingers together. "They offer to buy our rights and pay us immediately, but it seems to me that they'd be taking an awfully high percentage of the claim for themselves."

"I probably wouldn't call them brokers, Miranda," Daniel said, feeling the muscles of his jaw clench. "But I won't use that sort of language in front of decent ladies like yourselves."

He brought out the card he'd slipped into his cummerbund in expectation of the answer. Whites deliberately made no provision for carrying objects, but Daniel hadn't wanted to call on the Dorsts in company of a servant when he knew they couldn't themselves afford one.

"Go to this bank, the Shippers' and Merchants' Treasury, and ask for the manager, if you will," he went on as Miranda read the card with her mother at her elbow. "She's expert in this sort of matter, and I think you'll find the bank's rates are very moderate."

"Deirdre Leary," Madam Dorst said. She looked up. "Is she a relation, Commander?"

"As a matter of fact, she's my sister," Daniel said. "But I assure you, Deirdre would make sure that any member of the RCN got a fair shake."

What Deirdre *wouldn't* ordinarily do was immediately pay the full amount of the claim with no discount. That's what would happen in this case, because Daniel had directed her to take all fees out of his own considerably greater share.

Dorst had been killed carrying out Daniel's orders. Commander Leary would give those same orders again, because they'd been necessary to defeat the enemies of the Republic. But Daniel was also a Leary of Bantry, and as such he wouldn't leave his retainers in want while there was money in his own pocket. Deirdre would understand.

"Oh," said the older woman. "Oh. Oh." And then she started crying again.

"I can find my own way out," Daniel said, but as he was turning to the hall Miranda caught his hands in hers and pressed them together.

"Please come back," she said. "Please do."

"Yes," said Daniel. "I, ah, I'll be sure to do that."

She was a *remarkably* pretty girl on third glance.

CHAPTER 2

Southwest of Xenos on Cinnabar

Daniel stood with his hands crossed behind his back as the tram rocked to a halt at the end of the spur line. His convoy's five cars were from the RCN pool. They were made of pressed metal with no pretense of comfort, and the cush drive standard on civilian vehicles had been left off the suspension units in the interests of cost and reliability.

Adele was in the first car with Daniel. She grabbed a stanchion to keep from being thrown forward; he just shifted his angle slightly, keeping his balance by practiced reflex.

Daniel grinned, though not *at* his friend. Signals Officer Adele Mundy had by now spent a great deal of time on starships under way; a common spacer of comparable experience would probably have been rated Able. Adele was still a landsman in both the RCN and general senses of the word.

The double doors ratcheted open. Daniel didn't let anything show on his face, but he sighed mentally to see that the view was just as bleak as it'd seemed through the grimy portholes that served as windows. He'd known it would be, of course, but he regretted it. Officers on ships as small as the *Princess Cecile* live too close to their spacers to ignore the fact that they're human.

The slough was an even darker gray than the overcast sky. The reeds were a sullen green that might as well have been gray; likewise the algae-smeared mud from which they grew. The only brighter colors were iridescent patches of scum. The air was muggy even this early in the day, and Daniel smelled the bite of kerosene. They must've used fuel oil as a carrier when they fogged the site with insecticide.

He stepped onto the gravel slip. Well, it'd been graveled once, but that'd been too long in the past: the soft soles of his boots settled noticeably in the mud.

He slapped his cheek to crush a biting fly. The insecticide had been at best a partial success.

"But where are the barracks?" Adele said, her eyes scanning the bleak scene. "That isn't it, is it? It won't house sixty-two . . . well, I suppose it could, but . . ."

The other monorail cars clattered up, stopping directly behind Daniel's because there was no sidetrack as there would've been in Xenos proper. There wasn't a stretch of double track in the seven miles from where this spur left the great naval facility at Harbor Three on the outskirts of the city. There was very little traffic to this storage facility, and what little there was fell under tight RCN control.

"That's just the guard room," Daniel said. It was a standard modular structure, two stories high with an overhang at both levels. An officer of the Land Forces of the Republic came out the front door; the two soldiers who'd been playing cards on the bench outside got up and ported their stocked impellers.

"Those're the receiving barracks, so called," he said, stretching out his left arm to indicate the starships anchored almost a half mile offshore. "The hulks out there."

The swamps around this backwater of the Ancien River was too muddy to support the heavy structures of a working port without expensive site preparation. They were, however, a good place to store ships that'd reached the end of their useful lives but weren't to be sent to the scrap yard yet. The hulls had considerable storage volume, especially since the fittings and fusion bottles had been removed.

Now they were storing spacers. Admiral Vocaine and his staff viewed RCN crews as goods to be warehoused between periods of use.

"Yes sir?" said the officer of the guard, a lieutenant. He'd apparently donned his tunic hurriedly when he heard the convoy pull up: the press closure down the front was sealed askew.

"I'm Commander Leary," Daniel said, "here to pick up a draft of spacers." He handed over a coded chip but with it the usual printout that was all anybody really looked at. "I hope you got the warning order so that you could have them prepared for transfer."

Daniel knew perfectly well that the guard detachment had received the warning order: Adele had seen to that, as she'd seen to every other electronic jot and tittle of the process. Now that he'd met the officer in charge, though, he doubted that the order'd been read. Though a lieutenant and by several steps Daniel's junior in rank, the fellow was in his late thirties. The RCN didn't hold the Land Forces in high regard in general, but this one—the name on his left breast was PLATT—seemed to be dull even for a pongo.

The personnel accompanying Daniel, one per vehicle, were walking toward him down the muddy trail paralleling the monorail line. He'd brought Woetjans, his long-time bosun and Chief of Rig; Pasternak, the engineer and Chief of Ship, plus Midshipmen Cory and Blantyre.

Rather to Daniel's surprise, the middies had volunteered for the mission. They'd been among the personnel of the *Hermes*, the tender on which Daniel had served as First Lieutenant in the Gold Dust Cluster, but that was the first time they'd served with him.

Platt scratched his groin as he peered at the document doubtfully. *He could read, couldn't he?* After a moment he turned and shouted back toward the open door of the building, "Higby! Ready sixty packages now!"

"Your orders state sixty-two spacers, not sixty, Mister Platt," Daniel said. He didn't raise his voice, but there was a rasp to his tone. "And they're named individuals, not random personnel."

"Look, spacehead," said Platt, starting back toward the building. "We got a system here, and you're not in my chain of command. First in, first out, and you'll take who we give you."

"One moment, *Lieutenant*," Daniel said. The metal in his voice stopped Platt in mid-stride and turned his head.

To emphasize the expected distinction in ranks between him and the Land Force officer, Daniel'd worn his Whites with award ribbons instead of utilities like Adele and the others. There shouldn't have been a problem in getting the draft of spacers, but there generally *were* problems when you had to deal with base personnel.

That the administration of the receiving ships had been transferred to the Land Forces made the situation worse. The fact that the new head of the Navy Board chose pongoes instead of RCN Shore Police to enforce his regulations damned him utterly.

"You're right, I'm not in your chain of command," Daniel said, quietly again though he could feel the muscle at the back of his jaw twitching. "And I'm not in the chain of command of your battalion commander, Major Joinette."

He paused, giving time for Platt to realize that Daniel knew his CO; if Platt was smart enough to understand the implications, of course. It'd been Adele's idea and her research as well, of course. Daniel'd come to believe what Adele had always claimed, that there was no useless information.

"But Marshal of the Land Forces Leaver does report to the Senate Defense Committee under Lord Manco," Daniel continued, smiling now, "and the mission for which these spacers are required is one decreed by Lord Manco personally. Now, Lieutenant, why don't you just carry out your orders so that we don't have to look at each other any longer than necessary."

"I'll give the orders," Platt muttered, tracing a figure-8 in the ground with the toe of his boot. "I'll send a signal to the *Hopeless* and they'll have your, ah, spacers ready by the time the barge gets there. Except—"

He frowned at the hardcopy again.

"—it'll take fuck knows how long to enter all these names."

"Don't bother," said Adele. "I've already sent the request. You have, that is."

Daniel glanced at where his friend had been standing a pace behind while he dealt with the Land Forces officer; then he looked down. Adele'd seated herself cross-legged in the mud and taken out her personal data unit; her slanted wands flickered like the forked tongue of a snake, licking information out of empty air. With a nod of self-congratulation, she shut down the unit and slipped the control wands back into the case.

Platt gaped at her. "What're you doing there?" he said.

Daniel hid a smile. Adele was wearing utilities; they were meant for this kind of use, but Daniel knew perfectly well that she'd have done the same in a dress uniform. Funnier still was the fact the lieutenant was more amazed at seeing a spacer sitting on the ground than what she'd just told him: that she'd entered his command console and issued orders in his name, albeit much more efficiently that Platt could have managed on his own.

"Got some trouble to sort out, Captain?" asked Woetjans, a little ahead of the others because she'd been in the second car. Her big hands clenched and opened again.

The bosun was six and a half feet tall, raw-boned rather than bulky, and immensely strong. She was just as plain as the vehicles they'd arrived in. When Woetjans taught newbies the rigging on the ground, she used a starter of flexible cable that raised welts through utilities; in a brawl, her weapon of choice was a length of high-pressure tubing that broke bones with every stroke. She didn't carry anything now, but she wouldn't need tools for the likes of Platt.

"Not at all, Woetjans," Daniel said. "They appear to keep the ferry on this side, so we'll ride over to the hulk with it. Lieutenant, would you like to come along?"

He was going to offer Adele a hand up, but Pasternak was already doing that. He wasn't a man for a fight, and helping the signals officer gave him something to do with his hands in case Woetjans belted somebody.

Pasternak was in late middle age; his service cap hid the fact he was bald above a fringe of red hair. He never moved fast, but neither did he waste motion or hesitate. His skills and seniority rated a post on a heavy cruiser if not a battleship, but he'd chosen to accompany Daniel on an unrated private yacht—which was all the *Sissie* was now.

He liked serving under Daniel because he understood the details of the Power Room and propulsion machinery better than most captains; but Pasternak was an officer who took the long view as well. Lieutenant, now Commander, Leary had a remarkable record of taking prizes from the enemy, and the spacers who'd served with him had earned more florins than any other crews in the RCN. Pasternak was one of the exceptions who'd saved his money, and at least one element of his calculation must've been how much he was likely to get from another voyage with Mister Leary.

That was perfectly all right with Daniel. He was lucky to have so able a Chief Engineer, even if the fellow's thinking was completely foreign to him.

"You can't go over to the *Hopeless!*" Platt said to the backs of the spacers who'd walked past him toward the ferry—a double-ended tub, originally a barge for carrying bulk cargo. "That's not allowed."

"Of course it is, my good man," Daniel called brightly over his shoulder. "Come along with us, please."

Though Daniel hadn't expected it, he was pleased when Platt followed. The guard officer's mere presence might be useful in convincing his staff that what was going on was proper even if it was unusual.

Adele, either reading Daniel's mind or having decided Lieutenant Platt's spine needed a little stiffening, said in a mildly testy voice, "This has been approved at the very highest naval authorities, Lieutenant, and they *are* RCN personnel, after all. Admiral Vocaine simply wanted a picked crew for the mission."

"Right, well . . ." Platt muttered. He didn't look happy, but he seemed to accept the explanation. It was completely true, except that Commander Leary rather than the Chief of the Navy Board had made the decision.

Two soldiers wearing utility trousers but undershirts rather than tunics were taking the boardwalk from the back of the building toward the barge. They were obviously surprised to see the spacers and their CO walking across the mud to meet them.

"Sir?" one of them asked. The other tucked his khaki undershirt into his trousers with a sidelong glance.

"It's quite all right," said Daniel with a breezy confidence that he knew reassured other people more than words alone could do. "We're all going over together."

He waved cheerfully. It reassured *him*, to tell the truth.

A twelve-inch outside-diameter steel tube had been driven deep in the bank of the slough to anchor a heavy line of beryllium monocrystal. The rest of the line was coiled on one of two large drums in the center of the barge; a similar line ran from the second drum to the hulk, though it lay in the water for most of the distance. An electric motor drove both drums through a gear train so that one line paid out while the other was taken up.

The barge's interior was empty except for the drive train, the controls—a six-foot lever, now in neutral, which could be thrown into forward or reverse positions—and metal ladders welded to both sloping ends.

Water pooled in places on the deck plates. It'd probably slosh onto Daniel's boots and possibly his trousers when the barge got under way, but that couldn't be helped. He grinned as he boarded after the two soldiers: if they got through this business at no worse cost than him replacing a pair of dress trousers, he'd count it a win.

"I'll give you a hand, Lieutenant," Woetjans said. Daniel glanced back. Platt must've hesitated on the landing stage after Pasternak and the midshipmen clattered down the ladder. The bosun picked him up with one arm and followed, facing forward into the barge like the other spacers instead of back toward the ladder. Platt yelped, but he had better sense than to squirm.

Daniel grinned more broadly. Adele'd come down the ladder facing the bulkhead. She was RCN though, even if she wasn't a spacer!

"Cast off if you will, my good man," Daniel said to the soldier at the controls. He wished the pongoes were wearing proper uniforms so he could address them by their ranks, but behaving as a good-natured noble toward menials would do in a pinch. "The sooner this is over, the sooner we can all go back to doing things we prefer."

Daniel thought the soldier'd check with his CO, but he just threw the lever forward. The motor whined and the drums began to rotate in opposite directions with a hollow thumping. The line running over the bow and through an eyelet added a high-pitched squeal to the general racket.

It didn't bother Daniel: a starship under way frequently had as much equipment working at the same time, and there the noise was enclosed in a steel tube. The ferry was open to the sky.

On the other hand, the cable snaking up from the slough sprayed everybody aboard with algae and dirty water as it wound onto the take-up spool. Cheap at the price. . . .

The other soldier'd climbed the ladder at the bow end. To conn the barge, Daniel supposed, since the hull was too deep for anyone in her belly to see the surface. The receiving ship would be a looming presence ahead as they neared her, but Daniel supposed there could be some floating object in the way.

He couldn't imagine what—and the ferry couldn't maneuver around such an object anyway—but no doubt having a lookout was the proper procedure. Besides, it wasn't as though the guards had something better to do.

"That's a battleship, isn't it?" Adele said, making a visor of her hands to keep the filthy spray out of her eyes. She reached for her data unit, then caught herself.

The flying droplets were probably why she wasn't sitting in the bilges with her wands flickering. Her data unit was sealed—Daniel'd seen it dunked in salt water and perform flawlessly moments later—but Adele nonetheless lavished care on the tool that she'd scorn to expend on her own person.

"She was," Daniel agreed. They stood close enough together that he didn't have to shout to be heard over the noise of the ferry's jolting passage. "The *Lucretius*, built before my father was born."

Not that Corder Leary knew or cared about any aspect of the RCN unless one of his companies was making money from it. Which they might well be, even here.

"She served as a guardship on Plenty for a decade," Daniel went on. "Longer than that, I believe. They brought her back to Cinnabar some five years ago when she'd become too decrepit even for a guardship, but instead of scrapping her they stripped her for a hulk. They renamed her when she left service, the *Hope*. And of course either the guards or more likely the spacers billeted here renamed her again unofficially."

"Yes," said Adele. "The *Hopeless*. Well, perhaps not for the Sissies."

" 'Ware the dock!" shouted the lookout. "Twenty yards, Feeley!"

Daniel put his arm around Adele's shoulders, correctly anticipating that the bow wave rebounding from the battleship's outrigger would make the ferry lurch violently. He felt Adele tense, then relax as intellect overcame instinct. For a moment she didn't know *why* Daniel was bracing her, but she knew there must be a reason.

The bow juddered with a quick rhythm that made Daniel more uncomfortable than he'd expected. The physical shock was slight, but a vibration at that frequency on a starship meant that something had gone seriously wrong with the High Drive motors. A problem in a system that involved matter/antimatter annihilation could get lethal in an eyeblink.

The helmsman—if that's what you called him—walked around the control lever so that he could push it into reverse instead of pulling. A squeal rose to a shriek as the ferry's inertia fought the torque of the big electric motor. At the very instant the barge slammed the outrigger and lost the slight remainder of its way against log bumpers, the soldier brought the control to neutral.

"He's not the most military fellow I've met," Daniel said to Adele in a lowered voice, "but he's done a professional job getting us here."

"I dare say your superiors have often made similar remarks," Adele said, her expression deadpan.

The lookout had jumped into the belly of the ship rather than riding the bulkhead into collision. Before he could get to the ladder again, Woetjans had scrambled up it while still carrying Platt. She set the lieutenant down and tied the coil of vegetable-fiber rope that Cory tossed her around a stanchion.

"Shall I pipe you aboard, Cap'n?" the bosun offered with a grin. On her rough-hewn face, the expression was ferocious.

"Bite your tongue, Mistress Woetjans!" Daniel said as he climbed, as easily as she had but no quicker for being unburdened. "I'll willingly leave the command of the *Hope* here to Lieutenant Platt."

"I'm not in command!" Platt said with frightened emphasis. "I just have first platoon of the guards, that's all!"

Everybody ignored him. That must've become a familiar experience during his military career.

Daniel strode across the catwalk connecting the outrigger with the main hatch. All—well, most—of the *Hope's* ports and hatches were open; those that weren't had probably jammed closed. Spacers sat on the coamings, looking down at the open barge. A man—Daniel thought it was Barnes—cried in delight, "By all the Gods and their buggering priests! It's Mister Leary!"

Daniel waved, but faces were already disappearing from the hatches. His face hardened into a frown.

Barnes and his friend Dasi were excellent spacers. If Daniel'd known what was going to happen when the *Milton* reached Cinnabar orbit, he'd have rated them as bosun's mates. The new regulations covered only common spacers, not warrant officers, and those two were due a chance to spend their accumulated pay and prize money anywhere they pleased.

Indeed, all the Sissies were due that—and so far as Daniel was concerned, the same was true for every one of the spacers putting their lives on the line for Cinnabar. Sure, most of them were going to blow their wad down to the last trissie in the bars and brothels fronting Harbor Three, but that was their choice to make.

Daniel's usual smile reappeared as he walked through the *Hope's* main hatch. Given that Commander Daniel Leary's tastes were pretty much the same as his crew's—albeit of a somewhat higher class now that he could afford better liquor and women—he wasn't about to take a moral stand on the matter.

In the entrance foyer were a squad of guards and a Land Forces clerk. The clerk's self-powered console and folding chairs the soldiers had brought themselves were the only furnishings. The internal hatches were dogged and locked, as were three of the four companionways that would've given access to the decks above and below.

The swinging grate that replaced the hatch of the remaining companionway was also locked, but there had to be some opening at the other end; the compartment echoed with the happy excitement of spacers shouting down the armored tube. The guards had grabbed their weapons and were staring nervously at the grate, while the clerk was shouting into the console's audio pickup.

The soldiers didn't notice Daniel until Woetjans bellowed, "Atten-*shun!*" in a voice that snatched their heads around. Several of the gun muzzles swung around also.

Platt had followed the bosun into the foyer. She grabbed the squawking lieutenant and thrust him in front of Daniel.

"Sir!" the clerk cried, jumping up from his console. "I've been trying to raise you! The packages've all gone crazy!"

"There's no problem," said Daniel. "Do you have a PA system?"

The compartment stank; he could only imagine what the rest of the hulk was like. The *Hope* hadn't had power since her fusion bottle was removed, so her environmental system and plumbing didn't work. The open hatches would circulate air to a degree, but they also let in rain every time it stormed. And with no officers present, there were inevitably going to be spacers who relieved themselves into the vessel's interior instead of hanging their equipment out a hatch.

Woetjans walked to the grating, secured with a padlock. "Pipe down!" she shouted. "All the Sissies are going home shortly, but keep your bloody mouths shut!"

"No, no," the clerk said, looking from Daniel to Platt and then quickly back to Daniel. "We go to the head of the stairs and call through the grille, but we can't do that when they're in a state like this. What got into them?"

Daniel glanced at the padlock; it wasn't substantial. He gripped the nearest stocked impeller and pulled it out of the guard's hands before she realized what was going on. "I'll borrow this if you don't mind, mistress," he said calmly.

"You can't!" she said, but of course he already had. Woetjans stood in front of her and walked the soldier back slowly.

Daniel raised the impeller, then brought it down in a crisp blow that cracked the steel buttplate into the lock's body between the arms of the hasp. The lock popped open.

Daniel really looked at the impeller for the first time and noticed that the LED on the back of the receiver was green: it was ready to fire. He thumbed the safety on. He doubted that the slug would've penetrated a battleship's decking if the bloody thing'd gone off, but there'd have been about a hundred grains of osmium ricocheting hypersonically around the compartment.

"You can't go up there!" a soldier said. None of them wore insignia but the speaker was older than the rest and so probably a noncom. "Bleeding hell, sir! If they get loose like this they'll have us for breakfast, guns or no guns!"

"*My* gun!" protested the guard he'd taken the impeller from.

"Don't act a bigger fool than God made you, pongo," Woetjans said contemptuously as she stepped into the companionway. "But I'll lead, sir. Just to make sure everybody hears it's Mister Leary."

"You can have your weapon in a moment, soldier," Daniel muttered over his shoulder. "Right now I need to unlock the other end."

"Wait!" cried the clerk. "How'll we close it again if you knock the bloody lock off there too! Here, take the key!"

"I have it," said Adele, plucking the chip-implanted tab from the clerk's fingers. "Shall we go?"

She was smiling as much as she ever did, but Daniel noticed that she'd taken the key with her right hand; her left was in the pocket of her tunic. He was sure Adele didn't expect to need her pistol, but she was a very careful person.

"Right," Daniel said, nodding Adele ahead just in case some of the soldiers tried to push in and crowd her. There was small chance of that, but—well, Adele wasn't the only careful person present.

Woetjans' bellowed threats seemed to have brought a degree of order if not silence to the crowd outside the hatchway on E Deck. Dasi was on the other side of the grating. Daniel didn't see Barnes, but he didn't have much of a view between the bosun's legs and past Adele's torso. Kumara, a Power Room tech, was there, though.

"Back up!" Woetjans said. "Give me'n Mister Leary room to stand, damn your eyes! D'ye expect us to stand here in the bloody companionway tight as bloody maggots in a corpse?"

"Back, give the cap'n room!" shouted half a dozen Sissies on the other side of the grating; not all in unison, but close enough. A space opened.

The shift in the bodies in the corridor probably took physical effort beyond just words, but there wasn't anything like a brawl taking place. The Sissies would work as a team, whereas the other spacers had nothing to organize them. As short as the RCN was of personnel, they at least wouldn't have to be in this tubular steel latrine for very long.

Adele reached past; Woetjans then jerked the grille open. Instead of hanging the padlock from its staple, Woetjans dropped it on the deck as she led Daniel's delegation out of the companionway. Daniel suspected she'd have preferred to knock the lock apart; in any case, she didn't feel a need to make it easy for the soldiers to keep fellow spacers in what amounted to prison.

"Atten-*shun!*" Woetjans repeated, making fittings rattle. "Listen up for Mister Leary, damn you!"

Daniel stepped forward to give Pasternak and the two midshipmen room to get onto the deck proper. "Fellow spacers!" he said. He didn't have lungs like the bosun, but everybody up and down the corridor could hear him. "I'm here with a draft for the crewmen who arrived with me on the *Milton*. I'm taking only those personnel, but I'm taking *all* those personnel. If there's any Sissies who aren't in earshot, I want you who are to go fetch them now. We don't leave shipmates behind, spacers!"

"Sir?" said Claud, a rigger. "Hergenshied and Borjaily're up on K Deck with fever. The Medicomp here don't work and the pongoes won't take 'em off to shore, saying they's faking."

"Which is a bloody lie!" somebody shouted from too far back in the crowd for Daniel to be sure who she was. The only light in the corridor came from hatches open on compartments whose inner hatches were open also. "There's a hundred and fifty down with the crud and three died since we been here!"

"Yes," said Daniel, a placeholder while his lips smiled faintly and his mind fantasized about standing on the spine of the battleship and hurling Admiral Vocaine into the slough. "Midshipman Blantyre, take Claud and a party to K Deck and bring the sick personnel down immediately. The medicomp of the *Princess Cecile* is functioning, I assure you."

"Sir, we're going back to the *Sissie*?" Kumara said. "Oh, bless you, sir, bless you for a saint!"

"Sissies get moving," Daniel said. "We've got trams waiting. The sooner you're in the barge, the sooner we can get back to a job that'll benefit ourselves and the Republic. And Kumara?"

"Sir?" said the tech who'd bolted for the companionway.

"Don't talk like a *bloody* fool, if you please. Otherwise I'll leave you here to your religious exercises!"

"*Six,*" said Midshipman Blantyre in the entrance foyer. "*We've got a full load down here for the barge. Shall I take them across and Cory catch the rest as they come down, over?*"

Adele nodded approvingly: though Blantyre'd addressed Daniel directly—Ship Six, the Captain—she'd used the general channel so that everybody involved in the operation could hear her. Adele wouldn't claim she'd warmed to Blantyre during the months they'd served together, but both midshipmen had absorbed what Adele felt were correct communications principles.

That didn't necessarily mean what the RCN considered proper commo protocol: Adele herself was very poor at that. It *did* mean passing on information to everybody who might need it, without saying anything that wasn't necessary. That required a degree of intelligence, Adele supposed, which was praiseworthy as well.

She smiled faintly. And after all, she didn't warm to many people.

Daniel turned to face Adele before answering. He was using an earclip communicator since while he was in Whites he couldn't wear a commo helmet. The *Hope* was enormous, and without a PA system it was taking a considerable while to get word to Sissies in distant compartments.

"*Blantyre and Cory?*" he said, holding Adele with his eyes as he spoke to the midshipmen on the deck below. "*I want the two of you to cross with thirty of the lot you have and run them to the* Sissie *in two tramcars. I'll come down and take your place as a catcher, and I'm sending Officer Mundy along with you. In case there're any questions along the route. Over.*"

He raised an eyebrow to Adele; she nodded and put away her data unit. She hadn't been using it—there was no need to sit on the slimy floor of the corridor—but the familiar presence in her hands was comforting.

She understood perfectly why Daniel wanted her to accompany the midshipmen. The tramline was dedicated to RCN traffic until it got to the other side of Harbor Three. There was a good chance that an officer—perhaps a senior officer—would try to snatch some of these picked personnel on the way. Signals Officer Mundy only technically outranked the midshipmen; but Mundy of Chatsworth had a presence that would make even an admiral hesitate before crossing her.

Daniel turned. "Woetjans and Pasternak?" he said to the chiefs who were sorting spacers as they pushed forward in the corridor. "Carry on here. When all the Sissies are accounted for, follow the last one down to me below."

"Please, Commander?" said a spacer who must've been in his sixties as he tried to slip past Woetjans. "I served with your uncle on the *Beacon*."

The bosun shoved the fellow back contemptuously. "If you're not a Sissie, it don't matter that you served with God Herself!" she said. Switching her attention to someone farther back in the corridor—Adele wasn't tall enough to see who—she went on, "Yermakov, bring your ass forward! Do I have to go fetch you myself?"

Adele went down the companionway with one hand on the railing—not gripping it, but ready to grab if her boots went out from under her. That'd happened often enough in the past, and the filthy patina covering all the hulk's interior surfaces meant it could happen again.

She grinned mentally. She'd spent too many years in poverty to be overly concerned about embarrassing herself, but she *wasn't* going to embarrass the RCN in front of Land Forces personnel.

Cory, a middling youth in all senses—average height and weight with sandy-blond hair—was facing the guards at parade rest, his back to the happy spacers coming out of the companionway and crossing to the open hatch. In a verbal description he'd sound similar to Daniel, but nobody seeing them could possibly mistake one for the other. Cory was earnest, whereas Commander Leary was as vivid as raw flame.

"Join Blantyre in the barge, Cory," Daniel said as he followed Adele from the companionway. "I'll take your place here. Oh, and Mundy'll be going back with you."

The clerk, seated at his console by the entrance hatch, called, "You know, I'm supposed to be checking off every one of them packages before they're passed outa here."

Adele walked to the console. Her anger was an icy thing. Recordkeeping was a necessary prerequisite for civilization, but this *pismire* was using it as a club to bully others. "Keep a civil tongue in your head while addressing an officer of the senior service, sirrah!" she said.

"You watch your own tongue, spacehead!" the clerk said. He was covered in rolls of flesh that must've made the muggy heat unbearable. "*You* don't rank me and—"

Adele slapped him. Her left hand was in her tunic pocket. She felt rather than saw Daniel's presence at her side, but he was no longer part of what was happening.

"I'm Mundy of Chatsworth," she said without raising her voice. She never raised her voice. "In the future you will address me as Officer Mundy or as Your Ladyship. I will not warn you again."

The fingers of her right hand throbbed. The clerk's cheek was bright red and already beginning to swell.

The clerk's mouth worked but he couldn't get words out; his eyes were wide and staring. After a moment he managed to nod.

Adele turned and strode through the hatchway. Behind her Daniel said something to Cory, but she didn't hear the words.

She felt sick with reaction to the surge of adrenaline that hadn't been burned off by action. If the fellow'd said the wrong thing—if he'd said almost anything—Adele would've fired a shot into his console. She'd considered but rejected—initially at least—the plan of shooting *him*, because with soldiers present that could easily have led to a massacre. She'd considered that sequence all the way to the end before she'd confronted the gross bully—

And she'd done it anyway.

"Here you go, mistress," Dasi said, offering Adele a hand down the ladder. She'd walked all the way to the ferry with her mind filled by visions of possible futures, most of them bleak.

She chuckled. "Ma'am?" said the big spacer, walking her down while stepping only on the edges of the treads himself.

"There was a long period in my life," Adele said, "when what I now consider a bad result wouldn't have made my situation worse. There are philosophers who would say that I was better off then."

"Then they're bloody fools," said Dasi after a moment to parse what she'd just said.

"Yes," said Adele, "they are. Or rather they would have been if they'd really believed what they were saying."

The barge wasn't crowded now, but doubling the number of people in its belly would be uncomfortable if not dangerous. Cory freed the hawser from the bitt on the battleship's outrigger and tossed it into the ferry, then jumped to the gunwale and walked along it before dropping into the barge at a relatively clear spot. He was bragging, Adele supposed.

The soldier who acted as lookout had shifted to the other end of the ferry. "Get us under way!" said Blantyre, standing beside the helmsman; the fellow threw his weight onto the control lever. Adele found the rumble of wire cables circling the spools to be oddly soothing; the low frequency seemed to muffle the jagged edges in her mind.

The clerk hadn't done anything that made him worthy of shooting; but his like had been responsible for the worst of human behavior all through history. They were the ones who killed and brutalized not out of belief but simply because they were permitted to. Speaker Leary had ordered the Mundys to be exterminated for what he saw as the good of the Republic, but the soldiers who cut off the head of a ten-year-old child did so merely out of bestial whim.

The ferry grounded in the mud more gently than it'd brought up against the battleship. When Adele swayed forward, she found Dasi and Cory waiting to grab her arms and keep her on her feet.

"Take care nobody tramples Officer Mundy, Dasi," the midshipman ordered officiously as he scrambled up what was now the stern ladder.

"Aye aye, young gentleman," Dasi said, but he was grinning and speaking to his friend Barnes instead of making the irony bite. He and Barnes were both riggers; Adele thought there was a degree of affection in the way they watched Cory scampering along the gunnel to get to shore as soon as possible.

The spacers who'd just been released from the receiving ship weren't waiting for the ladder either. Making steps of their hands for one another and reaching down to help their comrades, they emptied the ferry in thirty seconds or less. Adele looked at Barnes and Dasi—her keepers—and said, "I think I can manage not to fall on my face in an empty boat, so shall we go?"

The riggers chuckled. Dasi led the way through the empty barge while Barnes followed Adele. "We don't mean no disrespect, ma'am," Barnes said with a hint of embarrassment. "It's just, you know, Mister Leary'd have our guts for garters if anything happened to you."

Dasi climbed—the word was too clumsy for the smooth grace of his motion—the bow ladder, then looked back down. "If you need a hand—" he said.

"Thank you, no," said Adele, taking each rung as she went but not slipping or making a fool of herself in some other way. She glowered for a moment, then smiled at her brief pet. In allowing for her awkwardness, Barnes and Dasi were doing the jobs Daniel and their shipmates expected them to do. She had no more right to be irritated at that than she did if they were careful while loading cases of ammunition for the ship's plasma cannon.

As Blantyre and Cory shouted directions, the Sissies boarded the first two tramcars. They carried their belongings in bags or occasionally in small lockers, hand-carved and inlaid: works of art rather than merely functional.

Their possessions were pitiably meager, yet they seemed as cheerful as any gathering of the rich and powerful Adele remembered from her father's day. Indeed, they were clearly ecstatic—because they were returning to service under a captain renowned for hard runs and hot fighting.

"Sir?" said somebody. Adele tramped toward the lead car, glaring at the muck she was stepping in. When they reached Bergen and Associates, she'd hose herself off. Being wet was better than being filthy.

"Sir?" the voice repeated.

"Ma'am, I think he means you," Barnes said diffidently. Adele jerked her mind out of its dark reverie and looked toward the Land Forces warrant officer standing in front of the guard barracks. He'd donned full utility uniform including rank tabs on his collar.

"Yes?" Adele said, suddenly cold again.

"Sir, you don't have an escort," said the soldier uncomfortably. He wasn't a spiritual brother to the clerk aboard the receiving ship after all. "Ah, usually replacements come in and outa the *Hopeless* under escort."

"Under guard, you mean," Adele said, feeling another wash of cold anger. "Your concern is misplaced."

She got into the lead car before she said—or did—something she'd regret. The problem was with Admiral Vocaine, not that soldier. Spacers made way for her to join Blantyre at the controls in the front of the car.

"*Car Two ready, sir!*" chirped Cory over the command channel. Blantyre raised an eyebrow, then stabbed EXECUTE on the control screen when Adele nodded. The vehicles lifted on their magnetic levitators and began to shake and rattle their way toward Daniel's shipyard and the *Princess Cecile*'s berth.

"Can you tell us what this mission is about, sir?" Blantyre asked, speaking directly to Adele instead of using the helmet intercom. The other spacers were keeping their distance, and the sound of the car provided as much privacy as a white-noise generator.

There was no need for privacy, of course.

"It's purely transportation," Adele said. Outside the blurry circular window, mudflats were giving way to factories. A canal paralleled the monorail track for a distance. Its surface was as black and still as bunker oil.

"Commander Leary's going to Ganpat's Reach as an envoy," Adele said, "and the *Princess Cecile* was his best available means of getting there. Navy House rated the *Sissie* an RCN Auxiliary for this purpose so you'll continue to accrue time in grade, but the same would be true on a provisions ship."

"Navy House" in this instance (as with most other things involved with support for Daniel's mission) meant Signals Officer Mundy, hacking into the system and changing entries to what they would have been if the bureaucracy was doing its job. Adele hadn't been indoctrinated by RCN specialist training to do things by the book, and the Mundys had never been known for obeying somebody else's stupid regulations.

Adele gave Blantyre a searching look. It didn't bother her to know that people she focused her eyes on this way thought she was angry, though in the present case she wasn't.

"I was surprised," she said, "to learn that you and Midshipman Cory had signed on with Commander Leary, as a matter of fact. There won't be opportunities for promotion aboard the *Princess*

Cecile. I've been assured that with your record during the fighting in the Bromley System, you could easily find berths on a larger vessel with a good chance of an acting lieutenancy during a long voyage."

Blantyre's face stiffened; she looked out the porthole. The tram was juddering past a squatter camp; children and adults stared at the gray vehicles with listless expressions.

"Look," she said, turning sharply. "Can I talk to you straight?"

"Yes," said Adele. She didn't bother to dress the truth in empty protestations.

Blantyre cleared her throat and looked down again for a moment. She was a solid woman, muscular rather than fat. She was certainly no beauty, but Adele had seen her spiky drive make an impression in gatherings of other women who were better-looking in a merely physical sense.

"Look, sir," she said. "Cory and I were aboard the *Hermes* with Dorst, right? He'd served with Mister Leary his whole time after Academy."

"Yes," said Adele again. "And Lieutenant Vesey as well."

"Sure," Blantyre agreed, "but Vesey's sharp. I didn't have an instructor at the Academy who could navigate better'n Vesey does, not to notice, anyway. But Dorst was thick as two short planks."

"Go on," Adele said. She thought of adding, "And if you use that phrasing in Vesey's presence, she'll probably shoot you without the formality of a duel," but she didn't bother. Blantyre had made it clear that she was talking to Officer Mundy, not to the world in general.

"But if Dorst hadn't been killed, he'd have been the first of his class to make captain!" Blantyre said. "When he gave an order, spacers jumped. Not because of anything the regs said but because he was an *officer.* And Vesey too, sure, but she'd have had that anyway, like enough. Though she herself says that it's Mister Leary who taught her astrogation."

"Commander Leary says the credit is Vesey's alone," Adele said. She'd almost said, "Daniel says," but a discussion with Daniel's subordinates could never be allowed to become that informal. "Personally though, I suspect Vesey has much of the right on her side of the argument."

"So sure," Blantyre continued, "Cory and I could've shipped aboard the *Zoroaster* and had a good chance of making lieutenant, assuming we pass our boards. Which we will. But we talked it over and decided we'd be better off learning to be officers under Mister

Leary than get our pips on a battleship and not know how to use them."

Adele sucked at her lips for a moment. "I see," she said.

"And if you're thinking, well it didn't work out for Dorst in the long run," Blantyre added fiercely, "well, that's what the job is. That's what being an RCN officer is, you take chances like that or you shouldn't have requested a commission!"

Adele gave the midshipman what was for her an unusually broad smile. "I don't usually consider the chance of death to be a determinative factor, Blantyre," she said. "It's a matter of historical record that every other member of my immediate family has died, and I don't expect to be the exception."

"What?" said Blantyre. Then the words penetrated and she blanked her face in surprise. "Oh. I didn't mean . . ."

"I apologize for shocking you," Adele said. "My sense of humor asserts itself at inappropriate times, I'm afraid."

She smiled wryly. "We seem to be approaching the Harbor Three reservation," she said. "Let's keep an eye out to make sure that nobody poaches the best-trained spacers in the RCN, shall we?"

CHAPTER 3

Bergen and Associates Yard near Xenos

Adele settled herself at the *Princess Cecile*'s signals console and adjusted the familiar seat restraints. It was a good six months since she'd been aboard the corvette. In the interim she'd served on cutters, the smallest craft capable of interstellar travel, and on cruiser-sized vessels with vastly more room than the *Sissie*. More room by naval standards, that is: to a landsman, quarters on even the 12,000-tonne *Scheer* would've seemed a cramped steel prison.

The *Sissie* felt right. That was an emotional judgment but—Adele smiled wryly—all human judgments are based on emotion, even those of librarians who conceal their emotions under a thick curtain of intellect.

The bridge had five consoles: the captain's in the center, with the signals and gunnery officers' along the starboard hull and missileer's and astrogator's to port. Each console had a jumpseat and duplicate display on the back side, intended for a striker being trained to carry out the officer's duties in an emergency.

At present, Adele's servant Tovera sat on the other side of the holographic display. She was a thin, colorless woman, a sociopath who acted the part of a responsible member of society out of an intellectual concern for the consequences of anti-social behavior.

"*Ship, this is the captain*," said Lieutenant Vesey over the *Sissie*'s PA system. "*Prepare to lift in ten, I repeat ten, minutes. Close all hatches now, out.*"

Vesey's presence at the command console was the only discordant note in Adele's homecoming to the *Sissie*. Daniel was a passenger being transported to Ganpat's Reach, and he'd insisted that Vesey take command in fact as well as in name. He was astern in the Battle Direction Center, the duplicate control room. Signals Officer Mundy was on the bridge to demonstrate to the world and to Vesey both that this, her first command, was a real one.

In a way Daniel was fully present, of course, since to Adele virtual reality was more comfortable and familiar than the thing itself. Keeping her commo data as a sidebar, she shifted her display to a real-time image of the BDC. Commander Leary was explaining something on an astrogation screen to Cory and Blantyre.

Hogg—Hoggs had been retainers of the Learys ever since they settled at Bantry long before the thousand-year Hiatus—watched with a sleepy expression that convinced most people that he was a harmless rural bumpkin. In fact Hogg viewed his surroundings with a poacher's constant alertness, and his baggy garments were likely to conceal more weaponry than a squad of Shore Police carried.

Adele switched back to the transmissions within the Bergen and Associates office and those from ships and equipment operating in the small basin shared by three private yards. For an instant the holographic curtain parted in a flash of Tovera's face; she looked faintly amused, as perhaps she was. She studied human beings with an unusually concentrated intelligence.

Tovera had no conscience; indeed, she didn't even understand what other people meant by the word. Nevertheless she considered her every deed and never acted out of anger. She was just as safe to be around as the pistol in Adele's pocket, which didn't fire unless Adele pulled its trigger. Because of the training Tovera'd gotten as a member of Guarantor Porra's personal intelligence agency, however, she was a great deal more deadly than that pistol.

Sun, seated beside Adele at the gunnery console, looked over to her and grinned. "Good to be back on the old girl, isn't it? Mind, I'm looking forward to the *Milton* when they get her into service. She'll rate a real gunnery officer, but I figure Mister Leary'll tap me for turret captain on a pair of them twenty-see-emma guns. Don't you think?"

"Ah, if the circumstances arise . . .," Adele said. *There were so many variables behind the gunner's question! It was like being asked the date of the first frost of two years in the future.* "I, ah, assume from the fact Commander Leary continues to employ you that you have good efficiency reports, but a commander wouldn't usually be given so large a ship, would one?"

"Oh, they'll give Six the *Millie!*" Sun said cheerfully. "You know they will!"

Adele didn't know anything of the sort, but neither did she see a reason to argue about something so speculative. Pasternak's warning, "*Lighting thrusters One and Eight,*" provided an excuse to end the conversation.

The pumps had been circulating reaction mass—water—through the plasma thrusters for some minutes with a deep thrumming. Now two flared nozzles buzzed, gushing plasma into the slip in which the corvette floated. Rainbow ions mixed with steam, swathing the image of the *Sissie* on Adele's display.

"*Two and Seven,*" said Pasternak. The buzz grew louder but the hull's vibration damped noticeably. "*Three and Six, Four and Five. All thrusters lighted and performing within spec, over.*"

Rather than turn her head to look, Adele brought a panorama of the *Sissie's* bridge across the top of her display. No one was at the consoles intended for the chief missileer and the astrogator.

Daniel had generally acted as his own missileer, and the *Princess Cecile* wasn't carrying missiles on this mission anyway. Likewise there was no need for a separate astrogator since Vesey was skilled and Commander Leary was aboard as a passenger. Nonetheless, the empty places reminded Adele that the *Sissie* had normally operated with a complement of a hundred and twenty, while the entire crew for this voyage was seventy-five.

She looked at Sun, turning her head this time instead of switching her attention electronically. He noticed the movement and raised an eyebrow. The gunner had as little to do as the riggers during liftoff.

"Sun," she said, keying a separate channel so that they wouldn't disturb personnel who had duties. They couldn't talk without the intercom; the thrusters were running up and down, making every object aboard the ship rattle against its neighbors. Instead of finishing the question she'd intended to ask, Adele said, "Why is there so much noise? There isn't usually, is there?"

Sun grinned. *"The Chief's checking mass flow and the nozzle petals, mistress,"* he said. *"The* Sissie's *been rebuilt since we last ran her, you see. That oughta be good, but it's not the sort of thing you take a chance on. At any rate, you don't if you serve under Mister Leary, right?"*

"Ah," said Adele. "Thank you."

She didn't say, "Of course," as another person might've done, because it hadn't been obvious to her. She'd known the corvette's modular hull had been tightened since she'd been sold out of service to Bergen and Associates, but she hadn't realized that Daniel'd replaced the plasma power plants.

"And the High Drive too?" she said to Sun.

"Motors and antimatter converters both," Sun agreed with an enthusiastic nod. *"D'ye suppose Six knew he'd be needing the old girl for a run like this?"*

Adele considered the question. "No," she said, "I don't. And I don't even think it was a case of Mister Leary being careful. I think he loves the *Princess Cecile*, and he spent on her all the money he thought she could use simply because he could afford to."

I love the Sissie *too*, Adele realized, *though I'd never say that out loud*. Even as the thought formed in her mind she realized that it wasn't true. What she did love, as much as the word had any meaning, was the community of which the corvette was the symbol. The RCN was the first real family she'd ever known, and the son of the man who'd had her blood kin murdered was her first real friend.

"Ship, this is the captain," Vesey said. *"The hatches are sealed and environmental systems are operating normally. All personnel proceed to their liftoff stations. Repeat, take liftoff stations, out."*

"Well, we're lucky he did," Sun said with a chuckle. *"And I'll tell the world, Mister Leary isn't just the best officer I ever served under, he's the luckiest too! Wouldn't you say, mistress?"*

"I think we're all lucky," Adele said after a moment's reflection. It wasn't a question to take lightly; well, no question should be taken lightly, for all that most people seemed to respond without considering what they were saying or even what they'd really been asked.

That wasn't a thought she wanted to pursue so closely on the heels of remembering that Speaker Leary and the Proscriptions had been absolutely necessary for Adele Mundy to find a friend and a family.

The universe posed questions that a human mind, even a mind as good as Adele's, simply couldn't answer.

To change the subject, she returned to the concern she hadn't gotten out a moment before: "Sun, are we going to be able to manage with so short a crew? I know we're not meant to be fighting, but—"

"*Lord love me, mistress!*" the gunner said in surprise. "*We handled the* Millie *well enough, didn't we, ten times the size? And jury-rigged too!*"

"Well, yes," said Adele, feeling a little defensive but trying to keep it out of her tone. "But we came from Nikitin to Cinnabar without maneuvering any more than absolutely necessary. I know that Mister Leary normally replots the course from a masthead every few hours."

Without Adele consciously intending to, her wands flicked her display back to the Battle Direction Center. Daniel was still talking with animation to the midshipmen, but this time they were examining Power Room readouts.

"*Oh, aye,*" said Sun. "*But don't worry, mistress. Woetjans had her pick of riggers from the whole Gold Dust Squadron, though I don't think she took anybody who hadn't shipped with us before. Between them and the ship having a fresh rig with no frays or splices, we'll show our heels to most anybody. With Six conning us, of course.*"

"Of course," said Adele, but her mind was full of wonder at what her life had become and who she shared it with. *I am lucky beyond human understanding. . . .*

"*Ship, this is the captain,*" Vesey said. "*Before we lift, I'd like Commander Leary to say a few words. Break, Commander Leary, over?*"

Vesey hadn't warned Adele that she was going to do that—*had she warned Daniel?*—but Adele's wands moved by reflex to export Daniel's real-time image to every screen and commo helmet aboard the *Princess Cecile*. Where the screen was already busy—the displays in the Power Room bubbled with data—Adele placed the image as a variable that waxed and waned with the gaps in the existing display.

Daniel smiled engagingly at the crew whom he saw only in memory: Adele hadn't seen any point in filling Daniel's display with seventy-odd expectant faces.

"*Fellow spacers,*" he said. "*And you are that, but you're also my brothers and sisters by now. We don't know what we'll be facing on this mission; it's not to a theater of war, at least not war the way you and I* know it. Space and the Matrix have enough dangers without the Alliance getting involved, though, don't they, Sissies? And from what I hear of Ganpat's Reach, we might at least find ourselves alongside a pirate for long enough to keep our reputation as the best fighting crew in the RCN."

Adele heard Sun cheer even over the sound of the thrusters, now settling into a dull drumming from below. The whole crew was cheering, she knew... and as Daniel had known. He had a real talent for telling people what they wanted to hear, perhaps because they knew he meant every word of it.

Adele echoed Vesey's display out of curiosity and saw what expected: across the top a line of green lights indicated closed ports and hatches. A red telltale at the end showed a pump sucking water from the slip to replace the slight amount of reaction mass being expended in running up the thrusters. It was unlikely that the difference between "tanks topped off" and "tanks down by a hundred gallons" would ever matter, but Lieutenant Vesey'd been trained by an officer who only took chances deliberately.

"We don't know what we'll face," Daniel repeated, "but there's one thing for certain: we know we can trust our shipmates. The spacers next to us will do their jobs, just as surely as we'll do ours. And so far as I'm concerned, that makes us the luckiest folk in the RCN. Cinnabar forever!"

Daniel raised his right fist on the display. Sun raised his too and cheered again. Faint echoes came down the corridor from riggers suited up to go onto the hull when the *Princess Cecile* reached orbit. Adele, affected but smiling at herself, blanked the image.

"Ship," said Lieutenant Vesey, "this is the captain. Prepare to lift in thirty, repeat, three-oh, seconds. Out."

The rumble of the thrusters built into a snarling roar. Adele settled herself against the seat cushions. Her mind was lost in memory.

En Route to Bennaria

Daniel shifted slightly to bring his helmet in contact with midshipman's and said, "I don't think there's anything as beautiful as this, Blantyre. On my oath as a Leary, I don't!"

"Sir?" said Blantyre, her voice thinned by contact transmission. "I can sort of see what you mean, but . . ."

Casimir Radiation, the sole constant among the infinite bubble universes of the Matrix, impinged on the microns-thin sails of charged fabric. Even an intercom signal or the electromagnetic field of a tiny servomotor on the ship's exterior would be sufficient to modify the charge and incalculably distort the ship's course. The yards were worked by hydraulics rather than electricity and communication on the hull was by hand signals, semaphores, or occasionally helmet-to-helmet contact.

"Sir," the midshipman repeated more forcefully, "maybe it'd be beautiful if I didn't have to work in it, but I do. You expect me to see courses the way you do and I *want* to. But to me it's like porridge, a porridge of light instead of oatmeal. Until I learn to read it, I won't be able to call it pretty."

Daniel took his head away from Blantyre's helmet so that she wouldn't hear his laughter and think it was directed *at* her. The *Princess Cecile* was a cylinder with six mast rings numbered from bow to stern, each with a mast at the four cardinal points: Dorsal and Ventral, Starboard and Port. He and Blantyre were on the highest yard of mast D6. Facing the bow they viewed not only the rippling light of the cosmos but also the corvette herself.

The *Sissie* was a trim vessel, but even Daniel knew that the ship's beauty was in his eyes rather than being an objective thing. Her sails were set in the asymmetric pattern which he'd chosen to match the conditions of the present, and the web of cables bracing the masts and yards was as confusingly complex as a black widow's web.

The High Drive motors recombined matter and antimatter to impart velocity to a ship, but it was only by shifting from the sidereal universe into bubbles with different constants of time and velocity that interstellar travel became practical. The sails didn't drive a ship through space: they moved it among the manifold bubbles of the Matrix, multiplying its sidereal velocity so that it could reenter the normal space light-years or hundreds of light-years from where it'd inserted.

Daniel brought his helmet back against Blantyre's with his usual care. They were in rigging suits, stiff and bulky but intended for the knocks that spacers got when they moved at speed on the hull. There were enough dangers inherent in standing on a ship in the Matrix, though, that he didn't intend to increase them by tapping helmets clumsily.

"Blantyre," he said, "the sensors and the astrogational computer treat the Matrix as a problem. They do a better job of analyzing it than you or I could. What people can do that the machines can't is to *feel* the patterns."

He stretched his arm toward the sky, being careful to bring it within the midshipman's field of view. Rigging suits traded field of view for strength. Skilled riggers—and RCN midshipmen were trained to do the work of the spacers they'd be commanding—allowed for that instinctively, both in their actions and in the way they turned constantly to compensate for the peripheral vision they lacked.

"You said you couldn't see the beauty in this sky till you'd learned to read it," Daniel said. "It's the other way around: find the beauty and the Matrix gives up all its secrets. They used to say my uncle Stacey knew what the sky would be in six hours from when he last glimpsed it. I thought it was magic, but it's not—I can almost do that myself. And when Lieutenant Vesey's on, which she is more and more every day, she's very good too. You and Cory can learn it, Blantyre. Just open yourself up."

"Sir," Blantyre said. It wasn't just the awkward means of communication that made her voice sound desperate. "I hear what you say, but I don't understand. I really don't!"

Daniel moved his arm to call attention to it, then pointed toward the flaring ambiance below the starboard bow. It wasn't the sky, though that's what spacers called it; it was the edge of the bubble around the *Princess Cecile*, the limits of the miniature universe surrounding the ship herself.

"You see the sequence of bright spots, there between the topsail yards of Starboard Two and Three, right?" he said. "Seven of them, ranging from ruby down through deep amber."

"Yes sir," said Blantyre, wary but more relaxed. "Those are universes."

"That's right," Daniel said, "and the bluish-whitish cloud they shine through is a universe as well. You can see the energy gradients. Now, you've studied the computer's course plot, haven't you?"

"Yessir!" the midshipman said. "I've memorized it! Ah, I think I've memorized it."

"Then you know the computer would send us through the fourth in the line there, MDG446-910," Daniel said. "That will get us to the next stage. What will happen if we enter MGD446-833 instead?"

Blantyre didn't respond instantly. "The lowest of the seven, the amber one," Daniel said, his voice calm. He couldn't expect a midshipman to have the Universal Atlas at her fingertips. It'd taken him years to understand how Uncle Stacey did it, not by memorizing numbers but rather by understanding the dimensional relationships of the cosmos.

"The gradient between us and it's lower," Blantyre said quickly, "so we'll enter quicker and with less strain. That's good. And those bubbles are a set—"

Daniel smiled. She was probably guessing as much from what he'd said as from anything she understood herself, but a good RCN officer learned to use any data available to solve a problem.

"—so the constants'll be similar. So we should steer for MGD446-833 instead of the plotted course!"

Beneath them, 6D's topgallant yard began to rotate ten degrees clockwise along with those of the other dorsal yards. The port and starboard rigs were shifting also; as were, Daniel knew from the semaphores, the unseen ventral masts.

"Which is just what we're doing, because Vesey saw the opportunity when she took a view three hours ago," Daniel said. "It's not magic, Blantyre, it's just common sense and a feel for the most perfect beauty there is."

The furled sails spilled out, trembling minusculely. D6 deployed properly, but half of D5 hung on a kinked cable. A rigger scrambled up the mast even before the semaphore relayed Vesey's instruction from the bridge.

"I'll try, sir," Blantyre said. Her tone might pass for hopeful, but it certainly wasn't optimistic. "I'll keep trying, I mean. But . . ."

Daniel chuckled and patted the midshipman on the shoulder, his gauntlet clacking on her vambrace. "We'll land on Pellegrino to get a look at things from their side before we go to Bennaria, Blantyre," he said. "We're twelve days out from there now. You and Cory'll be aloft with either me or Vesey on every watch. By the time we touch down, you'll both be able to conn the ship as well as any merchant captain and not a few in the RCN."

"I hope so, sir," said Blantyre. "I'll try."

Daniel looked at the spreading, flaring sky, the most beautiful sight in all the universes. It was perfect and splendid, and for this instant it was all his.

CHAPTER 4

Above Pellegrino

Daniel'd moved onto the bridge after liftoff from Cinnabar. He figured he'd made his point and—unlike Adele—his world was primarily what he could touch with his hands, not within a computer display. He was at the astrogator's station, however, leaving the command console to Vesey; Hogg sat on the jumpseat, whittling a block of structural plastic into a chain. The knife he was using looked much too big to do such delicate work.

The *Princess Cecile* was in a powered orbit above Pellegrino to maintain the illusion of gravity. Many worlds required that vessels wait in free fall until they'd been boarded and inspected—Cinnabar did for one—but according to the *Sailing Directions*, Pellegrino had a more relaxed attitude toward visitors, at least under normal circumstances.

Vesey's dialogue with Pellegrino Port Control was running on Daniel's audio channel, but his attention was on two ships: the freighter *Rainha* rising from the port, and the Pellegrinian light cruiser *Duilio* waiting in orbit to escort her to Dunbar's World. The cruiser was a fairly modern ship, built in an Alliance yard or at least to an Alliance design.

Six of the *Duilio*'s thirty-six masts were telescoped and apparently out of service, suggesting she was short-crewed. Conned by the right

53

officer, the light cruiser could still show her legs to the smaller *Sissie*. Daniel doubted Pellegrinian navy had anybody who could put so potentially handy a vessel through her paces, but he wouldn't bet his life on that belief.

He smiled. Unless he had to, of course.

The airlock just aft of the bridge cycled open for a team of riggers to clump ponderously into the foyer. They'd removed their helmets in the lock chamber. Their fellows from the other watch helped them out of the heavy suits, talking with loud enthusiasm about the task just completed and the ground leave to come.

Woetjans would normally've put both watches on the hull to telescope the masts and fold them against the hull in preparation for landing. She hadn't done so this time because the size of the *Sissie's* crew would've given the lie to the tale Vesey was spinning to Port Control.

Vesey sounded determinedly bored: "*Pellegrino, we're a private yacht carrying our owner to Ganpat's Reach. No, he's not a merchant, he's a Cinnabar nobleman. We're setting down here to refill our reaction mass tanks and to give the crew ground leave. We've got two turrets, each fitted with a pair of four-inch plasma cannon. I'm not crazy enough to come so far beyond the established trade routes without at least that. Yes, the* Sissie *used to be a naval vessel, but she isn't now. Our missile magazines are empty.*"

The story was mostly true, and more important it was perfectly believable. Chancellor Arruns wouldn't willingly provoke the RCN into sending a fighting squadron, but it wouldn't be a good idea to tell him and his bureaucracy that Commander Leary'd come to Ganpat's Reach to thwart the plan that'd absorbed half of Pellegrino's military. An accusation of smuggling could delay the *Sissie's* departure for months and risk nothing worse than a note from the Ministry of External Affairs on Xenos.

The *Rainha* was an ordinary regional freighter, a plump cylinder of three thousand tons burden and sixteen masts—as many as such a small crew could handle properly. She was rising ponderously on four plumes of plasma; when she reached orbit her captain would switch to the High Drive to build the velocity that she'd take with her into the Matrix.

High Drive was vastly more efficient than plasma discharge, but the process of turning matter and antimatter into energy was never perfect. If the High Drive was used in an atmosphere, there was always enough antimatter in the exhaust to destroy the motor and its mountings in spectacular fashion.

As soon as Daniel was sure the *Rainha* was an ordinary freighter, he shrank her image to a cameo in one corner and expanded the *Duilio* across his full display. His trained eyes could pick out tags of dangling cable and smears of leaking hydraulic fluid. One of the missile tubes was missing the hatch that should've closed it, though that didn't mean the launcher itself wasn't working; even if it were, the cruiser had seven others.

The corvette's lack of the missiles that should've been her primary armament worried Daniel. If he'd had time on Cinnabar he'd have gotten missiles one way or another, but if the *Sissie* hadn't lifted immediately somebody would've noticed her crack crew.

How many missiles were there in the cruiser's magazines, though? That was the important question, and there was no way to tell from an image of the ship's exterior.

The *Duilio* mounted two pairs of 15-cm cannon, powerful weapons but much slower firing than the *Sissie*'s. Wondering if all the guns were in operating condition, Daniel boosted magnification and focused on the forward ventral turret. As he did so, vivid purple letters crawled across the bottom of his display:

TOUCH HERE * FOR MANIFEST AND PAY LIST OF *RAINHA*.

TOUCH HERE * FOR MANIFEST AND PAY LIST OF *DUILIO*.

He glanced over his shoulder reflexively, seeing only the back of Adele's head at her console across the compartment. *She's probably watching me on her screen—and laughing*, he thought. Well, not laughing. He'd heard Adele laugh, but no more often than he could count on one hand.

Signals Officer Mundy was entirely a marvel. His friend Adele was something even better.

Daniel touched the second button with his right index finger, stabbing it hard as though the empty air could feel the difference. Data for the *Duilio* flashed up as a sidebar, shrinking the main image to make room.

Nineteen officers—far too many; naval commissions must be a perquisite of the Chancellor's friends and their families—and 229 enlisted personnel, where 350 would've been the bare minimum to handle the cruiser properly. Sixty-seven missiles in magazines which could hold 120.

The *Duilio* wasn't nearly as formidable an opponent as she might've been. Nonetheless she hugely outclassed the *Princess Cecile*, even if the corvette'd carried her maximum load of twenty missiles.

The *Rainha* had reached orbit and shut down her thrusters. Now she and the cruiser began to accelerate together on thread-fine ultraviolet jets from their High Drive motors, slowly building momentum against the moment when they shifted out of the sidereal universe.

"*Sir?*" said Vesey on the channel she shared with Daniel—and with Adele, of course. "*We've got clearance for Central Haven as requested. We'll be inspected on the ground, but they're not putting anybody aboard here in vacuum. Shall I proceed, over?*"

"Take her down, Vesey," Daniel directed. The *Rainha* and *Duilio* were drawing slowly away; they'd remain in the sidereal universe for an hour or hours, but there was nothing to gain from watching the vessels further.

Even as Daniel spoke, he felt the corvette's plasma thrusters kick as the landing program engaged. The ship's computer ordinarily did a cleaner job of setting down than a human on the controls could manage; besides, manual landings were unusual, and the *Princess Cecile* didn't want to call attention to herself.

Braking effort increased. The High Drive motors were on the outriggers where the oleo struts damped their vibration somewhat, but the buzz of liftoff and landing came directly through the ship's fabric. The thrusters were mounted on the lower hull, clear of the water in which a starship normally put down.

Daniel grinned: there was a fish-processing plant at Bantry. To this day, the odor of fish offal made him nostalgic. Similarly, the vibration of plasma thrusters at maximum output hinted at adventure and homecoming instead of making him feel that someone was sawing his joints apart.

He switched his display from the starships on their way to Dunbar's World to a view of Central Haven. The port was on the other side of the planet from where the *Sissie* was on her long curving descent, but the computer brought up the most recent image. If Daniel'd wished, he knew that Adele could've imported a real-time view from a ship or satellite in a suitable location, but he didn't have anything that time-critical on his mind.

Central Haven appeared to be natural in outline, but a major engineering project had diverted a river to fill a valley that'd been cut by a tributary. There were extensive slips along the south shore and a considerable city below them; quite a number of lesser vessels were moored on the north side also, though the facilities there were rudimentary.

By now the *Princess Cecile* was deep in the atmosphere. Even with masts down and locked, a starship wasn't a streamlined entity. The buffeting was fierce, completely masking the snarl of the thrusters.

"*Daniel?*" said Adele over a locked channel. The fact she used his given name rather than calling him Commander Leary indicated that what she had to say wasn't in her opinion a part of their professional duties. "*There's a disabled Cinnabar freighter in the port below, the* Stoddard."

She highlighted a ship near the southwest end of the haven. Daniel expanded the image from its initial matchstick size to his full display. It was quite an ordinary vessel, probably a little over 6,000 tons.

"*Something went wrong with her antimatter converter,*" Adele continued. "*It and all the High Drive motors have to be replaced, but they've been waiting for parts for over a month. I mention it because the owner—well, the owner after you go back through several corporate entities—is your father.*"

"Ah," said Daniel. "As a matter of courtesy, I'd visit distressed Cinnabar spacers regardless. I'll make a particular point of doing so because of the relationship. Thank you for telling me."

"*Two minutes to touchdown!*" Midshipman Cory warned from the Battle Direction Center. "*Two minutes!*"

The captain of a Cinnabar ship that'd been in Central Haven for a month would be a good source of information on support for the war on Dunbar's World. A captain who was being questioned by his employer's son was likely to be an even better source. Estranged son, of course, but that wasn't a fact Daniel intended to dwell on.

"*One minute!*" Cory warned. Daniel settled back in his couch, smiling broadly. He didn't know what he'd learn, but he expected the visit to be worth his time.

Haven City on Pellegrino

Chancellor Arruns and his government were on a plateau three hundred miles away at Highlands, but Haven City on the port's south shore was the commercial capital of Pellegrino. Hijaz Nordeen, the Cinnabar consular agent, lived in a Haven City townhouse, and it was there that Adele and Tovera had traveled on one of the electric minicabs which wound their way through the streets however the whims of their drivers chose.

The front door opened. The room beyond was dim, lit solely by a skylight in the roof thirty feet above. "Yes?" said the doorkeeper.

A child, Adele thought, but she was wrong. The fellow was a short, slight adult, bald and beardless in a loose tunic and trousers.

"Mundy of Chatsworth," she said. "To see Master Nordeen, as arranged."

"Come in, my lady," called the man standing across the atrium. The room's only furnishings were a high-backed chair and portrait busts along the walls. "A pleasure indeed to see you."

Nordeen was as small as the doorkeeper and much, much older. Adele followed him around the central fishpond into a small side chamber. Tovera stepped ahead of them, then gave Adele a sardonic glance and backed out again. Nordeen dipped his head to Tovera and closed the door.

"So, Lady Mundy," he said, gesturing toward the bottles and glasses waiting on the sideboard. "How can the House of Nordeen help you?"

Adele glanced at the offered drinks and shook her head curtly. "Tell me about the invasion of Bennaria," she said. "Can Pellegrino be convinced to back away from it?"

Nordeen was a native of Cesarie, a world independent alike of Cinnabar and the Alliance of Free Stars. He'd been a merchant on Pellegrino for more than forty years. The amount of direct trade between Cinnabar and Pellegrino was too slight to justify an officer from the Ministry of External Affairs, so Xenos had arranged for Nordeen to carry out such consular duties as might be required.

"Perhaps some tea or coffee?" Nordeen said, walking to the sideboard. "Or water, milady; I drink water myself. Water and knowledge, the finest things in life."

Nordeen was also an agent in Mistress Sand's organization. This windowless room had the deadness of active sound cancellation. Adele was confident that she'd learn it was shielded as well if she tried to connect through her data unit.

"Some water, then," Adele said. The muted illumination diffused across the ceiling from hidden fixtures. "Though that wouldn't have brought me away from the *Princess Cecile*. Its distillation unit has proved quite adequate to my palate."

Nordeen giggled as he filled matching glasses from a carafe with a fishing scene inlaid between two layers of crystal. His skin was the color of fresh bone, faintly yellow with a hint of texture.

Adele couldn't guess Nordeen's age. He'd been an adult fifty-three standard years ago, but he gave her the impression of being a great deal older than the minimum that implied. Mistress Sand's records on her agent were surprisingly incomplete, even granting that the region wasn't of great importance to Cinnabar.

Nordeen gave her the glass. The inlays were remarkable; shadings were conveyed by the use of gold, copper, and their alloys. Adele had been wrong about the subject, though: the fish were nibbling at a human corpse.

She sipped water and raised an eyebrow toward her host.

"There is no chance of Pellegrino withdrawing," Nordeen said, seating himself across from her. The chairs were straight-backed and simple; delicate to the eye but very uncomfortable to sit on. "Not while Chancellor Arruns lives, that is."

He made a chirrup that might have been laughter and added, "Perhaps you plan to assassinate the Chancellor, then?"

"I do not," Adele said without emphasis. "It appears to me that when Pellegrino's initial quick stroke failed, the long-term cost of carrying through had become greater than the tributary value of Dunbar's World."

She kept her disgust out of her words; or mostly out. She knew there were people within the Republic's government who thought that murder was a simple—they sometimes used the term "elegant"—solution to political difficulties. In Adele's opinion, they were too stupid to understand how vast a web of side effects their 'simple" action set atremble.

And as for elegant: she'd seen the face in her sight picture bulge as brains sprayed out the back of the skull. There was nothing elegant about killing. Nothing at all.

"The invasion wasn't about turning Dunbar's World into a tributary," Nordeen said, watching Adele over the rim of his glass. "The Chancellor is in some ways a kindly man, unwilling to execute his son and heir Nataniel. Nataniel is a bold, *manly* young fellow, a born leader. A credit to his father."

Nordeen's face looked like a minimalist ivory carving. His smile could've been etched with two strokes of a sharp burin.

"But not one to stand in his father's shadow for the next twenty years, you mean?" Adele said. She sipped again but washed the water around the inside of her mouth instead of swallowing it directly. There was nothing unusual about the taste.

"More than twenty, in the normal course of things," Nordeen agreed. "The Chancellor's scarcely fifty; fleshy, perhaps, but a man who takes care of his health. Occupying his ambitious son away from Pellegrino was part of that care. Bringing Nataniel back to Pellegrino in disgrace would be . . . say rather, would not be survivable for the Chancellor."

Nordeen shrugged, more a nuance beneath the thin, slick fabric of his robe than a gesture. "The war isn't popular here," he said, "but it isn't seriously unpopular either. There was a Grand Patriotic Levy to defray the initial cost—renting twenty-one large vessels, and at rates that made the owners willing to accept the risk. That was a ten percent surcharge on merchants—on citizens, that is. It was twenty percent on resident aliens."

He chirruped again and cocked an eyebrow at Adele. "You're *sure* you wouldn't like to assassinate the Chancellor?" he said. It was a joke. "Well, I thought not."

Adele set down her glass—on the floor; there was no table save the sideboard—and brought out her data unit. The information it held on Pellegrinian trade was old and of doubtful reliability, but it calmed her to have the control wands in her hands.

"The running costs aren't serious, though," Nordeen continued. "A cargo of munitions and replacement equipment on a twenty-day cycle, five days each to Dunbar's World and back, and five days turnaround at either end. There's no return cargo, not even wounded returning; for fear of alarming the Pellegrinian citizenry, I believe. Even so emptying the ship on Dunbar's World takes as long as loading it here does. The invasion base on Mandelfarne Island is primitive in the extreme."

He spread his left hand, as delicate as a feather. "It adds up, of course, and eventually it will cripple the economy; but not for two years. Or perhaps three. But what is a father to do?"

"Does the *Rainha* carry troops as well as materiel to Dunbar's World?" Adele said. She wore a hard expression as she scrolled through data.

Her information on Pellegrino came from commercial sources—largely from the Mancos, in fact. It was obvious to her that Nordeen could've provided far more precise figures and analysis, but nobody'd asked him to do so. The failure wasn't important except in the sense that it *was* a failure; but that mattered very much, to Adele Mundy if not to the Republic more generally.

"No more troops, no," Nordeen said. His face had never lost its almost-smile. "Nataniel would like more troops, I am informed, and perhaps the Chancellor would like to send them, but the army is the government's real base of support. Half of it is already far away from the Chancellery. If more troops should embark today for Dunbar's World, who knows who would be Chancellor tomorrow?"

Adele shut down her data unit and looked at her host. If the invasion remained bogged down there would come a time when Arruns needed more money, probably much more money. It might well be more cost effective for merchants, particularly merchants who were resident aliens, to finance a change in government instead of paying another ruinous assessment.

"Do you personally have a prognosis of whether the invasion will succeed, Master Nordeen?" she asked. Her expression of cold disgust wasn't meant for him, but he nonetheless stiffened noticeably.

"I am not clairvoyant, my lady," Nordeen said softly. "Until now I thought it would succeed, yes. The polity of Dunbar's World fragments further every day, and Chancellor Arruns *can* not give up for the reasons I described. But today . . . who knows?"

He repeated the graceful gesture with his left hand.

"What happened today?" Adele said carefully. The data unit remained in her lap though she'd slipped the wands back into the case.

"Why, today the redoubtable Commander Leary arrived in the region," the old man said, "and with him Lady Mundy, whose deeds are even more storied in certain quarters. More storied in my quarters, I assure you. I do not see how they can turn the tide with no resources but those of Bennaria to draw from, but age has shown me the wisdom of judging men rather than mere objects. I will not bet against that pair."

Adele stood up and put her data unit in its pocket. "I'll want a complete list of all the personnel and material that's been committed to the invasion," she said. "Along with the rate of usage and your best estimate of losses to date."

"I have prepared this," Nordeen said, rising also. He bowed to her and stepped to the door.

"You are a good servant of the Republic, Master Nordeen," Adele said, smiling faintly. "Commander Leary and I will do our best not to disappoint you."

CHAPTER 5

Above Bennaria

Adele focused on images of Bennaria in real-time through the ship's sensors and in the data she was pulling out of a dozen computers on the ground below. Bennaria Control wasn't particularly efficient—though there were only five ships queued to land or lift off, the *Sissie*'d been waiting half an hour already—and the controllers insisted arrivals remain in free-fall orbits while they were being processed.

Adele disliked weightlessness a great deal when she let herself think about it, so she lost herself in work. That wasn't difficult; indeed, her problem tended to be the reverse. She was sometimes oblivious of what was going on in her immediate surroundings under circumstances which made her detachment insulting to others or dangerous to herself. That wasn't likely now; and anyway, nobody'd benefit from Signals Officer Mundy vomiting across her console.

Data cascaded in. Adele was vaguely aware that she was smiling and as happy—as content—as she was ever likely to be in this life. Charlestown, the planet's capital, was on the west side of a roadstead fed by two major rivers. A long island—it'd probably been a mudbank initially and still wasn't much above sea level—bulged away from the mainland. The port facilities were on the island's landward side, reasonably sheltered though port records indicated that storm surges sometimes swept the island.

She'd assumed the fenced enclosures in the island's interior were cattle sheds. Being Adele Mundy she'd checked her assumption against the records of port duties instead of just accepting it.

She grimaced. They were cattle sheds in the broader sense, but the cattle in this case were human slaves rather than cows or sheep. She'd known that Bennaria based its foreign trade on the export of rice throughout Ganpat's Reach and beyond. The major landowners appeared to have decided that slaves were more cost effective than machinery. Here on the fringes of the settled universe, one could expect pirates to supplement the natural increase of the existing labor force.

"*Officer Mundy?*" said Daniel over the command channel; all the *Sissie*'s commissioned and warrant officers were included in the conversation. "*I don't see any warships in the harbor below. Is the Bennarian fleet off-planet, or—*"

Before Daniel got the unnecessary remainder of his question out, Adele imported an image to the upper right quadrant of his screen. He'd been viewing the harbor at the largest possible scale. She'd expanded it to include the area fifteen miles to the north, then thrown a red mask over the pool in the river where six slim destroyers were moored.

"*Ah!*" said Daniel. "*Many thanks, Mundy.*"

It shouldn't have been possible to adjust another officer's display unasked except from the command console where Vesey was dealing with the port authorities. In general that was a reasonable safety feature. It barely crossed Adele's mind that she was acting improperly to override it: *she* wasn't the general case.

She'd searched immediately for naval message traffic—and found none of any significance. She'd followed that by searching for facility locations in the database of the Armed Squadron. There were squadron terminals on the Charlestown premises of twelve of the Counciliar Families and an office building on the harbor esplanade, but the ships themselves were some distance from the city.

Only two vessels, the *Sibyl* and the *Tenerife*, appeared to have crews aboard, and even those were of a few dozen spacers. A destroyer's normal complement would be two hundred.

A score of communication streams ran as text crawls across the lower half of Adele's display. They included anything from the ground that might have bearing on the *Princess Cecile*, as well as the ship's internal chatter. A new incoming signal shouldered its way onto the screen, this one highlighted red because it was a response to the message Adele had sent as soon as the *Sissie* reached orbit. She opened the channel immediately, routing it also to Daniel on a one-way link.

"*Manco One to Mundy*," a male voice said. The transmission was microwave from Bennaria's communications satellite system, but it'd been scrambled using Manco Trading Company's commercial encryption system. "*Please identify yourself. Your message didn't make sense! Over.*"

"Master Luff," Adele said, "I'm Signals Officer Mundy, aide to Commander Leary whom the Navy Board has sent in response to the Bennarian Council's request for help. I—"

"*What!*" said Luff without waiting for her handover. Adele was using separate input and output channels so it didn't matter, but he was clearly too rattled to care. "*There's an RCN fleet in orbit and I haven't been warned about it? Oh my God, Councilor Waddell will, will—I don't know what he'll do!*"

By virtue of being manager of Manco Trading's operations here, Adrian Luff was Cinnabar's consular agent on Bennaria. Were it not for the Mancos, there probably wouldn't have been an official Cinnabar presence on Bennaria, so Adele'd contacted him through commercial rather than government channels.

She hadn't had time to learn much about Luff before leaving Cinnabar. The man's obvious panic over their arrival didn't positively impress her, but she'd learned over the years to make allowance for her impatience with other people's poor performance. She wasn't wrong to be disgusted, of course, but letting it show was counterproductive.

"Master Luff," Adele said calmly, "Commander Leary leads a Cinnabar advisory mission. There's no squadron and indeed no warship; we're aboard the commander's yacht. And since the Senate requested the RCN respond with all possible speed, we've outrun word of our coming."

"*Oh my God,*" Luff repeated. "*I'll have to inform the Council at once. But—no ships? The RCN isn't sending real help?*"

"I assure you," Adele said, feeling her voice grow even colder than it'd been, "that our presence constitutes real help and that you should so inform the Council. That would be the Bennarian Council, over?"

The *Sissie*'s thrusters roared, braking for descent. The sound and the sudden shove from the couch startled Adele, though she knew Vesey and Pasternak in the Power Room must've given the usual sequence of warnings. She'd been concentrating too hard on Luff— the whimpering fool!—to pay attention.

"*Yes, of course, the Council!*" Luff said. "*Oh my God, they'll blame me, I know they will!*"

Braking thrust built rapidly, squeezing Adele against the cushions. A starship's hull wouldn't accept really heavy accelerations, though, so this was nothing that she couldn't speak through without noticeable effort. Her voice was already as thin and hard as a razor blade, of course.

"We'll be landing within the half hour at—" Adele began.

A text block flashed onto her screen reading CHARLESTOWN HARBOR SLIP W12, followed by a digital clock in minutes reading down from 17:04.

"We'll be landing in seventeen minutes at Slip W12," Adele resumed. "Commander Leary would like a meeting with you as soon as possible, so—"

"*With me?*" said Luff. "*Oh, no—he'll have to meet with Councilor Waddell immediately. Perhaps some of the others too. I'll be waiting for you as soon as you touch down. Oh, there's so little time to set this up!*"

The *Princess Cecile* was deep enough into her descent that atmospheric buffeting added to the thrusters' predictable vibration. Raising her voice minusculely before she caught herself, Adele said, "Commander Leary will be pleased to meet with the Bennarian government, but he was expecting a briefing from you before he did so. A delay of a few hours or even less to consult with you will permit him to—"

"*Look, I'll talk to him on the way!*" Luff said. "*I don't have an aircar so there'll be time. But if you think I'm going to have Councilor Waddell thinking I've deliberately delayed him, you're out of your mind. Now goodbye, I have a great deal to attend to!*"

The transmission cut off abruptly. Adele pursed her lips, staring at her display in a mixture of anger and amazement.

"*Adele?*" said Daniel over a two-way link. "*Is that gentleman a Bennarian native, over?*"

"No, he's not," she said. The degree of her anger surprised her. "He's a Cinnabar citizen; a distant cousin of Senator Manco, in fact. That disturbs me in itself. In addition he's probably convinced the local elite that all Cinnabar citizens are contemptible worms so our own dealings with them will be more difficult."

"*Oh, well,*" said Daniel cheerfully. His image on a corner of her display grinned. "*I dare say an RCN officer and Mundy of Chatsworth can correct them on that point quickly enough.*"

He grinned wider. "*It could even be fun.*"

Charlestown on Bennaria

Daniel, standing in the *Princess Cecile's* entrance hold with Adele and the ship's officers, tugged the trousers of his first class uniform. He was trying, without much luck so far, to loosen them or least keep them from riding up so badly. Hogg tutted, gripped the hem of Daniel's tunic with both hands, and twisted hard.

"Now *don't* you go splitting a seam," Hogg grunted. "Behave like a gentleman, why don't you? We don't have another of these monkey suits along and I don't want to have to sew you up with a bunch of wogs watching."

"I hope that's the last time you'll refer to wogs while we're here, Hogg," said Daniel. Because of the way the trousers pinched his crotch, he was able to sound more severe than he usually managed with the servant who'd raised him.

"Hope's a fine thing," said Hogg, stepping back and eyeing the hang of Daniel's uniform critically. Then in a vaguely conciliatory tone he added, "Anyway, it's just us Sissies, right?"

"You can open up, Woetjans," Daniel said; the bosun, two decks above on the bridge, activated the hydraulic rams. The hatch released with a clang and began to lower into a boarding ramp, letting in a gush of Bennaria's atmosphere—breathable, though the back of Daniel's throat suddenly felt as though he were trying to swallow a sheet of plastic—and the usual remnants of steam.

Because Charlestown harbor was open to the sea, the water vaporized by the thrusters had almost completely dissipated. Daniel'd kept the ship closed up for a full ten minutes, longer than he'd ordinarily have done, to give him time to put on his Whites. He'd expected to change from his utilities at leisure while he met with the Manco agent here aboard the *Sissie*; more fool him to have assumed, of course.

He grinned. Given the choice was to sit squeezed into his Whites during landing—and it was *always* possible for something to go wrong during landing—he'd have made the same decision anyway. If that meant the Bennarian Council waited, well, who cared if a gaggle of wogs had to twiddle their thumbs for a while?

He glanced at Adele; she smiled in response, though you had to know her to realize it was a smile or an expression at all. She was in her second class uniform, gray with black piping, because she hadn't brought a set of Whites along. If necessary she could appear as Mundy of Chatsworth in an expensive civilian suit, but Grays were sufficiently formal for a junior warrant officer on Commander Leary's staff.

Daniel's grin broadened. The thigh sheath holding Adele's data unit and the weight of the pistol in her tunic pocket were less obtrusive than they'd be on closely tailored Whites, too.

The ramp clanged into its locking seat on the port outrigger. Dock personnel had already floated a wooden boarding bridge into place between the outrigger and the concrete quay, and the civilian waiting on it started up the ramp immediately.

Normally Lieutenant Vesey as the ship's captain would receive the delegation, but Daniel realized from Luff's flustered call that this was no time to stand on ceremony. He stepped forward, saying, "Master Luff? I'm Commander Leary. I'm—"

"Yes, of course," said Luff. "Come along quickly, *please*. They'll be arriving by aircar; some of them are probably at Manco House already."

The Manco agent was short and, if not exactly fat, still plump enough to make Daniel feel a tiny glow of superiority. Luff wore a bicorn hat with a feather and a magenta tunic with puffed sleeves—presumably the local fashion—but there was still a touch of Xenos nasality in his speech.

"This is Signals Officer Mundy, my aide," Daniel said as he fell into step with Luff. Adele'd followed on Daniel's other side, with Hogg and Tovera a little behind their principals. "I believe you've spoken to her already."

Daniel glanced back to wave goodbye to the *Sissie* and her crew, resisting the reflex to call, "Carry on, Vesey." Vesey, blond and slight, was already in charge. She saluted but she didn't match his smile. He hadn't seen her smile since Midshipman Dorst died. A fine officer, though.

"Yes, yes," Luff said. In a burst of sudden anger he added, "They snap their fingers on Xenos and expect everything to be done just as they say. They have no idea what it's like out here for a foreigner!"

A good-sized barge rocked on the other side of the quay; sailors waited to cast off the bow and stern lines. Luff led the Cinnabar contingent toward the glazed cabin aft; the considerable bay forward was covered with chain link fencing.

"You're the representative of one of the most powerful families on Cinnabar," Adele said in her usual tone of cool dispassion.

"And Cinnabar is very bloody far away!" Luff said. "Do you think Senator Manco would care if he had to replace his manager on Bennaria? *I* don't, and I don't imagine Councilor Waddell believes he'd care either."

A crewman opened the cabin door. Luff gestured Daniel ahead of him but followed without waiting for Adele to enter. Tovera entered the cabin also, but Hogg stayed on deck. Leaning against a railing, he seemed every inch the amazed rube just off the farm. Hogg had gambled very profitably with people who mistook the costume for the man underneath.

Tovera, on the other hand, looked like nothing at all: a small woman with a briefcase, colorless and completely devoid of personality or interest. The description wasn't entirely untrue: Daniel had never been quite sure whether or not Tovera had a personality. Occasionally she displayed a flash of one, but that could be an intellectual construct like her grasp of morality.

Tovera was a very drab, very dangerous, reptile. It was a great relief—to Daniel, to Adele, and probably to the parties themselves—that she and Hogg got along well together.

The launch pulled away from the quay with a slap of propellers and the higher-pitched vibration of electric motors. The city half a mile across the strait sprawled on the left side of the Gris River; there were only shanties on the right bank. Though the sun was still well above the western horizon, a mist blurred the landscape.

Most of the buildings Daniel could see were low, but a number rose to six or more stories; an aircar was landing on the roof of one of the latter. Luff noticed Daniel's attention and said, "Yes, that's where we're going, Manco House. The meeting's being held there because it doesn't belong to a Councilor. Not that there's any real animus, not among the families that'll be present, but Councilors Knox and Fahey at least would feel insulted to be told to meet at Waddell House."

"What do you ordinarily carry in this barge, Master Luff?" Daniel asked. The wire netting over the hold wouldn't protect a loose cargo, grain for instance, and it was too heavy simply to retain something bulky.

"Before Master Luff answers that," Adele interjected, her tone as thin and cutting as a snare of piano wire, "I'll remind him that slavery is against the laws of Cinnabar—"

"Mistress!" said Luff harshly. "The Republic's laws do not apply on independent worlds!"

"—and that the RCN enforces this prohibition on Cinnabar citizens no matter where they happen to be found at the time," Adele continued. "Now, Master Luff, you may make what answer you please to the question of Commander Leary."

The Manco agent looked from Adele to Daniel, his face in an angry scowl. That faded to wariness when he saw the expression Daniel felt stiffening his own cheeks.

"I'll retract the question, Adele," Daniel said. "I was naive to have asked it."

The launch nosed into a concrete slip; its walkways were heavily fenced. The barriers wouldn't do for long-term confinement, but backed by a few armed guards they'd prevent human cargo from making a break for freedom while they were being transferred to some other form of transportation.

Daniel looked at Luff. The agent hunched away and said to the bulkhead, "Look, you were sent here about Dunbar's World. That's all that need concern you."

Daniel reached past him and opened the hatch, stepping onto the concrete. He didn't reply to Luff; the fellow hadn't asked a question, after all.

Hogg was whistling a song called "Lulu"; he grinned and Daniel grinned back, and with the others from the cabin following they walked toward the waiting landau with Cinnabar flags fore and aft. The driver, a thin, nervous-looking man in magenta and cream, held open the door of the enclosed passenger compartment.

"You can ride up front this time," called Tovera.

"Who died and made you Speaker?" Hogg grumbled, but it was a good-natured comment. He walked around the front of the vehicle and slid onto the driver's open-topped bench seat.

"Commander," Luff said in surprise, "there's a platform for servants behind the passenger saloon."

"Right, and I'll be on it," said Tovera. She smiled at the agent, or at least the corners of her mouth curled up. She'd opened her attaché case just wide enough to stick her hand inside. It rested on the grip of her compact sub-machine gun, Daniel knew, though the pose was unobtrusive to anybody who *didn't* know what Tovera was.

"My servant's eccentric, Master Luff," Daniel said, getting into the passenger compartment. There were two plush-upholstered benches within; he gestured the manager to the seat opposite him so that he and Adele would be facing forward. "He's from the country, you see."

"Yes, I certainly do see!" said Luff, who didn't see at all. Hogg, a dumpy man in tastelessly garish clothing, grinned at Daniel through the front window; then he resumed his search of roofs and doorways for anybody who might be a danger to his master.

The car pulled out, turning down a street leading away from the water. The building on one corner was a theater with gilt columns down both frontages. The corner opposite was a bar with what must be a bordello on the second floor; the woman lounging over the railing with a drink in her hand was probably off-duty at this early hour, but she gave Daniel an appraising look.

"What resources does Bennaria plan to put toward aiding Dunbar's World, Master Luff?" Adele asked. She had her data unit out, though the wands were still for the time being.

"You'll have to ask the Council," Luff said firmly. "I don't know, and if I did know I wouldn't say anything. That's the Council's business, and the Councilors don't like outsiders meddling."

The harbor area was obviously Charlestown's entertainment district. Spacers could find it easily and locals wouldn't care. There were thirty-odd ships docked on the island, most of them of only moderate size. For a block or more from the waterfront, small bars, restaurants, and amusement arcades squeezed into the spaces between more pretentious establishments.

Beyond that were ramshackle buildings, many of them missing windows or even doors. People sat on steps and window ledges, watching the limousine with angry expressions.

"Sometimes they throw things," Luff muttered, looking at his feet. "They don't all know what the Cinnabar flag is, and anyway some of them don't care. I *tell* them in Xenos that I need an aircar, but do they listen?"

He looked up at Daniel and said fiercely, "It wasn't always like this. Councilor Corius stirred them up! He's all right, he has an aircar, but what does he think it's like for me having to drive to the harbor to check shipments and pay suppliers?"

"Will Councilor Corius be meeting us today?" said Daniel. He wasn't a politician himself, but Speaker Leary's son had seen this sort of gathering in the past: members of the elite meeting at an out of the way venue to determine policy.

"Of course not!" Luff said. "Corius meet with Councilor Waddell? Absurd!"

It wasn't absurd, but the fact Luff thought it was told Daniel that neither the Manco agent nor the political process on Bennaria was very sophisticated in Cinnabar terms. Sophisticated didn't necessarily mean subtle. The Proscriptions following the Three Circles Conspiracy hadn't been in the least subtle, but they'd brought everyone who wasn't on the list strongly out in support of what was happening lest their names be added.

On the left was a shoulder-to-shoulder block of solidly built buildings; only a few narrow windows faced the street. Beyond them rose one of the six-story towers.

"Are those warehouses?" Daniel asked, nodding toward the structure.

"That?" said Luff. "That's Fahey House and the apartments of the Fahey retainers around it. There's a courtyard on the inside, of course. The Councilor's been living at his estate since the troubles started, though he's flying in for this meeting."

Luff cleared his throat. "Look," he said, "I haven't told the Councilors, even Waddell, that you're not . . . that Cinnabar isn't sending a squadron. I'd like—"

He looked at his shoes again. "I'd like you not to have told me, all right?" he said at last.

Daniel opened his mouth to speak, but he reconsidered his words. In the tone his father would've used to an erring client, he said, "I would not expect to discuss the business of Cinnabar citizens with representatives of a distant planet, Master Luff. Especially a planet as peculiar and backward as Bennaria seems to be."

They were approaching another of the towers that dotted Charlestown, though this one wasn't surrounded by housing for clients. A solid metal gate opened in the wall; the landau turned in to the tunnel beyond.

"Welcome to Manco House," Adele said ironically as she put away her data unit.

The gate clanged shut behind them.

CHAPTER 6

Charlestown on Bennaria

Adele looked about the meeting room. Pink-patterned marble faced the walls to shoulder height; above that were mirrors framed with gilt pilasters. All the furniture had ornately carved gilt legs. The central table—though the chairs were pushed back from it—had a malachite top of surpassing tastelessness, and the overfilled upholstery was of contrasting pastel shades picked out with gold embroidery.

Adele's mother had sincerely believed in the Equality of Man and the natural good taste of simple people whom society had not trammeled with artificialities of culture. She would've been horrified if she'd learned that her daughter, eyeing these furnishings, was thinking, *This is precisely the sort of ugly trash one expects to find when a member of the lower orders comes into money.*

On the other hand, Evadne Mundy, born Evadne Rolfe, had spent all her life on the rarefied peaks of Cinnabar culture, while Adele had lived for many years among the poorest of the poor. And of course Evadne hadn't been able to learn anything since a couple of soldiers—simple, uncultured people—had fixed her head to a spike on Speaker's Rock. *Rest in peace, mother.*

When Luff led Daniel and Adele into the windowless room on the top floor of Manco House, there were already four men smoking fat cigars as they waited. The smoke had a stomach-turning sweetness. Adele's briefing materials had mentioned that the Bennarians steeped their tobacco in molasses before smoking it, but she hadn't realized that the fact would have any direct bearing on her mission.

It would be harmful to the Cinnabar mission if the Commander's aide vomited during his initial meeting with the Bennarian Council. They were tasteless cretins from the look of them, but they'd nonetheless take offense.

Adele was the only woman present. The briefing materials also mentioned that the Bennarian attitude toward women was unenlightened by the standards of Cinnabar or, for that matter, the Alliance. Adele supposed she'd eliminate slavery before she worried about gender equality, but in any case, her present duties didn't involve doing either.

"About time you got here, Luff," said a grossly fat man in puce, sprawled on a loveseat. An ordinary armchair would've been uncomfortably tight. "You called us, so the least we can expect is that you show up yourself."

"If it please you, Councilor Waddell," Luff said. "I'd like to present Commander Leary of the—"

Ignoring him, Waddell turned to the balding, bearded man on his right and said, "Where's Layard, do you know, Knox?"

"How would I know?" Knox said with a scowl, but he turned his head so that he didn't blow his powerful jet of smoke directly at Waddell. "You were the one who called him."

"We can go on without him," said a third man, probably the oldest of them. He wore a gold waistcoat over a red tunic with puffed sleeves; he'd dribbled cigar ash on it.

"Do you think so, Fahey?" Waddell said. He sucked in a deep puff of smoke, then let it curl out through his nostrils. "*I* think we'll wait."

Fahey turned his head and pretended to be studying the trio of gilt lions supporting a globe whose continents and seas were inlaid in semiprecious stone. The world it depicted wasn't Bennaria nor any other planet Adele recognized off the top of her head.

Another local man entered. His clothes were relatively sober in color—white, cream, and tan—but included tights, a skirt, and ruffs at throat, wrists, and ankles.

"You took your time, Layard," Fahey said.

"I had things to do," Layard snapped. "What's this all about, Waddell?"

The fat man blew a geyser of smoke toward the ceiling. "That's for Master Luff to tell us. We're waiting, Luff."

"If it please you, gentlemen," the Manco agent said obsequiously, "this is Commander Leary of the Cinnabar navy. He says he's come in response to your summons. I at once informed Councilor Waddell. Commander?"

"Say, that was good time!" said the man who hadn't spoken to that point. He was the youngest of the five, though well into his thirties. "How big a fleet did you bring, Leary?"

Adele unobtrusively settled onto one of two straight-backed chairs in an alcove setting off a large allegorical painting: a man in armor—though helmetless to display his flowing blond hair—was strangling a dragon in a forest while other people knelt in attitudes of prayer. Adele placed the data unit on her lap.

It would've been easier to stand and place the unit on the sideboard which held a display of ornate silver, but work wasn't the only thing on Adele's mind. She didn't need to observe the meeting, but she knew she'd feel uncomfortable with her back turned toward this crew.

"I'm here as head of an advisory mission, gentlemen," Daniel said easily. "The Senate sent me to aid our friend Bennaria in its present difficulties on Dunbar's World."

"Yes, but how many *ships*?" the man said, leaning forward to emphasize the question.

"The Senate sent me and my support staff, Councilor," Daniel said, still smiling. "I'm aboard my private yacht, though if you'll permit me the use of missiles from your own naval stores I'm sure—"

"A staff!" Knox said. "By *God*, sir! We made it quite clear that we needed a fleet, not some junior officer! Luff, didn't you—"

"If you please, Councilor Knox!" Daniel said. "The Mancos represented your interests ably in Xenos; *but*."

Adele felt the corners of her mouth twitch. Daniel hadn't precisely shouted, but he was used to being heard in the midst of a battle; he'd certainly been heard this time. Hogg and Tovera in the outer room would be planning how to kill all the other servants and guards waiting with them . . . though knowing that pair, they'd done that within the first thirty seconds of arrival.

Daniel smiled more broadly than she did—than she ever did. "Guarantor Porra," he said, "has attempted to give the Senate direct orders without any notable success. Senator Manco is far too wise to pass on a client's request in a form that the Cinnabar Senate, the most respected deliberative body in the human universe, would find insulting. The Senate, you'll appreciate, is a proud entity."

He looked from one Councilor to the next. When Adele saw her friend's face in profile it was grinning cheerfully, but even Councilor Waddell stiffened for an instant when Daniel's eyes flicked over him. *Waddell looks like a plump rabbit meeting a snake. . . .*

"I'm an officer of the RCN," Daniel continued, "and as it chances I'm also the son of former Speaker Leary. I understand the Senate's fully justifiable pride. It sent me with an able staff in the Republic's name."

"He's *that* Leary!" said the man in ruffs to Fahey. He gave Daniel a look of appraisal and, to a degree, respect. Though he hadn't identified himself, Adele now knew from his electronic communications with his aides that he was Councilor Tortoni.

"I'll do my best to answer any questions you may have," Daniel said. He remained standing, his hands crossed behind his back as though he were an officer at Parade Rest, briefing a group of Senators. "I've just arrived on your planet, however. I won't formulate a plan of action until I've familiarized myself both with the situation on Dunbar's World and the resources you yourselves have available."

He cleared his throat, letting the Councilors glance among themselves and whisper into the throat microphones that connected them with their aides. Adele smiled faintly as her wands quivered.

She'd already entered the systems of Manco House. Now, through the Councilors' to-and-fro commo streams, she was adding their databases to her store. She'd require the special equipment aboard the *Princess Cecile* to break some of the encryptions, but that shouldn't take long.

Adele hadn't been sent to Bennaria in order to penetrate the information systems of the Republic's friends, but she firmly believed that there was no useless information. And in the particular case—

Some people were friends in name alone; with others the word "friend" had a much deeper meaning. The Bennarian Council, at least the portion she was meeting today, were not in the latter group, and she was beginning to doubt that this lot were friends even in name. No doubt that was an example of her regrettable tendency to cynicism.

But that cynicism was something which experience of the world had taught her early and which additional experience had consistently reinforced.

At age sixteen, Midshipman Leary had been assigned to the training vessel *Gannet*, a former patrol sloop now configured for the basic instruction of would-be RCN officers. The *Gannet*'s warrant officers had tongues like wood rasps, and they used starters of braided conduit to punctuate their words. Daniel and the other midshipmen of his rotation were rightly terrified of them.

Now he looked at the five most powerful men on Bennaria. Their moods were, judging from their expressions, anything from sour to seriously angry.

It was all Daniel could do to keep from laughing. He'd seen *real* politicians, with his father the fiercest and most powerful of all. Did these bumpkins think they could frighten Daniel Leary?

"Gentlemen," he said. "Councilors. I take it that you're a select committee of the Council chosen to deal with the emergency? I wonder—"

"We *are* the Council," Fahey said. "There's twenty-seven houses with chairs, but the others know to vote as they're told or it'll be the worse for them."

"No one else matters," Knox agreed with a fierce nod.

"Well, Councilor, there *is* Councilor Corius," Luff said nervously. "I only mention this because he's called what he calls an Assembly of the People for tomorrow midday. Not that *I* believe—"

"Corius thinks that Corius matters!" Waddell snarled, raising his bulk on the loveseat. "Corius thinks too bloody much, and he supposes that by stirring up the rabble he can get us to notice him. Well, I've got news for him!"

He glared at Daniel. Waddell was fat, but he was a genuinely big man as well, six feet four inches tall, as best Daniel could judge from seeing him seated.

"I can sit on my estate and let the whole of Charlestown rot!" he said. "*I'll* be no worse for it. We all can do that! Are Corius and his gutter sweepings going to hike through the marshes to change my mind? I don't think so! And they'll pretty quickly learn that Charlestown eats food that the estates send, not the other way around."

"I appreciate that there are domestic political aspects, Councilor," Daniel said. "My own duties are limited to what you asked the Republic to help with, however—the invasion of Dunbar's World."

He felt as if he were dancing on ice. With a partner who'd *much* rather be dancing with somebody else. The humor of the image—Waddell in a tutu—struck him; he grinned broadly, shocking the fat man into a coughing fit. Jets of cigar smoke spurted from his nostrils.

"As I said, I can't offer a detailed plan until I have more to go on," Daniel said to take attention away from Waddell. He'd met the fellow's sort before. They were even more unpleasant as enemies than as allies, so Daniel preferred not to embarrass him. "Still, it's clear from the information I've already gathered that Nataniel Arruns can't continue attacking without resupply from Pellegrino. That seems the obvious weak point."

"Yes, it *is* bloody obvious," said Waddell. "Which is why we asked for help that Cinnabar could readily provide but decided not to."

He turned and said—to Fahey but obviously speaking to all his fellows, "It seems we need to consider our next move, gentlemen. It might be better to cut our losses now and open negotiations with Arruns."

"You know the kind of bargain he'll drive, Waddell," Fahey said peevishly. "Besides, my family's had a relationship with the Pentlands on Dunbar's World since back in my grandfather's day—and yours with the Retzes. I don't like the idea of selling them out."

"If I may interject, Councilors?" said Daniel, who didn't need the permission of fat wogs to do *any* bloody thing but who intended to keep it polite. "My understanding is that Bennaria has a fleet of its own that should be more than sufficient to interdict supplies from Pellegrino, especially given your advantage of position. I believe—"

"Look, Commander," Waddell said. "I'll try to put this in words short enough that you can understand me. First, the Armed Squadron isn't in any kind of shape to be fighting a war."

"Well, the *Sibyl* is," said Knox unexpectedly.

Everybody looked at him. "Well, I am head of the squadron committee, you know," he said defensively. He toyed with his beard. "I asked Admiral Wrenn for a briefing just the other day and he assured me that the *Sibyl* could lift as soon as she had a crew aboard."

"*I* wouldn't take Wrenn's word that the sun rose in the east," grunted Councilor Layard, tapping cigar ash onto the malachite table.

"And just where did you think the crew was coming from?" said Fahey. "Don't you remember the Concordia Day celebrations last year? Wrenn had to rob the whole staff out of the Pool just to lift the *Sibyl* off and do a fly-past. If somebody wanted to steal the fittings off every bloody ship in the squadron, he could've done it without worrying about a watchman."

"Well, I wasn't suggesting that we do it!" Knox said, glaring angrily at Daniel. The Councilors obviously didn't like each other very much, but they all knew it was safer to lash out at foreigners than at one another. "There's nothing wrong with the ship, though."

"Wrenn says," said Layard. He sneered.

They think *it's safer to take it out on foreigners.* Daniel continued to smile mildly at the Councilors. Maybe in the case of Luff that was true. He, however, was an RCN officer. So long as his duties to the RCN required it, he would be polite to them. When that ceased to be the case, Councilor Waddell was going to find himself dangling from a sixth-floor window with Daniel's hand on the scruff of his neck.

If Adele didn't shoot the fat bastard first, of course.

"It doesn't matter whether the ship can fly," said Waddell. "It doesn't matter if all the bloody ships can fly! If we attack one of Arruns' warships, we're at war with Pellegrino. Our trade stops right there, period. Nothing goes out of Ganpat's Reach, and no ship that trades with us will be allowed to go through Pellegrino even if they don't have Bennarian cargo aboard. Period, I said!"

The stub of Waddell's cigar had gone out. He looked at it in sudden fury and flung it onto the carpet. Luff started to bend forward to pick the butt up; he caught himself instead and straightened.

"Commander," said the man whose name Daniel didn't know, "what's happening on Dunbar's World is a private affair that doesn't involve the Pellegrino government. Officially. If Cinnabar chose to get involved, even by attacking Pellegrinian ships, well, that'd be a matter between Cinnabar and Chancellor Arruns instead of us."

"They wouldn't have had to fight, for God's sake!" Knox said. "If they'd just come with a few ships, Arruns'd have found a way to back off without war."

He'd been looking from one to another of his fellows as he spoke. Now he glowered again at Daniel and added, "But they didn't!"

"I understand the political sensitivity of the affair," Daniel said, smiling just as mildly as before. "I still hope and expect to be able to carry out my assignment to aid your government in repelling the invasion of Dunbar's World. And simply as a matter of gaining information, I wonder, Councilor Knox—"

He made a slight bow toward the man.

"Would you please authorize me to examine your fleet? It's possible that an outsider would see something that your own officers are too familiar with to notice."

That was more polite than saying that anybody who'd take orders from this lot was certain to be incompetent. It was his *duty* to be polite.

"Well, I don't see what . . .," Knox said, looking sidelong at Councilor Waddell.

"Yes, all right," Waddell said. "You've come this far, I suppose. My secretary's in the outer office. He'll give you a chit in my name."

"Ah, sirs?" said Luff. "There's the question of transport. The only vehicle I have that could reach the Squadron Pool is the lighter, and that would be very slow."

Waddell grimaced. "I begin to see that being a Friend of the Republic isn't worth as much as I thought," he muttered. "You come without ships, and you don't even have an aircar of your own!"

Daniel didn't speak. The fat man turned to Knox and said, "Have your driver carry him to the Pool. You can spend the night with me in town. We'll want to see what it is Corius is up to tomorrow, after all."

"Is that safe, do you think?" said Councilor Layard, frowning.

Waddell shrugged and said, "I've got all the boys in from the estate. I don't intend to leave Waddell House empty—that'd be an invitation to burn it down. If there's real trouble, we'll have time to fly out."

"*Damn* Corius," Knox said, rising. "All right, Commander, my man will take you to the Pool. Though I don't see what you plan to do there."

"Thank you for your kindness, Councilor," Daniel said, bowing again. "Thank you all, gentlemen."

He didn't know what he was going to accomplish at the Pool either, but he was determined to find some way out of this political tangle. It wasn't simply duty: he was Daniel Leary, and he liked to win.

CHAPTER 7

Charlestown on Bennaria

Adele filed and sorted the data cascading across her holographic display. She was alone in the landau's passenger compartment—Luff had simply sent her back in his car—but it wouldn't have mattered if there were five other people present. Given half a chance, Adele focused on work to the exclusion of all else. That'd been her saving grace, the quirk that had made life bearable for so many years when nothing else redeemed her existence.

"Mistress," said Tovera—on the rear platform again—through the bead receiver in Adele's left ear. *"He's not driving back the way we came. There may not be a problem."*

Adele looked up. Though Tovera was so paranoid that she honestly couldn't imagine circumstances where she might not need her sub-machine gun, she wasn't an alarmist. "There may not be a problem" meant that she thought there definitely might be one.

Traffic, most of it pedestrians and bicyclists, was heavier than it'd been earlier; that in itself might've caused the driver to change their route. There were tenements on both sides of the street, indistinguishable to Adele from those she'd seen earlier, but just ahead was a block of row houses surrounding a central tower. They were of white stone recently sandblasted to a dazzling luster, definitely something she'd have remembered if she'd passed them on the way to Manco House.

Adele frowned, considering options. Hogg was off with Daniel, looking at the Armed Squadron, so the driver was alone in the front.

She tapped on the glass; the driver didn't give any sign of hearing her. There was probably a way to release the glass, but she didn't see a catch or button.

A bronze-finished gate, the only gap in the block of white houses, opened; the landau turned hard and drove down the passage beyond. Adele reached across her body with her right hand and unlatched the door. It hadn't been locked from the front; that was something.

The landau stopped in a landscaped courtyard facing the white tower. Bronze moldings made the building a subtle work of art, but that was a matter to consider another time.

Adele stepped to the ground, keeping the open door between her and the two men standing twenty feet away in the tower's entrance. Her left hand was along her thigh. She didn't look behind her— Tovera would handle anything there as well as it could be handled. The driver, obviously bribed, had thrown himself onto the floor of his compartment when he'd seen Adele take the pistol from her pocket.

She'd been wrong about facing two men. *One* was a man in his mid-thirties who wore a flowing white robe with gold accents. His companion was a humanoid reptile nearly seven feet tall. Its body was as lithe as a snake's.

"No!" the lizardman said, wrapping its long arms around the man and shifting to put its body between him and Adele. "This is a mistake! We come to talk with you only!"

The creature was speaking Standard. Its voice was perfectly intelligible, but it had a noticeable plangency as though its vocal cords were metal.

"What are you doing, Fallert?" the man said, trying to fight clear of the creature holding him. Its gripping arms were too strong. "What's the matter?"

"Good mistresses, this was a mistake!" the lizardman repeated. Its jaws were longer than a man's and its teeth were triangular. The creature wasn't so much dressed as draped in harnesses; a wallet and equipment hung from them. "My master wishes your friendship only!"

"You can let him go, then," Adele said. She felt the corner of her mouth lift, though she wasn't sure it was enough to count as a smile. The lizardman's body was too slender to prevent her first shot from killing the human he was trying to shield. If she'd wanted to, of course; most likely she'd have started by killing the creature itself.

The creature *him*self. His accouterments weren't intended to conceal his gender, and there was no doubt he was male.

He set the man back on his feet and stepped to the side, his hands open and slightly raised. He had three fingers and an opposed thumb on each. He was grinning in a fashion that was probably intended to be reassuring despite his pointed teeth.

"Lady Mundy," the human said, twitching his robes to adjust their hang, "I'm Yuli Corius. I'm sorry to have had to arrange to see you through subterfuge. I'm sure you understand. And I can't imagine what got into—"

He looked at the lizardman with a combination of astonishment and anger.

"—Fallert. That's never happened before!"

"My family were populists, Master Corius," Adele said. "You may call me Mistress Mundy or Officer Mundy. And as for why Master Fallert behaved the way he did—"

Ordinarily she'd have put the pistol away unseen. To make her present point she closed the door of the landau and stepped away from it. Only then did she slip the weapon back in her pocket.

"Mistress," said Corius. "I had no idea."

"Regardless of whether or not I understand the reason for your behavior, Master Corius," Adele said, "it was extremely discourteous. I am Mundy of Chatsworth: do not treat me with discourtesy again."

"My deepest apologies," Corius said. He sounded as though he were sincere. He turned to the lizardman and said, "And my apologies to you, Fallert. My bad judgment—"

He looked at Adele again, bowed, and continued, "My stupidity. It could have led to the most serious results."

The lizardman also bowed to Adele. The weapons dangling from his harness jingled. "Fallert, Mistress," he said, still grinning. "I am merely Fallert."

"He's real, mistress," Tovera said unexpectedly. She giggled and added, "He's flashier than I am, but he's real."

"Yes-s-s . . .," said Fallert, looking past Adele. To Corius he said, "You did not tell me about this one, master. This one is even more interesting than her mistress."

Corius cleared his throat, obviously disconcerted by events. He was strikingly handsome, tall and blond with regular features. He smiled. The expression was forced at first, but it spread into real welcome.

"Please," he said. "Since we've gotten through the preliminaries, however ineptly on my part, allow me to offer you the hospitality of Corius House while we talk. I assure you, mistress, that our getting to know one another is as important to your mission as it is to me."

Adele looked around for the first time. To her surprise, the balconies overlooking the courtyard on all sides were empty. The four of them were the only ones visible.

"I requested that my people remain indoors during your visit, mistress," Corius explained. "I regret the appearance of discourtesy in my actions, but I assure you that I was alive to the possibility that you would feel threatened. I minimized that as much as I could."

"And Fallert?" said Adele, raising an eyebrow.

"Fallert is my companion," Corius said. "I don't think of him as a threat."

"Then you're a fool," said Adele. "Or perhaps you think I am. Regardless, I'm willing to talk to you. But not in your house."

She opened the door of the landau. "In here, I think," she said. "That gives us privacy, and it's reasonably neutral given where it's parked."

"While you and my master speak, mistress," Fallert said, "I will become acquainted with your attendant."

He grinned wider. "Do you have a name, attendant?" he said.

"Yes, of course, mistress," Corius said, walking toward her without hesitation. "I'd offer to have drinks brought out to us, but I'm sure there's a full bar in the vehicle. And I don't require anything myself."

"We can talk from where we're standing now, Fallert," Tovera said. Adele would've sworn she heard warmth in the sociopath's voice. "I'd like to stay out of claw range since I don't have a set myself, you see. And the name's Tovera."

Fallert made a sound by sucking air into his throat pouch. It seemed to be his version of laughter.

Corius got into the landau and slid to the far end of the rear-facing seat. He crossed his hands on his lap, waiting expectantly. Adele seated herself kitty-corner and closed the door.

"Go ahead," she said as she took out her data unit. "Since you called the meeting."

"Just so," said Corius. He gave her an engaging smile. Someone less cynical than Adele might've even thought he meant it. "When I heard who Cinnabar had sent in response to the Council's request, I immediately examined the information available on you. On both of you, that is: the dashing young officer *and* the aide who merely seems to be present at all the victories."

He leaned against the door cushion and smiled again, this time a triumphant expression. "I'm sure that rural gentlemen from Cinnabar are an estimable group of people, brave and steadfast and all those splendid virtues, but it seems obvious to me that the brain that planned those brilliant coups was that of the scholar at the gentleman's side. Not so?"

Adele looked at him, uncertain as to how to respond. Anger was her natural reaction, but it was generally her reaction so she'd learned to control it.

"Master Corius," she said, "you obviously have a good mind and a very complex one. I won't surprise you if I say that your colleagues on the Council didn't have sense enough to research Commander Leary and myself; they simply noted that we weren't a fighting squadron and dismissed us."

Corius laughed with real humor. "Did they really?" he said. "I don't have a report on the meeting yet, but you're correct to assume that I will before long."

He pursed his lips and added, "Don't completely discount Waddell and his cabal, though. Especially Waddell himself. He probably felt snubbed and let his ego overrule his intelligence. This happens not infrequently since Waddell's ego is the most distinguishing aspect of his character, but he really does have a good mind. Very nearly the equal of my own."

Corius laughed again, suggesting that his words were a joke. They weren't, of course; not in his heart of hearts. And perhaps his self-image was correct. She and Daniel had outrun news of their coming, so the fact that he had information about them at hand showed that he took a broader view of the future than most members of the Cinnabar Senate.

"Sometimes someone who thinks in convolutions can miss the obvious, though," Adele continued, speaking without emphasis but locking his eyes with her own. "In this case, let me assure you that Mister Leary is exactly what common report makes him out to be: an officer who wins battles more by strategy than by luck, but with his share of luck also."

And by ruthlessness, but Adele didn't say that out loud. Daniel was a friendly, personable man, but she'd never seen him hesitate so much as a heartbeat before doing *anything* he thought was necessary for success.

She cleared her throat. "Now that we've gotten that out of the way, I'm sure you had some purpose for bringing me here besides mistakenly flattering me. What is that purpose?"

"I intend to defeat Nataniel Arruns' attempt on Dunbar's World," Corius said, suddenly sober. He leaned forward slightly. "The rest of the Council resent me. They'd probably even block me if I gave them the opportunity, which I won't. Now: you'll hear things about me. Maybe you already have."

He raised an eyebrow to draw a response.

"Go on," Adele said. Her duties didn't include spying for Yuli Corius.

"Yes," said Corius. "I want you to be very clear that my purpose is to defeat the Pellegrinians on Dunbar's World. I intend to do that and I will do that. You're welcome to believe that this is a ploy to increase my political standing here on Bennaria . . . and perhaps you'd be correct in that belief. But I *will* defeat Arruns."

He chuckled, appearing to relax again. "Since you've been sent here to accomplish the same purpose—you have, haven't you?"

"That is correct," Adele said. Her words had no overtones of emotion. Well, they usually didn't.

"And I don't suppose you care about the political situation here on Bennaria one way or the other?" Corius said. He raised an eyebrow in question again.

"Go on," Adele repeated. The fellow kept pushing. He was probably used to getting a good result from the technique, but it irritated her. She wouldn't let that get in the way of her decision-making processes, however.

"I would be very appreciative of the support of the Cinnabar mission," Corius said. "In turn I will endeavor to help you and Commander Leary in any fashion that I'm able to."

He leaned forward. "I know that I'm facing a difficult task," he said. "I'll need allies, and I don't expect to find them on Dunbar's World. It didn't have much of a planetary government at the best of times, and by the time we arrive there may be none at all. I'm hoping, Officer Mundy, that I've found those allies in yourself and Commander Leary."

"I'll report this conversation to the proper quarters," Adele said. "The decision will be made by persons other than myself. Now—"

She gestured with her right hand to the door beside Corius.

"—it's time for me to get back to the *Princess Cecile*. Since the driver appears to work for you, please direct him to take me to the waterfront by the most expeditious route. If he doesn't—"

Adele smiled tightly.

"—he should hope that I will kill him myself. If Tovera takes care of the matter instead, it's likely to be a much longer affair. Do you understand?"

Corius opened the door and got out. Before he closed it, he bent to meet Adele's eyes. "I understand completely, mistress," he said. "I understand everything you've told me."

Shut inside, Adele couldn't hear Corius' conversation with the driver, but she saw the servant's face in profile. It appeared that Corius was passing on her message with enough detail to make sure the fellow believed it.

Corius might indeed be as smart as he thought he was.

The Squadron Pool on Bennaria

Nodding toward the driver on the open bench in front of them, Hogg said to Daniel, "Not in a hurry, is he?"

Councilor Knox's black aircar was certainly older than Daniel and not a great deal younger than Hogg, but the fifteen-mile flight from Charlestown had been as smooth as the *Sissie* in free-fall orbit. The driver was middle-aged and handled his vehicle sedately. Knox obviously didn't set much store by flashiness.

Though Hogg insisted he could drive an aircar, the few times he'd gotten one into the air had ended in controlled crashes; more often he hadn't managed to lift off. He made up for his failure by complaining about anybody who actually could do the job.

"Well, we're here now," Daniel said as they dropped from the thousand-foot height at which they'd been cruising. They spiraled down toward the landing ground in the hollow of the U-shaped building on the edge of the water. "And anyway, it gave us a chance to see how the land lies."

Hogg sniffed. "It lies pretty bloody flat," he said, "and wet. The only thing I've seen yet that isn't marsh is rice paddies, and then the only difference's the green being brighter than what just grew. Though if we're going to be here awhile—"

As the car descended, a flock of birds lifted from the reeds fringing both banks of the river. Their bodies were blackish green, lost in the vegetation, but each had two pairs of wings whose flight feathers were brilliantly white. Their sudden appearance was like watching glass shatter.

"—I wouldn't mind snaring a few of that lot." He slid the forward window open. "Hey buddy? You in the funny hat. How do those birds taste, huh?"

The driver wore a pink-and-black skullcap that hooked under his ears. The colors were those of the Knox family, Daniel supposed, though that was just a guess.

"I have no idea, sir," he replied. "I suggest you ask some field hands, as low fellows of that sort are the ones who'd consider doing such a thing."

Hogg guffawed. "Got me that time," he admitted. "Hey, you don't happen to play poker, do you?"

"Your cards or mine?" said the driver. His tone was just as flat and respectful as it'd been when he first threw Hogg's insult back at him. Hogg guffawed again.

The LeBlanc River meandered so broadly that Daniel hadn't always been able to see both ends of the loops during the aircar's straight flight from Charlestown. The Squadron Pool was formed by a low concrete dam across the channel proper and by its extension into a quay around the eastern edge of the impoundment. An overgrown chain-link fence closed the perimeter.

There were destroyers in four of the five slips while the last held a large river barge and several smaller watercraft; two more destroyers were moored against the mud banks. One had been hauled partway into the reeds, presumably to keep it from sinking.

The car flared to a hover, then settled onto the landing plaza. Puddles flashed briefly into spray before the driver shut his motors down. Faces appeared at several windows of the surrounding building; a moment later the door in the middle of the central section opened and three men came out. They wore blue jackets and white vests, though one man was still buttoning his. Daniel didn't know anything about Bennarian uniforms, but presumably these were something fancier than utilities.

"Sirs?" said the last man through the door. He was in late middle age and missing the little finger of his left hand.

"I'm Commander Daniel Leary of the RCN," Daniel said as he and Hogg got out, leaving the driver in the vehicle. "I have authorization from Councilor Waddell to examine your squadron here."

Hogg stepped forward and gave the handwritten note to the man whose name was either Brast or Grast, depending on how the light struck the pin on his left breast pocket. One of the disadvantages of first class uniforms—one of many disadvantages—was that they didn't have pockets; when Daniel was wearing Whites, Hogg carried anything too big to slip into a cummerbund.

"The RCN?" Grast/Brast said. "Cinnabar? Oh, sir, we're honored to meet you! I'm Basil Brast, the port commandant. Oh! Though—"

His face fell. The two younger men were whispering together behind him; one scurried back into the building.

"—I'm afraid you won't be very impressed by what we have to show you," Brast went on. "To tell the truth, things have been so quiet hereabouts the past ten years and more that Bennaria might as well not have ships."

"From the way the appropriation's been going down," said the junior officer who'd remained with Brast, "the Council pretty much thinks that too."

"That's not our place to say, Tenris!" Brast said sharply.

"If I can just see the ships, I'd be much obliged," Daniel said. "Starting with the *Sibyl*, which I understand is operational?"

"Well, yes-s-s . . .," Brast said. "But yes, come along, Commander. This is a great pleasure, meeting a Cinnabar officer like yourself!"

He took Daniel into the administration building and down the central hallway. Men wearing baggy gray uniforms stood in doorways to watch.

A grizzled old fellow saluted Alliance fashion, fingertips to brow and palm outward. Daniel returned it by reflex, then smiled mentally. *At least there's one spacer in the Bennarian navy who can be expected to know what he's doing.*

"As for being operational," Brast said, "the *Sibyl* hasn't lifted in the past year. That's longer in Standard, fourteen months I think. We check her regular, I don't mean that, but—

He pushed open the back door and nodded Daniel through; beyond were the concrete quay and the silent destroyers. Hogg followed them at a respectful two paces. He'd been looking in doorways as he went by with a blank smile.

Brast gestured to the left, though Daniel already knew from Adele's data that the *Sibyl* was in the second slip. The *Tenerife*, the other potentially operational ship, was in the first.

"But you know . . .," Brast resumed. "Things go wrong that don't show up till the thrusters fire."

"Indeed I do," Daniel said, stepping from the concrete to the destroyer's boarding ramp. The familiar springiness beneath his boot brought a happy grin to his face. "To be honest, I'm surprised that the Council isn't more concerned to have the fleet in readiness. The *Sailing Directions* for Ganpat's Reach mention piracy as a problem."

The *Sibyl* had been built on Pleasaunce only a decade before. The Fleet Dockyard had been accepting foreign commissions to keep its labor force together during an interval of peace between Cinnabar and the Alliance. Indeed, they'd probably been bidding against the construction yard at Harbor Three on Xenos.

"I can't say to that, sir," said Brast, activating the vessel's main hatch from a faired-over switch plate. "There's some who claim that the Council, some of the Councilors anyhow, have come to other ways of dealing with pirates. But I wouldn't know."

Tribute to the pirates, in other words, or simply the slave trade which the pirates found too profitable to harm by preying on Bennarian cargoes. As a naval officer Daniel thought that was a bad long-term strategy and as a man he found it a despicable one, but—

"Well, that's not for me to judge either, Brast," he said aloud, showing to the commandant that they *were* both judging the matter and agreeing in their distaste for it.

Ten years could be a long time in the life of a destroyer since they tended to be over-sparred. A hard-charging captain could strain not only the masts but the hull as well. That hadn't—that *certainly* hadn't—been the case with the *Sibyl*, but one bad landing could do as much damage as a year of throwing a ship through the Matrix without concern for the gradients between universes.

The hatch rose without sticking, a quick and nearly certain way to prove the vessel was sound. Destroyers were long in relation to their beam, so any sort of twisting would make the main hatch bind and leak.

The interior lights were on and the climate control system was running at low cycle. "I'm glad to see you keep her powered up," Daniel said, walking toward a companionway. There were two of the armored stairways here in the main entrance hold, Up and Down, and according to the *Sibyl*'s plans there was another pair astern. Those would primarily serve the Power Room crew.

All communication between decks was by steps. The stresses when a starship entered or left the Matrix were likely to trap an elevator cage in its shaft, and the shock of a hard landing could do the same. What was true even for a merchant vessel was doubly so for a warship faced with higher acceleration, the recoil of its own weapons, and the impact of hostile ordnance.

"Well, to tell the truth," Brast said, "we're running the ground facilities from the *Sibyl*'s fusion bottle. The dirtside power plant went out last year. The lines won't carry enough to run the heavy equipment in the shops, but we haven't had any call for that. We were thinking about taking the bottle out of one of the old ships, maybe the *Admiral Kalinin*, for a replacement, but we haven't gotten around to it."

Despite her greater tonnage, the *Sibyl* was a five-deck ship like the *Princess Cecile*; the destroyer's additional mass came from having half again the length with a slight increase in beam. She'd be quick as moonlight on the right heading, but a cack-handed captain could tear her in two. Daniel'd never served on a destroyer. . . .

"Shifting a fusion bottle is a job and no mistake," Daniel said agreeably as he climbed through B Level to A.

What he *really* thought was that a maintenance yard like this was equipped and intended to do just that sort of work. As a boy he'd helped Uncle Stacey change a fusion bottle by manpower, pulleys, and a jury-rigged shear legs because another ship was already in the small dry dock where all Bergen and Associates' power equipment was built.

He grinned, sobered, and then smiled again as he thought of the gentle old man. He missed him, but so long as Uncle Stacey remained in Daniel's memory a part of him was still alive. Stacey lived in memory and in the skills he'd taught his nephew.

The light at the top of the companionway was out, as were alternating banks of lights in the ALevel corridor. "Oh, dear," Brast murmured when he saw it.

Daniel strode down the corridor toward the bridge. "It's probably just a dirty contact," he said. "An easy fix, I'm sure."

It was the first maintenance failure he'd seen on the *Sibyl*; she was in much better shape than he'd counted on. It really was a trivial matter. He could probably troubleshoot it himself in half an hour with a borrowed electrical kit.

He grinned broadly. *And ideally with borrowed coveralls over my Whites.*

The bridge was similar to that of the *Princess Cecile*, though it followed the present Alliance fashion of placing the striker's jumpseat and screen to the right of the main display instead of on the same axis. Daniel brought the navigator's console live. The port commandant watched nervously; concerned that it might malfunction, Daniel supposed.

The console responded quickly and as crisply as you could wish. Instead of pearly radiance the initial display was a bar spectrum, red at the base and shading upward to violet. Seating himself, Daniel rotated through the standard displays—navigation, maintenance, Power Room, Plot-Position Indicator, and finally to an attack board. Everything came up without hesitation.

Someone was shouting below, the voice drifted unintelligibly up the companionway. Brast trotted to the hatch in the corridor and called back a reply as Daniel continued to examine the *Sibyl*'s electronic heart.

There were more red pips on the maintenance display than Daniel liked, but a quick, frowning assessment didn't find anything more serious than a leaking hatch seal in the Warrant Officers Day Room. Worst case, they could dog the internal hatch and leave the compartment open to vacuum.

Now, if the *Tenerife* were only as in as good shape . . . or almost as good . . . or even just good enough to lift off and look threatening. With two destroyers whose crews were leavened by the *Sissie*'s veterans, Daniel would be willing to fight a partly functional light cruiser manned by Pellegrinians. A bluff would probably be enough, after all.

In all truth, he'd try it with one destroyer, though he wouldn't do that with any enthusiasm.

Daniel glanced down the corridor. Brast stood stiffly in the corridor facing the companionway; whatever was happening wasn't good news so far as he was concerned.

Daniel would deal with that situation when and if he had to. For now he brought up the stores status. Somewhat to his surprise, the food compartments were full or at least listed as full. Cutting corners on the quantity and quality of comestibles was a common fiddle for dishonest pursers and administrators, so it'd take a physical inventory to be sure. Still, there was at least a chance that the vessel had thirty days' rations aboard.

Munitions, though. . . . Not so good.

The magazine holding ammunition for the forward 10-cm turrets was full; the aft magazine was empty. The actual quantity was greater than a maximum load for the *Princess Cecile*, but it'd take work to shift enough of the charges sternward to enable the *Sibyl*'s full eight-gun battery to fire. There wasn't a conveyor as there might've been on a vessel of greater beam, so it'd mean lines of spacers staggering between magazines with yokes or hand-trucks.

"Brast, what in Hell's name do you think you're playing at!" bellowed the man who stepped out of the companionway. "And you there! Get off the bridge *now* or I'll have you arrested as a spy!"

"Admiral, Councilor Waddell gave him permission," the port commandant said. He'd been standing at attention but stepped back when the newcomer shouted in his face.

Daniel got up from the console, taking only enough time to switch the display back to the initial spectrum. So long as the unit wasn't shut down completely, Adele could enter the system and access all data. Though he'd already seen all he probably needed.

"Do you think Waddell's the Admiral Commanding the armed squadron, Brast?" the newcomer said. "By Hell, do you think *you* are? I'm in charge and I decide who's allowed aboard my ships!"

Daniel walked to join the other men. Half a dozen more, junior officers by the look of them, had followed the admiral from the companionway. Daniel stood politely erect in his Whites, but he very deliberately didn't come to attention.

The plasma cannon were the *Sibyl*'s defensive armament. For attack she had only sixteen missiles in her magazines. They were of the expensive dual-converter style that accelerated twice as fast as what he'd expected to find here in the boondocks, but that still wasn't much to fight a cruiser with.

"Sir?" said Brast desperately. "He's from *Cinnabar*."

"I know he is!" said the admiral turning to stare at Daniel. He was no more than five and a half feet tall, probably trim-looking on normal occasions but now disarrayed from running up three decks. His face was red with exertion and anger. "And Hell take Cinnabar too!"

"I'm Commander Leary, RCN, sir," Daniel said calmly. "I'm here at the request of the Bennarian Council to advise—"

"I don't care who you are!" the admiral said. His name tag read WRENN, the name which Councilor Knox had mentioned during the meeting at Manco House. "Nobody has permission to board my ships unless I give it, and Hell *take* me if I'll give it to some weasel who thinks he can do as he pleases because he's R-bloody-CN!"

"I assure you, sir—" Daniel said.

"Don't assure me!" said Wrenn. "Get off my ship! Now!"

Daniel nodded politely to the Bennarian officers. Wrenn's aides were huddled as closely together as sheep in a storm. Whatever they thought of the RCN, Daniel was pretty sure that they had doubts about denying Councilor Waddell's authority.

"Good day, gentlemen," Daniel said. The aides jumped to either side to let him through the companionway hatch.

Daniel had considered thanking Brast, but that would just get the fellow into worse trouble. He'd also considered asking about getting missiles from Bennarian stores for the *Princess Cecile*, but he'd rejected that even more quickly.

Hogg followed Daniel down the companionway. He was singing "Never Wed an Old Man" in a low voice, but instead of "old man" it was coming out "'admiral."

CHAPTER 8

Charlestown Harbor on Bennaria

The water taxi that brought Daniel and Hogg from Waddell House to the *Sissie* was a flat-bottomed skimmer driven by an air-screw astern. It was only marginally stable, extremely wet, and more than a little dangerous because the power plant was a nacelle cannibalized from an air-cushion vehicle.

The high-speed intake stream would've sucked off Daniel's saucer hat if he hadn't kept it on his lap. He could imagine a drunk who'd stood too close when the nacelle pivoted for a turn having worse problems than a lost hat.

Half a dozen other watercraft, bumboats rather than taxis, were tied up to the starboard outrigger. As a safety precaution, locals weren't allowed aboard the corvette in harbor and the lower decks remained sealed in accordance with Daniel's orders. He'd given half the crew liberty, though, and the other half—save a minimal anchor watch—was free to trade with local entrepreneurs so long as they didn't leave the ship.

The floating crib, an open-topped canvas shelter on a boat small enough to be rowed with a single set of oars, was stretching the point a trifle, but only one man left the *Sissie* at a time and that only by the length of the bow rope. Vesey'd been right to interpret the orders loosely. Spacers waiting in line greeted Daniel cheerfully as the taxi glided to a halt, and Plastin, a tech on guard duty in the entrance hatch, bent to give him a hand up.

Hogg had paused to pay the driver with a handful of local scrip—and when had he found time to gather that? He scrambled onto the ramp a moment later, glaring at Daniel's spray-sodden Whites. "Bugger-all use they'll be till I get 'em cleaned!" he grumbled.

"It may be some while before I need them again, Hogg," Daniel said. "The quality people of Bennaria don't seem to have warmed to my charms."

"The Lieutenant's on the bridge, sir," said Plastin as he retrieved the sub-machine gun that Fairfax, his partner on guard, had been holding while Plastin helped Daniel aboard.

"And Mistress Mundy's in the BDC, sir," Fairfax added. "By herself."

"I thought Tovera was with her," Plastin said, frowning.

Fairfax gave his partner a broad grin. "Like I said," he replied.

"I'm glad she's aboard," said Daniel, striding toward the companionway. It was a pleasure to hear the familiar echoes of his boot soles on the steel deck plates. "Thank you both."

"I've seen better-quality people working the Harbor Three Strip," said Hogg in a low voice. "I've seen better quality people lying in the *gutter* on the Harbor Three Strip!"

Daniel didn't respond except perhaps to smile a little broader; but then, he was generally smiling. He more or less agreed with Hogg. Any Cinnabar citizen would.

A brief frown touched his forehead. Well, almost any; Master Luff was a disturbing exception.

Vesey was coming out of the bridge to meet Daniel as he stepped from the companionway into the A Level corridor. "Good evening, sir," she said. "Mistress Mundy was hoping you'd drop in on her in the Battle Direction Center when you came aboard."

"That's where I'm headed, Vesey," Daniel said. "You've had no excitement, I trust?"

Vesey'd been alone on the bridge, running a simulation at the command console. Daniel couldn't make out the details at this distance, but his mind made an intuitive leap at the sight of a few blue specks maneuvering among the large number of orange ones.

"There haven't been any angry calls from the groundside authorities," said Vesey with a perfunctory smile. "Ah—I gave the starboard watch liberty, as we'd discussed, but I let both Blantyre and Cory go tonight. I hope that's all right?"

"I'd have done the same," Daniel said as he turned toward the BDC at the other end of the corridor. Over his shoulder he added, "And regardless, Captain, it's your decision."

Tovera cycled open the heavy hatch as Daniel approached; the BDC was armored, like the bridge and Power Room. She gave him a smile that made him think—as usual when he was around Tovera—of snakes, then said, "Come have a drink with me, Hogg. They won't need us for a little while."

Daniel glanced at his servant. "Yes, of course," he said. He didn't know what Tovera wanted to discuss with Hogg, and he *did* know that asking wouldn't gain him anything. "For that matter—I intend to go out later myself, but there's no reason you need to accompany me."

Hogg sniffed. "No reason the sun needs to rise in the morning either, young master," he said. "But I guess it will."

To Tovera he added as the hatch closed, "I've got a pint of what they call whiskey on Blennerhasset. Leastwise we can make room for something better, eh?"

The consoles of the BDC were arranged petal-fashion around the center of the compartment, with five jumpseats along each side wall. Adele, alone in the room, didn't turn when Daniel entered behind her.

"I've been busy," she said as her wands flickered; she'd slaved the console to her little data unit as she generally did. She was so familiar with its controls that she gained minusculely by the circumlocution. "I assume you want to know about Admiral Wrenn?"

"Yes-s-s . . .," said Daniel carefully, patting his head by reflex to be sure that he wasn't after all wearing a commo helmet that would've transmitted the business aboard the destroyer back to Adele here in the *Princess Cecile*. He wasn't—of course.

He settled onto the console to the left of Adele's. Text spilled across the display, broken up with images of Wrenn at various stages of his life. Mostly he was dressed in one or another comic-opera Bennarian uniform, but in one he appeared in the unpiped gray of a probationary RCN midshipman.

Understanding dawned, filling Daniel with relief. "I turned the *Sibyl*'s console on!" he said. "You used that to see what was going on aboard her. And then you gathered the rest of this because you knew I'd want to know what had gotten into Wrenn."

"You would, and I did also," said Adele, cocking her head just slightly sideways and offering Daniel a smile. Well, a smile for Adele; a slight tick of the lips for anybody else. "And I suspect the answer is that Wrenn was sent to the RCN Academy at Xenos as a foreign student but was dismissed after the first year. He doesn't seem to have showed up for classes. The Wrenns are a Conciliar House, of course."

She frowned. "I'm a little surprised that he wasn't simply waved on through," she said. "Since he wouldn't be entering the RCN, after all."

Daniel shrugged. "If he'd been from somewhere more important," he said, "Kostroma or the Danziger Stars, say, I suspect that's what would've happened. Bennaria doesn't matter enough for External Affairs or Navy House either one to worry about offending the local nobility."

He laughed. "I suppose I ought to regret that choice," he said, "but I don't. I don't care that some dimwit from Bennaria gets angry any more than the Academy Provosts did."

"I was puzzled by the timing of Wrenn's appearance on the *Sibyl*," Adele said, cascading additional text across Daniel's display. He glanced at it but kept his attention on his friend instead; she'd give him the information he needed in an organized and compact fashion, a much better plan than him trying to sort the raw data himself. "Since it didn't seem random. I found—"

More text in the corner of Daniel's eye; he continued to watch Adele and to smile as she worked, completely absorbed with her task.

"—that as soon as Councilor Fahey had returned to his town house, he called Admiral Wrenn and informed him you were inspecting the ships and installations at the Squadron Pool. You see from the transcript—"

"Summarize it, please," Daniel said mildly.

Adele looked up, caught his smile, and managed one of her own. "Yes, of course," she said. "While the Councilor doesn't refer directly to the fact Wrenn flunked out of the Academy, he's obviously wording his comments in a way to remind Wrenn of the fact. 'These Academy-trained Cinnabar officers think the sun shines out of their asses' was one of his lines. It strikes me as an effective job of goading Wrenn into actions that he'll reasonably regret."

She frowned and added, "I don't see why Fahey's opposing us, though."

"He's not," said Daniel. "He resents Waddell's power, so he's using my visit to embarrass him. Fahey doesn't gain anything, but he irritates his rival. And he doesn't think his involvement'll be traced back to him."

Daniel shrugged. He smiled, but he felt suddenly tired.

"It's the sort of thing my father'd do," he said. "Except that my father would probably have done it better."

"I have enough to regret about my own actions," said Adele coolly, "that I'm not going to become depressed over the behavior of foreigners whom I neither know well nor care for. And as it chances, my trip back to the ship wasn't as uneventful as I'd expected either. I've met Yuli Corius. He arranged to meet me, rather."

"Did he indeed?" said Daniel, his expression sharpening. "And what was that in aid of?"

"He told me he intends to defeat the Pellegrinian invasion of Dunbar's World," Adele said. "By himself, if necessary; but he'd like us to work with him."

"By himself?" Daniel repeated. "Can he do that, do you think? From the way Waddell was talking. . ."

He let his voice trail off. Adele had been at the same meeting; he didn't have to repeat what was said there. Besides, anything Councilor Waddell said had to be taken with a grain of salt.

"I'm still working on that," Adele said. "Corius has rented four large transports, which implies he's serious about moving a significant number of troops somewhere. They're at his estate eighty miles up the River Noir from Charlestown."

More data appeared on Daniel's display; this time he did look at it. The ships were the *Greybudd*, *IMG40*, *Todarov*, and *Zephyr*; 3,000-ton freighters of the type standard in Ganpat's Reach.

His hope had been wrong: they weren't warships and couldn't be converted to warships. Two of the transports mounted single 10-cm plasma cannon; the other pair had pods of unguided eight-inch rockets, the sort of light armament that pirates used to cripple their prey. By no stretch of the imagination could they tackle a cruiser, even a cruiser crewed by Pellegrinians.

"On a short run," said Daniel. He was thinking out loud as much as he was informing his companion. "You could pack three thousand people aboard them. A run from here to Dunbar's World, that is. But soldiers—not nearly so many, not if they've got any kit at all. And even three thousand troops won't throw Arruns off Dunbar's World. Corius's going the wrong way about it if that's really what he plans. He ought to be looking for warships."

He pursed his lips. "Do you believe him?" he asked.

"I don't disbelieve him," Adele said. "He's a clever man and clearly a bold one." She smiled faintly. "Rash, in fact. He nearly got himself killed this afternoon, and I can easily imagine him miscalculating other risks just as badly."

She paused. "I don't disbelieve him, Daniel," she said. "But I certainly don't trust him."

Daniel laughed and got up from the console. "Based on what I know thus far," he said, "I see no way to accomplish our mission. That doesn't mean I'm giving up."

Adele sniffed. "I didn't imagine you were," she said dryly.

"No, of course," said Daniel in mild embarrassment. "Sorry."

He'd been talking for effect rather than talking to Adele. He didn't need to convince her of anything, and she wasn't the sort to be swayed by words alone anyway.

"We need more information," he said. "We'll get it—here, I think, though I'll go to Dunbar's World if we've explored all the avenues here."

"Corius may be the answer," Adele said. "There's his assembly tomorrow."

"Right," agreed Daniel. "And tonight I'm going out to see what I can learn around the harbor. Spacers may tell me what the Councilors wouldn't."

He grinned and added, "Besides, it's been a long voyage. I'm looking forward to having a drink on the ground."

Adele nodded. "I'm going out myself," she said. "I'd like to get a neutral opinion about the situation here on Bennaria before we pick a side—whether Waddell or Corius."

Daniel felt his lips purse; he knew Adele was a spy, but that wasn't a business he felt comfortable around. "Well, I trust your judgment, of course," he said, and turned toward the hatch.

"Oh, not one of Mistress Sand's people, Daniel," she replied with a hint of amusement. "His name's Krychek, and I have an introduction to him from an old family friend. His ship's berthed at the other end of this island. From the way he responded when I called him this evening, he'll be very glad to talk to someone whom he considers civilized. The members of the Council of Bennaria and their associates don't qualify as civilized in his opinion, I gather."

Daniel laughed as he cycled the hatch open. "Well," he said, "Master Krychek and I agree about something, at any rate. Good luck to you!"

The water taxi's electric motor began to arc and spit before it'd carried Adele and Tovera more than halfway to Krychek's ship. They wallowed.

"Can you get us to shore?" Tovera said. Adele couldn't see her face in the darkness, but her voice was cold. "We'll walk the rest of the way."

"No no!" said the boatman, pulling on a rubber glove. "Is not a problem, you see!" He put his index finger on the motor's control panel, apparently holding down a relay. The motor buzzed back up to speed and they proceeded, a nimbus of sizzling blue wrapping the boatman's hand.

"There's no road on the island," Adele said mildly. That was why she'd called a water taxi for the trip to the *Mazeppa*. "It's just mud except for the individual slips."

"Yes," said Tovera from her seat in the far bow. She was wearing RCN goggles which gave her several-light enhancement options as well as magnification if she wanted. "But even so we wouldn't sink as deep."

The boatman cut inshore toward a freighter hulking against the tip of the island. The stars were thick enough to silhouette dorsal turrets at the vessel's bow and stern; there were rocket clusters also, bolted on awkwardly between the folded masts.

Krychek's *Mazeppa* displaced nearly 6,000 tonnes, nearly twice the size of anything else in harbor. Lights shone through open hatches on the upper levels, though the hull at the waterline was dark save for the vast square of the entrance hold.

Adele had examined the *Mazeppa* through its computer. The vessel didn't carry missiles so it couldn't engage a real warship with any chance of success, but its array of short-range armament was enough to warn off a pirate—or squadron of pirates.

"There's two automatic impellers aimed at us," Tovera said. She didn't sound frightened, but she'd raised her voice more than she usually would.

"Sheer off!" a man shouted. "We don't want visitors!"

A powerful searchlight above the entrance hatch blazed down at the taxi. The boatman yelped, jerking his hand away from the relay. The motor spluttered, leaving the boat to wallow again.

Adele had expected the light and was already squinting. In the side-scatter of the beam she saw a pintle-mounted automatic impeller aimed at them from the boarding ramp. Tovera'd opened her attaché case, but she used the lid to conceal her right hand from the vessel.

"This is Mundy of Chatsworth!" Adele said. "Visiting Captain Krychek by arrangement!"

"Bloody hell!" somebody muttered from the *Mazeppa*. The searchlight cut off, turning the night into a pit of total darkness.

"Come aboard, Mistress," a different voice called. "Sorry for the confusion."

The taxi coasted against the *Mazeppa*'s outrigger. The boatman was hunched with his hands clasped over his head, so Adele herself grabbed the rope ladder hanging from the metal. Tovera remained as she'd been, smiling faintly but focused on other concerns than whether the taxi would drift away from the freighter.

Adele didn't have local currency, so she dropped two florins beside the boatman and climbed the ladder. "That's too much, mistress," Tovera said mildly as she waited for Adele to reach the outrigger.

"He may have trouble changing Cinnabar money," Adele said, waving aside the spacer bending to offer her a hand. "Besides, he just had guns pointed at him."

Tovera tittered. Adele didn't ask what her servant had found funny. Perhaps it was the thought that an automatic impeller was more dangerous than she was.

A hatch squealed open; full illumination flooded the entrance hold in place of the yellow watch light that'd been on before.

"Mistress Mundy!" said the big man coming toward her with his arms out in greeting. "I am Krychek! Pardon my men's mistake. The Bennarians do not welcome us, and we do not encourage drunken louts to speed past and hurl garbage. As has happened in the past."

Krychek was about sixty, with close-cropped hair, a full beard, and a wrestler's build. He wore closely tailored trousers and tunic of blue fabric with red piping. The outfit suggested a uniform but had no unit or rank markings.

"I regret to hear that," Adele said, clasping Krychek's right hand in both of hers to prevent him from embracing her—if that was actually what he'd intended. "I was hoping for a neutral assessment of the political situation here."

Adele'd looked up Krychek as soon as Claverhouse mentioned his name, though at the time she hadn't expected the information to be of importance. He was hereditary Landholder of Infanta, one of the founding worlds of the Alliance of Free Stars.

From the beginning Infantans had been more notable for military prowess than scholarship; Adele didn't remember ever meeting one in the Academic Collections. She didn't know what the culture considered a friendly greeting, and she had no intention of adapting her own upper-class Cinnabar reserve to anything more physical.

"A neutral assessment?" said Krychek, taking her firmly by the elbow and guiding her toward the companionway. "A difficult task, mistress. Flies, I am sure, can find all manner of subtleties in garbage, but for such folk as you and I—what can we say about a stench and an abomination? Still, come with me to my library and I will do what I can to inform you."

The first segment of companionway would've been dark except that a work light hung on a length of flex running back into the corridor behind. Adele had noticed that the floor of the entrance hold wasn't level, a more serious maintenance problem. The port outrigger must leak enough to float lower than the starboard one.

"Do you appreciate fine wines, mistress?" Krychek asked. "Or liqueurs, perhaps?"

He was immediately behind Adele, which meant Tovera brought up the rear. She'd presumably decided that she could best protect her mistress from that position, though Adele couldn't imagine what criteria she'd used. Tovera didn't have the emotional concern for Adele that Hogg did for Daniel—she didn't have emotions at all, so far as Adele'd been able to tell—but she would stolidly and efficiently do the best job she could through intelligence and ruthlessness.

"I can't say that I do, sir," Adele said, honestly but for effect also. She wasn't here to socialize. "I might say that I'm a connoisseur of information, but even there I have catholic tastes."

She stepped out in the A Level corridor and turned left—toward the bridge—by reflex. "This way, if you please," Krychek said, opening the hatch across from the companionway. The interior lights went on automatically.

In a compartment down the corridor men—she was sure they were all men—were singing, "*Rosy dawn, rosy dawn, will today my grave-mouth yawn?*"

Krychek nodded toward the voices. "The crew are my retainers," he said. "My children and closer than children. They came into exile with me—*for* me."

"*Soon I'll hear the trumpet sound,*" sang the hidden chorus. One of the group had a guitar. "*I to death am surely bound, I and my dear comrades.*"

"I'll join them, mistress?" Tovera said, flicking her eyes toward the singing. Adele nodded agreement.

"I understand," said Adele as she followed Krychek into the compartment. The hatch was an ordinary steel valve, but the inner surface was veneered in the same dark wood as the cabinets and other furnishings. "The circumstances of my own exile were rather different, of course."

"*I never thought, I never thought—*"

"Exile?" repeated Krychek, pausing with his hand on the hatch. "But of course, I should have realized—you were an associate of my friend Maurice!"

"*—my joy so soon would come to naught,*" the chorus sang with lugubrious gusto.

"Yes, my family was implicated in the Three Circles Conspiracy," Adele said simply. "I spent most of my adult life on Bryce, until the Edict of Reconciliation permitted me to return to Cinnabar."

She was using the massacre of her own family as a tool to elicit the sympathy and thereby cooperation of this Infantan noble. Part of her was horrified at such callousness, but that was an intellectual thing. Emotionally she was quite content to use any tool available to accomplish her task.

Krychek closed the hatch. "So!" he said. "We have much in common, mistress, you and I. Though I've never been to Bryce."

"The Academic Collections suited me better than they might you," Adele said with a faint smile. Sometimes she was afraid that she had no more conscience than Tovera did.

The compartment was built on two decks. A hardwood mezzanine circled this level, giving access to the books in shockproof cases, but a broad staircase led down to cushioned chairs and curio cabinets. The ceiling was white and double-vaulted, with unfamiliar—to Adele, at least—coats of arms at the eight corners.

"Come, please," Krychek said. "We can sit as we talk. And surely you'll drink *something* with me?"

"A light wine, then," Adele said, walking down the polished steps with the care they deserved. Neither the staircase nor the mezzanine had railings. Krychek was presumably used to it, but even so it'd be a bad place to be caught if the ship had to maneuver unexpectedly.

"How is dear Maurice, eh?" Krychek said as he unlocked a tantalus and withdrew the decanter of pale yellow wine. "He wasn't sure how he'd find Xenos. One doesn't really return after so many years, you know; what had been home is a different place."

"Yes, I do know," said Adele dryly as she accepted the offered wineglass. "As for Claverhouse, he seemed as well as anyone his age could expect. Judging from the restaurant where we met, he's comfortably fixed at least."

"Yes, we made a good deal of money," Krychek said, waving Adele to a chair. Its leather upholstery was the same polished brown as the paneling. "And Maurice's expenses are lower than mine, of course; he has only himself to care for."

He looked up at the ceiling. "This library is a replica of the one on my estate, as you'll have guessed," he said, lowering his eyes to Adele's. "I cannot return to Infanta till God rips the tyrant Porra from the throne he disfigures, but I have brought a little of my home with me."

"Including your retainers," Adele agreed, tasting her wine. She was no more of a connoisseur than she'd claimed, but she was quite confident that her father—who was remarkably knowledgeable—would've approved the vintage.

"Yes-s-s . . . ," Krychek said, sipping his wine with a harsh expression, his eyes focused a thousand miles away. "That is so."

Rather than probing while her host was lost in a brown study, Adele glanced at the curio cabinets to either side of her chair. The one on her right held pipes for smoking; tobacco pipes, she was almost sure. They were of a remarkable variety, ceramic, vegetable, and mineral. One was of white material, possibly ivory but stone or synthetic with equal likelihood. Its bowl, bigger than her clenched fist, was decorated with a forest scene in high relief.

The case on the left held . . . more pipes.

"They are my whimsy," Krychek said. "I began collecting them before my exile."

He walked to the case on Adele's left and rotated it, then pointed to a simple pipe with a bowl of dark rootstock and a stem with noticeable wear. Many of the others didn't appear to have been used.

"This was my grandfather's," Krychek said musingly. "He was smoking it when he died. That and his name are the only things that remain to me of him."

He met Adele's eyes. "I do not smoke myself," he said. "But I collect."

Krychek settled into his seat again and cleared his throat, frowning. "You wish to know about Bennarian politics," he said. He shrugged. "There are four great magnates, Waddell above all; Fahey and Knox; and there is Corius, who sets himself against all the others. Waddell leads the Council, but he's not greedy. Not *too* greedy. He leaves some cream for the rest; more than they'd get fighting him, at least."

"If Waddell isn't interested in driving the Pellegrinians off Dunbar's World . . .," Adele said, pursing her lips as she looked into the display of her data unit. "Then Corius is our only hope?"

She'd brought the unit out without really being aware of what she was doing. A flick of the wands brought up a graph of payroll records for the five Counciliar Houses represented at the meeting in Manco House. It was the first thing she'd checked after entering the Councilors' databases.

"Perhaps," said Krychek. "He's a reformer, this Corius. He thinks the common people of Bennaria should have some of the cream themselves. A victory on Dunbar's World would give him greater status."

"Do you mean that he *says* the common people should have more?" Adele said harshly. "What other evidence is there that he believes what he says?"

Lucius Mundy had said similar things as head of the Popular Party, but he'd literally ridden on the backs of his supporters down Straight Street to the Senate House a month before Adele left to complete her schooling on Bryce. Representatives of the poor districts of Xenos dined at the Mundy table in the run-up to every election that Adele could remember . . . but they were clients dining with Mundy of Chatsworth. None of them was likely to misunderstand the fact that their role was to aid Senator Mundy in his plans for the betterment of their position.

"You're a cynical one, Mundy!" Krychek said with a laugh. "More wine, then? No? Well, Corius says the people should have more, I'll leave it at that. But he's gathering soldiers, two thousand of them."

Adele said nothing for a moment, staring at the graph already on her display. Councilor Waddell had some three hundred armed retainers, allowing for the possibility that she'd misallocated men who might be clerks. None of the other Councilors had more than two hundred, putting Corius' private army on a different scale from those of his rivals.

"Do you think he's planning a coup here on Bennaria, then?" she asked, meeting Krychek's eyes calmly. She didn't bother asking whether he was sure of his figures; that would simply insult his intelligence and make him less forthcoming. Besides, the numbers matched the capacity of the transports Corius had rented.

"No," said Krychek. "No, he doesn't have men enough to defeat all the Councilors put together—and they'll unite against him if he tries, you can be sure of that."

He snorted. "*Corius* is sure of that, he'll have no doubt," he went on. "His family's always been powerful here, so he was born knowing how the rest of the Councilors think. And besides . . ."

Krychek rose swiftly and smoothly to his feet. His right arm lashed out, hurling his empty glass into the dummy fireplace set into the bulkhead across from him. He was a strong man; the impact smashed the glass to little more than dust.

"And besides," Krychek resumed calmly, looking down at Adele, "if Corius intended a coup, he would hire me and my good fellows, would he not? A hundred and eighty men, trained as shock troops and long experienced in crewing a ship, this ship. Experienced in holding their own among the dregs of the galaxy."

Adele took her left hand out of her pocket. She bent to retrieve the wand she'd dropped when her host moved unexpectedly, but she didn't take her eyes off his face.

She didn't speak, either. A matter that so raised Krychek's emotional temperature was nothing for her to start dabbling in verbally unless she had to.

"I owe you an explanation," Krychek said, though from his tone he was more bragging than apologizing. "Why I behave in this way."

"You owe me nothing but common courtesy," said Adele calmly. "If you want to break a glass in your own residence, the reasons are none of my business."

Though if you startle me like that again, she thought, *you may not survive the experience. Which will pose problems for me as well.*

"We had to leave Port Dunbar very suddenly," Krychek said, turning to stare at a display of pipes. "We were the only ship to lift from the harbor after the invasion. Their shots were hitting our hull and pierced an outrigger. There was danger, yes, but less danger. Arruns would certainly have hung us all had he captured the city. Maurice didn't come with us—he went by land to Ollarville and took commercial transport from there."

The flamboyance was gone from Krychek's tone and demeanor. He seemed a sharp man; Adele suspected he'd noticed that her reaction to violence wasn't to cower.

"I recall him saying that," Adele said, a politely neutral comment. She met her host's eyes, but the little data unit was busy gathering all the information available from the *Mazeppa*.

"We'd just come back from a trading voyage," Krychek continued, facing Adele again with a leisurely movement that couldn't be mistaken for a threat. "We hadn't restocked yet, and our thruster nozzles were thin. Very thin, I learned, but there was no choice. We lifted for Bennaria while the Pellegrinians shot at us, and landed as quickly as we could."

He shrugged expressively. "There was no choice," he repeated. "Two thrusters failed as we landed, and we cannot lift until the whole set is replaced. Or at least half—we can manage with twelve. We have no payload, you see."

"Are there no yards on Bennaria that can do the repairs?" Adele said. She knew full well that there were—docks and repair facilities were among the first subjects she researched on any new planetfall—but it seemed a useful comment to keep the conversation flowing.

"Ah, but that will be expensive," Krychek said. "The bankers here are the Councilors themselves, you knew that?"

"Yes," said Adele. She would've expected it anyway, since close-knit oligarchies rarely gave outsiders a chance to become wealthy.

"None of them will loan me enough for the repairs," he said, glowering. "Our latest cargo was just off-loaded into warehouses in Port Dunbar. The banks won't accept it as collateral, even at a ruinous discount; nor will they loan money against the *Mazeppa* herself."

Krychek stalked back to the sideboard. Instead of pouring more wine from the tantalus, he opened the cabinet underneath and took out a squat green bottle. Adele sipped from her glass, until now barely tasted, to forestall being offered some of the liquor. She needn't have bothered; for the moment Krychek appeared to have forgotten her.

He took a deep draft of the oily, pale yellow fluid and wiped his mouth with the back of his hand. "It is not just business, you must see," he said harshly to a bookcase. "They fear me. They will not accept the sworn oath of a Landholder of Infanta!"

Krychek threw himself into his chair again. There was something innately theatrical about the man. He wasn't putting on a show for Adele, high emotion was simply so much of his nature that he couldn't help but put on a show.

"If the thrusters would lift us, I would take us to Ferguson," Krychek said, his voice rising and falling in measured periods. "The new Headman would treat us as we deserve! *He* knows the Cispalans will stop at nothing to renew their tyranny over Ferguson."

Adele hadn't studied Ferguson in detail, but current events were her trade. From what she'd gathered in passing, Daunus Fonk had been the notably rapacious Cispalan governor of the wealthy Cispalan colony of Ferguson. He'd changed his name to Headman Ferguson when he declared the planet independent, using his whole administrative budget to hire mercenaries—and then used those mercenaries to raise additional money. The wool from Terran sheep raised on Ferguson grew up to eighteen inches long and was remarkably fine, but the Headman was shearing his citizenry closer than ever they did their sheep.

"As it is," Krychek said, "were I to try the thrusters, we would rise only to plunge to the ground like a doomed comet. Yet what choice is there? If we stay here, I will shortly be unable to purchase even food for my men. Better to die in flaming glory, do you not think?"

Headman Ferguson was at best unbalanced, at worst certifiably psychotic. He *was* hiring mercenaries, though, and Adele appreciated that a former pirate trader was unlikely to have a delicate conscience. Still, Ferguson didn't seem the best available choice for employer.

"I'm puzzled," she said, ignoring what she assumed was a rhetorical question, "as to why Councilor Corius isn't willing to hire your men. No matter what he intends to do with them."

Krychek looked at her. The half-full liquor glass in his hand seemed forgotten. "Corius would hire my men," he said. His faint smile hardened as he spoke. "Buy them from me, if you will. But he would not allow me to lead them. Am I such a brute that I should sell my own people?"

No, thought Adele as she put away her data unit, *you wouldn't sell your retainers. But God help anybody who got in the way of you taking care of yourself and those retainers. Yuli Corius seems to understand that too.*

Adele stood, setting her glass on the end table beside her chair. "Master Krychek . . .," she said.

"Krychek, just Krychek," her host interjected, rising also.

"You've been of great help to me," she said. "I'll do what I can about your problem if a means occurs to me, but I'm afraid that at present I don't see one."

"No man can escape his fate," said Krychek portentously. "Perhaps this is mine, to die in flames on this wretched planet!"

Adele looked at the man; he was posed as though modeling for a heroic statue. For all his histrionics, Krychek was just as sharp as she'd have expected a partner of Maurice Claverhouse to be. He'd made the connection that many would've missed: if Yuli Corius were planning a coup on Bennaria, he'd have hired the Infantans under Krychek simply to prevent his rivals from doing so as soon as the fighting started.

"I won't discuss religion with you or anyone else," Adele said aloud. "I have neither knowledge nor interest in the subject. But speaking analytically, Krychek, I will point out that the situation on Bennaria strikes me as very unstable. If I were you, I wouldn't be in too great a hurry to convert myself into a fireball."

Krychek laughed with honest gusto. "Come," he said, offering Adele his arm. "I will have my men take you back to your ship. We have a crawler—from our business, you see—that does very well on muck like this island. The places we met our clients to trade were ones that others did not visit, you see?"

"I do see," Adele said, mounting the steps arm in arm with her host. She'd intended to have the water taxi wait for her, but it seemed unlikely that the boatman would ever come within impeller range of the Infantans again. "And thank you."

Krychek's information meant that Corius planned to take his private army to Dunbar's World. That didn't mean she and Daniel could trust Corius, but they could trust his intentions and act accordingly.

"*Now shine your cheeks like milk and wine . . .,*" sang the chorus as Krychek pulled the hatch open. "*But ah! all roses wither.*"

Tovera turned out to be a lyric soprano.

CHAPTER 9

Charlestown on Bennaria

Daniel was whistling a tune from the production number that'd climaxed the show at the Diamond Palace. The dancers were only a slender cut above what he could've found on the Harbor Three Strip and the comedians' jokes hadn't gotten any fresher for having traveled across the galaxy, but live entertainment never came amiss to a spacer.

There were any number of recordings aboard the *Sissie*, music and dance, comedies and dramas, but human beings on a stage of boards and chintz drew Daniel as surely as they did the riggers and motormen. Perhaps their greatest virtue was that a live performance proved to the audience that they were on firm ground in sidereal space once more.

"*Little white snowdrop, just waking up!*" Daniel caroled, giving each word a hammered emphasis very different from the saccharine blonde who'd sung the piece half an hour before. "*Violet, daisy and sweet buttercup!*"

Besides, the strength and quality of the Palace's cider made up for any deficiencies in its performers. "That was bloody good cider, Hogg," Daniel said. "*Bloody* good."

"And you drank enough of it to float the *Sissie*, so you did, master," Hogg said, "but fortunately there was some left for me. And since you bring that up . . ."

They'd walked past the mouth of an alley. The street was crowded with pedestrians and slow-moving vehicles, but the only lighting was the garish mix of colors on the building fronts. A couple paces back from the entrance, the alley was dark as a yard up a hog's backside.

In practiced unison, Daniel and Hogg reversed course and strode into the alley. Daniel was already fumbling for the fly of his third-best set of Grays, the uniform he wore when he was looking for entertainment at harborside instead of in the parlors of the wealthy.

A cat or a dog—or perhaps a drunk—scuttled into the deeper darkness. Daniel wasn't worried. A mugger foolish enough to set on him and Hogg together would just be more entertainment.

Judging they were far enough in, Daniel turned to the wall—the back of the Diamond Palace, he supposed—and relieved himself with a feeling of enormous relaxation. He really *had* put down a lot of that cider. . . .

"You know, Hogg," he said, "I've often thought that the simplest things are the most satisfying. Somebody should write a book—"

A car turned into the alley from the other end, its headlights filling the passage with a blue-white glare. Trash cans, downspouts, and short flights of steps up to back doors sprang into harsh silhouette.

"Always said wogs didn't know squat about courtesy till you knocked it into 'em," Hogg muttered as he tied his fly shut. He sounded amused rather than really put out by the incident, though.

The closed car pulled up just short of the steps near which Daniel'd been standing. The car's front door opened and an attendant in magenta livery got out, lit by the headlights reflecting from the concrete steps.

Four men came quickly from the building, metal in their hands. "Bugger off!" one growled, but as he spoke he clouted the attendant over the ear.

The attendant shouted, staggered, and ran down the alley toward Daniel and Hogg. The side of his head was bleeding. A thug came around the front of the vehicle; the driver got out and ran the other way.

"Hold up!" said Daniel, grabbing the attendant. The man had a baton as long as his arm. It might've been intended for show but it made a good weapon regardless. He shrugged free, bawling with fear, but he left the baton in Daniel's hands.

"You lot!" Daniel shouted. "Sheer off!"

"You want some of this, you Cinnabar space turds?" said the thug who'd struck the attendant. He stepped toward Daniel, waving a knife with a long, curved blade and a knuckleduster hilt. "Here it is, then!"

Daniel broke the fellow's knife wrist, then lifted the baton in a quick backhand that smashed his jaw as well. The thug had been clever enough to recognize Daniel's accent, but it didn't seem to have occurred to him that a Cinnabar warship in harbor might mean people who knew how to handle themselves in a brawl.

Daniel went left, toward the steps. There was no slowing down now. The thug who'd pulled open the car's rear door turned toward him. Daniel lunged, using the baton like a foil. The fellow got his hand up in front of him, but the tip of the baton rammed through and punched him in the chest. His breastbone was broken if Daniel'd read the crackle under the impact rightly.

It was good Daniel'd ducked as he lunged because a *bwee!* passing his left ear meant that Hogg had swung his weighted line at the thug standing at the top of the three concrete steps. "Bloody—" the fellow shouted, then screamed in disbelief as Hogg jerked back.

Hogg's weapon of choice was ten feet of monocrystal deep-sea fishing line with a two-ounce sinker on either end. He could bring down a running man a hundred feet away or—gripping one end with a steel-mesh glove—use the line as a flexible sword. It was too strong to break and thin as the working edge of a knife.

The last thug was the one who'd had gone around the front of the car. Daniel stayed low, waddling toward the fellow. He'd seen the damage Hogg's fishline did too often in the past to risk losing a finger—or his throat—to it.

Something flew through the air, flapped against the car's windshield, and then bounced to the ground. *The gun the guy on the steps was holding*, Daniel thought; and it was, sorta, but the fellow's hand was still locked on the grip. The muscles must've spasmed when Hogg jerked the monocrystal through the wrist.

The man on the steps was blubbering prayers; the one Daniel'd punched with the baton had shambled off toward the street; and the one with the broken arm and jaw hunched in the headlight beam, clutching his face with his good hand and moaning. Daniel rose and shoved that last fellow ahead of him, hoping he'd take the first bullet if their remaining opponent had a gun.

The two thugs collided. One screamed—maybe they both did. The injured man collapsed and the other hurled his spiked club at Daniel before turning to run. Daniel started after him but halted when his intellect took control again.

Let the silly bastard go. He wasn't a danger to anybody now, and Daniel'd had *quite* enough exercise. He leaned against the car, sucking air through his open mouth and wondering if he was going to spew up the rest of the cider.

The car's back door opened, switching on the dome light; a man with delicate features leaned out and said, "My manager, Lonnie. Please, I've got to find him. Is he inside?"

The fellow's voice was familiar.

"I'll check," said Hogg. He was gathering his line for further use, wiping it with a patch of chammy.

"I'll do it," said Daniel, moving toward the steps. "I need to move a bit."

His shoulder ached from the flung club. Nothing broken, though. A spike had torn the fabric and he seemed to've split his tunic up the back when his muscles bunched, but that's why he'd worn this uniform.

Daniel hefted the baton. It was made of dark, fine-grained wood and was a *very* nice tool for a street fight. If the person using it had balls, of course; which the original owner hadn't.

The would-be gunman staggered down the alley, holding his stump with his remaining hand and shouting frightened curses. Daniel patted the baton into his left palm. He'd have broken the fellow's knee if he hadn't run away on his own.

The outside door opened to a short hallway. The firedoor to the right was bolted shut from this side; directly opposite was an open dressing room with a small light on inside.

Daniel stepped into the dressing room, the baton ready to block or strike. He recognized the smell; the smells.

A man was wired to the room's cane chair. He'd been tortured to death, tortured and mutilated. The killers hadn't been trying to get information: they'd taped his mouth shut before they started, judging by the way blood and humors from his eyes coated the gag.

Daniel backed from the room and out of the building. Hogg was in the driver's seat; he'd turned the headlights off. "Say," he called, "this fellow's the singer we heard, you know? The pretty blond girl, Elemere. Only he isn't a girl."

Daniel got into the car. "Your manager's dead," he said to the man in the backseat. "I'm sorry. Hogg, get us back to the ship."

"Oh, God," said Elemere. "Oh *God*. You've made a bad enemy for yourself, sir. Councilor Waddell sent them."

"The people who did this aren't folk I'll ever want for friends," Daniel said savagely.

Hogg turned the lights back on. The man with chest injuries had crawled halfway to the street before collapsing on the pavement. "Ah . . .," said Hogg. "Should I back, young master, or—"

"Drive on!" said Daniel, his hands clenching the baton in mottled fury. He was thinking of Councilor Waddell's fat throat.

The entertainer who called himself Elemere sat at the rotated astrogator's console of the *Princess Cecile*, facing the gathered officers. He was drinking brandy that Hogg'd borrowed from a spacer just back from liberty. Adele didn't suppose the liquor was of the best quality, but Elemere wasn't complaining. He held his mug in both hands, huddling over it and taking frequent gulps. He was shivering and seemed on the verge of going into shock.

"I have a galactic reputation," Elemere said. "I've sung to the rulers of a score of worlds. My family's of the Pleasaunce nobility, you know."

It seemed odd to Adele that the fellow didn't sound as though he were bragging. He must've repeated the lie so often that in a crisis his brain went back to it by rote. Adele had tapped a background check in the files of Waddell House, showing to her satisfaction that Elemere had been born Albertus Mintz on Planchett, a minor planet. *Nobody* on Planchett qualified as "noble" by the standards of Pleasaunce, and Albertus' father had been a watchman at an open-cast copper mine.

"Bennaria wasn't on the planned tour," Elemere said, "but Bestin, the owner of the Diamond Palace, caught my act on Pellegrino. He offered us a bonus for a one-week engagement. I said this place is already Hell's sewer but Lonnie said, 'Come on, kid, for this kinda money we can hold our breath a week.'"

His eyes shut; he was crying. "Oh, God," he whispered. "Lonnie's dead."

Woetjans was on shore. Vesey, the two midshipmen—Cory wide-eyed, Blantyre stern but lacing and unlacing her fingers—and Pasternak listened with Adele and Daniel; Hogg and Tovera had left the ship on business they considered important; Adele was willing to accept their judgment.

"Go on," said Daniel, standing at parade rest with his hands crossed behind his back. That Elemere would be shaken was only to be expected, but Adele didn't recall ever seeing Daniel in such a state as he was at present. His torn uniform showed he'd been in a fight, but in the past that'd exhilarated him. Now he looked as though he were ready to chew through the pressure hull.

"We took the offer," Elemere said in his dead voice. He paused to empty the cup. Pasternak held the bottle ready, but the entertainer didn't signal for a refill. "It was Lonnie's idea but I said, 'Sure, why not? At worst it'll make Cranston look good.' Cranston was the next stop on the tour. A stinking place. They process wood pulp there."

Adele glanced at her display, shifting and sorting. Elemere was no nobleman, but he really did have a reputation. The accounts of the Diamond Palace indicated his salary was forty percent of the theater's talent budget for the week.

Elemere shook his head in despair. He'd worn a hooded cloak when he boarded the *Princess Cecile*, but he'd taken it off inside. Now his hair, blond and as fine as spiderweb, fell to his waist.

"So the first two nights were all right," he said. "Good houses and the theater, well, I've played worse."

He raised his mug and found it empty. Pasternak made a slight gesture to call attention to the brandy bottle. "Yes!" said Elemere, holding out the mug. "Yes, for God's sake!"

He drank deeply again. "After we closed the second night," he said, "there was a man waiting for me—Councilor Waddell. I could tell by the way Bestin treated him that he was a big deal—on Bennaria. Which is a mud puddle, is *nothing*. But I was polite and when he asked me out to his country estate, I said I'd talk to my manager and let him know. Oh God."

Elemere's hands began to shake, spilling a little of the brandy. He leaned forward to set the mug on the deck, but he'd have dropped it if Daniel hadn't squatted beside him and taken the mug.

Daniel held the brandy. His face was that of an angry statue.

"I've had arrangements like that in the past," Elemere said. "It's a matter of how good the money is. Waddell was a fat pig, but that's not unusual either."

He looked around the compartment, obviously prepared to respond to an expression of disapproval. *I, with as many lives as I have on my conscience, should judge you?* Adele thought; and perhaps the others had similar reactions. At any rate, all the faces were still.

"But Lonnie checked with people," Elemere said. "Not just Bestin. Bestin said it was a wonderful opportunity, that Waddell would bring me back and forth in his aircar, but others—there were whispers that some of the people Waddell took to his estate didn't come back at all. Some men, but women too. And when he came to me the next night, I told him no, that I didn't want to go."

Elemere reached out for the mug; his hands were steady again. While he drank, Daniel said quietly, "I've met Councilor Waddell. Perhaps I'll meet him again when I'm not representing the Republic."

"He got . . . threatening," said Elemere. "It worried me. I think it worried Lonnie too, though he said it was just the usual thing, the sort of business we've shrugged off a hundred times. You know. But Lonnie said he'd get us passage off-planet tomorrow night, that's tonight. We'd go before the last show, and if Bestin didn't like it when he learned, well, he had the second half of my fee to console himself."

The entertainer drank, paused, and drank again before lowering the mug. "I cut my last performance tonight and went straight to the harbor," he said. "Lonnie was supposed to be waiting with a boat. We'd pay off the car and attendants that we'd hired here and go straight over to the *Varta*. She was a tramp. She'd make two more planetfalls in Ganpat's Reach, but she was leaving tonight. I just wanted to get off Bennaria."

He lowered his head. "Oh God," he whispered. Tears were running down his cheeks. "Oh God."

Vesey turned to Daniel and said in a quiet voice, "The *Varta* lifted for San Felipe an hour ago, sir."

"Yes?" said Daniel. He shrugged. "Chances are their captain was the one who informed Waddell anyway. Nobody who trades regularly to Bennaria is going to want to get on the wrong side of Waddell."

"Lonnie wasn't at the waterside," Elemere said thickly. "Nobody'd seen him tonight. I turned around and came back. I thought maybe he'd gotten confused so he was waiting back at my dressing room."

"They brought him back," Daniel said. His tone was quiet but not calm. "I believe they expected to find you there. They waited when you weren't since they knew you didn't have anywhere else to go. And found ways to occupy their time."

"Sir, I'll stop liberty," Vesey said. "Should I call the port watch back, too?"

"Yes," said Daniel. He rubbed his forehead with both hands. "They recognized my accent, though they probably don't know it was me in person. Waddell's likely to decide that grabbing a couple Cinnabar spacers as hostage'll convince us to give him Elemere."

The entertainer looked up from his chair. "Will you . . .?" he said. His voice rose to a squeak that choked off any additional words.

Daniel stared at Elemere. "No," he said, enunciating clearly but not raising his voice. "I won't. I'll burn this city down before I do that."

The private security force patrolling the Charlestown entertainment district hadn't had time to make a written report on the murder in the Diamond Palace, but Adele'd made a text crawl of their excited calls to their supervisors. She looked up from reading how the manager had been mutilated.

"Yes," she said, speaking very distinctly. "We will."

"Blantyre and Cory?" Daniel said. "Take our guest to your quarters and show him how to lock the hatch. You'll bunk with your watches until further notice."

Adele noticed that he wasn't pretending Vesey was really in command anymore. Vesey had the active cancellation field up around the command console, but that didn't affect Adele's ability to overhear, of course. She was sending armed parties ashore to roust the spacers on liberty back to the *Sissie*.

Cory helped Elemere to his feet. As they shuffled to the hatch, Pasternak held out the brandy bottle. Blantyre turned toward Daniel with a worried look; he nodded. She took the bottle before closing the hatch behind them.

Pasternak let out a deep breath and knuckled his ear. He was flushed; his rosy scalp clashed with the color of his thinning red hair.

"Look, sir," he said, looking at the floor. "The hull's my business. What you want to do with it's yours, I know that. But I swear sir—"

He met Daniel's eyes with a shame-faced expression.

"—if that fellow's aboard any length of time, there's going to be trouble. I'm not saying it's his fault, but ... bloody hell! You know what I mean."

"Yes, I know what you mean," Daniel said heavily. He seated himself at the console that Elemere had vacated; he looked very tired. "That's one of the problems I'll be working on until I get it solved."

"Sir?" said Vesey. "You and Mistress Mundy were planning to go to the Council meeting tomorrow morning? Maybe that isn't safe now."

"It doesn't matter if it's safe, Vesey!" Daniel said. "It's our duty so we'll do it."

Adele didn't let the frown reach her forehead; Daniel wouldn't have spoken like that—his tone more than his words—under normal circumstances. He was remembering the manager's body.

"I believe we'll be safe, Captain," Adele said, bending her lips into a smile as she looked at Vesey. She tapped her tunic pocket. "At any rate, we'll be safer than the first twenty of Waddell's men who try to hold us."

With the words came a rush of what Adele could only describe as bloodlust. Her forced smile became quite real.

CHAPTER 10

Charlestown on Bennaria

The Council Hall was a round, domed building. The center of the polished stone floor was white; twenty-seven backless chairs were set around the black border. There were balconies on both sides. Neither would hold more than a dozen people, but Adele, Daniel, and Luff had the left-hand one to themselves.

The balcony opposite had six in it, the chief aides to the five Councilors who'd met with them at Manco House—and Corius' servant Fallert. The humans were clumped in the corner farthest from the snakeman.

Fallert grinned and made a sweeping bow to Adele when she entered the box with her companions. Luff flinched away. Adele responded with a curtsey, thinking of how pleased her deportment teacher would be that she'd remembered her lessons after twenty years of disuse.

"Our distinguished guests from the Republic of Cinnabar are present," said the Chairman of the Council, an eighty-year-old with a walker who looked to be a hundred. Adele's vantage point emphasized the fellow's hunch, of course. "Does anybody know if we can expect more of our colleagues to join us?"

"That's Monson," Luff whispered. Adele knew the Chairman's name; so did Daniel if he'd read the briefing she'd prepared for him.

"He doesn't have any real power. The chairmanship is a rotating office."

"We have a quorum, Honorable Chairman," said Waddell. He sat on his chair like a gross golf ball perched on its tee. "I don't think we need delay this matter if the constitutional requirements are met."

Only fifteen of the places were filled. Three Councilors were ill, and two houses were headed by youths below the minimum age of sixteen.

Judging by the private discussions among the five chief members—which Adele had perused in detail—the remainder of the absentees were simply unwilling to come to the capital when the populace was in a state of unrest. They were largely the less wealthy Councilors who didn't trust the size of their private armies to protect them.

The meeting was already past its scheduled midday start time, but a ship had landed in the harbor just as Monson was laboring to his feet. He'd had to wait till the echoes from the thrusters died away before starting to speak.

Though the Council Chamber wasn't quiet even now. The public wasn't allowed inside, but by tradition the double front doors were thrown back so that in theory they could listen to the deliberations.

Today the Councilors' retainers stood outside shoulder-to-shoulder in front of the building, each group wearing a colored beret or similar livery to mark their affiliation. The crowd beyond made a sound like an angry sea, washing in and out of the domed chamber. It half smothered the Chairman's voice.

"This is a special meeting, called by Councilor Corius," Monson quavered. "As is the right of any of us. I therefore turn the floor over to the honorable Councilor."

He made a slight gesture with his hand, then settled cautiously onto his chair. His walker trembled.

Yuli Corius rose with a flourish. His choice of unadorned white robes made him stand out among the garish colors of his peers like a marble faun in a tulip bed. He was standing almost directly beneath Adele's balcony, so mostly she saw only the top of his head.

She wasn't terribly interested in looking at Corius anyway. There were no seats in the balcony so she'd placed her personal data unit on the floor between her and the railing. Its holographic display was capable of projecting images twenty feet with reasonable sharpness, so raising them from the floor to a short woman's working height was no trouble at all.

"Fellow Councilors, I'll get right to the point," Corius said; his delivery was breezy. "Our friends and allies on Dunbar's World—our close business associates on Dunbar's World—are faced with a threat which at best will overturn all existing trade arrangements unless it's successfully countered. I propose to counter it in the name of Bennaria but at my own expense. Do I have your approval?"

The other Councilors reacted in everything from laughter to the stark anger of Councilor Fahey, who leaped to his feet and pointed his finger across the room at Corius. Waddell made a small gesture. When that didn't work, he spoke sharply enough to get Fahey's attention. Fahey sat down, flicking his angry eyes from Corius to Waddell and back.

"You can't expect us—you couldn't expect *anybody*—to give you a blank check, Corius," said Councilor Waddell. He smiled at his rival, but his face was hard under the feigned amusement. "That's particularly true when you're making promises that you can't possibly fulfill."

"Well, Waddell, we differ on that matter," Corius said. His smile was wider than Waddell's but equally forced. "And on so many others, of course. But this one's easy to test: as soon as the government of Bennaria authorizes me, I'll go to Dunbar's World and either succeed or fail. Not so?"

The aides in the other balcony were taking calls from retainers outside the building; expressions of horror settled onto their faces. Fallert's grin was a predator's gape.

"*Mistress?*" said Tovera through the bead receiver in Adele's ear. "*Troops're joining the mob in the square outside. I think they came from the ship that just landed.*"

She paused, then added, "*They've got their right sleeve blue over battledress and they just carry clubs, but they're pushing a cart that could carry guns for fifty or sixty.*"

Adele didn't have a microphone to reply orally, but she used her data unit to send a text acknowledgment. Her servant would read it on the miniature display she was using to monitor sensors outside the building. Tovera was an information technician, not an artist like Adele herself, but she was a very well-trained and painstaking technician.

Adele already knew about the men advancing from the harbor, though. The aides on the opposite balcony had been informed as soon as the first of the prepositioned barges crossed the strait and unloaded in Charlestown.

Fallert had presumably known earlier than that: these were the mercenaries Corius had been hiring. Adele frowned, still sure that Corius wasn't planning a coup. He was too smart to believe he had enough men to succeed, and the weapons he'd brought were basically defensive.

"Corius, it's not news to me that you're pushy and full of yourself," Waddell said, losing even the semblance of good humor. "It shouldn't be news to you that you can't push *us*. Now—when you provide the Council with a detailed plan of the proposed operation, that'll be time for the Council to begin deliberations on whether you'll be allowed to carry them out."

He turned from Corius to sweep the circle with his eyes. "Or so I would propose to my colleagues," he added. The smile was back, this time with an oily sheen.

"Full of myself, Councilor?" said Corius pleasantly. He patted his belly with his left hand, striking hard enough to slap the fingers audibly against the hard muscles beneath his robe. "Not words I'd have expected to hear from you, to be honest."

Several of the Councilors grinned. Knox, seated at Waddell's right hand, blurted an open laugh which he quickly suppressed with his hand. He didn't meet Waddell's eyes.

"But for the rest . . . ," Corius continued, meeting the eyes of his fellows one by one as his expression settled into speculative lines. "Councilors, every hour we delay makes success more difficult. Besides, I don't have a detailed plan; it'd be impossible to make one without knowing more than we *can* know until I'm on Bennaria with my troops. Give me the authorization, and I'll give you—give Bennaria—the victory. That or die trying."

The aides were signalling furiously to their principals beneath. "That's odd," said Luff in a husky whisper. "Nobody's allowed to step onto the floor while the Council's in session. I think those fellows are trying to get their masters to leave the chamber so they can tell them something!"

Adele said nothing. Luff was correct, of course, but it was so obvious a conclusion that she couldn't imagine why he'd thought it necessary to voice.

Councilor Layard started to rise, his eyes on the balcony. Waddell gestured him back with curt anger.

"Honorable Chairman?" Waddell said. "Our colleague demands we vote on his proposition immediately. I therefore move that we deny his request and adjourn to our homes!"

"Second," said Layard, still glancing up at his aide in obvious discomfort. "Call for an immediate vote."

Adele smiled coldly. *He probably thinks a vote's the quickest way to learn what crisis had just broken. He was right about that.*

"Well, ah . . .," said Monson. "Why yes, ah, will the honorable Council please vote on the motion before it."

"That we reject Corius' proposal!" Waddell said forcefully, staring at his rival.

Yuli Corius remained standing, his head cocked. He wore a faint smile.

"Yes, of course," said Monson. "Ah, a voice vote, I believe."

"Aye!" said Waddell, and the remaining Councilors echoed him with, "Yes," or "Aye," or—from Councilor Fahey—clearly audible over the chorus of murmurs, "Too bloody right!"

Councilor Waddell wobbled to his feet. "I don't know about the rest of you," he said, "but I'm going home now. Corius, I suggest you either drop this notion or work out a plan that the rest of us can consider."

"I'm afraid I won't have time for that, Waddell," Corius said, raising his voice to be heard over the shuffle of chairs and feet on the stone. "I have to chair a popular assembly in the square outside. I'm going to ask the people of Bennaria to authorize my proposal, since the Council hasn't seen fit to do so."

"Popular assembly?" Fahey said, his face growing blotchy with anger.

"Yes, indeed, Councilor," Corius answered brightly. "I suggest you all come to watch. And I can assure you there'll be no violence: I've brought two thousand men from my estate to keep order!"

"Oh my God!" said the Manco representative, wringing his hands. "Oh, what does this mean?"

"Well, Master Luff," said Daniel. "I suggest you come with me and watch as Master Corius suggested. That way we can learn firsthand."

The noise from the crowd outside was vibrantly excited, and the Councilors who'd reached the anteroom were talking in spiky concern as Daniel led his party down the balcony stairs. He stretched his arms, overhead and then back behind him, to loosen the muscles. His left shoulder throbbed from the knock the club'd given him, but he had full strength and movement in the limb.

He grinned cheerfully at the milling nervousness below: the RCN was ready for action. As usual.

"Daniel?" Adele murmured, but just then Yuli Corius reached the outer door with Fallert behind him. Corius raised his hands high and the mob beyond the line of armed guards bellowed in response. Daniel paused, lifting a hand to warn his companions.

The aides from the other balcony were with their principals in the anteroom now, relaying orders over radio links. The guards outside parted, some of them glancing back with set expressions. Corius passed out of the building and into a troop of his own blue-sleeved retainers. He raised his hands again, gesturing toward the steps at the other end of the plaza.

When Corius had moved out of sight and the noise had abated a smidgen, Adele leaned close again and said, "Daniel, I have business that'll prevent me from attending the assembly. I'll explain later."

"Yes, of course," he said, turning his head slightly; Adele might not be able to hear the words but at least she could see his lips moving. "Good luck."

Now that Corius had taken the crush away from the plaza outside, the other Councilors were leaving. Daniel started down again. He didn't know what Adele had in mind, but she wasn't somebody whose work he had to oversee.

And looking out through the open doorway, it was pretty obvious that he had enough on his plate already.

"Commander Leary?" Councilor Waddell called as Daniel reached the bottom of the stairs. "I wonder if I might have a word with you on a personal matter."

It was a question only in form. Daniel looked at him. He half expected Adele to wait to hear this, but she and her servant slipped past and out of the building with the stream of Councilors. Waddell stood with a single aide, the young man with curly hair and broad shoulders who'd been present at Manco House the previous day.

Tovera's intelligent and frequently very useful, but how Adele can stand to have her around is beyond me. That was a thought for another time, though.

"I'm not aware of any personal business between us, Councilor," Daniel said, but he turned into the alcove under the stairs he'd just come down. There was enough room for them despite the presence of a statue of a robed orator with two fingers raised.

Hogg lounged against the wall, picking his nose and looking completely the rustic buffoon; his mouth drooped slackly as he eyed Waddell's aide. Daniel would've thought Hogg was overdoing the act, but he'd learned—as his servant had known from the beginning—that city folk would believe any lack of culture or intelligence in a countryman. Hogg made himself so easy to underestimate that opponents frequently didn't know what'd hit them.

"I think you found some property of mine last night, Leary," Waddell said, coming within arm's length. His voice was pitched to be lost in the continuing background of crowd noise at any distance from the two of them. "I know you'll want to return it for the sake of friendship."

"I have no property of yours, Councilor," Daniel said. "Nor friendship either, I'd have said."

He cleared his throat and went on, "You referred to 'personal business,' but I might mention my plan to hire some additional crew here. If so, they'll be RCN personnel to be tried by their captain for any infractions they happen to commit on Bennaria. Though of course that won't have any bearing on matters between you and me in our private capacities."

He knew that his face had stiffened from its usual smiling pleasantry, but he kept remembering the body he'd found in the dressing room. That needn't have been at Waddell's orders and might even have been against them, but it was a predictable result of hiring the sort of scum Waddell had picked.

The anteroom had emptied except for the two of them and their retainers. Guards wearing green-and-yellow rosettes like the aide's cap badge looked anxiously through the doorway but they didn't enter.

"I see," said Waddell. "I see indeed. Well, Commander, I'm sure that Nataniel Arruns will be in real danger if so resourceful an officer ever begins doing the job for which he was sent to Ganpat's Reach. Good afternoon, sir."

Waddell turned on his heel and stalked toward the doorway, flanked by his aide. Just before he exited, he turned and snapped, "Until we meet again, of course!"

Hogg scratched his right armpit. "Still want to push into the ruck on the other side a the square, master?" he asked, his eyes focused on the plaza.

"Yes, Hogg," said Daniel. "I'm sure the crowd will be full of whores and pickpockets and the usual run of city layabouts."

He paused, smiling again. "They'll raise the average tone over what we've been dealing with thus far today."

CHAPTER 11

Charlestown on Bennaria

Luff waited outside the entrance of the Council Chamber. Either he'd gone on to give Daniel and Waddell more privacy, or he was simply trying to keep out of the angry Councilor's sight. Regardless, Daniel nodded to the Manco agent and said, "Hogg and I are going to move toward the speaker's stand, Master Luff. Care to join us?"

Luff hunched himself together reflexively. He grimaced and said, "Yes, if you think it's safe. I suppose I should hear what he says."

"Oh, I think this assembly should be safe enough," Daniel said. He smiled, thinking, *For me at least it's much safer than almost anywhere else on Bennaria.* He doubted Waddell would attack the *Princess Cecile* directly, but other places were all a possibility.

With Luff in tow and Hogg at his side, Daniel began maneuvering forward. It was a hot day but the haze that seemed to be normal here in Charlestown kept the sun from being the hammer it might otherwise have been. Daniel was in his best set of Grays, not garments he wanted to wear in a brawl but less restrictive than his Whites. He was comfortable enough.

The plaza was full of civilians, but they grew thicker toward the center like that of stars in a cluster. To Daniel's surprise, Corius had disposed the bulk of his force to protect the crowd from a sudden onslaught by his rivals' massed retainers. He had only fifty or so men around him personally.

The cordon of guards eyed Daniel grimly as he approached. Corius'd had their two-foot truncheons decorated with tinsel streamers. That wasn't to hide the fact they were weapons, Daniel supposed, but to permit the other Councilors to pretend the troops weren't an armed threat.

A redhead in his mid-thirties appeared to be in command of the section Daniel approached. He was speaking into a microphone on his wrist; responses would come through his earclip, a larger version of the unit Adele was wearing. His frown cleared, becoming a smile of professional welcome.

"Sorry sir," he said. "I didn't recognize your uniform. You're very welcome here, but we're not letting in troublemakers wearing livery, you understand?"

"I do indeed," Daniel said, passing between two of the blue-sleeved guards, but he might as well have saved his breath; they couldn't possibly hear him. Councilor Corius was climbing the steps at the far end of the plaza, sending the crowd into shrieks of rapturous enthusiasm.

Corius raised both hands high, building the mob's excitement; the air of the plaza reeked of sweat laced with adrenaline. The speaker's stand was still a hundred and fifty yards from Daniel; he resumed working his way forward. There were too many people in the way for that to be easy, but a determined push generally made an opening. People prefer not to be in actual contact with one another; Daniel exploited that instinct to move through them.

"Fellow citizens of Bennaria!" Corius called. His bodyguards stood two steps below him, so that he could easily see and be seen by everyone in the plaza. "My brothers and sisters!"

"Bloody hell!" Hogg muttered angrily. "Does he think he's bulletproof? He's an easy shot from any roof around the square here. *Any* roof."

"We're not here to talk, Hogg," Daniel said, as quietly as he could and still be heard. With luck, none of the spectators *had* heard Hogg's comment. It would've sounded like a threat rather than the professional observation it was.

Hogg wasn't an assassin, but all his life he'd been a hunter. He was scarcely the only one on Bennaria today to view Councilor Corius as potential prey.

"It's been two generations since you, the people of Bennaria, met in solemn assembly," Corius said. "Now is the time to resume exercising your sacred rights of governance!"

The crowd had thickened further. Daniel thought he might be able to worm a little closer to the steps, but only a little.

Being close turned out not to be necessary for him to hear clearly. Not only was Corius using a concealed public address system, the plaza's acoustics were remarkably good. Behind the steps from which he spoke was the Port Administration Offices, the largest government building on the planet. The side facing the square sloped back at a 70-degree angle. Daniel wasn't sure that made it a better sounding board than a vertical wall would've been, but it was *very* effective.

"Our friends and neighbors on Dunbar's World have been attacked by a murderous warlord who plans to turn their planet into a base for pirates," Corius said. "If Nataniel Arruns is allowed to succeed, how long will it be before he or another like him grinds his iron heel on your neck and mine, fellow citizens?"

The crowd bellowed agreement, though many of its members must've known the claim was a farrago of nonsense. Pellegrino—unlike Bennaria—didn't trade with pirates. There was no likelihood that Nataniel Arruns planned to turn Dunbar's World into a pirate haven.

In the unlikely event an outside power conquered Bennaria, Corius and his fellow Councilors would come up short—probably a head short. The common people who made up the bulk of this mob would see little change in their status, though. Like the disenfranchised islanders on Dunbar's World, they had nothing to lose.

Still, whenever you tell a man that foreigners are dirty swine determined to cheat him, you're likely to get enthusiastic agreement. You're playing to his existing beliefs, after all. Speaker Leary's son had seen those tactics used more than once in the past.

Daniel smiled. That sort of realization made Adele angry to the point of despair. To him, it was like seeing a rambunctious puppy knock over a table. Puppies and people would be puppies and people, that's all there was to it.

"Your Council has failed you, fellow citizens!" Corius said. "Not only is the Council unwilling to act in the face of this immediate danger, the other Councilors are unwilling to permit me, acting as a private citizen, to work at my own expense to preserve the honor and safety of Bennaria. Therefore I've come to you. Will you, the people of Bennaria in sacred assembly, send me to Dunbar's World in your name?"

"Corius!" the blue-sleeved guards began to chant. "Corius! Corius!"

"*Corius!*" took up the crowd, twenty thousand strong if there was a man in it. "*Corius! Corius!*"

Daniel glanced over his shoulder. Hogg stood stolidly, his fists on his hips and his elbows flared outward to give him a little more room. He wore his usual vacant expression.

Luff's mouth was open also. His eyes were turned toward the speaker but they didn't seem focused. His right hand was cupped over his ear, shielding it from the noise around him so that he could hear what his in-canal earphone was telling him.

Corius raised his hands. For a moment the shouts grew even more fevered, but when he first crossed, then lowered them the crowd noise abated.

"My friends, my brothers!" Corius said. "Do you, the assembled people of Bennaria, authorize me, Yuli Corius, to act on your behalf but at my cost to drive the Pellegrinian invaders from Dunbar's World? If so, signify by—"

"*Yes!*" screamed the crowd. The citizens closest to Daniel were red-faced and sweating with excitement. Many pumped their fists in the air. "*Yes! Yes! Yes!*"

Daniel looked at Hogg, who nodded. They turned to ease their way back. There was nothing more to learn here, though the excitement would continue for as long as Corius chose to milk it.

Luff lowered his hand from his ear; he seemed transfixed. Daniel gestured him to turn, but it wasn't until Hogg put his hands on the Manco agent's shoulders and physically rotated him that he started to move.

Luff looked sour, angry, and very, very frightened.

"I had Hogg buy the boat for us," said Tovera at the tiller of the taxi. She wore a waterman's garments: baggy shorts, baggy shirt, and a vest with bright red embroidery. Her hat was a flat cone woven from split reeds and shaded her face completely. "He's better at that sort of thing than I am."

She tittered. "I suppose he bought the boat," she added. "Perhaps he cut the owner's throat instead. Though I could've handled that myself."

"I'm sure Hogg wouldn't kill anyone unless he thought they really needed it, Tovera," Adele said with a deadpan expression. "Unless we were shorter of money than I believe to be the case at present, of course."

Elemere wore one of Tovera's pale-gray suits; his blond hair was cropped short under Tovera's usual cap. He looked from Adele to her servant and back again with a horrified expression. His mouth trembled, but he didn't speak.

"It was a joke," Adele said. "Don't be upset."

Tovera *had* made a joke, the sort of thing normal human beings did. Adele felt it was her duty to encourage her sociopathic servant every time she attempted to act human. She didn't suppose Tovera would ever be good at it, but the effort deserved support.

It wasn't something Adele was very good at herself, after all, but she too kept trying. Being part of the RCN family helped a great deal. Spacers who daily risked death in exotic and horrible fashions were an eccentric lot. They had room for other eccentrics who were good at their jobs. Adele and Tovera qualified on that score.

The taxi was driven by a power unit clamped to the starboard side; the massive battery pack to port balanced the motor's weight. The vessel purred and slapped down the strait toward the *Mazeppa*; very slowly, but that was probably a good thing.

Krychek didn't know they were coming—Adele hadn't radioed ahead for fear of interception—and the last thing she wanted to do was to race toward the armed freighter. Krychek's crew must be as frustrated and depressed as their captain. There was no point in goading somebody who's got a gun with which to let out his anger.

"No one could possibly mistake me for that woman," Elemere said pettishly, glaring at Tovera on the seat ahead of them. "It's a waste of time to bother!"

"If they're looking for you, that's true," Adele said. The complaint—the stupid complaint—irritated her, but she understood how nervous the singer must be. Elemere was reacting to fear in an unhelpful fashion, but that's what people generally did. "We're doing this during the popular assembly because it's unlikely that you're at the top of anybody's mind at present, especially Councilor Waddell's."

The guard manning the impeller on the *Mazeppa*'s boarding ramp watched them, but he hadn't actually trained his big weapon on the puttering taxi. Adele waved. She was wearing the suit in which she'd visited the night before, but she knew it wasn't very distinctive.

She thought of standing up to make her approach even more obvious and therefore peaceful, but she'd probably tip the boat over if she tried. That *would* make them look less threatening, but she trusted it wouldn't be necessary.

"Most likely those we need be concerned about," she continued, in part to keep the singer from flying into hysterics, "are either watching Corius or getting ready to defend themselves if the mob goes on a rampage. There may be observers keeping an eye on the harbor, but they'll be worried about another transport full of troops landing."

"I should never've come to Bennaria," Elemere muttered, looking at his hands clenched in his lap. Adele didn't see any reason to disagree with him.

Three more crewmen walked onto the ramp to watch the taxi approach. All three wore horizontally striped shirts and loose, grubby trousers, but the peaked hat of the man in the middle marked him as an officer.

"Good day, sir!" Adele called as Tovera curved them toward the hanging ladder where they'd landed the night before. Lubricating oil slicked the water iridescently and hung as a miasma in the thick air. "Please tell Landholder Krychek that Lady Mundy wishes an audience with him."

"The Man's coming down, Your Ladyship," said the officer. "C'mon aboard. He says you're a friend, and we've *bloody* few friends on this mudball."

Tovera in the guise of the boatman lashed the taxi's painter to a recessed eyebolt on the outrigger instead of simply gripping it while the passengers disembarked. The Infantan spacers didn't comment.

"Go up," Adele muttered to Elemere. Then, peevishly, "Take your case with you!"

Elemere climbed the swinging ladder gracefully despite the burden in his left hand. The attaché case resembled Tovera's, but of course it wasn't. The contents of hers—the little sub-machine gun and similar pieces of equipment—were concealed under her baggy clothing.

Adele followed Elemere, but much more awkwardly; he was a dancer as well as singer. As she stepped onto the outrigger with deliberate care, Krychek strode from the hatchway and boomed, "Lady Mundy! A pleasure indeed to see you, an unexpected—"

He stopped, staring at Elemere. He raised an eyebrow.

"Go on into the ship, Tovera!" Adele said, then prodded Elemere with an elbow to start him moving. He'd forgotten the name he was using this afternoon; he obviously wasn't a natural conspirator.

"Let's go into your library, Landholder," Adele said, following close behind the singer to shield him from lenses that might be watching from across the strait. She didn't think anyone on Harbor Island could see them here. "I want to discuss the situation on Bennaria further."

"But of course, dear lady," said Krychek. To the officer nearby he added in a clipped, harsher, tone, "Keep an eye out. It's possible that these mud-wallowing pigs will think to interrupt us."

"To the left," Adele said in an undertone when she and Elemere were well into the entrance compartment. "The companionway."

They entered the helical stairs with Tovera immediately behind them. Krychek banged closed the hatch below, then said, "And now, my dear Mundy—what is all this? I recognize Master Elemere. While he's very welcome, I don't understand him arriving in quite the present costume."

"When we're in the library, if you will," Adele said over the echoing *shoof, shoof,* of their soles on the metal stairs. "Where we can talk more easily."

She stepped ahead of the hesitant Elemere and led the rest of the way to the freighter's uppermost level. Tovera's feet didn't seem to make a sound, which was remarkable but not surprising.

A hatch facing the strait and Charlestown beyond was open in the foyer; another automatic impeller was mounted there. It hadn't been manned when the taxi approached, but two Infantans were unlocking the mount and switching on the gun's power. They gave Adele a look of appraisal as she entered the library, but they didn't speak to her or to Krychek himself.

Tovera remained outside with the gunners, exchanging nods with Adele. Krychek closed the door—the hatch—behind them and gestured graciously toward the chairs on the level below. "Please," he said, "sit and make yourselves comfortable. Mundy, will you have another glass of wine? And Master Elemere—"

"Elemere," the singer said sharply. "Just Elemere."

"As I am Krychek!" said the captain with boisterous good humor, linking arms with Elemere and leading him down the stairs. "I fear your tastes may be too sophisticated for my poor cellar, but please—will you do me the honor of drinking a tot of Landholder Reserve cognac with me? The run was bottled at my birth."

"Why, I . . .," Elemere said, allowing himself to be guided to a short loveseat. Krychek opened the cabinet beneath the tantalus and brought out a slender green bottle with fluted sides. "Yes, a brandy would be . . . I would like a brandy."

Krychek poured an ounce of pale yellow liquor into each of two snifters but left them on the cabinet until he'd served Adele another glass of white wine. He seated himself beside Elemere and only then offered him the snifter in his right hand.

After breathing deeply from his own glass, Krychek looked over the rim of it and said, "Now Mundy. I'm pleased by this visit, very pleased; I saw Elemere perform on Lompac only last year. But there is a story behind it, is there not?"

"Yes," said Adele austerely, still standing. She watched the interaction of the two men. It was what she'd hoped, of course, but still it—

Never mind. "Landholder, you and your crew aren't the only people on Bennaria who aren't afraid of Councilor Waddell, but you may well be the only people besides us aboard the *Princess Cecile*. We're about to lift for what I may well be combat. We can't take Elemere with us."

"So . . .," Krychek said, tilting the snifter till the brandy touched—but only touched—his lips. He turned from Adele to look at the man beside him; his expression of cool appraisal gave way to a broad smile. "So, Elemere. Tell me why it is important that I am not afraid of Councilor Fat Pig Waddell?"

"He wanted me to go with him," the singer said, meeting Krychek's eyes. "He killed my friend when I wouldn't."

The glass in Elemere's hand trembled. He took a convulsive drink, probably a terrible thing to do to a stellar brandy, but Krychek didn't protest. He patted Elemere's knee and looked at Adele again. His smile remained.

"So," he repeated. "I understand much, but one thing I do not understand. You Cinnabars are here to help the government of Bennaria, and Waddell—for all that he is fat, and a pig, and utterly disgusting—is the government of Bennaria himself. I have no love for him—he is why I cannot get credit of any sort on this mudball—but it would seem your duty is to hand Elemere over and go on about your business. Not so?"

"Certainly not," said Adele without emphasis. "Our chief of mission is a Leary of Bantry; he's made this a matter of honor. I won't say Commander Leary's personal honor would take precedence over his duties to the RCN. Nonetheless, turning the matter over to brave and honorable men like yourselves makes it unnecessary for him to make such a decision."

Krychek laughed harshly. He sipped his brandy again; Adele took a drink of her wine. Her lips and tongue were extremely dry.

"I should help the RCN, that is what you say?" Krychek said musingly. "An interesting thought. Because I am an exile, I must be a traitor, that is what you think, Mundy?"

Adele set her barely tasted drink down on the display cabinet beside her. She realized she was standing very straight.

"Landholder Krychek," she said. *I sound like my mother,* she thought. *When she was very, very angry.* "You pointed out correctly that my actions here and those of Commander Leary verge on being in conflict with our RCN duties."

She made a peremptory gesture with her right index finger. "Master Elemere," she said, "get up. I can't leave you with a fool."

"You can't call me a fool!" Krychek shouted, lurching to his feet.

"I just did!" Adele said, her left hand in her pocket. "Elemere, get up *now* or on my oath as a Mundy I'll shoot you dead! That'll solve both Daniel's problem and the RCN's!"

The snifter shattered as Krychek's big hand clenched; blood and brandy sprayed. Elemere keened wordlessly and cupped Krychek's fist in both hands.

"Oh you've hurt yourself!" Elemere said. "Please, please, there's been enough pain! Let me bandage that, please!"

Adele took her hand from her pocket and held it away from her as if it were hot. She felt sick to her stomach from embarrassment; her skin burned as though she'd been buried in hot sand.

"I apologize," she said. She forced herself to meet Krychek's eyes. She was dizzy and afraid she might faint. "This is your ship, your house, and I insulted you in it. If you wish satisfaction, I will of course—"

"Stop that," said Elemere fiercely. He'd teased open Krychek's fist and was picking bits of broken glass from the blood. "*Stop* that! You'll not fight a duel, you'll not do any more stupid things, either one of you. There's been enough pain."

The singer jerked the lace doily out from under the tantalus with a sudden, sharp pull; the stand and decanters rattled against the wood. He wadded it in Krychek's palm, then poured the rest of his brandy into the lace.

"Now close your hand again," he said to Krychek. "This'll hold it till we get real medical help."

"There's a medicomp on C Deck," Krychek said. He sounded stunned. "But this is nothing, nothing."

"Elemere," Adele said, "we need to leave while the assembly's still going on. Landholder, I—"

"Wait," said Krychek. "Lady Mundy, the fault was mine. You came to me, a lady to a gentleman, and I acted a spoiled child."

He bowed at the waist to her, stepped back, and bowed even more deeply to Elemere. "Mistress," he said. "You are a great artist, a *great* artist. It would be an honor to me and my men to shelter you from your enemies. It would be an honor to die if we can shelter you with our very bodies. To die!"

"I don't think that will be necessary, gentlemen," Adele said dryly. She felt a smile twitch the corners of her mouth; in relief, largely, she supposed. "Waddell should believe that Elemere is aboard the *Princess Cecile* when we lift, and I trust that will be very soon. Tovera is arranging for one of your men to take us back in the boat, wearing the costume she came aboard with; she has her ordinary clothes on under it. Ah, with your permission, that is."

Neither of the men was listening to her. Elemere still held Krychek's fist.

"Would you help me?" the singer said. "I'm so alone. Lonnie was . . . Lonnie took care of everything."

"It is an honor," Krychek repeated. He put his free hand on the dancer's shoulder. "A very great honor."

Adele stepped briskly up the staircase. She didn't look around, but it wasn't until she'd banged the hatch closed behind her that she let out the breath she'd been holding.

"I suppose you're used to this sort of thing," Luff said bitterly as he started around the Council Hall with Daniel, toward the enclosed parking lot in back. There were clots of spectators at the rear of the plaza, watching but unwilling to be said to have joined the mob. Corius' voice through the PA system was audible though individual words weren't always clear. "Because your father's Speaker Leary, I mean."

I wonder who told him that? thought Daniel. He was pretty sure Luff hadn't known that Daniel was anything more than a young middle-ranking officer when the *Princess Cecile* landed on Bennaria.

"I've seen other mass gatherings, yes," Daniel said carefully. He had no reason to be abrupt with the question, but neither did he want to get in a discussion about Corder Leary. "This is quite a polite one, it seems to me. But that has nothing to do with who my father is. I grew up on our country estate, Bantry, not in Xenos. I saw bird migrations and file-fish runs, but not political demonstrations."

There'd been political *meetings*, though. Not this sort of thing, but the discussions which the public never learned about. One man, or three, or on a single occasion twelve, arrived at Bantry separately and separately slipped away again. On the night of the largest meeting began the Proscriptions that crushed the Three Circles Conspiracy.

They'd reached the steel-scrollwork gates of the parking compound. Luff's driver was inside talking with three attendants. Daniel pulled at the leaves, but they were locked.

Hogg'd been walking behind Daniel and Luff as they moved away from the crowd. He glanced back once more, then stepped to the gate and rattled it in irritation. "Hey!" he called. "You there! Look alive!"

The four men muttered uncertainly for a moment. Finally an attendant walked toward them while Luff's driver got into the black landau. It was the only vehicle still in the lot.

"They'd *better* get a move on," Hogg muttered, resuming his watch on the plaza. In a different voice he went on, "There were people waiting down some of the streets leading to the square, you know, master. They don't wear their colors, but they're somebody's bullies for sure."

"Master Luff?" Daniel said. "Do you think the other Councilors will attack Corius today?"

He wasn't sure how the Manco agent would respond. He'd remained in sullen silence while the three of them pushed back through the crowd, and the comment about Speaker Leary hadn't been made in a friendly tone.

Instead of growling some angry variant on, "How would I know?" though, Luff said, "No, no, they won't do that. The whole city would be burned down if they did that. Waddell may have observers, but attack? No."

He looked over his shoulder at the plaza. "The Councilors've all gone to their estates, I'm sure of that. Those who think they have enough retainers may leave a guard on their townhouses, but some won't even do that."

Luff shivered. "What if the city burns anyway?" he asked plaintively. "What will I do? This is a terrible thing, *terrible.*"

The driver had turned the car and was moving toward them. The attendant unlocked the gate's crossbar and slid it sideways. Hogg shoved the leaves fiercely, deliberately making the attendant jump back. The fellow'd delayed them, but Hogg was capable of taking his anger out on anybody who happened to be close.

Any wog, that is; Daniel didn't catch his servant's anger unless he personally was the cause of it. Which was often enough, in all truth.

"Sir?" said the attendant unexpectedly as he pulled one leaf fully open; Hogg was pushing the other back. "I—"

The fellow looked back at his fellows, standing against the wall. Each had his hands locked together to keep them from twitching. "I mean we, we were wondering if, you know, we should leave the Council Hall?"

"Ah," said Daniel, the syllable replacing, "Why in the world are you asking me?" because as soon as he framed that question mentally, he knew the answer: the attendants were terrified. They feared not only what the mob might do but also equally irrational violence by the Councilors who were their masters.

"I think you should go home, now," Daniel said quietly. He was the closest thing to authority the poor fellow had; it was simple human kindness to give him the answer that might save his life. "You want to be with your families in case things get, well, confused later."

Luff had gotten into the car. "Come along, for God's sake," he said. "We can't be sure the streets are safe even now!"

Hogg moved deliberately to put his shapeless bulk between Daniel and the Manco agent. He was looking back at the crowd, whistling "Waiting to Grow" between his teeth. That'd been Elemere's signature tune. . . .

"Even though Councilor Waddell told us to lock the doors and watch the place tonight?" the attendant said. He sounded as desperate as a mother asking a doctor about her child.

"If the building's still here in the morning," Daniel said, "you can come back before Councilor Waddell's likely to. If it's not, well, you're still better off, right?"

He smiled and clapped the man on the shoulder. Hogg climbed into the open cab with the driver, and Daniel slid into the passenger compartment with Luff. The car was accelerating out of the lot before he got the door fully closed.

Daniel glanced through the opera window in the back panel. The attendant he'd spoken to was waving to his fellows to join him. Even before they did he'd trotted out into the street, leaving the gates open behind him.

"Well, you're off the hook now, at least," Luff said. He was tight-faced and glared straight ahead, though Daniel doubted that he was looking at anything beyond the sheet of one-way glass between them and the cab. "Are you going to go straight back to Cinnabar?"

Daniel pursed his lips, wondering how to respond. Before he decided, Luff added, "I wish I could go back with you. I wish I'd never taken this bloody job, but I had no choice!"

A gang of children, the oldest of them no more than twelve, stood in a side street. They shouted something unintelligible when they saw the car and several threw stones; the driver accelerated. Hogg rose to his feet so that he could shoot over the driver's head if he had to, but in the event he kept the squat pistol down by his side.

"I'm not sure what you mean by me being off the hook, Luff," Daniel said quietly. "My assignment is to help oust the invaders from Dunbar's World. It would've been simpler to do that if the Bennarian government were more forthcoming, but that wasn't part of the orders I was given at Navy House."

Luff stared at him in a mixture of anger and resentment. "Look," the agent said, "your orders have changed. You're here to help Bennaria, and the best thing that could happen to Bennaria now would be for Yuli Corius to be killed on Dunbar's World. If you don't believe me, just ask any of the Councilors."

"With all *due* respect, Master Luff...," Daniel said, giving the adjective a slight emphasis to make the insult unmistakable. "I cannot imagine circumstances in which an RCN officer would ask tin-pot foreign politicians to interpret orders given him by his superiors."

"You know what I mean!" Luff said angrily. His clenched fists quivered on his knees in an access of frustration. "You're not here because of the Cinnabar navy or the Cinnabar Senate or the Cinnabar bloody anything! You're here because the Mancos had you sent here to make their trading partners on Bennaria happy. That's the Councilors, and I'm telling you—the Councilors *don't* want Corius to succeed!"

Daniel looked out the front window as he considered what Luff had said. They were nearing the harbor; the only people he saw out were those nailing sheets of plywood or structural plastic over the windows of the larger houses of entertainment.

"Well, Luff . . .," he said, keeping his eyes on the buildings rather than facing the man with him. He and Hogg'd come from the *Princess Cecile* in an ordinary water taxi, but those might no longer be running. Of course the crewmen of the Manco barge were locals also, as apt to be part of Corius' assembly as the independent watermen were.

Daniel'd let his voice trail off. He grimaced and said, "Sorry. Yes, you may well be right about the motivation behind my orders, but—"

He turned and smiled directly at the Manco agent.

"—you see, the orders themselves don't say that."

The car slowed and turned left down Harbor Street. Hogg stood again, this time to see past the embankment to where boats might be riding on the ebb tide. The *Princess Cecile* was a low shape among the bulkier freighters in the mist across the strait.

"You don't have to be that literal!" Luff said. "You've got leeway, I know that. I've seen your record, Leary, so don't pretend you're some kind of by-the-book robot."

"No, I'm not," Daniel said. "I've used my judgment to interpret orders in the past, and I'm doing the same now."

He paused, considering how much more he really ought to say. *Nothing more* was probably the right answer, but he was Daniel Leary.

"You're wondering if this is happening because I dislike Councilor Waddell," Daniel said. "Again, no. I wouldn't compromise my duty, let alone risk the lives of the crewmen for whom I'm responsible, simply because I feel Councilor Waddell's best use would be as fish bait."

As he spoke, he thought of Waddell bouncing along on a cable behind the *Bantry Belle*, with Hogg at the controls and himself manning the harpoon gun. The trench eels off the east coast grew to over a hundred feet long.

The image made him grin broadly; Luff started back.

"As I say, my personal feelings don't matter here," Daniel continued, a lie but a small one. "The Pellegrinians have been developing increasingly close ties with the Alliance, however. I don't see any benefit to the Republic in letting an Alliance supporter expand its power into Ganpat's Reach, and I'm confident that my superiors will feel the same way."

The car stopped abruptly. Daniel leaned back, compensating with a spacer's reflex, but Luff rocked forward hard enough to thump the divider with his shoulder. Hogg jumped out and called to someone unseen beyond the seawall.

"They'll blame me, you know," Luff muttered, again to his clenched hands. "Not that *you* care."

"He'll take us, young master!" Hogg said, gesturing toward the presumed boat and boatman. The closed compartment muffled his voice. "And I won't mind having the Sissies and a couple plasma cannon around me, I'll tell you now."

Daniel got out of the car. Before he closed the door, though, he leaned back and said, "Master Luff? I've told you what I intend to do as an RCN officer, but I should add that if I were a civilian I'd do the same. I prefer to think that any Cinnabar gentleman would put his heritage ahead of the wishes of unpleasant foreigners."

As he swung the door to, he added, "It's something you might keep in mind yourself."

CHAPTER 12

Bennaria

The spacer from the Armed Squadron unlocked the riverside wicket in the fence surrounding the Pool; he gave it a tentative push. The vines growing through the wire meshes held it closed. "It's stuck," he said to Daniel in apparent surprise.

Woetjans stepped past Daniel and gripped the frame with both hands. Planting her left boot on the gatepost, she pulled hard. The gate opened; the thicker woody stems popped like burning brushwood.

"Bloody hell," the Bennarian said when he got a good look at the bosun. Unlike the Sissies he didn't have light-enhancing goggles and Bennaria's moon, though full, was too small to be more than a gleam in the haze. "You're a big one, ain't you!"

"Yes, she is," said Daniel. "Now—seeing how short we are on time, let's get to the missile warehouse at once, shall we?"

"You're not the only one on duty tonight, are you?" Woetjans said harshly. "Where's the rest of you?

The bosun had spent much of her working life on the hull of starships in the Matrix, an environment utterly hostile to any kind of life. Clearly she wasn't a coward, but she didn't like darkness. Daniel

151

knew the long ride upriver in the water taxi must've been slow torture for her.

Hogg was a skilled boatman, but the river wasn't marked; they'd twice run onto mudflats that were indistinguishable from rafts of floating weed. Besides, the taxi was overloaded with five. Daniel'd brought two Power Room techs, Kaltenbrenner and Morgan, for their expertise in handling missiles. Woetjans was in a bad mood.

"Look, they're in the admin building," the Bennarian said. "We cut cards and I lost, so I'm the one letting you in. I'll show you the missiles and the lighter, then I leave too. What you do then's your business. We don't know a thing!"

"Let's go," Daniel said quietly. He'd made the deal with Commandant Brast over a channel that Adele swore couldn't be tapped by anybody on the planet except herself. The missiles were costing a fortune because every member of the detachment on duty at the Pool had to be paid off; but Daniel had money, now, and he couldn't think of a better use for it than to arm the *Princess Cecile* before she lifted tomorrow for Dunbar's World.

If it worked, of course. The trip upriver had already taken two hours longer than planned, and Daniel didn't kid himself that returning to the harbor in a heavily laden barge was going to be any easier. They'd still be transferring the missiles to the *Sissie* when dawn broke.

Well, one problem at a time. If Daniel had to use his cannon to keep the Bennarian authorities away while he finished loading the missiles, that's what he'd do.

Their guide didn't have a vehicle. The path from the gate was covered with pierced steel planking, slick and likely to trip the unwary where the sections fitted together.

The local man had more trouble with the surface than Daniel and his crewmen did, only in part because they had night vision goggles. They also had much more experience moving in difficult conditions. As rarely as any Bennarian warship lifted, the Squadron's spacers must spend most of their time playing cards in the administration building.

Hogg didn't wear goggles: he'd been a poacher too long to allow machines to come between his senses and the night around him. He walked beside the track in soft, shapeless boots that wouldn't leave identifiable tracks. In his arms was cradled a stocked impeller. Just in case, he'd said, and Daniel hadn't been disposed to argue the point.

The Bennarian skidded; he'd have fallen over backward if Daniel hadn't caught him by the shoulder and held him upright. He fumbled a light out of his belt pouch, muttering, "I never have no luck!" he muttered angrily. "Bloody *never!*"

He switched on a small light, but its razor-thin beam did more to conceal than illuminate the path. He resumed slipping and sloshing toward the row of barrel-vaulted warehouses backed against the Pool itself. Kaltenbrenner said something to Morgan; both men chuckled.

There were five warehouses, though Daniel wouldn't have been able to tell that in the darkness. The front lights of the U-shaped administration building were on, throwing a faint glow skyward, but the floods on the sides and rear had been switched off.

The warehouse aprons were concrete, a pleasant change after the PSP. The path to the water was for maintaining the downstream locks, but it must not get much use. Well, no part of the Armed Squadron seemed to get much use under the present Council.

The guide took them around to the back where loading docks jutted into the water. He stopped at the second warehouse and fumbled with a switch. The full-width door began to rumble upward; it didn't appear to have been locked.

"There!" the Bennarian said. "The missiles're against the north wall and the boat's tied to the dock. Now you're on your own, all right?"

He started off in the direction of the admin building. Daniel caught his arm again. "Where are the lights, please?" he said.

"Look, they'll show up for miles with the door open," the Bennarian said peevishly. "Can't you use your handlights, all right?"

"I'm afraid we can't, no," Daniel said. "The sooner we finish this job, the sooner—"

As he spoke, a red bead appeared in the field of his night vision goggles and pulsed to the right. Adele was obviously listening to what was going on and—as now—always offered help when she thought it was useful.

Daniel turned to center the bead, then put out his hand to a switchbox with a row of toggles. He threw them in pairs; fluorescent lights with a distinctly greenish cast flickered on in the ceiling.

"Do as you please, then," the spacer muttered. "Since you're going to anyway."

Woetjans and the two technicians strode into the warehouse and stopped. The bosun muttered, "Well, what'd I bloody expect?"

"There's an overhead crane," said Morgan. He started for the back, where a ladder led to the tracked crane above. "I'll get it going. If it will go, I mean."

The southern half of the building had racks, but crates and a jumble of loose gear were piled in the aisles. Daniel saw the noses of several missiles facing out from the other half of the building, but there were boxes in front of them and more on top. From what he could tell at a quick glance, much of what was stored here was junk.

The guide started off again; Hogg thrust the barrel of his impeller out like traffic barrier. "Come look over the boat with me, buddy," he said. "It won't take a minute if everything's the way it should be, and I guess you can straighten things out for us if it's not."

"It's all right," the Bennarian said sullenly. He turned without objection, though. "Anyway, what do I know about boats?"

As they walked toward the water, Hogg said, "You know, that's like me and missiles. I don't know squat. But with this little darling—"

He slapped his palm against the fore end of his impeller.

"Why, one of these I can just about make sit up and beg," Hogg said, his voice brightly cheerful. "Even at night, like now."

They started down the short ladder to the barge moored to the end of the dock, the Bennarian leading. Ten missiles would be an overload for it.

Woetjans climbed onto the pile covering the missiles, then turned to look down at Daniel. "Sir?" she called, her hand on a swivel chair with a broken seat. "We need to clear the eyebolts so we can hook the crane to 'em. D'ye care what happens to the stuff on top?"

"No," said Daniel without hesitation. Quite obviously the Bennarians didn't care about it either or the warehouse wouldn't have been treated like a rubbish dump. "Just don't throw it where we'll have to move it again."

Woetjans snorted. "Right," she said as she hurled the chair deeper into the warehouse. "That's the sorta thing a mere bosun like me wouldn't've figured out, sir."

"Sorry, Woetjans," Daniel said contritely, making his own way up the heap of heaven-knew-what-all. The overburden covering the missiles was five feet deep and occasionally more. "I was thinking out loud. And not thinking as clearly as I should have."

He grabbed a crate that'd originally been for signal rockets, judging from the stenciled legend; it now held light fixtures and their cords in knotted confusion. Daniel shoved it away like a shot put instead of using an over-arm motion the way he'd started to. All he'd need was to throw his arm out by being hasty. . . .

The lights in the cab of the crane came on. The mechanism squealed, then began a rhythmic thumping. "Now if I can just—" Morgan called down. There was a loud clank and the crane began to crawl forward along its track down the middle of the vault.

"Sir?" said Kaltenbrenner. He held the rim of a transmission casing in both hands. Though light metal and empty, it was a full meter in diameter. "Give me a hand with this and I think we'll be able to hook the crane to the forward attachment point. We can shake her free if we do."

"Right," said Daniel, moving toward the tech. What he thought was something solid under his right boot started to tilt up as soon as he started to put his weight on it. He stepped over it, balanced a moment to make sure he had firm footing, and heaved himself up opposite Kaltenbrenner.

"I think we'll be all right if we just roll it toward the shelves behind me," he added, looking over his shoulder. With the power of the crane to lift, the casing wouldn't be a problem even if it were pressing against the flank of the missile. "On three."

Daniel braced himself. "One, two, *three!*" He lifted and at the same time pivoted at the waist.

The casing resisted, then came away with unexpected ease: it'd seemed much heavier than it really was because it'd been caught under other trash. Daniel followed it down with a crash, barking his knuckles but not doing himself serious damage. There wasn't any real distance to fall.

"Oh, bloody hell," Kaltenbrenner said. "Bloody *fucking* hell. Sir, we're screwed. On this one at least."

Daniel climbed back up the trash hillock, using his hands to help himself this time. He looked down into the opening they'd created by digging out the casing.

The hole was deeper than that. An access panel in the missile's hull had been removed. The missile's antimatter converter had been taken out through the opening.

"Hell, the bastards cannibalized this one, sir!" Morgan shouted from the cab. His vantage point didn't show him any more than Daniel could see from thirty feet below him, of course. "D'ye suppose they gutted the rest of this lot too?"

"Drop the hook!" Daniel called. "Jerk this one out of the way, just shift it against the back wall, and we'll be able to check the next one pretty easily. Maybe we'll be lucky."

It took an hour and a half to examine the ten missiles. All were missing the converter and High Drive motor: they were steel tubes, no more weapons than so many empty well casings.

Hogg entered the warehouse while the last missile hung tilted on the hook. Daniel and the spacers with him stared at it glumly.

"Young master, we're screwed," Hogg said. "The lighter they got moored here, the motor shorted out when I switched on the power. There's two barges up by the admin building, a little bigger even, but neither of them's *got* a bloody motor in it! We can't carry a missile in the boat we came in, no way."

"Well, that's not a problem, Hogg," Daniel said. He laughed at the absurd humor of it. "All the taxi has to do is get the five of us back to the *Sissie*. We'll be going to Dunbar's World without missiles."

"What about that Pellegrino cruiser, sir?" Woetjans asked.

"We'll try not to get in a fight with it," Daniel said, stretching some of the kinks out of his back. He'd managed to tear his left sleeve badly, he now noticed. "And if we have to engage, well, who knows? Maybe Pellegrinian supply and maintenance is no better than what we've found tonight on Bennaria."

He laughed so cheerfully that the other spacers joined him, though they seemed a little doubtful.

Adele wouldn't have said that she liked liftoffs, but so long as she was at her console aboard the *Princess Cecile* she liked them as much as she liked any other part of life. She was running a panorama of the harbor as a narrow band on her display, but her attention was on the communications traffic as usual.

She grinned slightly as her wands danced, sorting messages. The last of Councilor Corius' troops were boarding his four freighters. One of those, the *Todarov*, was sealed for liftoff. The *IMG40* and *Zephyr* were fully loaded also, as best Adele could tell, but peevish intercom transmissions indicted their crews were still trying to settle their military passengers into the available space.

She checked on Daniel by echoing his display on hers, the way most natural to her. The upper half was a real-time view with the four freighters broken out as icons in a sidebar so that he could quickly expand them if he thought he needed to; the lower half was a schematic of the *Sissie's* plasma and High Drive systems, all comfortably in the green. None of that was critical, so—

"Daniel?" Adele said over their two-way link. *Should she've said "Commander"? But no, this was her personal curiosity.* "Why is Corius taking four ships to Dunbar's World when he was able to get all the troops in one when he brought them from his estate here to Charlestown? Are the ships themselves important? Over."

"*No, the ships are still just transports,*" Daniel said. His face smiled cheerfully, but there was a tight readiness in the muscles that they always got when he was preparing for action. "*And it's not a long run to Dunbar's World, that's true—a day or two, even for freighters. But that's still far too long to keep two thousand soldiers aboard one or even two ships the size of those. When they lifted from Corius' estate, there must've been men packing every corridor and compartment.*"

His tiny image grinned at her from the top of her display. "*You couldn't feed them like that,*" Daniel added, "*which is a good thing because you certainly wouldn't be able to cycle them through the heads. And then there's their equipment too. They aren't tourists, they're carrying all their weapons and munitions, remember. Over?*"

"Ah," said Adele. "Yes, thank you."

She focused for a moment on her display. She'd started to say "Out"—she was getting much better about RCN communications protocol—but before the word reached her lips it became, "Daniel, Commander, the *Todarov* is starting liftoff."

Blast, I've done it again! Switching to the command channel she repeated, "Captain Vesey, the transport *Todarov* is preparing to lift off. The *IMG40* and *Zephyr* should be ready in a few minutes. The *Greybudd* hasn't sealed its hatches yet, but Corius is aboard that one himself and both the crew and his soldiers seem to be better organized than the remainder of the force. Out."

"Thank you, Mundy," Vesey said. "*Break, Commander, all our systems are go. I propose to wait for the last of them to actually get floats up before I light our thrusters. Is that acceptable to you, over?*"

"*I'd do the same if I were captain, Vesey,*" Daniel said carefully. "*Though of course I'm not.*"

To take the sting out of what Adele knew was a rebuke, he added, "*Six out.*"

It was clearly an uncomfortable situation for Vesey, because Daniel was not only the former captain but also the ship's owner. Using Ship Six, his call sign from when he'd been captain, was a way of acknowledging her problem while the form of the statement itself made it clear that she had command of the corvette and that he expected her to exercise it.

Adele smiled broadly enough that a stranger seeing her would've recognized the expression. The duties of both her present positions—signals officer and spy—required her to be skilled at breaking codes. Not all the codes she'd learned to deal with were formal ones, however.

The *Todarov's* image wrapped itself in fireshot steam, plasma mixing with the water vapor. The *thump-p-p* of the thrusters lighting in quick sequence was followed by a buzz as they settled into a low-output flow. Static from atoms changing phase washed across the RF spectrum.

Councilor Waddell had left a twenty-man section in Charlestown to observe events in general and particularly to see what Corius would do. Adele knew as much about the Councilors' secret deliberations as anyone on the planet; more than any single Councilor, even Waddell, because she had tapped the internal conversations of the various cliques as well as what they told each other.

Waddell and his fellows were nervous. They were willing to sacrifice the city to riots that'd leave the mob starving and homeless, but they feared Corius would try to conquer the whole planet with his two thousand troops. They were sure he'd fail, but he might try anyway—

And barely whispered among themselves was the thought that just possibly Corius could conquer Bennaria after all. They couldn't imagine how he'd do it, but *if*.

Waddell's observers were split into four posts and a command unit on the roof of Waddell House. The squads kept up a running dialogue, and the command unit sent a constant flow of information back to Waddell on his estate. Either the observers were too low-ranking to've been told that Corius might be planning a coup, or they were remarkably phlegmatic individuals. Their tone and words suggested nothing more than bored professionalism.

The curtain of steam shrouding the *Todarov* billowed into an anvil-topped cloud. Shock waves transmitted by the water made the *Princess Cecile* shudder an instant before the roar reached them through the air. The transport lifted high enough for the savage rainbow beauty of her exhaust showing through the steam. The

IMG40 and *Zephyr* lit their thrusters also, unnoticed in the thunder of their colleague's liftoff.

It was natural that the other Councilors wouldn't know what Corius had in mind. What bothered Adele—and what she absolutely refused to consider proper—was that *she* didn't know what Corius would do.

The ships' captains, all civilians, and the mercenary commander on each vessel had sealed orders to open after liftoff. Nobody knew what was in those orders except Corius himself. Adele's skills and equipment were both of a very high order, but they wouldn't take her inside the skull of a man wise enough to keep his own counsel.

The *Todarov* must by now be at mid-sky, out of range of the visuals Adele had chosen to import. She tracked the ship's transmissions—the normal clutter of a working vessel, nothing more—but she had no reason to adjust her imagery.

The thrusters of the *IMG40* and *Zephyr* were building volume also. Adele expected the ships to stage their liftoffs at least a minute apart, but instead they broke from the harbor's surface within seconds of one another. The *IMG40*, starting marginally behind its fellow, climbed faster and soon was leading the track into the sky. Either her thrust to weight ratio was significantly higher than the *Zephyr*'s or her captain was overstressing his thrusters. The latter behavior would be nonsensical, but it was well within what Adele had come to accept as normal for human beings.

She quirked a wry smile, directed at herself. She'd generally felt like an outsider, not really a member of the human species. In this particular case, she was capable of exactly the same sort of pointless rivalry. Perhaps she was more human than she thought.

"*Adele?*" said Daniel, using their paired connection rather than an official channel. "*Can you get me access to what's going on aboard the* Greybudd? *I want in particular what's being said on the bridge and ideally an echo of the command console. Over.*"

"Yes," said Adele, her wands opening links to shunt to Daniel information that she was already gathering for herself. She'd almost said, "Of course I can!" but people—even people like Daniel who knew her very well—didn't understand quite how completely information was her life.

She'd entered the *Greybudd* through an automatic channel intended to exchange course and operational data with a similar unit at port control. In Charlestown—and generally on the fringes of civilization—port control was conspicuous by its absence, but the transponder was a standard fitment in every astrogational computer.

It was possible to isolate the telemetry channel from the rest of the computer, but almost no civilian vessel bothered to do so; and Mistress Sand's technicians had supplied Adele with tools to defeat most firewalls as well. There was no need for that here: Adele had better access to the captain's console than the *Greybudd's* other officers did: the output relay to the Power Room and mate's consoles was sticking.

And because Daniel'd asked her, he now had that access.

She returned to her task for the *Princess Cecile* as opposed to the *Princess Cecile's* owner. "Captain," Adele said over the command channel, "the *Greybudd* is about to test her plasma thrusters. She'll be lifting in a few minutes, over."

"*Roger, Mundy*," Vesey said. "*Break. Mister Pasternak, prepare to light your thrusters. Over.*"

"*Been ready this hour past, Captain*," the Chief Engineer said. "*Just say the word, over.*"

"*There!*" Daniel said. "*Adele, you're a treasure that a squadron of battleships couldn't match! Break, Captain, may I address the ship's company? Six out.*"

"*Go ahead, Six*," Vesey said. Adele frowned at the flat tone, professional and nothing more. Vesey had become a skilled machine with no emotions save anger which she primarily directed at herself. Adele had spent too many years in that gray world to wish it on anybody else.

Still, so long as skill remained, so did a reason for living. Perhaps something would eventually change for Elspeth Vesey, as it had for Adele Mundy.

The *Greybudd* lifted with the same shivering grace as the previous three ships of Corius' argosy. Its image immediately rose out of Adele's display, but sound diminished with a suddenness that was equally vivid to her now-experienced ear.

"*Fellow Sissies*," Daniel said, "*this is Six. You may've wondered why we're sitting here in harbor, waiting for Councilor Corius to lift for Dunbar's World. Well, the answer is that I wasn't sure he was going to Dunbar's World. You and I have been places where politics get played with guns.*"

You and I come *from a place where politics has been played with guns, Daniel,* Adele thought. She blinked but then opened her eyes very quickly. If she kept them shut for as much as a second, she'd imagine something she hadn't really seen: her sister Agatha's head nailed to Speaker's Rock.

"*The first of those transports has just switched to High Drive and set a course for Dunbar's World,*" Daniel said. "*That means it isn't going to set down again on the plantation of some Councilor who doesn't approve of the way Yuli Corius does things. So we're going to Dunbar's World too, Sissies, with nothing to worry about except a few thousand Pellegrinians and probably half the wogs who're supposedly on our side. That's nothing to the RCN, right Sissies?*"

From the volume of cheers echoing through the corvette's interior, you'd scarcely have known that she was short-crewed compared to what Adele was used to. And by now Adele was used to hearing the *Sissie's* crew cheering Daniel's Leary's words.

He plays them like a flute, Adele thought, *and they love it. We love it.*

"*Six out,*" Daniel said.

He'd scarcely spoken the closing before Vesey said, "*Power Room, light your thrusters. Break, Ship prepare to lift in sixty, six-zero, seconds. Captain out.*"

The high-pitched roar of plasma discharging into the water beneath the *Princess Cecile* blanketed ordinary sounds within, but noise cancellation by the commo helmets kept Daniel's voice clear as he said, "*Adele, we won't be in company with the transports so I expect to reach Dunbar's World six or more likely twelve hours ahead of Corius. We'll have enough reaction mass left to hold a powered orbit for days, probably. Unless you see a reason to land immediately, I propose to spend that time in orbit to get a better look at what's going on than we would in Ollarville harbor. Over.*"

"I think that's an excellent idea, Daniel," Adele said. "You go ahead and look, and I'll be listening to their transmissions. Out."

She didn't add, "And I'll learn more than you will by an order of magnitude." That would've been discourteous.

And besides, Daniel already knew it.

CHAPTER 13

Dunbar's World

Adele wasn't too lost in her world of data to notice that the buffeting was worse than usual as the *Princess Cecile* dropped through the atmosphere of Dunbar's World, but she didn't care very much. It was very unlikely that something had gone so badly wrong that Daniel wouldn't be able to save them from a crash. If it did, well, it wouldn't have happened because Signals Officer Mundy had failed.

Carrying out her duties in an accurate and efficient manner was one of Adele's highest priorities; personal survival was not. She'd seen death too often to doubt that it would come for her also, later if not sooner; and she'd meted it out so frequently that her death would only be delayed justice.

"*Adele?*" said Daniel through the intercom. "*There's an anti-ship missile battery at the Pellegrinian base on Mandelfarne Island. It's point-defense, but they might try something as we slant past to Ollarville. If you get anything before the ordinary threat-warning alarm sounds, it could be a lifesaver. Over.*"

"Yes, I'll try," said Adele, her wands sorting before she'd given them conscious orders. Any craft carried to the level of art—and Adele's ability at information retrieval was art—required more than intellect and training. "Oh. *Oh.* The ventral turret's extended; that's why I'm smelling ozone!"

"*That's correct,*" Daniel said. She heard the smile in his voice even without looking at the image on her display. "*Sun is looking forward to shooting down missiles. I'm much more interested in avoiding a situation in which he has to try. We may be able to do that with a little forewarning, over.*"

"I've copied the inputs from the installation's targeting computer to you," Adele said. *I should've said, "Over," when I spoke before, but I forgot. Again.* "I didn't see anything of concern, but you may . . . that is, I'm not competent to judge. Over."

"*Right,*" said Daniel. "*Excellent. The battery's default is to track only objects on a course approaching within one degree and to launch at thirty klicks unless countermanded. Since the computer is in default mode, we're safe. And so, I presume, are Corius and his force. Over.*"

That explained the severe buffeting also. Starships, even with their antennas telescoped and folded, were nothing like streamlined. Turrets, particularly belly turrets, were normally retracted into the hull during reentry since they were offset—toward the stern in the case of the *Sissie*—and the gun barrels acted as lever arms on the leading edge besides.

Adele pursed her lips and glanced at Sun hunched over the gunnery console beside her. His lips were spread in a smile of bright anticipation.

"Daniel?" she said. "Would he actually be able to hit missiles at such short range? Over."

The plasma cannon were intended to deflect incoming missiles at ranges of hundreds of thousands of miles in vacuum. Plasma bolts were extremely effective against nearby ground targets even in an atmosphere, but the chances of destroying hypervelocity missiles launched from a few thousand miles away seemed remote to Adele.

"*He thinks he can,*" Daniel said. The smile was back. "*I think the possibility that he's right is worth a little extra turbulence—and perhaps some water leaking in when we land.*"

He paused, then added, "*There, we're below the missiles' horizon. Break.*"

He'd switched to the command push.

"*Captain, this is Six. We're clear of the battery on Mandelfarne Island. Over.*"

Adele felt rather than heard—she couldn't hear anything over the wind noise and the thrusters blasting at high output—the turret begin to retract. Though the turret race rode on a magnetic suspension, a gear train raised and lowered the barbette. The regularity of the vibration made it noticeable through more violent but arrhythmic noises.

She nodded to herself in understanding. Daniel couldn't—well, chose not to—give Sun orders, but the gunner was sharp enough to understand what Six said on the command channel. If Daniel'd given the information to Vesey alone for relay through the formal chain of command it would've been delayed too long to be of any use.

The *Princess Cecile* flared to a hover, suspended on thrust in a pillow of steam ten feet above the surface of Eastern Harbor. Adele glanced at a topographic display for an instant, though in a manner of speaking it didn't matter to her where they landed.

The jaws of the shallow bay were open, and there were no moles to extend them. According to the *Sailing Directions*, before the war the harbor'd served only the immediate region and hadn't been important enough to rate expensive improvements. Now it was too late: the ships carrying military supplies and entrepreneurs drawn by the chance of quick profits in a war had to take their chances with the southeast storms that sometimes wracked this coast.

Until recently Ollarville, the city which spread halfway around the bay's curve, had a population of ten thousand. The federal authorities now estimated it was double that. Adele had also entered the data banks of the Eastern Provinces League, a political party before the invasion and now the self-proclaimed government of the East Coast. The EPL claimed Ollarville was over a hundred thousand, half again as big as Port Dunbar, but even party activists seemed to treat that figure as a pious wish rather than a fact.

The *Sissie* settled in tiny jerks, the minuscule overcorrections of a landing using the automatic system. The computer never made a huge error that'd splash waves over the neighboring quays, but neither did it anticipate conditions the way a really skilled human pilot seemed to do.

"Adele?" said Daniel. "*Do you see what Vesey's doing?*"

Probably realizing the answer would be either, "No," or more likely, "Yes, but it doesn't mean anything to me," he continued without waiting, "*She's doing a dummy manual landing while the ship lands itself. She'll go over the recordings later to see where she could improve. It's an exercise I set my junior midshipmen, and she's still doing it. Out.*"

"*Ship, touchdown in ten seconds*," announced Midshipman Blantyre from the Battle Direction Center.

Adele heard and understood the sadness in Daniel's voice. Vesey was through study and practice doing everything possible to make herself an accomplished officer. What both Adele and Daniel knew was that machines would always be better at the mechanical aspects of command.

The things that machines couldn't do were the really important ones. These required humanity, and Vesey was determinedly walling herself off from all that'd been human in her.

Adele smiled without even a hint of humor. The core of being human was the ability to feel pain. She'd had too much personal experience of that to want to call it a virtue, but perhaps she was wrong.

The *Princess Cecile* settled into her slip with the usual deafening roar. The sound of steam cut off the way fabric tears, quickly but not quite instantaneously, when the buzz of the thrusters stopped.

"*Ship, this is Damage Control*," said Midshipman Cory, trying to sound magisterial from the BDC. Vesey'd instituted more formal procedures than Daniel had thought necessary. "*All compartments report green, over.*"

"*Pasternak, you may open the main hatch*," ordered Vesey. The chief engineer was Chief of Ship as the bosun was Chief of Rig, though Pasternak was of course busy in the Power Room with shutdown procedures and damage assessments. A pair of techs would cycle the hatch with a few off-duty riggers present for extra muscle in case something'd warped enough to stick.

Adele heard the squeal and clang of a score of hatches all over the ship opening—without orders and by implication against orders. Vesey was rising from the command console. Her pale face flushed. She sat down again hard and reached for the commo switch.

"I wonder, Captain Vesey," said Daniel very loudly. Despite the pings of differential cooling, the bridge was quiet enough for normal talk now that the thrusters had shut down. Daniel's volume was suitable for shouting across the harbor. "Would you come here for a moment and see if my course plot agrees with yours?"

Vesey hesitated between what she'd started to do and obeying Daniel's summons. Adele disconnected the command console from all communications links save the cable going to the signals console. She supposed that was mutiny, though she doubted that she'd be tried for it. In any case, it was better than letting Vesey give an order that Daniel was obviously trying to prevent.

Sun was raising the dorsal turret to make room in the hull. Ollarville wasn't a bad place to have the cannon available besides, though the turret power was off so that the guns couldn't be loaded, let alone fired.

At the sound of Daniel's raised voice, Sun turned to look. Adele caught his eye and pointed one of her wands—disconnected for the purpose of the gesture—toward the hatch. The gunner's mate scrambled up from his console, pausing only to shut it off.

Adele rose also, moving more deliberately than Sun but not wasting time either. Hogg and Tovera stood on either side of the hatchway, awaiting developments.

Vesey had gone white again. "Sir," she said, "I gave no orders to open any hatch but the main one where we can control access."

"Mundy, I'd appreciate it if you'd stay and chat with me and Vesey here," Daniel said easily. He remained seated, apparently at ease. "And Hogg, please close the hatch behind yourself and Tovera."

"Yes, of course, Commander," Adele said. Her mouth was dry. She considered sitting down again but decided not to.

"Guess we know when we're not wanted, don't we, Tovera?" Hogg said cheerfully. "Come on up on the spine with me and let's pick fields of fire."

The hatch closed with a sigh and a restrained clink, automatic mechanisms completing the task they were directed to do by a human push. Daniel's eyes flicked to the portal, making sure the sound hadn't deceived him.

"Not 'Commander,'" he said, "because this is just a chat. Three friends together, you see?"

Vesey didn't speak. She looked worn beyond life, a mummy draped in loose utilities.

"Yes, of course," Adele said. "We're all friends."

That was true, but it was also true that she'd shoot Vesey dead if Daniel ordered it. Daniel knew that and surely Vesey did also; but it was equally true that Daniel wouldn't have kept Adele Mundy present for her willingness to do a job that Hogg or Tovera would've handled with less concern and equal skill.

"And you're right that you didn't order the crew to ventilate the ship now that we're down, Vesey," Daniel said, his fingers laced on his lap. He leaned back in his console. "But I don't see why you thought that would be necessary. The *Sissie*'s fortunate to have an extremely experienced crew who've made, oh, tens of thousands of landings in all, wouldn't you say?"

"Sir, do you want my resignation?" Vesey said. She was trembling and her eyes, though focused on the bulkhead beyond Daniel's right shoulder, didn't appear to be seeing anything but the misery in her own soul.

"No, I don't," Daniel said calmly. "But I will ask for your resignation if you attempt to turn this crew into robots. You won't succeed, of course. But you might just push them to mass desertion, which would be almost as bad as ruining the best lot of spacers who ever graced the RCN. Now, what about it?"

"Sir, there ought to be discipline," Vesey said. She sounded desperate. "There has to be discipline!"

"Yes, there does," Daniel said. His tone was much harder than it would've been if he'd been agreeing. "And if you think either Woetjans or Pasternak doesn't know how to enforce discipline, then you haven't seen them put a draft of landsmen through their paces with a starter of flex to get their attention. A crew like this one doesn't have to be told to pull their utilities on zipper-end front, though. *Do* you understand?"

"If I'm captain, I have a right to set procedures," Vesey said. Her voice had sunk from desperation to despair. "Isn't that so?"

"Certainly," said Daniel. "But these aren't dogs you're training for the circus. Vesey, you're a crackerjack officer and that's why I hired you. But if you decide you have to regulate everything around you just to say you did, then I'll recommend you for a training post in the Academy. You certainly won't be of any use on a ship that I own."

Vesey didn't speak. She looked as though she was tied to a stake, waiting for the firing party to execute her.

Adele suddenly realized why Daniel had asked her to be present. "Elspeth," she said. She wondered if she'd ever used Vesey's given name before. "I'm not sure that Daniel understands why you might react to loss in the way you have. I understand very well."

Vesey turned to look at her. The movement had an odd jerkiness as though Vesey's conscious mind had to control actions that were usually instinctual. "What do you mean?" she said, her voice soft.

"The need to control things, because all you cared about has melted away like sand in the ocean," Adele said. "I was an orphan on a distant planet, living on sufferance. The only thing I could control was myself, and I got very good at that."

She grinned at Vesey. It was actually as broad a smile as she ever managed.

"I'll bet I was better than you could be," she went on. "I think I was always missing a piece of what it means to be human. But if you think you can top my record, go right ahead. Just don't try to apply the same degree of control to anything beyond your own skin, because it's improper to treat human beings as though they're game pieces. Besides, as Daniel said, it won't work on anybody worth having around you."

Vesey swallowed, then forced a smile. "Sir?" she said. "I understand and I'll try. But I can't lead the way you do. Nobody can! But I'll try not to . . ."

She let her voice trail off. Daniel's smile was warm as a summer day. He rose from the console with compact grace and said, "We're just friends talking, Elspeth, so I'm Daniel. Now, we've got the local authorities to deal with. After that we'll reconnect with Corius, since I hear his ships coming down now. But at some point, this evening I hope, the three of us can have a friendly drink in the owner's cabin. If you're amenable, that is?"

"Thank you," Vesey said. "I'll try to make you proud of me. I—"

She turned her head away quickly. "Thank you, *Daniel*," she blurted and put her hands to her face.

Adele was closer to the hatch, but Daniel reached the latch plate before her. They were both mumbling inconsequential things to mask the sound of Vesey's sobs as they stepped into the corridor. The tears were a release of course, nothing to be ashamed of. Still, as a matter of courtesy and duty both Adele and Daniel had reason to get off the bridge.

More than two minutes ago Blantyre had excitedly reported that a local delegation was on the quay demanding access. Woetjans with a squad of armed spacers was keeping the officials from stepping onto the boarding ramp.

But Daniel'd always been good at prioritizing. First things first.

The *Greybudd* had landed two slips away from the *Princess Cecile* and the air still roiled with hot steam and the sharpness of ozone from her thrusters. Rust obscured the transport's number, but a checkerboard of replacement hull plates made Daniel sure of his identification. Besides, Corius would've brought his own vessel down first.

He and Adele walked down the boarding ramp to meet the four officials. They wore berets with a red-and-white rosette. Two were in khaki uniforms; one wore a uniform jacket with shapeless blue trousers; and the last had similar trousers, a horizontally striped shirt, and went barefoot.

All wore pistols and belt knives. The barefoot fellow carried a crude-looking shoulder weapon with a drum magazine, probably a shotgun powered by chemical explosives.

Daniel continued to smile, but in all truth they weren't a prepossessing bunch.

"I'm Pennant-Leader Onsbruck," said the huskier of the men in full uniform. He was in his mid-twenties, a little older than Daniel but younger by a decade than the other uniformed man and the thug with the shotgun. The fellow in the khaki jacket was a slight teenager with acne and close-set eyes. "We're here to take charge of your ship till the full Committee can assess it."

"And your guns," said the older uniformed man. He was over six feet tall but stooped and soft-looking. *A bookkeeper before the war,* Daniel thought. *Some sort of office worker, at any rate.* "Foreigners aren't allowed to have guns in Ollarville."

Woetjans, standing on the ramp with five husky spacers ready for anything, spat into the water. She cradled an impeller in the crook of her left arm, but Daniel suspected that if trouble started she'd kick the man with the shotgun in the balls and then strike right and left with the stock of her weapon. The bosun was a good shot and big enough that the impeller's heavy recoil didn't faze her, but shooting was just a job to her. She took personal pleasure in breaking bones, however.

"Yes," Daniel said, nodding agreeably. "I think for now it's best that you consider us Dunbar citizens since we're here to help your government against the Pellegrinians. And there's no question of turning over an RCN warship without a decree of the Cinnabar Senate, of course, so you'll have to pass on that also."

"Who do you think you're ordering around?" Onsbruck demanded, his face getting red. The kid with acne looked even more like a rat than he had to start with; his hands were twitching. "If you foreigners come here, you either obey our regulations or you're no better than those pissants from Pellegrino!"

Hogg was on the *Sissie's* spine, sitting on a telescoped yard and goggling at the harbor. An impeller was concealed in the furled sail beside him. Given how quickly Hogg could snap off a shot, Woetjans might not get much chance to crack skulls after all.

Daniel's smile grew broader. This lot wouldn't make trouble, though. Not when Yuli Corius was landing with two thousand troops even as the discussion took place.

Adele's eyes had a bright, unfocused look that Daniel had learned to interpret: she'd been listening to something through her commo helmet. Her gaze suddenly locked on the chief of the local delegation.

"I assure you, Master Onsbruck," she said, snapping out syllables like a series of mousetraps closing, "that as representatives of Cinnabar, we'll be punctilious about dealing with the Federal Republic of Dunbar. We have no right to become involved in your domestic politics, however, nor do we intend to do so. Whether you're here as private citizens or as members of the Eastern Provinces League, you have no right to involve yourselves in our mission."

"We *are* the government here!" the little rat said. "We've got the power!"

"You've got shit," said Woetjans in an even voice. When the youth reached for the pistol under his belt, Woetjans stepped forward and stiff-armed him into the water.

The thug with the shotgun looked at Onsbruck and said, "What? What?"

"Don't!" Daniel said, but talking didn't seem a sufficient way to deal with the situation. He grabbed the shotgun at the balance with both hands and twisted counterclockwise. The thug twisted back. Daniel reversed his effort, swinging the weapon in an arc that ended when the gunbutt thumped the thug's right temple.

The thin fellow dropped his clipboard and stood transfixed. Onsbruck himself threw his hands in the air and cried, "I'm not fighting! I'm not fighting!" in a voice that rose into the treble range.

"I am!" said Dasi. He grabbed Onsbruck by the throat and right arm; his partner Barnes seized the other wrist and elbow and started to twist them the wrong way.

"Belay that!" Daniel said. "Barnes, let him go!"

"Aw, sir...," said Dasi, but he was grinning. He released Onsbruck's neck but kept hold of the wrist. His now-freed right hand drew one the knives from the local's belt and cut the belt itself through. It fell to the ramp with the other knife, the holstered pistol, and a trio of grenades.

"Somebody fish the little one out of the water, will you?" Daniel said peevishly. "Woetjans, pull him out, if you please."

He was breathing hard and he'd lost his cap. He looked at the shotgun. The closed breech showed a gap of over an eighth of an inch; the casing of the chambered round was readily visible. *I wonder which end's the more dangerous.* He grimaced and tossed the weapon into the harbor.

Woetjans bent over but apparently decided that she couldn't easily reach the man struggling in the water. Grinning she poked the muzzle of her impeller down while gripping the stock with both hands. "Here you go, sonny," she said. "Just catch hold. And don't worry, the safety's on—I think!"

Simkins, another of the spacers on guard, was looking over the other side of the ramp. "Hey!" she called. "There's a body here. Bloody hell, there's two bodies!"

Daniel stepped to her side. The bodies were so ripe that they bulged at the necks and wrists where their clothes constricted them. One wore a striped shirt and workman's trousers like the EPL thug; the other had pantaloons and a tunic with puffed sleeves, female fashion on Pellegrino and the planets trading with it.

The corpses had been shot in the back of the neck. The wounds were red and swollen; the flesh was black everywhere else it was exposed.

"What's this?" Daniel said sharply, glancing at the EPL officials. Onsbruck was rubbing his left elbow with his right hand. He looked up sullenly and said, "It's nothing to you. They were traitors, probably. We don't coddle traitors in Ollarville."

Daniel noticed his hands were clenching and unclenching. He deliberately spread his fingers wide. He'd really like to throw this fellow into the harbor and hope he couldn't stay afloat as well as the boy accompanying him had, but that wasn't the job of an RCN officer. What happened between citizens of Dunbar's World was a domestic affair.

"Go on back to your kennel, Master Onsbruck," he said pleasantly. "And take the rest of your pack with you, if you please."

Onsbruck bent to pick up his equipment belt. Daniel shoved him: not a blow, simply a matter of placing his hand on Onsbruck's head and pushing. The EPL official shot backward, off the ramp and several feet beyond. He sprawled on his back when his feet couldn't backpedal fast enough to keep him upright.

"I believe I gave you directions once already, Onsbruck," Daniel said, his voice still quiet. He used the side of his boot to skid the belt into the water with a loud splash.

Daniel looked over his shoulder. There were automatic impellers mounted in three open hatches, and the dorsal turret was trained on the city. Another twenty spacers stood in the main hatch under Cory; they were armed to the teeth. Hogg and Tovera slipped through them, grinning like the fiends they were.

"Master Cory," Daniel said, "take charge of the security here if you will, till Captain Vesey gives you other orders. Woetjans, you and your squad to accompany Officer Mundy and myself just down the quay to the *Greybudd*. I have some matters to discuss with Councilor Corius."

CHAPTER 14

Ollarville on Dunbar's World

Troops in gray-green battle dress were marching off the *Greybudd* via two of the ship's three ramps. Most of them carried sub-machine guns, but there seemed to be one stocked impeller per ten-man squad.

The ramp closest to the bow had stuck halfway down. Spacers from the *Greybudd* were looking at it from the quay and the hatchway, but there wasn't the sort of bustle that Daniel liked to see in a crew when something goes wrong. He frowned.

The troops were forming a perimeter, closing off the quay and politely—reasonably politely—but firmly moving out the handful of idlers and dockworkers who were there at the moment. As Daniel and his escort approached, one of the soldiers began talking urgently into a handheld radio. Another man stepped out of the line with his arm raised in bar.

"Sorry, gentlemen," the second soldier said. "This area's closed to everybody but the Bennarian Volunteers unless you've got a pass from—"

"Let 'em through, Rajtar!" said the man who'd been on the radio. He shoved forward and put his hand on the second man's—Rajtar's, presumably—shoulder for attention. "The Councilor's on his way down right now to see them. It's the RCN mission, you see?"

Rajtar looked surprised and uncertain. "Ah, right, sir. Sorry, thought you were more of this lot."

He waved a hand at Ollarville generally. The port was being forced to handle cargoes well beyond its normal capacity. Much of the overage was piled in vacant lots or stretches of street frontage. Existing businesses were supplemented by shanties, and the buildings themselves were being raised by additional stories made of bamboo and wicker.

"Glad to have the RCN on our side. Bloody glad."

"Sorry," Adele murmured to Daniel as they led his entourage through the cordon. "Corius' staff didn't get the word to the troops in time. If I'd been back at my console, I could've routed the orders through myself."

Daniel smiled broadly and waved toward Yuli Corius, trotting down the stern ramp behind his reptilian bodyguard. Three men in uniform, aides rather than guards from the look of them, followed. He said quietly, "I prefer you here."

That was certainly true, though he wasn't sure he could give a reason that'd mean anything to other people. Adele was a friend, certainly; but Hogg and Woetjans were friends as well in their different ways.

Learning was all very well and Daniel valued it, but he had more interests in common with Hogg or even the common spacers than he did with Adele Mundy. If Daniel'd thought knowledge for its own sake was important, he'd have lived a very different life. Time spent poring over books that didn't advance a particular interest of his— natural history, for example, or anything to do with the duties of his profession—was no better than so much time spent in jail.

It wasn't even Adele's intelligence or at least not only her intelligence. Perhaps it was the way Adele applied her intelligence as dispassionately as a scalpel; no matter how she felt or what she felt. She'd provide a clear, cogent analysis of a question even if she knew the result would be her own death.

He could trust her. He could trust her judgment in any and every situation, and you could hardly ask for a better definition of who you wanted at your side in a chancy negotiation.

"Commander, I was on my way to see you," Corius said. He wore a field gray uniform like those of his Volunteers, but without any indications of rank. Corius didn't carry a weapon, though, an oversight that'd mark him as a worthwhile target to any hunter as practiced as Hogg . . . or as Daniel himself, come to think. Though hunters that skilled weren't thick on the ground either.

"This is Colonel Quinn, my field commander," Corius went on, gesturing to the short, extremely fit, sixty-year-old at his side. "We're going to the military routing office here in Ollarville and I want you to accompany me. With Lady Mundy, of course."

Quinn responded with a Cinnabar salute, touching his right index finger to his brow with his stiff hand and forearm in perfect line. "Sir!" he barked. "A pleasure to meet you!"

Daniel returned the salute, but not nearly as sharply. Quinn was obviously Cinnabar—but not a Cinnabar officer, not with that demeanor and accent. Very likely he'd been a noncom in the Land Forces before retiring into what was supposed to be a cushy billet in the sticks.

It must not've worked out the way Quinn had expected, though, since the man's nose and ears were oddly pinker than the rest of his tanned features. They were synthetic, not real skin. At some point in the recent past Quinn had been mutilated, and reconstructive surgery hadn't been able to put the damage quite right.

"And to meet you, Colonel," Daniel said. Part of him—the RCN officer and the Cinnabar gentleman both—was irritated at Corius' phrasing: *I want you to accompany me.* On the other hand, he wanted to see the nearest central government officials also, and it'd be foolish to cavil about some wog's unfortunate terminology.

Daniel grinned brightly. "Yes, I'm planning to talk to the locals myself. We'd be pleased to have you and the colonel join us."

After all, he could horsewhip the fellow on the ramp of his ship some other time, if that seemed like a good idea. The humor of the thought made Daniel smile—and the thought of the Councilor's face if he knew what caused the smile made him chuckle audibly.

"Quite," said Corius, but a puzzled look flashed across his face. "The Federal Building's three blocks down the waterfront."

He nodded; toward a four-story building clad in tan brick, Daniel thought, but that was just because it was prominent. Though he'd learned over the years that the chance of a government building being strikingly ugly were very good, and this one qualified. The brick had a violet undertone that made Daniel queasy when he concentrated on it.

"I've got an aircar aboard the *Greybudd*," Corius continued, "but rather than wait for it to be unloaded, I propose that we walk. With a suitable escort, of course."

"I haven't seen anything in Ollarville that a couple crossing guards couldn't handle," Hogg said, picking his nose. "What do you guess, Woetjans?"

Woetjans spat again. The gobbet wobbled ten feet as straight as a chalk line, then plopped into the slip.

The lizardman, Fallert, made a noise in his throat like a loose gear train. That was apparently laughter.

Corius looked even more disconcerted. He cleared his throat and said, "Let's go, then. Colonel Quinn, detail a squad to accompany us."

Tovera said something to Hogg in a low voice. Daniel couldn't be sure, but he thought it was something like "ten crossing guards." Whatever the precise wording, it put Hogg and Fallert in boisterous good humor as they sauntered through the cordon.

Spacers aren't trained to march in unison, and Corius' Volunteers were individually recruited mercenaries who hadn't spent a lot of time on drill and ceremony either. It struck Daniel that the body of them looked more like a well-armed street gang than they did professional soldiers.

That seemed to be quite in keeping with the conditions prevailing in Ollarville. He grinned and began to whistle "The Patapsco Shanty" cheerfully.

Adele intensely disliked using her visor and its simple cursor controls in place of a proper display linked to her wands, but while she was walking down Water Street she didn't have a better option. She was uncomfortably aware that Barnes and Dasi kept step, poised to catch her if she stumbled. It was embarrassing, but falling on her face would be still more embarrassing. That was a real possibility, given the state of the pavement and the fact she was seeing through a 70 percent mask of projected data.

The half-dozen guards at the entrance to the Federal Building were in laborers' clothes, loose dark trousers and striped shirts, but they all wore the red-and-white EPL rosette somewhere on their garments. They bent their heads close and buzzed to one another as the combined Bennarian and RCN contingent approached; one man scurried inside. None of them had been in the delegation which had visited the *Princess Cecile* earlier in the afternoon.

"Colonel Quinn?" said Corius in a carrying voice. "If those ruffians open their mouths, I want you to have them soundly thrashed."

"Very good, sir," said Quinn, sounding like he meant it.

Hogg turned to Fallert and said conversationally, "Say, I could come to like your master."

The lizardman laughed again. "He won't let me eat the hearts of those I kill for him, though," he said. His pronunciation of Standard was excellent, though he didn't or couldn't give labial consonants their proper emphasis. "I don't know why. It's only cannibalism when it occurs within a single species."

"S'pose he means it?" Barnes said in a husky whisper, ostensibly to his partner but of necessity speaking across Adele.

She didn't reply. She simply didn't know the answer, and she wasn't good at making empty conversation.

The EPL contingent backed out of the doorway; two even walked quickly away as if late for a distant appointment. A man whose crossbelts supported two pistols remained to glower at the foreigners, his hands on his hips.

Woetjans grinned and butt-stroked him in the pit of the stomach, knocking him out into the street. He thrashed, curling up in a ball and retching uncontrollably. There was general laughter from Sissies and the Volunteers alike.

The entrance hall was empty except for a desk littered with wine bottles and papers. The desktop was marble; somebody'd carved his initials on it with a knife and one corner'd been broken off. A door down the back hallway banged behind whoever'd been in the hall before the foreigners arrived.

"The Federal governor has the suite of offices to the right," Adele said, gesturing with her right index finger. "His name's Zorhachy, and a personal assistant named Moorer has remained on duty also. The rest of the Federal staff have either resigned or left Ollarville for points west."

"How does she know that?" said Quinn in surprise. He was looking at his employer when he started the question but had moved his eyes onto Daniel by the time he finished it.

Neither man answered him, but Dasi tapped the side of his nose and said, "That'd be telling, little feller. But if Mistress Mundy says it, you can take it to the bank."

Councilor Corius knocked firmly on the door Adele had indicated. "Governor Zorhachy, I'd like to speak with you," he said. His tone didn't make it a question.

"You can't come in!" called a voice from inside. There'd originally been a frosted glass panel in the top half of the door, but it'd been replaced with a sheet of plywood nailed from the inside. The points of several nails stuck out through the panel.

"Sir, this is Councilor Yuli Corius!" Corius said. "It's necessary that I speak with you."

He rattled the door, then shoved. It was bolted shut. "Please!" Corius said. "I don't want to break it down!"

"I'll get it," Woetjans said, measuring the distance and turning slightly so that a perfect halfturn would bring the heel of her boot squarely onto the latch plate. "Just move aside!"

"Don't shoot!" called a different voice from inside. "My God, Governor, I'll not be shot just because you want to be a hero!"

A crossbolt slid back; a plump man in frock coat and vest jerked the door open. Behind was a younger man in similar garb and a much older one wearing a long-sleeved shirt and a string tie. Behind the desk at the back was the man Adele recognized from file images as Governor Zorhachy; the blond youth beside him must be Moorer. A pistol lay on the desktop; both men were studiously not looking at it.

"Look, we're shippers, Beltras and Conning and me," said the man who'd opened the door. He was probably ruddy at most times, but now he was pale except for hectic patches on both cheeks. "We've nothing to do with politics, nothing! We just came to talk with the Governor, that's all. Let us go and you can do what you please with him!"

"For pity's sake!" said Corius. "What are you afraid of? I'm Councilor Corius of Bennaria, come here to aid you against the Pellegrinian invasion. I just want to arrange supplies and billeting for my men until they can be transferred to the seat of the war."

"The only way you'll get supplies here is from the EPL," said the man who'd opened the door. "And they won't be getting any more either because they pay with their own scrip. As isn't worth wiping your ass with!"

All Adele knew about the speaker was that he was a shipper and his name probably wasn't Beltras or Conning. She stepped into the office; there was an occasional table by the door. She put the file boxes stacked there on the floor and sat on the table, bringing out her personal data unit. It was a relief to have proper apparatus instead of directing a cursor with tongue motions.

Barnes and Dasi followed, forcing the merchants back by their presence; then the whole mixed entourage flowed into the room. Moorer surreptitiously scooped up the pistol and dropped it into a desk drawer.

"We've been trying to get the Governor to act," said Beltras, the man in the string tie. His tone started out resigned but quickly rose into anger. "Will he? No, not him!"

"The EPL commandeers our property and the Governor says, 'Too bad,' that's all!" said Conning. "Some governor. Some government!"

"Well, what do you expect me to do?" Zorhachy demanded. "Do *I* have an army? There's me and Moorer, that's all, and I don't know why he stays!"

"I won't leave you, sir!" Moorer said.

Perhaps brave but completely ineffectual, Adele thought. *And young. Though in years, as old as Daniel.*

She had her information—from the Federal data banks—in the form of a petition for redress by shippers named Worthouse, Beltras, and Conning. It stated that their cargoes of agricultural produce had been taken without pay by members of the Eastern Provinces League claiming to be the government. The shippers demanded that the Federal authorities either recover their property or pay them compensation at market value.

Good luck, Adele thought. And the shippers probably felt the same way, but they were following up their petition sent to the Federal capital, moved from Port Dunbar to the inland city of Sinclos, with a visit to Governor Zorhachy himself.

"All I have is my office, this room!" said Zorhachy, rising to his feet. He was a tubby little man with a pencil mustache and a receding hairline. Withal, he managed to project a certain dignity. "I thought when the good Councilor appeared that it was Rasmussen and his animals come to take that too. Perhaps they would shoot me as they have shot so many."

He waved his arm. "Master Worthouse," he said. "If the sacrifice of my life will return your property, I will give it now! Only show me how this can help you?"

"You sir," said Corius, pointing to Worthouse. "Can you supply rations for two thousand men for a period of a week or so? Till I decide on my next step."

Worthouse shrugged. "The three of us can," he said. "We can bring in that much food over the next week or month or year. *If* we're paid—"

"You'll be paid," snapped Corius.

"*And* if the EPL doesn't hijack it, the way they did what we had in our warehouses," Worthouse concluded. "It was ready to be sent on to Port Dunbar like we were contracted to do."

"How many armed men does the EPL have, anyway?" Daniel asked. Adele noticed that although he didn't seem to raise his voice, his words rang clearly through a room which was by now full of people.

"A thousand," Moorer said. "Perhaps a few more, but they aren't well armed. If the Ministry of the Interior in Sinclos would just listen to us and send a battalion, we could return law and order to Ollarville. Instead they badger us to ship supplies we can't gather because of the EPL!"

"I think between me and the Councilor, we can open normal supply routes, Governor," Daniel said. He grinned. "I'd venture that my Sissies can do the job by ourselves, but in that case I'd have to use the ship's cannon. I'm afraid your city wouldn't be the better for it."

"That won't be necessary," Corius said. "Quinn, meet with these gentlemen—"

He nodded to the shippers.

"—and get a plan in place. I want to start receiving local supplies by tomorrow morning at the latest, to conserve our present stocks."

"It'll be a pleasure, sir," Quinn said. "It'll be good to blood the boys before we take them to Port Dunbar, besides. You lot—"

In a peremptory tone, his eyes flicking from Worthouse to Beltras and Conning.

"We'll find a room right now and sort this. Boys, let us by. Blaisdel, I'll need you for the commo back to the *Greybudd*."

"I'll leave you to handle matters," Corius said to the room at large. He nodded to the Governor, then turned to the door.

"Commander Leary?" he added as quietly as the bustle allowed. "Lady Mundy? Might I have a word with you in the hall?"

Adele put away her data unit. Dasi and Barnes made room for her to step down into the milling crowd by bracing their arms and pushing forward. Corius and Fallert left the office. Hogg followed closely while Daniel waited for Adele. Tovera brought up the rear with a tight grin.

"What I'm planning to do," said Corius in the entranceway in a cocoon of his men and the Sissies, "is to fly my aircar to Port Dunbar, just me and Colonel Quinn. I have people I can trust to do the ash and trash jobs here while we're gone, but it's clear that I'll need to see the military situation for myself to be able to make a useful decision."

Daniel nodded. "I'm inclined to agree," he said. "The *Sissie* doesn't have an aircar, but if I can buy or rent one here . . .?"

"No, of course that's not necessary," Corius said. "I would be very pleased for you and Lady Mundy to accompany me. Shall we say, we leave at dawn tomorrow?"

"Adele?" Daniel said with a cocked eyebrow.

The *Princess Cecile* contained useful tools that she wouldn't be able to carry in an aircar, but she didn't expect to need particularly exotic equipment to break local security systems. And the *Sissie* couldn't approach the battle site directly without risking attack by the Pellegrinian missiles.

"Yes, of course," Adele said. "There's nothing in Ollarville that I'm going to regret leaving behind."

Everyone who heard her chuckled—but it was the simple truth, as were most of the things she said. She wondered if some day she'd figure out why her telling the truth struck people as funny.

Perhaps it was just that they heard it so rarely.

CHAPTER 15

Dunbar's World

Daniel rotated the command console inward and smiled at his assembled officers. The *Sissie*'s bridge was a tight fit even for the eleven of them, but Adele was projecting the address onto the display in each other compartment for the crew.

He remembered being surprised earlier in their relationship that she'd bent over her console while he was giving the ship's complement one of his pep talks. *Of course* she concentrated on her console: Adele preferred to get her information displaced by one or more filtering layers. It didn't mean she wasn't absorbing it.

"Well, Sissies," he said, keeping his tone light. The expressions on the faces watching him ranged from wary to angry. "In the morning Officer Mundy and I will go off with Councilor Corius to Port Dunbar, as I'm sure you've heard by now. This doesn't change anything since Captain Vesey's already in charge. Besides, we'll be in constant communication."

"Sir, what if the comsat net goes out?" Midshipman Blantyre said. The very effort she put into sounding coolly professional showed how worried she was. "The Pellegrinians might decide to take it down."

"We'll still be in communication, Blantyre," said Adele without looking up. She spoke calmly, but her wands were moving in jerks as

185

quick and seemingly meaningless as the legs of a sleeping dog. "There may be a delay of a few minutes, depending on what ships are in orbit. There've never been less than two in the whole time since the invasion, according to landing control database, and I assure you I can use their communications modules for relay."

Daniel nodded, knowing that Adele's unusually full answer was meant as a rebuke as well to provide information. She took her duties seriously, and the notion that she wouldn't have considered alternative ways of carrying them out obviously rankled. Blantyre hadn't intended the implied criticism, of course, but one of the things an RCN officer had to learn was that words could be just as precise as—and even more potentially dangerous than—pistol bullets.

"Sir, you ought to take a few of us along," Woetjans said, speaking in a forceful growl but looking at the deck instead of meeting his eyes. "Look, these wogs—half of 'em are against us and we can't trust the other half neither. You need somebody along to break heads when needs be!"

Everybody knew what she meant was "Sir, take me!" and knew also that if Six had been willing to do that he'd already have said so. Woetjans spoke anyway, because she had to.

"Well, Woetjans, there's a risk," Daniel said, allowing the hint of a frown to furrow his forehead. He meant what he was saying, but the *way* he was saying it was as calculated as any lie his father had delivered in the Senate Chamber. Speaker Leary would understand and probably approve.

"I don't believe it's an unreasonable risk, though," he continued. "Besides, there's only the single eight-place aircar to carry the whole party, and the Councilor is granting me four seats. Perhaps you think that I should say to him, 'Well, this trip's all right for a wog politician, but it's too dangerous for an RCN officer.' Eh?"

Daniel heard hoots of laughter through the closed hatch. He paused, grinning at the bosun and seeing everybody else on the bridge do the same.

Everybody but Adele, of course, her attention on her display. She probably disapproved of him using the word "wog" though she'd see the need to make his point to the crew in the language spacers themselves used.

"Look, sir, you can laugh," Woetjans snarled to the deck. "I haven't got the words, I know that. But you know what I mean!"

She was genuinely angry, at the situation rather than at Daniel for having created it. She'd have had a right to be angry at him, though; he'd made her look foolish, which she didn't deserve and which her courage and loyalty *certainly* didn't deserve.

"Woetjans, look at me," Daniel said sharply. "You're right. I apologize. But as for what you're asking—Hogg and Tovera are going with us. I've cracked a few heads myself when it was called for. I don't expect that to be the case in Port Dunbar, but you're right, it could be. And I guess we all know that Officer Mundy can take care of herself, right?"

This time the laughter, on the bridge and beyond it, was entirely positive.

"Mundy and I don't need more bodyguards than we've got on this . . .," Daniel shrugged, searching for a word. "On this reconnaissance. But it may very well be that we'll need a rescue party, and because of who I'm leaving behind on the *Sissie* I know that there'll be one. I trust Captain Vesey—"

He looked at her and nodded, avoiding the smile he'd have offered in a different context.

"—to plan ably if I'm not in a position to give detailed instructions. And I trust you, Woetjans, to lead the party executing those plans with your usual skill and enthusiasm. But to do that—"

This time Daniel did smile.

"—you have to be back here waiting for the word which we all hope will never come. Right?"

"Do I gotta say I don't want a chance to mix it with these wogs, sir?" Woetjans said. "Because I'll say it if it's orders, but I'll be lying."

Daniel joined the laughter. "No, Woetjans, you don't have to say that," he said. "But I'd appreciate it if you'd hope Mundy and I get back *before* the fighting starts, all right?"

There was general laughter again. Woetjans' guffaws were the loudest, perhaps out of relief.

"Fellow Sissies . . .," Daniel continued. "I don't know any better than you do what the next few days will bring. I've given Captain Vesey instructions about cooperation with the Bennarian Volunteers, as Corius calls his troops. They'll be policing up local political gangs. Not a big problem, I suspect, but if they ask for help we'll of course provide it."

Once it'd bothered him to see how he was using words to *make* his spacers react in particular ways. It was the sort of thing his father would've done—the sort of thing Corder Leary *had* done repeatedly over the years and probably still did. Daniel let his expression grow grimmer.

"Now," he continued, "here's the hard part. I've requested Captain Vesey to stop leave until I tell her otherwise. That's partly because if I call for help, I don't want the watch officers to have to comb every dive in Ollarville before the *Sissie* lifts to save my butt."

When he mentioned stopping leave, the watching faces had grown guarded. Nobody was going to argue with Commander Leary, but it wasn't the sort of news spacers liked to get. On a voyage they were confined to the ship of necessity, but they reasonably felt that they were owed a chance to let off steam as soon as they made landfall.

The explanation—that they were on call for a rescue attempt—was one they could understand and accept, but it wasn't the whole truth. Since Daniel expected shortly to be leading his Sissies into hot places—and maybe hotter than that—he wasn't willing to leave them with what at core would be a lie.

"Now," he said, "I told you 'partly.' Here's the other part: I don't want you fighting with Corius' men."

"What!" Sun blurted. There'd be other, similar cries from the common spacers in the other compartments. "Hey, it doesn't matter how many there is! We can handle that, sir!"

"I know that I can expect my Sissies to conduct themselves as credits to the RCN," Daniel said, letting a deliberate harshness enter his voice. "I also know that if push comes to shove, somebody'll decide that a pair of plasma cannon make up nicely for the other side having twenty, thirty times the numbers. I know that because that's how I bloody think—and what I'd bloody *do* if I had to!"

He cleared his throat and made a slight grimace, as though he were ashamed of raising his voice that way. The emotion was completely real, but the fact he showed it—there was the art. As Corder Leary well knew.

"It's because of that," Daniel said, "that I'm stopping leave. Because if you go out and the odds are so much on the side of the pongoes, they're going to push. And you'll push back—sure as *God* you will, because you're my Sissies. And then it'll go all the way up the line because we're the RCN, we do what we need to to win. And so I'm going to make sure by the only means I've got that we don't have to fight it this time. Do you understand?"

The officers on the bridge made muted, positive sounds. Some of the spacers outside shouted or even cheered.

"I'll promise you two things, fellow Sissies," Daniel said. "When all this is over, I'll buy enough booze to float the *Sissie* and all you'll have to do is drink it. That's the one promise."

Woetjans, Sun, and Cory—the midshipman looking startled an instant later—shouted approval. Louder shouts trickled through the closed hatch.

"And the other is this," he concluded. "Before we leave Dunbar's World, you'll have had your belly full of fighting. We don't need to start with Corius' troops, that's all."

There were more cheers. They were a good crew, the best, and they trusted their commander.

They have a right to trust me, Daniel thought as the cheerful enthusiasm rolled over him. *I haven't lied to them yet. But my God, the truths I've told them in a way to make them pleased to hear them!*

Adele looked without enthusiasm at the landscape a thousand feet below. She didn't object to rolling plains and thickets of darker green shrubs at the bottom of the valleys, but neither did the scenery—any kind of scenery—particularly impress her.

She smiled ruefully at herself. She'd be more interested in this if it were imagery rather than what she was seeing through an aircar's window. But to *really* engage her, the landscape would have to be something that somebody else had asked her to research. Perhaps she could trick herself by telling Daniel to demand she gather information on the terrain. . . .

"Ah . . .?" said Colonel Quinn, Adele's seatmate on the car's third crossbench. "You'd be from the Cinnabar family, Officer Mundy? I mean, I heard the Councilor call you Lady, so that's how I took the name."

The aircar was built slimly for speed, seating its occupants on four two-person benches in the enclosed cabin. Hogg rode in the front with the driver, a Volunteer with the rank of sergeant if Adele was reading his collar tabs correctly. Tovera and Fallert were on the rearmost bench, and since Corius had asked Daniel to sit with him, Adele was perforce left with Quinn.

It was theoretically possible to talk between benches. Even in a luxury vehicle like this one, though, wind rush and the fan intakes acted as effective sound dampers unless you really worked to speak over them. Adele saw no need for that, nor for talk in general; she had work she could be doing on her personal data unit. Quinn apparently had a different opinion on the latter point, however, so—

"Yes, I'm Mundy of Chatsworth," Adele said. "I'm here as Signals Officer Mundy, however, assigned as Commander Leary's aide on this mission. My family has nothing to do with it."

My family has very little to do with anything since the Proscriptions, Adele thought. Her closest living relative was a second cousin named Rolfe, a harmless enough man who'd had the misfortune of marrying a bitch from a nouveau riche family.

"I'm a Cinnabar man myself, Xenos in fact," Quinn said, apparently thinking that it wasn't obvious in his accent. "Not like you, of course. I, ah . . . well, I'm Colonel of Volunteers for the Councilor here—"

He nodded to Corius on the bench in front of them, talking with animation to Daniel.

"—and Headman Ferguson called me Supreme Marshal when I was with him, but the truth is I put in my twenty years with the Land Forces of the Republic and got out as Sergeant Major. I figured I'd go off to the back of beyond and make easy money with the wogs."

He grimaced. "I made money," he said, "but none of it stuck to my fingers any better than it did back in the LFR. And as for easy, I'll tell the *world*!"

Quinn tapped his nose, then patted his ears. "These're false, you know," he said. "Ferguson had'em cut off and put me on a transport to Pellegrino, bleeding like a pig and with no more than the clothes I was wearing. Fortunately, I did have a bit owing to me on Pellegrino from a business transaction. I was able to get patched up, more 'r less, and even managed to fall on my feet with the Councilor there."

The region they'd been overflying for the past hour wasn't as populous as that nearer the coast, but small-holdings frequently showed up as regular lines against the smudged yellow-green of the natural landscape. Often a farmer—and sometimes the whole family down to babes in arms—stood in the fields to watch the aircar, shading their eyes with their hands.

Quinn shook his head. "Never work for wogs," he added. Pursing his lips in sudden concern he muttered in a still lower voice, "Of course, there's wogs and wogs, you know."

"I'll take your word for it," Adele said austerely. Corius seemed to be completely engrossed in his own conversation, so presumably

Quinn hadn't compromised himself by speaking too freely—this time. "Why did Headman Ferguson expel you, if I may ask?"

"You know," said Quinn, nodded his head with enthusiasm, "I've often asked that very question myself. 'What did I do?' I ask myself, and what do I answer?"

He seemed to expect a response. Adele raised an eyebrow in interrogation; she wasn't willing to be drawn into a question and answer session like the straight man in some silly minstrel show, but she'd make a modest effort to accommodate Quinn's conversational style.

"Fuck all if I know!" Quinn said. "No reason in the world as I could see. The bastard just got up in the morning and said, 'Let's send old Quinn for the chop,' as best I could tell. No reason at *all*."

"Though you mentioned you were doing business...?" Adele said, not really stressing the point but nonetheless raising it. The colonel had chosen to have a conversation; he couldn't legitimately complain if Adele listened to what he'd said and asked questions on the basis of it.

"Ah, well, that," said Quinn, fluttering his hand dismissively. "That was nothing, no more than was expected. Why, the wogs wouldn't trust a man who didn't have some fiddle, don't you see? They wouldn't think he was natural. No, that wasn't why—and in all truth, I don't believe there *was* a why, milady. Just the Headman getting up in the wrong side of the bed, that's all it was, I truly believe."

"Perhaps so," Adele said, wondering if she had a right to dislike the now-colonel as thoroughly as she found herself doing. "I dare say you were lucky not to have been treated worse, in that case."

Quinn's attitude toward foreigners was narrow, prejudiced, and factually *wrong*—as Adele knew by her studies and through personal observation. On the other hand, the colonel hadn't voiced any slur that Hogg or any of the *Sissie's* spacers might not've spoken as easily. Adele accepted it from them, making allowance for the uneducated culture in which they'd been raised; she filtered their words through a rosy cloud of trust and friendship.

Still, there was this difference: Hogg scorned foreigners without exception, but he served a Leary of Bantry. Quinn treated foreigners as sheep to be sheared in order to provide a comfortable nest for himself. Sneering at people you prefer to avoid was very different from sneering at your benefactors behind their backs.

A road—a broad dirt trackway—curled over the contours of the hills on the northern horizon. Farms were strung along the crude artery like tourmalines on a necklace, but Adele had seen very little traffic in all the time the aircar sped west parallel to it. Now a plume of dust much higher and broader than any she'd seem before waved from the road like a brick-red flag.

Quinn saw that she was looking through the window behind him. He turned and unfolded a flat plate into a pair of electronic binoculars which he focused on the plume.

That reminded Adele of the RCN-issue goggles strapped over her forehead; she hadn't worn them long enough for their use to become second nature to her, the way winkling out secrets with her personal data unit was. Still, now that she'd remembered, she settled the goggles over her eyes, locked their stabilizer, and raised the magnification by steps to x64.

A huge tractor with caterpillar treads and a coal-fired steam engine pulled a train of six boxcars on puffy all-terrain tires. A bin in the back of the tractor held coal; there was a conveyor to load the firebox, but a human stoker watched the process with a shovel in his hand. The tanks swelling the sides of the vehicle carried water to replace steam losses.

"Army recruits," Quinn said. "Going off to Port Dunbar to learn about war. They don't give 'em any training, you know. They've got bugger all in the way of a cadre who *could* train 'em."

He made a disgusted sound in his throat; Adele feared for a moment that he was hawking to spit. Instead he went on, "They'll get their belly full soon enough, I'll tell you. Too soon for most of 'em. Fucking wogs."

The doors of the boxcars were slid fully open; men sat in the doorways, their bare legs out in the breeze. They looked like farmers being hauled to a harvest.

A few days ago they'd *been* farmers; the guns stacked in the cars' interiors didn't really make them soldiers. And even without Quinn's disgusted comment, Adele had no doubt that they would indeed be harvested in the near future when they were sent against Arruns' trained troops. They'd take a few of the Pellegrinians with them, though, and there were more farmers being born every day in the interior of Dunbar's World.

Adele understood the mathematics of the equation quite clearly. That didn't make her like it any better, but it wasn't necessary that she like it.

"You see the women?" Quinn said.

"Yes, of course," said Adele. They rode on top of the boxcars; there were even a few children with them, infants too young to be left behind.

"They're the commissariat," Quinn explained. "When the train stops to take on water, they'll get out and fix meals for their men. Ash cakes and whatever vegetables they can buy in the farms along the way, I'd guess. None of that lot'll run to the price of a chicken."

"I see," said Adele. She lifted the goggles up onto her forehead again. The train and its broad flag of dust had fallen far behind the speeding aircar; and besides, there was really nothing more to see.

The quicker this war could be ended, the better it would be, and Commander Daniel Leary was on Dunbar's World to end the war. Adele smiled faintly. She'd do her duty—and Daniel would certainly do his duty—regardless.

But it was nice to feel that your mission might actually do some real good.

CHAPTER 16

Port Dunbar on Dunbar's World

Daniel slid back the aircar's roof panel as they cruised slowly down the center of Southern Boulevard. They were only thirty feet in the air and the apartment houses on the right side of the street were mostly five or six stories high. He wanted to be able to see their roofs.

"I wouldn't do that," Corius warned sharply. "Those tents down there and the buildings're full of refugees from the northern part of the city. You don't know how they'll react to a limousine. They might start throwing things."

"And they might start shooting," said Hogg. He was standing beside the driver to watch the left side of the boulevard. He held his impeller across his body, ready to shoulder it. "Which is why the master and me're keeping an eye out. Sir."

"I'm afraid he's right, Councilor," Daniel said apologetically. "If it were only the chance of a flower pot or a roof tile, it wouldn't matter; but people can get very angry when their lives've been turned upside down. And there could be Pellegrinian agents, you know."

Daniel'd seen enough of mobs during his own short lifetime to appreciate the risks. He'd taken his service pistol from its holster and laid it on his lap, ready for use. He wasn't under any illusions about

195

his pistol marksmanship, but if worse came to worst he thought he could come close enough to disconcert a sniper.

He thought of suggesting to Adele that she take over the duties with his heavy pistol; her own wasn't intended for use at the hundred feet or so of slant distance to the rooftops. She was lost, though, in whatever flood of information she was gathering as the aircar proceeded toward the Emergency Ministry building. It was a converted secondary school, from what they'd been told in Ollarville.

Besides, Tovera and Fallert were standing in the back of the vehicle: she with her sub-machine gun and the snakeman holding a wide-mouthed weapon with a drum magazine. Daniel didn't know just what Fallert's gun did, but he was confident that it'd be adequate for whatever purpose he put it to. Tovera obviously respected him, which was as high a recommendation as you could give a conscienceless killer.

Corius grimaced. "Woodson, can't you get us up a little higher?" he said to the driver. "Over the roofs, I mean."

"Best not to, Councilor," the sergeant replied. He was a bearded man with a bland expression; a native of Pleasaunce from his accent, Adele said, but apparently happy to serve under a former Cinnabar officer. "They've got plasma cannon on Mandelfarne that'd eat us right up if we gave 'em a shot. I'm keeping low so they don't."

Daniel was wearing his RCN helmet. He brought up a topographic map of the region as a 30 percent mask through which his eyes continued to search for potential snipers. The coast of Mandelfarne Island was a good ten miles away.

While cannon the size of the *Sissie*'s—it was unlikely the actual guns were that big—might do lethal damage to an aircar at that distance, there was only the most remote chance of any gun crew managing to bring its weapon on target in the fraction of a second which a moving vehicle offered. Woodson was skillful and he'd managed the full ten-hour drive without relief, but he obviously wasn't a man to scoff at risk.

Daniel shrugged mentally. That was how a lot of old soldiers managed to have lived to become old soldiers, of course.

A snarl like giants ripping metal made Daniel hunch reflexively. The quick WHAM/WHAM/WHAM/WHAM/WHAM three seconds later was reassuring. The impacts were over a mile away, in the city's northern suburbs.

The Pellegrinians had launched a salvo of bombardment rockets at the Federal positions; it had nothing directly to do with the aircar. Black smoke rose beyond the buildings but quickly dissipated: residue from the warheads, not a secondary explosion.

"They've increased the number of shells they fire every week since the invasion began," Corius said, frowning. "By now half the *Rainha's* cargo on each resupply run is more rockets."

"I've never understood why . . .," Daniel said.

He paused, his attention drawn by something suddenly stuck over the cornice of a building they were approaching. It turned out to be a wooden pole. A woman began hanging diapers on it to dry.

"Right," Daniel muttered. "I don't understand why people seem to believe that filling the streets with broken rubble makes a city easier to attack. You could scarcely ask for a better place to conceal your enemies than a jumble of bricks and timber. Even an old woman with a wooden spear can be dangerous in a mess like that."

"I suspect Arruns is getting desperate," Corius said. He chuckled. "I'd certainly be desperate if I were in his shoes. But—"

He sobered as quickly as he'd laughed.

"—I *will* be in his shoes if I commit my troops to the fighting in the city itself. The only way I can really be effective is to turn their flank, it seems to me."

Daniel switched his visor display to imagery the *Princess Cecile* had captured from orbit; the Pellegrinian positions were highlighted in red. He didn't really look at it, though, because he'd absorbed the relevant details while he was waiting for the Bennarian ships to arrive above Dunbar's World.

"The Pellegrinians have brought heavy equipment," Daniel said. "There're earthworks around their entire position. Their flanks are on the sea. It seems to me that their supply routes are the only place they're vulnerable. Either destroy the barges they're using to ferry supplies from Mandelfarne to the mainland, or prevent them from bringing supplies from Pellegrino itself by threatening the *Rainha*."

"Can you do that?" Corius said sharply. "Keep the *Rainha* from landing on Mandelfarne?"

"Not so long as she's escorted by a cruiser," Daniel said. "At least not while the *Sissie* is the closest thing to a warship that I have to work with. I'm second to none in my belief in what the RCN can achieve with limited resources—"

He smiled to emphasize the humor of what he was saying, but it was the flat truth as well.

"—but I won't throw away my ship and the lives of my crew for a gesture on behalf of the Federal Republic of Bennaria."

Corius grunted and said, "Then we'll have to find another way to do it, won't we?"

The median strips on Southern Boulevard were as wide as the traffic lanes on either side. Originally they'd been grassy and dotted with flower beds, but now shanties made from scrap wood and plastic sheeting covered them. Downdraft from the aircar's fans ruffled the flimsy structures, though none actually collapsed.

Refugees looked up, their expressions unreadable. A surprising number were men of what Daniel thought of as military age.

Well, he wasn't here to help the Federal Republic reform its military recruitment policies. Though he was beginning to wonder why he was here at all, given the general lack of enthusiasm for his mission on Bennaria and the absence of resources on Dunbar's World.

"I think this is the place, sir," said the driver in a raised voice. Without waiting for direction, he eased back on the yoke and curved the aircar down toward a complex of two-story brick buildings ahead on the right. The complex filled much of a city block whose perimeter was bounded by chain link fencing. Vehicles, mostly groundcars, were parked inside the fence. The sandbagged blockhouses at each of the three driveway entrances were newly built.

Daniel laughed cheerfully. Corius gave him a wary look and said, "I'm not joking, Commander. I intend to defeat the Pellegrinians."

"And so do I, Councilor," Daniel said, "so do I. Because if we don't do that, why, the only reason I'd have for being here would be to keep me out of the way of Admiral Vocaine. I have too much confidence in the leadership of the RCN to believe in anything so cynical."

He laughed again as the car landed, but the Councilor's expression became even more guarded.

As Adele stretched, working out stiffness from the long ride, Hogg called to Tovera, "You want to stay with the car or shall I?"

"You're the sturdy outdoorsman, Hogg," Tovera said. "Besides, that great clumsy impeller wouldn't be nearly as useful inside a building as my attaché case."

She tapped the case of pebble-grained black leather that she always carried. The small sub-machine gun nestled inside wouldn't show up even under a fluoroscope.

"Yeah, right," Hogg said, but he wasn't arguing the decision. "I could maybe kick one in the crotch, don't you think, mistress?"

Corius turned in surprise and mild irritation. "You can both come in if you like," he said. "Woodson will stay with the car."

"That's all right, sir," Hogg said. "I'll keep him company."

The front entrance was up three broad, concrete steps. The uniforms of the two guards there didn't fit; the men themselves were very young and looked younger. They straightened as Corius, his bodyguard, and Quinn a step behind strode toward them.

Daniel leaned close to Adele and whispered. "Did you notice Fallert's throat sac? It's flushing. If he were a real lizard, I'd say it was a courtship display."

"And what makes you think it isn't?" Adele said, settling her data unit into its pocket as she and Daniel followed the Bennarians.

"But Adele," Daniel said, "there's no. . . . My God! You mean Tovera! That's . . . That's disgusting!"

"Well, Daniel," Adele said. "There are some of us who put all human reproductive behavior in the 'disgusting' category. Though I know you and I probably differ on the point."

Daniel laughed at the humor of it. "I know perfectly well that we humans are animals," he said as they climbed the steps together. "But I just don't think of us that way."

"Good," said Adele. "Because if you did, you'd be a different person."

A person more like your father, she thought, but she didn't let the thought reach her tongue.

"I'm Councilor Corius with my staff," Corius said to the sentries generally. From what Adele could see, they were untrained recruits and bored rather than worried. "I have an appointment with General Mahler."

Adele frowned: that wasn't precisely true. Corius had spoken to Mahler from Ollarville before setting out, but they hadn't—couldn't have—set an exact time for the meeting.

Her expression softened into the wry smile that'd become more frequent since she'd met Daniel: she was focusing on words again instead of on the purpose for which the words were spoken. That purpose, to get into the presence of the military commander of Port Dunbar, was a valid one, so she shouldn't object to the way it was achieved.

The smile grew wider: so long as she didn't have to tell lies herself.

"Sure, sir," said a guard—the one on whom Corius had fixed his gaze, probably at random. "His office's upstairs and all the way to the right. He may not be in, though."

"He's in," said Adele as she entered the building beside Daniel. Mahler was arguing with the Minister of Defense in Sinclos, the temporary capital, about his need for water purification equipment; the Pellegrinians had captured the water plant in their initial assault.

"How do you know?" Colonel Quinn asked plaintively as they stepped briskly up the central staircase.

Adele had been listening to Mahler's conversation among others from as soon as she'd gotten close enough to the city to conect her data unit through the aircar's transceiver. Federal communications security was appallingly bad, and the Pellegrinian field units weren't much better.

Arruns' headquarters on Mandelfarne Island, on the other hand, was thoroughly professional—and, judging from various recognizable quirks, was almost certainly staffed by an Alliance signals detachment. Given time and the full facilities of the *Princess Cecile* Adele could break their security, but for the present it remained impenetrable.

Adele simply shrugged; she was concentrating on the present situation. Besides, Quinn wouldn't understand any better if she described the process to him, so he might as well think she was a mentalist of some sort.

Fallert bounded to the top ahead of the rest of the party; his thin legs took three steps at a time without apparent strain. Tovera was backing up at the rear, her eyes on the outside door.

"They're well matched," Daniel whispered, indicating Fallert with a tiny nod. He smiled at his joke, but Adele thought the expression was strained. That made *her* smile.

The rooms to either side of the hallway were occupied by men in uniform—though not quite the same uniforms—and women, seated at one-piece writing desks which were bolted to the floor in neat rows. They were working with ledgers and loose sheets of paper.

Adele noticed only one computer as she passed, on the combination desk and lectern at the front of one room. The portly man seated there wasn't using the equipment or doing any other useful work that she could see. He watched with increasing outrage as Corius and his entourage walked by, then cried to their backs, "You there! This is a restricted area!"

A hand-lettered sign reading COMMANDER IN CHIEF had been taped over the original legend painted on the frosted glass of the room at the end of the corridor. Nobody was in the outer office. Corius opened the door to the inner office and walked through.

"What?" said the bearded man seated behind the desk inside. He'd been speaking into a phone connected to his computer. "What? Who're you?"

"I'm Yuli Corius, commander of the Bennarian Volunteers," Corius said. "I want to discuss the deployment of the two thousand troops I've brought to Dunbar's World."

"What?" said the man. Adele recognized General Mahler, a former district governor who in his youth had been a cadet officer on Novy Sverdlovsk. In the most recent image he'd had a neat goatee, but it had spread into a ragged brush in the past month. Into the phone he continued, "Minister, I'll get back with you!" and banged the handset into its cradle.

"General Mahler?" Corius said. "This is my staff. Commander Leary here is an advisor sent to me by the RCN."

Adele felt her lips purse in disapproval. Daniel simply smiled engagingly, though, clearly not troubled by the way Corius had described his mission. Daniel was doubtless correct as to what was important in the greater scheme of things, but Adele had rather different personal priorities.

Mahler ignored them both and didn't even blink at Fallert. "I didn't expect you so quickly," he said. "Where are your troops?"

"At present they're in Ollarville," the Councilor said, "but—"

"Ollarville!" Mahler said. "What bloody good is that? How quick can you get them here?"

There were two straight chairs in front of the desk. No one else was using them, so Adele sat down and brought out her personal data unit.

"We might differ about what's useful," Corius said in an increasingly distant voice. He wasn't, Adele surmised, the sort of man who took well to being interrupted. "And they'll stay in Ollarville until we've determined—"

"Do you have artillery?" Mahler said. He wasn't so much having a conversation as dropping questions into an answer machine. "If I had real artillery, I could—or tanks? By God, with tanks I can smash these pigs right into the sea, into the sea to *drown!*"

Adele had been sorting communications, as usual, but without really thinking about it she brought up a sidebar from the unit's internal memory. Normally she'd have the unit linked to far more extensive databases, but this was adequate for her present purposes.

As she'd expected, the cost of a tank of the sort in current use with the Cinnabar and Alliance armies was comparable to that of a moderate-sized starship. When one added in the expense of transporting the tank from, say, Xenos to Dunbar's World, Mahler's question became either remarkably uninformed or remarkably stupid.

Or both, of course. Nothing Adele had seen thus far convinced her that Mahler wasn't both.

"My troops are light infantry," Corius said, his tone as thin as piano wire. "It's my understanding that the Pellegrinians are also light infantry, so that isn't a handicap. Indeed, I can't fathom how one could obtain tanks and heavy artillery anywhere in Ganpat's Reach."

"Well, beggars can't be choosers," Mahler muttered. He sounded extremely tired; perhaps fatigue rather than stupidity explained his behavior. "They'll be a help even if they won't break the pigs once and for all. I can't get the conscripts to hold with the pigs blasting shells into them. No bloody discipline, that's the problem!"

"I didn't bring my Volunteers here as cannon fodder," Corius said. "I—"

"Look, Julie or whatever your name is!" Mahler said. "I'm the Commander in Chief, and I decide who goes where!"

"Shall I damage him, Councilor?" Fallert asked. His tone was pleasant but the slight lengthening of the sibilants gave it a hint of menace. "If I cut off his foot, perhaps he will listen."

"Chew it off, I would've thought," Tovera said.

Mahler stiffened in his seat. He started to open the middle drawer. Daniel leaned over the desk and banged the drawer shut again with his left hand, narrowly missing the fingers Mahler jerked out of the way.

"Let's not," Daniel said with a smile. "These utilities are rumpled after the long flight, but they were new when I put them on. I don't want to get blood on them, the way I certainly will if you try to shoot it out with my colleagues here."

"I would not shoot him, Commander Leary," said Fallert. "But yes, there's blood everywhere when one bites through human necks. It is very colorful."

The snakeman and Tovera laughed in their separate fashions. Adele wasn't sure which was the more unpleasant to hear.

"Enough!" said Corius sharply. His face lost its momentary blocky stiffness. Smiling again, he went on, "General Mahler, I wouldn't think of usurping your authority, but you must recall that I'm not a Federal citizen under your direct control. I want to work with you to defeat the invaders, but throwing my troops into a battle of attrition against five times their numbers will at best only delay a Pellegrinian victory."

Mahler leaned back in his chair and rubbed his eyes. "I'll take a delay," he muttered. "I'll take any bloody thing I can get."

He opened his eyes and said, "You know how I got this job? Because I was willing to take it and nobody else was! I don't have any real troops—the Port Police and the Federal Gendarmerie had some discipline but no training, and by now they're mostly gone. Not much in the way of guns and less ammunition. The main off-planet cargos come in mostly through Ollarville now, so bugger-all gets through to us who need it here!"

Another salvo of bombardment rockets slammed down. A moment after the fifth warhead detonated, a secondary explosion shook the school building; the windows rattled. Mahler winced.

"You say you're not under my control?" he said ironically. "Well, neither's the Port Dunbar Militia, the Farmers Brotherhood, the Federal Struggle Association—for all they were raised by the Federal Unity party that's supposedly the government in Sinclos. And we won't even talk about the Action Battalions of the EPL that've arrived here. Best I can tell, they're here to loot Port Dunbar before the Pellegrinians take it over. So why should you be different?"

"General," Corius said, nodding politely. "My staff and I will conduct a reconnaissance of the war zone, if we may, and then I'll get back to you. I'd appreciate it if you let people know who we are and ask them to give us full facilities, but we won't be a burden on your supply system."

"Supply system?" Mahler said. "It'd be a fine thing if I had one of those, wouldn't it? But all right, Councilor, do what you can. While I try to stop the pigs from eating the city away one block at a time because I don't have troops who'll hold their position while they're being shelled. Till the pigs get it all."

"Then we'll—" Corius said. The *whack!* of a powerful impeller firing outside the building ended the conversation.

Adele drew her pistol. She didn't have time to case the wands properly, but her right hand slid them with the data unit into her thigh pocket as she turned in the direction of the shot. At a conscious level it would've made more sense to leave the little computer on the desk, but she was operating on reflex.

And it was a good reflex. A workman who doesn't put her tools away when she's done with them probably isn't much of a craftsman.

Fallert faced the door, his weapon aimed down the empty corridor. *It'd be a bad time for office workers to run out waving their arms in panic,* Adele thought, but that wasn't a present concern.

Daniel and Tovera were at the outside windows. She held her submachine gun—of course—but Daniel hadn't drawn the heavy pistol he wore with his utilities as an officer on detached service.

Quinn had dropped to the floor and was trying to pull Corius down beside him; the Councilor was looking in the direction of the shot but seemed startled rather than afraid. Adele stepped on the small of Quinn's back in her haste to look down onto the parking lot, but she was off again as quickly and she didn't weigh enough for the accident to matter.

Six men in black shirts, workman's trousers, and black berets surrounded the Bennarian aircar thirty feet away. Two of them held pistols openly; the others wore holsters. It didn't surprise Adele to see that the red-and-white rosette of the EPL was pinned to the berets. Woodson had gotten out of the vehicle but was trapped against it, his hands half raised.

Hogg had backed toward the building to keep the EPL goons in front of him. He held the stocked impeller in his right hand like a huge pistol; it was pointed skyward. The weapon's powerful flux vaporized the aluminum driving band of its heavy-metal projectile. That glowing cloud had dissipated, but Adele's nose wrinkled with the sharpness of ozone.

"Any time, mistress!" Tovera said. Her voice had the quivering eagerness of a cat poised to spring.

"Don't shoot!" said Daniel. "We can't afford civil war!"

He jumped out of the window. It was twelve feet to the ground. Or perhaps fifteen? The only way Adele could've been sure would be by checking the building's blueprints, and she wasn't quite obsessive enough to go searching for them at the present instant.

Daniel scrunched heavily on the gravel but didn't fall. Straightening—his knees had flexed—he strode purposefully toward the car.

"Mistress?" Tovera said. "Any time!"

"You there!" Daniel called. He seemed to have forgotten his holstered pistol. "Do you know who I am? I'm Commander Daniel Leary of the RCN! See this?"

He fluffed out the left breast of his jacket with one hand and pointed with the other at the tape reading RCN in subdued lettering. It was probably unreadable against the blotched gray pattern of the utilities, but the bit of business consumed time enough for several more steps. "Cinnabar! Republic of Cinnabar!"

"Is this car yours?" said a red-haired thug whose darker mustache flared into his sideburns. He seemed to be a full head taller than Daniel, though the angle prevented Adele from being sure. "I'm Storm-Captain Pintada. There's a war on, buddy, and we're taking the car for military purposes!"

"That's a bloody lie!" shouted General Mahler, standing at the other window beside Tovera. "Get out of here, you thieves! Guards!"

"Right!" said Pintada. "We're taking the bloody car and anybody who—"

He put his hand on the latch of the car's front door. Daniel gripped Pintada's elbow. Pintada spun, jerking his arm free, then swung his left fist at Daniel. Daniel caught Pintada's wrist in both hands, kicked him in the crotch, and continued to twist and lift the bigger man's arm to keep him from doubling up.

"Mistress!" Tovera said.

Each of the six thugs wore a target in Adele's mind, over the eye or the temple or the side of the neck. She waited with her little pistol vertical beside her left ear because she'd been trained as a duelist rather than a combat shooter, but at this range she wouldn't miss; she never missed.

She'd only get one or possibly two of them, though. As soon as her shot started the game, Tovera's sub-machine gun would finish it. And Adele didn't shoot, because she knew—and Daniel knew, that's why he was risking his life down there now—that killing EPL thugs would mean civil war among those who'd been trying to stop the invaders. Navy House hadn't sent her and Daniel to Dunbar's World to decide the war in the Pellegrinians' favor.

"RCN!" Daniel bellowed, shaking Pintada like a cat toy. "Is that what you want, you backwoods dog turds? War with Cinnabar?"

A squat, black-haired thug was dancing about with his pistol drawn, trying to decide whether to risk a shot. The EPL contingent hadn't expected their victims to start the violence, and their leader was screaming too loudly to give coherent orders.

"I wouldn't do that, sonny," said Hogg. The gunman turned his head, saw the muzzle of the big impeller three inches from his right eye, and squealed. He tried to swing his pistol.

Hogg stabbed the impeller like a blunt spear, tearing the man's cheek open and smashing the thin bones behind it. The man threw his hands up, hitting himself in the face with his own pistol. He gave a gobbling cry and ran blindly into the cab of a parked truck. He bounced off, hit the ground, and collapsed.

The three men who hadn't drawn their pistols began to back away. The last had one hand on the grip of his weapon and the other on the muzzle. His mouth was slackly open. Daniel stepped toward him, holding Pintada close to his body, then shoved him hard against the gunman. The pistol fell to the ground. The man who'd dropped it fled toward the open gate, drawing his three fellows along with him.

Several men in Federal uniforms stood beside the blockhouse. They let the EPL squad run past unhindered, just as they hadn't interfered with the attempted car theft. Daniel let Pintada fall to the ground and bent over, leaning against the aircar so that he could gasp air into his lungs.

"We need to go now," Adele said crisply, swinging away from the window. The drop to the ground was too far. She hadn't trained as a midshipman, chasing like a monkey among the antennas of starships. If she jumped she'd at best make a fool of herself and very possibly wind up a cripple besides. She ran down the corridor, still holding the pistol.

Before Adele'd reached the stairs, Fallert bounded past. Tovera would be guarding the rear, then. A good team, indeed.

When they reached the parking area, Daniel'd stood up and was tugging at his utilities. Loose as they were, he'd torn the right sleeve off. Woodson stared in disbelief as Hogg lifted the groaning Pintada's head halfway into the driver's compartment.

"You want the car, wog?" he shouted.

And slammed the door with his foot.

CHAPTER 17

Port Dunbar on Dunbar's World

Daniel awoke in near darkness. In the instant it took for his eyes to begin working, Hogg whispered, "Wakie, wakie, young master. The fish won't wait."

"It's bigger game tonight, Hogg," Daniel said, pulling on the trousers he'd hung as usual on a chair by his bunk; his tunic waited under them. "Is Officer Mundy up?"

"Yes," said Adele from the hallway. "And I believe I heard Fallert speaking to the Councilor."

Daniel slid his feet into his soft-soled ship's boots. He'd been only a child when he got the trick of awakening at any set time without need for an alarm; he didn't know whether it was Hogg training him always to be ready on time for a fishing or hunting trip or if the training had simply uncovered an innate ability.

"Here you go, master," Hogg said, handing Daniel a stocked impeller. "You were never much use with a pistol, so I found you this instead of having you weight your belt down for no good reason."

"Thanks," Daniel said, turning the weapon over and trying the balance. It was a carbine, perhaps from Gendarmerie stocks. He didn't bother asking if Hogg was sure it worked: he wouldn't have given it to Daniel without testing it for function and accuracy.

Daniel also didn't ask how Hogg had "found" the weapon. It didn't bother Daniel that the means were probably illegal—so were some of the ways Daniel had used to arm and equip the *Princess Cecile* the way she needed to be—but there were things that he'd object to if he knew about them. Hogg had fewer scruples or better focus on the task in hand, whichever way you wanted to describe the difference. Best not to explore the details.

"Commander?" said Corius, entering the cubicle where Daniel had slept. "I've decided that Fallert will drive. We've decided, that is; he suggested it."

Daniel snapped his equipment belt around him. The communicator, handlight, and first aid pouch were there, but the pistol in its flap holster and the extra magazines had been removed: Hogg had spoken literally. He generally did, a habit that would've made many people uncomfortable if they'd realized he wasn't exaggerating.

They'd eaten and slept in a warehouse belonging to a merchant who'd done business with Corius in peacetime. The man—Adele probably knew his name, but it didn't matter to Daniel—had fled to Sinclos when the fighting started, but the armed staff he'd left behind had made Corius and his entourage as comfortable as the circumstances permitted.

"It's your vehicle," Daniel said. He'd never thought about the snakeman being able to pilot an aircar; there was no reason why he shouldn't. He smiled: Tovera had learned, after all.

Woodson was technically as good a driver as you could ask for, but Daniel didn't trust him to push a reconnaissance as close to the enemy defenses as was necessary for it to be useful. Daniel hadn't been alone in that opinion, apparently.

He put on his goggles. He'd planned to wear his commo helmet, but he couldn't get a proper cheek weld on the carbine's stock if he did; he'd make do with the earclip communicator attached to the goggles' frame.

They walked into the main bay of the warehouse where the aircar was parked. The long translucent panels in the building's roof let in enough light through years of bird droppings and general grime that Daniel didn't need his goggles.

A mélange of rich odors filled the big room: spices, Daniel thought, but of course they might've been from exotic forms of decay. Two attendants talked in low voices near the waterside door, watching the foreigners covertly.

Corius frowned when he saw Daniel's impeller. "I'm not proposing to attack Arruns' base tonight," he said. "Just to get a look at it. I wouldn't think those guns were necessary."

"They might be necessary," said Fallert unexpectedly. "Therefore they *are* necessary, Councilor. Hogg informs me that his master is expert; that permits me to drive instead of keeping watch."

"All right, if you feel it's the right thing to do," Corius said with a shrug as he got into the aircar. Its roof panels had been removed, leaving the tubular framework they were ordinarily locked onto. Daniel wondered if they were sturdy enough to act as a roll cage, though as the car'd be over water on most of this patrol it probably didn't matter.

"To be honest," Corius added, "I wouldn't have guessed that the Cinnabar navy spent much time on marksmanship training."

"The RCN doesn't," said Daniel, deliberately taking a seat behind that of Corius. Tonight Quinn could ride with the Councilor; Daniel wanted to be able to concentrate on the terrain and the data feed Adele would be providing. "It's an accomplishment expected of a country gentleman, however, which in my younger days—"

He smiled to suggest he was joking. In all truth, his civilian life seemed a lifetime distant. Though seven years didn't seem like a long time even to him when he spoke the words.

"—I was."

Corius nodded. "Yes, of course," he murmured.

"Daniel," said Adele, standing beside the vehicle. "I can monitor the spectra just as easily if I come along with you. I linked my data unit through the car's radio on the flight from Ollarville, you know."

Daniel frowned as he tried to puzzle out what she was actually saying. "There's not an advantage to your being in the car, is there?" he said.

"Well, no, but I *can* be," Adele repeated.

"Mistress," said Tovera, "neither of us can use long arms well enough to be useful tonight. Rather than add weight to the car, why don't you stay in the warehouse office as planned while I defend you against Pellegrinian infiltrators."

"And cockroaches," Hogg said from the front bench beside Fallert. "Some I saw tonight could carry away a rat."

"Officer Mundy?" Daniel said now that he understood the question, "I'd prefer that you be in a place where you can concentrate on keeping us alive, rather than worrying about being thrown out of the car if we have to maneuver. I'm fairly confident that there'll be other occasions soon on which you can demonstrate your manly courage."

"Yes, of course," said Adele. "I'll get up to the office right now."

She cleared her throat and added, "That was very foolish. Sorry, I'll be more careful."

"The RCN," Daniel said softly, "has built its reputation on the habit of taking the more dangerous course unless some other method could better achieve the desired result. In this case, I'm ordering you to stay on shore because you'll be more effective. But no, that wasn't foolish, Mundy."

Fallert fluffed the car's ducted fans, four of them in pairs forward and aft. "We are prepared, Councilor," he said over the intake noise. Dust whirled and eddied among the crates and bales.

"All right, open the door!" Corius shouted. When the attendants didn't act for a moment he waved violently. Finally they started shoving the heavy panel sideways. Fallert lifted and slid the car forward before the opening was sufficient; the attendants shouted and put their backs into the job.

Accelerating and with no more than inches to spare on either side, the aircar shot out over the barge dock. They skimmed the water for a moment before Fallert rose ten feet so that they no longer kicked up an obvious plume of spray. Mandelfarne Island lay ahead.

Adele stepped into the warehouse office and communications center, a small room on the flat roof. Under other circumstances you could call it a penthouse, but she didn't suppose the word applied here.

Under other circumstances, Adele Mundy could be called a librarian. Not now.

She glanced at the modern equipment. It was operating properly, just the way she'd left it four hours ago before she went to sleep. She hadn't thought she'd be able to get her eyes to close, but she'd been wrong. She'd learned a great deal since Daniel brought her into the RCN.

Instead of sitting at the console, Adele turned abruptly and walked toward the end of the roof overlooking the barge dock and the harbor beyond. There was no railing, and fitful breezes flicked across the water; she stopped a full pace back but even then felt uncomfortably close.

She smiled. Daniel would've gone to the edge without thinking about it.

"Is something wrong, mistress?" Tovera asked. She'd been standing just outside the office; she'd to step aside quickly when Adele reemerged.

"No, nothing," said Adele, looking out to sea. "Some people prefer seeing things with their own eyes, you know. I find that much less informative than my instruments."

An automatic impeller to the east pecked out short bursts. Even without her goggles, Adele could see the haze of light from the discharges; the gun was within the Pellegrinian lines, firing into the city.

Dust spurted skyward; several seconds later Adele heard the rattle of masonry collapsing. Another building had been reduced to ruin, or more complete ruin. She couldn't imagine that result aided anyone at all in the human universe, but that wasn't a question she'd been asked to answer.

Mandelfarne Island was in the direction she was looking, but it was under the horizon even though she was thirty feet above the water. The mast-mounted antennas behind her had a direct line on it, though. And somewhere in the darkness was an aircar heading out in a wide arc that would eventually carry it around the back of the Pellegrinian base.

Tovera didn't say any more. Did she understand why Adele was standing here?

Adele sniffed. She herself didn't fully understand, so it was unlikely that Tovera did. She returned to the office and closed the door between her and her servant before sitting down at the console and getting to work.

She'd been surprised at the quality of the commo suite, not least because government electronics on Dunbar's World had proven old, shoddy, and in poor repair. This wasn't the government, however. Though the Merchants' Guild collectively ran the planet much as was the case on Bennaria, the individual houses were in fierce competition with one another.

The office here—and presumably the similar offices in Port Dunbar's other warehouses—was set up to communicate by laser and tight-beam microwave with ships both in orbit and while floating in the harbor. Neither method was completely safe, but coupled with a good encryption program either would protect commercial information from rivals long enough to retain a competitive advantage.

Tovera had disconnected the identification transponder from Corius' vehicle. A transmitter could call enemy attention to the car whose best chance of survival would come from being ignored. Sensors sensitive enough to keep a laser beam aligned with a ship in orbit, however, were easily capable of tracking the electromagnetic signature of an aircar's motors a few miles away. All it took was the correct software, and Adele's personal data unit provided that.

Adele placed the car as a blue dot in a display centered on Mandelfarne Island; the scale changed as she watched, decreasing as the car neared the base and the image area shrank accordingly. Pellegrinian emitters—communications, range-finding, targeting, and even recreational—were red dots with brief legends indicating their type and intensity. Full data would appear as a sidebar if the computer determined the threat to the aircar had increased or if Adele moved her cursor over a particular dot.

Laymen were amazed to see what information Adele could draw from the simplest electronic signatures by matching them against the information in her database. A search radar with a particular pulse frequency and amplitude was a standard fitment for the command unit of Alliance ground batteries of 5-cm plasma cannon; the same weapon but with a different radar armed Alliance airborne armored personnel carriers.

Arrruns' troops used both types of radar. Twelve cannon in gun pits guarded the perimeter of Mandelfarne Island, and five APCs escorted the barges ferrying supplies from the island to Arrruns' fortified camp in the east of Port Dunbar. From personal experience as well as her data banks, Adele knew that the APCs were very lightly armored; even empty they weren't nearly as fast or as nimble as Corius' aircar.

But an aircar couldn't outrun a plasma bolt. Even the small guns the APCs mounted could turn an aircar into a fireball and memories from hundreds of meters away.

The blue speck moved outward, skirting the northern tip of the island at a distance of ten miles. It moved slowly, keeping close to the water so that only the most careful radar operator could separate it from the clutter of wave tops.

Adele would know when the Pellegrinians noticed the car, if they did; then she would warn Daniel. Until then she remained silent, doing her job with professional skill as she did all things.

She didn't pray. A prayer by someone who didn't believe in God would be hypocritical. She knew Daniel believed in an amorphously benevolent Being somewhere, however.

Adele hoped that Daniel's prayers would be answered.

Daniel could see scores of lights across Mandelfarne Island. A few were on moving vehicles. More were area lights on poles erected in front of pre-fab buildings—operations rooms and officers' quarters, presumably; Daniel's goggles easily picked out the details. The largest number were low-wattage incandescents which snaked on jury-rigged lines from the fusion plant on the north shore of the island and through the tents of the enlisted personnel.

From the lack of visual security at the base, one got the impression that the Pellegrinian garrison didn't think it was at war. To a degree they were right: the Federal troops had no long-range artillery, and an air attack would be quick suicide against plasma cannon. The sloppiness still made Daniel frown.

Though of course they're the enemy, he thought. He'd forgotten that. His face broke into a familiar smile.

Fallert was stooging along at thirty miles an hour so that he could keep the car's underside close to the wave tops without lifting spray. They'd raced northwest across the sea till they were out of sensor range of Mandelfarne, then dropped low and returned slowly to avoid notice.

Daniel wasn't sure what Corius and Quinn intended by this reconnaissance, but for his own part he wasn't particularly interested in what he saw at the present. The goggles, however, were gathering and storing multi-spectral data which he and Adele would analyze at leisure. They'd be just as useful with Hogg wearing them, and very nearly as useful strapped to the aircar's frame.

"Leary?" said the Councilor, leaning over the back of his seat. "The colonel here thinks there must be a thousand personnel on Mandelfarne. What do you think?"

Daniel adjusted his goggles as he eyed the speckles of light. They weren't going to tell him more than they already had, but the activity gave him a moment to consider.

"At least that, I should think," he said. It depended on the size of the tents and how densely Arruns packed his troops into them, but allowing for a similar number of lights on the other side of the island . . . at least a thousand. "We don't have to guess, though. I'm confident that Officer Mundy will have an accurate figure by the time we return."

"How's she going to do that?" said Quinn. "I thought she was waiting for us back at the warehouse."

Daniel shrugged, though he didn't suppose the gesture was visible in this light. "Pay records," he said. He'd worked with Adele long enough to have an idea of her methods, though in truth it still seemed like magic to him. "Movement orders. The location of unit HQs coupled with their tables of organization."

"She can do all that from the warehouse?" Quinn said. He sounded plaintive. "I thought she was just a signals officer."

"She's a signals officer," Daniel said dryly. "But no, she's not only that."

He switched his goggles to infrared; Pellegrinian equipment showed up as bright blotches on the cooler land. To see details he'd have had to raise the magnification higher than he could hold on target without engaging the stabilizer, but the four plasma cannon in pits near the shore were obvious. The psychological effect of plasma bolts would be as crushing to an assault as the bolts themselves— and those would blast any aircraft or troop-laden fishing boat into flaming debris.

"Check with her now, Commander," Corius said. "It'd be helpful to know the numbers immediately. You do have a link, don't you?"

"No sir," Daniel said. In strict honesty he *did* have a link, but he had absolutely no intention of using it for pointless chatter. "We'll have the data before we start the actual planning on our return, I'm sure."

"*The* Rainha *is beginning her approach*," said a voice in Daniel's ear. He knew it was Adele speaking only because it had to be; compression and the distortion-correcting algorithms in the laser communicator stripped all the personality out of the words. They were at the very limit of line-of-sight communication here.

Daniel picked out the shimmer of plasma thrusters in the western sky. The ship was still high enough that the atmosphere blocked the dangerous actinics, so the goggle filters didn't deploy.

He bent forward and said, "The *Rainha*'s coming in. If we can get closer to the island, I'd like a good view of their landing procedures."

He'd been speaking to Corius, expecting him to relay the instruction to Fallert if he approved it, but the reptileman was apparently able to hear better over the fans than a human could. Daniel felt the direction of thrust shift as the aircar swung slowly toward the island.

The distant ship's thrumming vibrated the night even over the car's intake whine. The flare of ionized atoms returning to their normal state was first brighter than any star, then brighter than the small moon. It continued to increase. Daniel's goggles dimmed the discharge, but a ghost of the thrusters' rainbow aura remained.

Only one ship was landing: the *Duilio* remained in orbit. The warehouse personnel had told Daniel that was the procedure. He hadn't doubted what they said—it was the logical way for the Pellegrinians to operate, after all—but he liked to see things for himself. He didn't have a plan or an inkling of a plan at the moment, but when he did he'd have the facts right.

The *Rainha* swelled into a fat, blunt-ended cylinder flanked by the lesser cylinders of its outriggers, bathed in its own exhaust. The roar of its descent sent ripples across the sea's surface, even miles away. Daniel smiled, unconsciously moved by the sight of a starship and all the wonder and delight that brought to his mind.

His earpiece blipped at him. He couldn't hear the message over the *Rainha*'s thunder.

"Say again, over," he said, cupping his hand over the earpiece. His response went out as VHF because the aircar's commo suite didn't have a laser emitter. Daniel was taking Adele's transmission's through the goggles, but the tiny RCN sending unit was useless beyond intercom range.

As he spoke, he switched his viewing mode from light amplification to IR. He saw an APC lifting from the opposite shore of Mandelfarne Island even as Adele said, "*You've been . . . The APCs they use to es . . . are to shoot you . . . . . . was manned when the alert sounded. O . . .*"

"Fallert!" Daniel said. He pointed his carbine as the snakeman's head turned enough to catch the motion with his peripheral vision.

Air compressed by the APC's fans was a warm plume spreading beneath the vehicle. "They're on us!"

Fallert shifted his throttles and steering yoke. The car stayed low as it accelerated, but to Daniel's surprise the stern lifted slightly. The downdraft threw up the expected roostertail, but because the car wasn't level the spray was nearly the length of the vehicle behind where Daniel would've expected it to be.

Oh, yes. Fallert knew how to pilot an aircar.

"I am returning to base!" the snakeman called. "We could not be fully recharged before we left tonight. If I let them chase us out to sea, I do not know that we will be able to return."

We ought to be able to make it, Daniel thought. He loosened his seat belt with his left hand as his head turned to follow the APC. No plasma cannon had much range in an atmosphere, and that was true in spades for the little popgun the APC carried.

It wasn't a popgun compared to an aircar, of course.

The faint hope that the APC didn't see them—that it'd been sent out because somebody on shore had heard sounds—was dashed when the big vehicle curved toward the aircar. It was seven miles distant but on an interior course, and the aircar had ten miles to go to the safety of the shore. Though the Federals didn't have plasma cannon of their own, a burst of multi-sonic osmium slugs from an automatic impeller would turn an APC into a colander in a heartbeat.

Daniel disliked using goggles for data display, but he'd been very wise to pick the headgear he had. He grinned at himself. Not that there'd ever been doubt: he'd always go for the tool that'd be best in a fight.

The APC fired. The dazzling bolt was on the right line but it sizzled out in a bottle-shaped plume a few thousand yards from the muzzle. Even the most incompetent gunner must've known the aircar was miles out of range, so why—

Two more APCs came around the west end of Mandelfarne Island, three miles from the aircar. They'd stayed low in the strait, but now that they were in sight they lifted to get a clear shot at their quarry against the sea.

Though the APCs were relatively slow, they'd be between the shore and the aircar before it could cross their line. The bolt's ionized track was fading, but sufficient glow still hung in the air to point the newcomers toward their prey.

"Between them!" Daniel said. "Stay low and get between them!"

Fallert swung the car up on its left side in a hard turn, deliberately overcorrecting; for thirty seconds only inertia was keeping them airborne. Instead of locking into a straight new course, he made them fishtail to the right as they settled.

The APC still over the island fired, hitting the sea a quarter mile from the car. The bolt slaked its energy in iridescent steam. An instant later the APCs on a converging course fired also. Daniel felt the bare skin of his face and hands prickle, but the nearer of the two bolts nonetheless struck well behind the speeding aircar.

Fallert nudged his steering yoke again, not hard—a serious input would slow the aircar in the kill zone—but enough that the trailing flag of spray pointed momentarily in a direction different from the car's present course. The APCs were dead ahead, high enough that the fan ducts on their undersides were visible from the sea skimming car.

Daniel aimed over the left side of the vehicle and squeezed off a shot—

And a shot—

And a shot—the osmium pellet ricocheting from the target's sidewalls of high maraging steel, a flash at the point of impact and a neon spark wobbling into the high sky—

And a—

Daniel's target banked hard to the right, making it more vulnerable. As he swung his weapon to follow the eight swelling ovals of the fan ducts, Fallert twisted to the right again. The carbine's barrel slammed the roof support, jarring the round off wildly into the empty night.

Hogg's target crashed into the sea sideways. Either the impact or the gunner's reflex triggered the plasma cannon while the muzzle was already underwater. The fireball lifted off the turret as the APC skipped upward like a flung stone.

"Got the bastard!" Hogg was shouting as he twisted in his seat— *good God, he must not be belted in at all!*—to point his heavy RCN impeller directly over Fallert's head. "Got him!"

Fallert steered through the geyser from the first impact while the APC—now a collection of scraps and fragments spraying out like a shotgun charge—hit a third time. A few of the bits continued on to splash in a wide arc. The aircar bucked. Falling water drenched the passengers, but they were through and headed for home at nearly 150 mph.

Daniel popped his own belt loose to aim over the back of the vehicle. To his surprise he had no target: both surviving APCs had dropped to the sea's surface to cover their vulnerable fan ducts. They hadn't a prayer of tracking, let alone hitting, the aircar, there.

The rainbow bubble of the *Rainha's* exhaust was dimming, but there was still enough to color the froth around the wrecked APC like a tapestry of jewels.

Adele was sitting at the checker's desk when the two attendants raised the overhead door. Noises from the night outside became louder and sharper: occasional shots, a klaxon in the far distance, and the growing murmur of the returning aircar.

The desk terminal was intended only for inventory control, but it was cabled to the database that the communications suite on the roof fed. Adele hadn't found it difficult to link her personal data unit to the terminal and through it to control the entire system. The display in the commo center was far better and so, she supposed, was the security; but neither of those things was as significant as being on hand when Daniel and Hogg returned.

The aircar paused on the loading dock, then turned slowly—counterclockwise—to back into the warehouse. Adele frowned. She hadn't thought about positioning the vehicle to leave quickly; Fallert had. It was his job, of course, but that was the sort of information which might be important to her present duties.

Echoes deepened the whine of the car's motors as it crawled inside. Adele couldn't make out the features of the persons aboard without pulling down her goggles, but there were five of them. That was all that really mattered, that they'd all come back. Against the lighter background of the night sky she saw that the left side of the windshield was crazed and milky.

"They hit something," said Tovera quietly. "Not bullet holes, a collision."

Had she been worried also? Probably not; the statement was analytical, though the fact Tovera made it aloud showed that she was at least trying to act the way a normal human who was worried would act.

The door rattled and rumbled down, stopping with a jangle against the lintel. Fallert had already shut off the motors, but the fans roiled the air still further as they spun down. Adele sneezed, then sneezed again. The downdraft had driven a strong vegetable sharpness—ginger root?—out of the wooden flooring.

"Turn a bloody light on!" Colonel Quinn shouted. "Now, dammit! All I bloody need tonight is to break my bloody neck besides!"

A panel on the right door pillar flickered into greenish life. "Make do, buddy," growled an attendant. "If we turn on the overheads, the pigs'll see it through the skylight. We don't draw rockets here, not even for the Lord God Incarnate!"

After nearly complete darkness, the luminescence was more than sufficient. Adele left her data unit on the desk and walked to meet Daniel as he got out of the back of the car. His uniform was wet—dripping wet, in fact—but he flashed her a brilliant smile.

"I'm glad to see you're safe," Adele said. Part of her mind observed that another person would've added flourishes, but the words she'd used were sufficient.

"You ought to be bloody glad!" Quinn said angrily. "Do you know how close we came to being killed? If that Hogg hadn't been luckier than anybody alive, we'd be cinders out there right now!"

I do indeed know how close it was, Adele thought. *I watched you. I watched the whole thing.*

Turning from Adele to Hogg, Quinn added, "I don't know why you're working for a living, bub. If you're that bloody lucky, you ought to just play roulette!"

Hogg ignored him. He'd walked over to a stack of crates which were unmarked except by stenciled numbers. He pried up the lid of the top one with his big folding knife.

"Master Hogg is indeed lucky," Fallert said with a little more than his usual emphasis of the sibilants. "I would guess that Master Hogg is often lucky with a long gun, not so?"

Hogg pulled a liter bottle from the honeycombed interior of the crate. He cut the foil seal and worked the stopper out.

"It's been known to happen," he said. His tone was mild enough, but his eyes had a look of hard speculation as they rested on Quinn. "But luck, sure. You know that as well as I do, Fallert. Just hitting the bastard was doing good, what with that wind and you throwing us around like granny jogging without a bra."

"You and the commander each hit twice," the snakeman said. "That is very good. I could not have done as well."

He bowed to Tovera. "I did not doubt you, mistress-s-s," he said. "But what I saw tonight was very remarkable."

"Here you go, young master," Hogg said, handing the bottle to Daniel.

Daniel drank and returned the bottle to Hogg. "I'm afraid I can only claim one," he said, turning the carbine over in his hands to look at the underside of the receiver. "And other than perhaps startling the crew, that didn't do any harm."

"You hit twice and Master Hogg hit twice," Fallert said. "One of our enemies fled and the other was destroyed. This was very good. This was worthy of great honor."

"Did you kill the driver, then, Hogg?" Corius said. "I thought the car just went out of control and crashed. And at a very good time, I must say."

"I put a round through a fan duct," Hogg said. "It's what I wanted, but I don't pretend I could do it more'n maybe one time in five."

Daniel raised an eyebrow.

"Well, one time in three, then," Hogg admitted. "And then it bounced the right way and put paid to the motor."

Hogg drank again and held the bottle out to Fallert. Fallert shook his head, but his whole long jaw was smiling. "I thank you, Master Hogg," he said. "But ethanol would kill me."

The snakeman laughed.

Hogg shrugged and looked at Corius. "I couldn't shoot through the driver's cage on one a those, Councilor," he said. "Not at two hundred meters, which is as close as we got, you'll recall. The armor's too thick."

"Those APCs weren't heavily loaded," Quinn said. "Even if you did shoot out a fan, it could still have flown. The driver just lost control."

He sounded frustrated, a man desperate to find an answer to a question that was completely beyond him. It didn't make Adele like Quinn any better, but viewing him as a mongrel dog invited to give a lecture permitted her to interact with him without getting angry.

"Yes, Colonel, he did lose control," Daniel said. Adele could hear the edge beneath his cheerful lilt, but Quinn probably didn't. "He panicked because his fan had been shot out—it hadn't just failed. He poured maximum power to the remaining units before adjusting his angles of thrust. That overbalanced the vehicle, and by then he had no chance to recover."

He patted Quinn on the shoulder. *Much as he'd pat a dog*, Adele realized, and wondered whether Daniel had formed the same mental image she had of the man.

"Let's all take that as a lesson not to panic," Daniel said with a smile. "In case the enemy has somebody as good as Hogg is, right?"

"As lucky, you mean, young master," Hogg said, lowering the bottle. Half its contents were gone. He'd been frightened too, though "frightened" wasn't quite the right word. He'd been very well aware of how close they'd come to being killed, him and the boy it was his duty to protect.

"Here you go, Tovera," Hogg said, offering her the bottle. He was making a point of not including Quinn in his forced camaraderie. "Finish it if you like. There's plenty more where this one came from."

"I'm working," Tovera said. Her smile was as wide as her thin mouth permitted and looked—at least looked—real.

"Mistress-s-s?" Fallert said. "Do you mean that if you became drunk, you would not be able to kill?"

"Not that," said Tovera, still smiling. "I might forget to stop, though."

She laughed, and Fallert laughed, and Hogg laughed so hard that some of his big mouthful of wine squirted out his nostrils. Corius looked a little queasy. Adele wasn't sure he understood all the by-play, but there was enough going on even at a surface level to disturb anybody who wasn't used to it. And he'd been in the car also when the APCs bore down on it shooting. . . .

"Look, I don't see that there's any more to do tonight," he said. "I propose to get some sleep and discuss the details in the morning."

"Adele, I have a few questions," Daniel said. "Can we go over them now, or—"

"Of course," Adele said, striding back to the desk and her data unit. If she was going to work, she'd have the wands in her hands. The wands or a pistol, and not the pistol tonight.

Corius had been heading toward the line of locked storerooms which the addition of cots had turned into sleeping quarters for him and those who'd accompanied him. He paused and without comment joined Daniel.

The desk was meant to be used standing, which didn't matter to Adele one way or another. Hogg slid over a crate and sat, but the others decided to stand also. The two attendants watched from beside the door. Adele wondered if she should order them to leave. For the moment she didn't see any reason to.

Tovera walked over the pair and spoke briefly. They left the warehouse through the pedestrian door.

"We've been told there're ship-killing missiles at the base," Daniel said. "Are there, and are they operational?"

Adele had been gathering electronic data simultaneously through the antennas on warehouse roof and from the pickups on Daniel's goggles. As she sorted them, she heard Quinn say plaintively, "How's she going to tell that? You'd have to be right there with the missiles, wouldn't you?"

No, of course you wouldn't. You could determine whether the targeting radar—and lidar, Adele learned on checking her database on Metex Group AS9 missiles—were active, whether the signals were being relayed to the missile battery, and whether the missile control panel registered the six missiles as being ready to launch.

"Yes," Adele said. "The missiles are here and are live."

She threw up a display of Mandelfarne Island, then shrank the scale to focus on the missile battery in a pit two hundred yards from the chalked cross on which the resupply vessel landed. This inventory-control terminal didn't have projection lenses, so she had to use those of her little data unit. They weren't really adequate at the present scale, but her audience would have to make do.

Daniel sucked his lower lip for a moment and nodded. "Well, I was willing to hope they were bluffing," he said. "I had visions of bringing the *Sissie* down and ending the war with her ventral turret while we hovered."

"But Arruns has plasma cannon even if he didn't have missiles, doesn't he?" said Corius. "We know he does—on the armored vehicles at least. They *shot* at us."

"There's twelve guns around the perimeter of the island," said Daniel, turning his head slightly. "But they're two-inch weapons, Councilor. Serious enough against boats and aircraft, but no danger to a starship. A ship's plating's thick enough to take half a dozen bolts on the same point—plasma doesn't have much penetration, you see. The missile battery's the problem."

There were only ten guns in working order, but Adele didn't correct Daniel on a point that didn't change the basic reality. And of course the *most* basic reality was that missile battery.

"They don't engage the *Rainha*, though," Daniel said, turning back toward Adele and resuming with his next topic for discussion. "Adele, can you forge her electronic signatures?"

"It doesn't matter if she can," Corius protested. "They'll see the difference between your corvette and a transport even if Lady Mundy mimics the *Rainha*'s transmissions perfectly."

He didn't raise his voice unreasonably, but his whole manner emphasized that he was an intelligent, powerful man who was proud of his ability to grasp situations better than those around him. In that and in other ways, Corius reminded Adele of her own father.

"Yes, we'll have to use one of your ships, I'm afraid," Daniel said. "I'd bring it in normally and then your assault troops would rush the positions. The ship-owners wouldn't approve if you told them ahead of time, but I doubt there'd be damage that my Sissies couldn't patch in whatever shipyard Port Dunbar offers."

"Commander," Adele said, "I can't do that. The landing procedures involve Base Control making coded exchanges with both the *Rainha* and the cruiser in orbit. The encryption is single-pass, truly random, and I can't enter the nodes where they're stored. Arruns has an Alliance communications unit with personnel on both ships. They won't be fooled, not by me at least."

"Then not by God Himself, eh, Councilor?" Daniel said with a rueful smile. "We need a starship to assault the base, and the Pellegrinians themselves have the only ship that can do it."

"So we capture their ship," said Hogg. "The *Rainha*. We've done that before, young master—captured a ship, I mean."

"Yes, but not a ship with a cruiser for escort," said Daniel. "Except . . ."

His smile grew wider. Adele saw the expression and smiled as well. "Yes, of course," she said. "The *Rainha* won't be under escort while she's being loaded in Central Haven."

She shifted her display, replacing Mandelfarne with an image of the transport built up from data recorded when it and the *Princess Cecile* crossed above Pellegrino. A moment ago Adele had thought it was a middle-sized vessel of no particular interest; now she highlighted the hatches through which the ship could be entered.

"I'll have to go myself, you realize," she said.

"Umm, no, I don't think that's a good idea," Daniel said. "I'll send—"

"Commander," said Adele sharply. "There's no one else available who can use the *Rainha*'s identification transponder to respond correctly to the ground interrogations. You can't, Tovera can't. And that's why we're planning to capture the ship, you'll recall."

"Ah," said Daniel. "Yes, I do recall that."

He turned to Corius. Hogg was standing again. "Councilor," Daniel said, "I need to get back to Ollarville—to the *Princess Cecile*, that is—as soon as your car's accumulators can be recharged. Do you agree with this course?"

"I agree," said Corius, "but it'll take eight hours to get a full charge. And we'll need a full charge—it ran completely flat flying here in the other direction."

"The forklifts in this warehouse use the same accumulators," Hogg said. "Only one apiece instead of three; they're a standard size. There's four forklifts *and* they're charged, which I checked before we went out tonight."

"Come along, Hogg," said Daniel cheerfully. "Let's swap accumulators. It's a good thing Woodson has had a chance to sleep, because he's going to driving straight through to Ollarville. And then—"

He and Hogg were trotting toward the bank of forklifts against the side wall, their boots scuffling against the timber flooring.

"—it'll be my turn to make the fastest run from Dunbar's World to Pellegrino that anybody's ever dreamed of!"

CHAPTER 18

Haven City on Pellegrino

"I *don't* bloody like the look of this," said Woetjans as a third police vehicle pulled in line with the others, completely blocking the end of the dock at which the *Princess Cecile* had tied up. "Sure you want to handle it this way, Six?"

"It's all going to plan, Woetjans," Daniel said. "I'd worry if they weren't waiting for me."

That was technically true, but he was injecting a little conscious cheeriness into his tone for the sake of the bosun and the nearest of the liberty party. Daniel could admit in the silence of his mind that the riot control vehicles were imposing even though he knew they mounted water cannon rather than plasma weapons,

Wearing his best second class uniform without medal ribbons, Daniel walked beside Woetjans at the head of the spacers going on liberty. His tailored gray-and-black garments looked out of place in that company. All members of the *Sissie*'s crew were veterans with many years of service to commemorate in their liberty rigs. Patches embroidered with scenes of exotic landfalls covered what had started out as utilities, and varicolored ribbons, some with legends, dangled from their seams.

The cops braced as the spacers bore down on them. Daniel had formed his Sissies into a column of twos so that they didn't fill the dock as they approached. The party looked formidable even when it wasn't deliberately threatening, however.

Daniel'd also ordered the spacers to leave behind the short truncheons and knuckledusters that were normally part of their liberty paraphernalia. That last had caused complaint, but the RCN encourages resource in its personnel. They could use bottles and barstools if the need arose.

They're spacers on liberty; when *the need arises.*

"Good—" Daniel called. Was it morning or afternoon? He'd forgotten to check local time! "Good day, gentlemen! I'm Commander Daniel Leary, RCN. I'm the owner and captain of the yacht *Princess Cecile*, and this is a liberty party from my crew. They're hoping to spend a month's pay in the entertainment establishments of Haven City."

"Yee-*ha!*" called a Sissie. As a breed, spacers were unlikely to be cowed by the presence of police, but Woetjans turned with a scowl to silence the enthusiasm. This wouldn't be a good time for things to get out of hand.

"Commander Leary?" said a pudgy civilian with receding hair and a brush moustache. "I'm Superintendent Otto. Some matters have come up since your previous visit to Central Haven. I'd like to discuss them with you in the Port Control Office, if you don't mind."

"Not at all," said Daniel. "To be honest, I rather expected that. Shall we walk—"

He nodded to the building kitty-corner across the broad street paralleling the harbor. It looked like a three-story pillbox covered with turquoise stucco.

Mostly covered. Patches had flaked off.

"—or would you prefer to drive me?"

"Look, sir," Woetjans said, trying to sound calm. "Why don't the two of you talk things over aboard the *Sissie*? That's where customs people ought to be, right, aboard the ship they're checking?"

"Go on about your liberty, Woetjans," Daniel said with a touch of sharpness. The bosun knew as well as he did that Otto had nothing to do with customs. "There's no problem with that, is there, Superintendent?"

Otto hesitated, then turned to a police officer with rings of silver braid around his billed cap. "Send your men back to their usual duties, Major."

"Shall I leave one truck—" the policeman began.

"You *shall* do what I told you, Major," Otto snapped. "Let the liberty party through and go on about your duties!"

The major stiffened. "Right, let 'em by!" he said.

As his men parted and two of the trucks pulled forward to open a passage, he turned to Woetjans. With something like professional unctuousness he added, "We don't mind you boys having a little fun, ah, madam, but keep it in bounds. Get out of line and you'll spend the rest of your leave in the pokey, understood?"

"Six . . .?" said the bosun plaintively.

"We're visitors, Woetjans," Daniel said. "The Pellegrinian authorities have some reasonable concerns. I'm happy to allay them. Go on ahead, but I'm sure I'll be rejoining you shortly."

The two civilians flanking Otto were tall, broad men, bigger than any of the green-uniformed police. From a distance Otto would be a slightly rumpled joke. His cheeks were soft, his mouth weak, and his eyes as hard and piercing as a pair of ice picks.

"I'm glad to find you so reasonable, Commander," he said. "We perhaps need not go to my office after all. We will sit in my car."

"Wherever you please, Superintendent," said Daniel. He started toward the nearest of the riot control vehicles, but Otto gestured instead to an aircar parked just beyond them. It looked nondescript, but when Otto opened the door of the passenger compartment Daniel saw a luxury that hadn't been hinted by the polarized windows.

Otto closed the door behind them. His aides remained outside, one standing at either end of the vehicle.

"You described yourself as owner and captain of the *Princess Cecile*, Commander Leary," Otto said. "When you docked here a week ago, you stated—stated on oath, I might add—that the captain was one Elspeth Vesey. She signed the port records."

"I hired Vesey," said Daniel. "Quite a clever young lady. I honestly thought she was up to the job, but by the time we reached Bennaria it was obvious that I'd been wrong. I'd brought her along too quickly, I suppose, or . . ."

He gave an expressive shrug. "To tell the truth, Superintendent . . . there's a lot written about a woman being every bit as good as a man and I dare say there's some cases where it's true. Though I gather you folks here around Ganpat's Reach have never bought into that as strongly as they do back on Xenos?"

"No," said Otto. "We are simple folk. We do not believe bullshit just because somebody who says he's a sophisticate from Cinnabar says it is true."

"Well, there's a lot to be said for that attitude," Daniel said, nodding firmly. "As one man to another, well—of *course* a woman isn't fit to captain a starship, not on a voyage like this one! I have no doubt that Vesey'll marry well on Bennaria, have a lot of children, and be a great deal happier than if she'd stayed on Xenos and tried to force herself to be something no woman is."

If Woetjans had heard the conversation, she'd have ignored it because it wouldn't have made sense to her. The bosun wasn't an intellectual and knew it. There was a lot in the world that she didn't understand, and that wasn't something that bothered her.

Adele, of course, would've understood that Daniel was telling Otto things that Otto already believed. That made him more likely to believe the other things Daniel would tell him.

Vesey would take the words as seriously meant for at least a few heartbeats, a betrayal of her trust and a damning indictment of her own competence. All that despite the fact that logic told her Commander Leary *couldn't* believe what he'd just said, that he was simply explaining to the Pellegrinian security police why the *Sissie's* former commanding officer was no longer aboard.

"Perhaps you've found wisdom in your visit to our region," Otto said. Daniel couldn't tell from his tone whether the words were meant as irony. "No doubt that by itself would justify the time and effort of your voyage."

He spread his fingertips against the burl inlays of the doorpanel beside him. His nails were painted with chevrons of dark blue against an azure background. "You returned from Bennaria to Pellegrino, then?" he asked, his cold eyes on Daniel.

"Not directly, no," said Daniel. "We went from Bennaria to Dunbar's World. Then from Dunbar's World to here, and back to Cinnabar as quickly as the sails can take us."

Vesey wasn't aboard because she was marching off toward the bars, brothels, and gambling hells of Center Street with forty-four other Sissies. She wore a liberty suit borrowed from Cui, an engine wiper who'd remained with the anchor watch. There'd be a lot of coming and going of the *Princess Cecile's* crew members over the next twelve hours. Unless the police were counting very carefully, the fact that thirty of those spacers were still on the ground when the ship lifted ought to go unremarked.

It wasn't a problem port policemen were used to dealing with. Though quite a lot of their duties involved searching for spacers who'd jumped ship, it was up to the ship's officers to report that there were missing personnel in the first place.

"Ah!" said Otto, his spread hand suddenly as motionless as a waiting spider. "You admit you were on Dunbar's World, then?"

"My mission was to aid Bennarian forces in repelling the recent invasion of Dunbar's World, Superintendent," Daniel said calmly. "This isn't a secret—it was debated and agreed in an open meeting of the Cinnabar Senate. And no, I didn't make a point of telling that to you or other officials when we landed at Central Haven on our way in—I'm not a complete idiot."

He shrugged and added, "But neither am I foolish enough to think you don't know all this by now from your own sources. I assure you that if my mission hadn't been a complete and total failure, I would've bypassed Pellegrino on my return."

Otto was obviously taken aback. He touched a set of controls on his armrest. A holographic display briefly brightened in front of him, then vanished. From Daniel's angle it'd been only a milky blur.

"You are forced to land on Pellegrino," Otto said with what was obviously feigned assurance. "Our location controls access to Ganpat's Reach!"

Daniel smiled. "Superintendent," he said, "I don't think there's a captain in the RCN who couldn't plot a course in and out of the Reach without touching down on Pellegrino. It's a convenience certainly—that's why I'm here. And besides—"

He let the smile turn rueful.

"—I figured you deserved a chance to crow at me on my way home with my tail between my legs. Because I was, I'll admit, less than candid with the authorities here when we landed the first time."

Otto blinked. He set his hand against the doorpanel, then brought up—and killed—the display again. Finally he said, "So, what is it that convinced you to return to Cinnabar, Commander?"

"Superintendent Otto," Daniel said, leaning slightly forward. "I'm an RCN officer, not a Pellegrinian spy. I have no intention of discussing the details of what I observed in Ganpat's Reach with you. I *will* tell you that while I don't expect people at Navy House to be pleased with the report I tender to them, neither do I expect the failure of my mission to seriously harm my career. Not on the facts I determined while I was in the Reach."

Otto chuckled like bubbles percolating through heavy oil. "Well, I'll withdraw my question then, Commander," he said. "To be frank, I doubt there's very much you could tell me about what you did and saw that we on Pellegrino don't already know."

He tapped the controls to the car's data unit but didn't switch it on.

"So," he continued. If his chuckle had implied good humor, it was certainly past now. "I will ask another question: what are your present intentions, Commander Leary?"

"I'm allowing the crew eighteen hours' leave," Daniel said. He grinned and added, "I don't think I'm giving away military secrets if I tell you that neither Charlestown nor Ollarville right now are places I was willing to give unrestricted liberty."

He hadn't started with, "I've already told you," because that further waste of time would serve only to sour his relationship with the Superintendent. At the moment the relationship was merely doubtful. Daniel was under no illusions that his Cinnabar rank and citizenship would protect him from real trouble if he angered Otto sufficiently.

"We'll top off our reaction mass here and take on local produce," he continued. "The usual business, of course. And then we lift for Cinnabar, which I hope to manage in a single insertion. All the way in the Matrix, that is, without dropping back into sidereal space for star sightings."

"Is that possible?" said Otto, looking puzzled but no longer hostile. "It is the voyage of a month, is it not? I'm not a spaceman, of course, but I understood if one spent so long in the Matrix without a break, one went mad."

Daniel shrugged again. "I judge thirteen days," he said. "I've gone longer in the past with this ship and mostly this crew."

He met Otto's eyes and grinned engagingly. "Not to put too fine a point on it," he said, "I intend to get back to Cinnabar before word of what happened does. *I* want to be the one who explains why my mission failed. If I come waltzing in after some merchant captain spreads the word—or the Manco agent through a courier, I shouldn't wonder—then they'll be on me with their knives out as I step down the boarding ramp. I won't have a chance to get the facts out."

"I see," said Otto, sounding as though he did. He let out another chuckle. Then, sober again, he went on, "You have permission to go about your business in Haven City then, Commander; but with a word of warning: if you have occasion to land on Pellegrino again, be sure you are fully forthcoming about your intentions. A failure to do so will be regarded as an insult to Pellegrino and to our benevolent Chancellor. No one, not even a son of the redoubtable Speaker Leary, would be immune to the righteous workings of justice in such a case."

"I take your point," said Daniel. He'd guessed already that Otto had taken the time to learn his background. He unlatched the door but didn't push it open for a moment. "And you've reminded me to mention something else I need to do while I'm in Central Haven. One of my father's ships is disabled here, the *Stoddard*. Either I or my aide will check with the captain and see if there's anything they need from us."

He leaned his shoulder against the car door but paused again and allowed it to swing closed. "I don't know how much your files have on me, Superintendent," he went on, "but I'll tell you that my father and I haven't spoken since I joined the RCN."

That wasn't *quite* true, but it was beyond the ability of anybody save the Learys, father and son, to disprove.

"He's no longer Speaker, but he's a powerful man in the Senate," Daniel said. "And I'm going to need help in the Senate to explain how my mission worked out the way it did in Ganpat's Reach!"

Otto was laughing again as Daniel got out of the car. The door's solid closing *thump* put a merciful end to the oily gurgle.

Master Nordeen's conveyance was a low-slung runabout which'd surprised Adele when his chauffeur first brought it out of the garage behind the merchant's townhouse. The vehicle was nearly silent because it ran on four hub-center motors but they were extremely powerful. The open wheels tilted on the axles, allowing the car to hold the road like molasses running down the side of a bottle.

Adele turned to her host as the chauffeur pulled up beside the *Stoddard* in slip West 35. The traffic passing on Harbor Drive was heavy; a large freighter was discharging a cargo of bales onto a line of lowboys, each pulled by a snorting diesel tractor.

"I didn't expect so sporting a car, Master Nordeen," she said, speaking over the noise of the tractors.

"Because I am old and feeble, I must ride in something old and feeble, mistress?" the merchant said as he got out on his side. He patted the flank of the car. "This is a whim, I admit; quite unnecessary to my needs. But at my age, there are few things that give me pleasure. I can afford my whims."

The *Stoddard* was slightly bow-down, enough so that the boarding ramp touched the quay on one corner instead of along the whole edge. Nordeen walked up step for step with Adele, showing no signs of discomfort. *Old certainly, but not feeble. . . .*

Though the freighter's hatch was open, no one was on watch on the ramp or in the entry hold beyond. Adele frowned, wondering if she should've radioed ahead. She hadn't done so because of what was now looking like a misplaced concern over communications security.

While waiting for Master Nordeen to awake from his afternoon nap, Adele had reviewed the intercepts she'd made already. Chancellor Arruns' secret police did quite a lot of electronic eavesdropping themselves, but their own protective measures were conspicuous by their absence. If they'd shown any interest in the *Stoddard*, Adele would know it—so they didn't.

Tovera stepped past Adele and Nordeen, walking on the balls of her feet. Her head moved in quick jerks, searching for movement in her peripheral vision. She was looking for enemies rather than trying to rouse a friend. That was no more than to be expected from Tovera, of course, but it wasn't very helpful. . . .

"Captain Evans!" Adele said. She walked over to the Up companionway. "Anyone? Will someone come down, please? We're here to see the crew of the *Stoddard*!"

"What's that?" someone called from above. "Come up to bridge level, then. We're on the bridge."

Adele glanced at Nordeen, standing impassively at her side. Putting her head into the companionway again, she shouted, "Get down here, and get down here *now*! Unless you want to spend the rest of your lives on this miserable excuse for a planet!"

Adele backed away and turned, drawing in deep breaths in an attempt to calm herself. She took her left hand out of her pocket. It appeared that she was closer to her personal edge than she had any reason to be. The *Stoddard's* crew didn't know the situation, after all.

They still needed to do their jobs promptly and without argument. Their jobs *now* were whatever Mundy of Chatsworth told them to do.

Adele had time to look around the compartment. Pressed-metal benches were folded against the bulkheads. She twisted the dogs to drop one with a bang. The third dog was stiff; Tovera murmured a warning and slammed it with the heel of her shoe, then backed to face the companionway down which the sound of boots echoed.

Nordeen settled onto the bench with a grateful nod. Starships didn't use elevators because the stresses of entering and leaving the Matrix warped the shafts and caused the cages to stick. Ordinarily that was of no great matter as even the largest ships were rarely more than ten decks high, with the entryways at midpoint or close to it. Master Nordeen wasn't an ordinary visitor to a starship, however.

"All right, what is this?" boomed the first man out of the companionway, a burly fellow in his fifties. His flaring beard was pepper-and-salt, but the hair on his scalp was thick and as black as a crow's wing. Two men and a woman followed. One of the men was bare-chested, scarred, and carried a short prybar.

"I'm Signals Officer Mundy of the RCN," Adele said crisply. She cocked an eyebrow at the bearded man. "I assume you're Captain Evans?"

The *Stoddard*'s officers brought themselves up short. Adele wore a civilian suit whose deep green cloth showed chartreuse undertones at certain angles. The tunic and trousers weren't flashy, but they were well made and expensive, obviously so even to the eyes of spacers who'd never shopped on the Golden Plaza in Xenos.

"Aye," muttered the man she'd directed the question to. His bluster of a moment before had vanished. The bare-chested fellow lowered the prybar to beside his leg, then concealed it behind him. "What do you want here?"

"Which of you are Cinnabar citizens?" Adele demanded, only answering the question indirectly. The bosun's name was Hartopp according to the crew manifest. She hadn't found pictures of the personnel, but it seemed evident that Hartopp was the bare-chested man and that the slim youth in a blue jacket was Stonewell, the mate.

"I am and Stoney is," Evans said cautiously. "Hartopp, are you?"

"My brother is," said the bosun, looking at his toes. "We're from Caprice."

Caprice was a Cinnabar protectorate, but the only citizens on the planet were immigrant bureaucrats and locals who'd done one or another kind of favor for those bureaucrats. Adele didn't care about citizenship in itself; the question was an indirect way of seeing whether any of the officers had been born on an Alliance planet, as they might very well have been.

"I'm Kostroman but I've been with the *Stoddard* the past three years," said the woman—the purser, Linde. From her diction, she was better-educated than the others. Quite well educated, in fact. "Why are you asking, please?"

"I'll get to that shortly," Adele said. She knew that Daniel'd do this differently; he'd probably have them cheering by this point. Nevertheless Adele was better off being herself than she'd be trying to ape Daniel's style. "Is there anybody aboard the ship besides yourselves? Anybody at all?"

The officers looked at one another again. "No," said Evans. "I paid off the crew when I saw how long repairs were going to take. I'll hire a new crew when we're ready to lift."

"Look, you can't just walk aboard and ask questions," said Hartopp. "What're you doing here?"

"You know the Consular Agent, Master Nordeen, I believe," Adele said, cocking her head toward the merchant without taking her eyes off the spacers. "I asked him to accompany me so you'd know that the orders I'm going to give you have the full weight of the Republic behind them."

"Me'n Boobs talked to Nordeen right after we landed," Evans growled. If Purser Linde had a problem with being called Boobs, she concealed it behind a mask of wary silence. "He did bugger-all for us, I don't mind telling you."

"I provided my good offices in putting you in touch with repair facilities," Nordeen said calmly, his eyes focused on the infinite distance. "Under normal circumstances it is not the place of the Republic of Cinnabar nor of Bright Dragon Trading Company to pledge its credit to effect repairs on a privately owned vessel."

"Which brings me to the purpose of my visit," said Adele. "Master Nordeen has arranged for eight antimatter converters to arrive by barge alongside the *Stoddard* this evening. A number of trained spacers will also arrive. They will begin the task of replacing your faulty units. They'll be staying on board the ship while they work."

"We need the motors too," Stonewell said quickly. "The converters were the problem, right, but we didn't catch them in time before they'd ate up the motors."

"New motors will be brought as soon as the work on the converters is complete," Nordeen said, still staring into nothingness with a beatific expression.

"Well, this is great," said Evans in surprise. "I'd like it happened a couple months ago, but I'll take it, sure. Ah—how's this being paid for? Because Nordeen, you said—"

"Master Nordeen is pledging his personal credit—"

"The credit of Bright Dragon Trading Company," Nordeen corrected mildly.

"The credit of his company, that is," continued Adele, angry with herself for the error, "to expedite the work. He in turn is protected by a guaranty by the Republic of Cinnabar, though that won't appear in any documents on Pellegrino. Ultimately Hinshaw Transit, the *Stoddard*'s owners of record, will pay the costs. We're merely expediting the process."

The ship's officers looked at one another. The men seemed puzzled, but Linde's expression had become perfectly blank. She didn't know precisely what was coming next, but she'd clearly guessed that if the Republic was putting up such a considerable sum of money, the Republic expected value for its investment. If she'd known that the guaranty wasn't from RCN funds but rather from a secret account controlled by Mistress Sand, she'd have been even more concerned.

"From this moment until the workmen leave the *Stoddard*," Adele said, "the four of you must remain on board also. I'm sorry for the inconvenience, but it's necessary to prevent any discussion of what's going on until the operation is over."

"Just who the bloody hell are you to be telling *us* we can't leave the ship?" said Hartopp with his voice getting louder with each word. "Now look! I don't care if you're RCN or one of God's angels, you don't give me orders here. This is Pellegrino! You're off your patch, girlie!"

"Can I give you orders?" asked Tovera, standing behind and to the side of the four officers. She'd set the attaché case down and was openly holding the sub-machine gun she kept in it. She giggled. "I'm not RCN. I'm not an angel either."

"Bloody hell," Stonewell said quietly. He stared at the gun as though it'd hypnotized him.

"I hope not," said Adele, "but it could certainly become a bloody hell if you attempt to violate my instructions. If you do as you're told, you'll be able to lift within ten days according to the estimate I was given by Commander Leary. Is the situation clear?"

"If you shoot us, it's piracy," Linde said. She'd been looking at Tovera's gun, but now she raised her eyes to meet Adele's. "It doesn't matter that you're RCN or that the honorary consul—"

She used the Kostroman term for the office both Cinnabar and the Alliance called a consular agent.

"—agrees with you. It'd be murder and piracy."

"Yes," said Adele, "you're quite right. More to the point, it'd bother me a good deal—"

She lifted the pistol in her pocket just enough to give them a glimpse of it. The barrel shroud had a faint rainbow pattern from one of the times she'd used it in rain heavy enough to quench the hot steel.

"—to shoot one or all of you. But I've killed people just as innocent as you are in the past, and I'm ready to do it again."

"It won't bother me, though," said Tovera, grinning. "In fact, I like shooting people."

That was quite true. Adele knew that Tovera was speaking for effect to help her mistress convince these strangers that cooperation was their only survivable option, but it was still bothersome to hear the quiet gusto in her voice.

Three Power Room techs in liberty rigs walked up the boarding ramp. "Ma'am?" called the leader, Tech 3 Samson. His companions were wipers. "Is this too soon to board?"

I'll need to get working outfits for the whole crew, Adele thought. She'd mention it to Nordeen before he left.

"This is fine," she said, raising her voice so that the Sissies could hear her. She returned her gaze to the *Stoddard*'s officers.

"These are the first of your workmen," she said. "There'll be thirty all told. My servant—"

She nodded to Tovera.

"—and I will be staying aboard also."

"The barge with the converters will arrive within the hour," said Nordeen placidly. His eyes were still directed—inward? Into the infinite? Elsewhere, at any rate. He was clearly following events, however.

"Master Hartopp, please show these men to their accommodations," Adele said. "And Mistress Linde, I need to discuss the workmen's rations with you."

She looked out of the hatch; another party of Sissies, riggers this time, was heading down the street. Several of them held bottles, but they weren't drunk as a spacer understood the term.

Adele looked at the *Stoddard*'s officers again; she found herself grinning slightly. "One further thing," she said. "The owner of the company you work for, Hinshaw Transit, is Corder Leary. The success of our mission here may well determine whether his son, Commander Daniel Leary, survives the next two weeks. Now—"

She paused, considering the way to phrase this. "You may think you can escape me and Tovera there," she said. "But I assure you, you will not survive if you cross Speaker Leary. And I'm as much an expert on that as anyone still alive!"

CHAPTER 19

En Route to Dunbar's World

Woetjans was already waiting for him in the airlock, but Daniel spent a further moment on the hull to watch the heavens. They flared in a splendor unglimpsed by those who never left the sidereal universe. Colors and hints of color—hues Daniel was sure formed in his mind rather than on his retinas—spread to infinity wherever he turned.

Every spark was a universe, every color was as meaningful as a woman's glance. At times like this, Daniel felt that the only reason for the sidereal universe was to permit a man to eat between visits to the Matrix.

Daniel grinned as he stepped into the lock, dogging the hatch behind him. There were important things besides eating that one couldn't do on the hull in the Matrix, but the social life of Ollarville didn't lend itself to them either. Unless one chose to pay, of course.

Light from the diodes in the ceiling softened as air filled the lock. Woetjans was glaring at Daniel. As they lifted off the helmets of their stiff rigging suits a moment before opening the inner hatch, she muttered, "You should've let me go, sir."

They exited onto the foyer just aft of the bridge. Off-duty Sissies stood in the corridor, waiting expectantly. The riggers were suited up, ready to furl the sails and lower the antennas in preparation for landing. Woetjans joined her people, still looking morose.

Riggers could remain outside while a ship transitioned from the Matrix to sidereal space, but the experience was disorienting—and therefore dangerous—even to veterans. Daniel would order it if the situation required, but otherwise he kept his crew within the hull during insertions and extractions. That was true even when the *Princess Cecile* had a full military crew, which she certainly didn't at present.

Cory had been in command of the *Sissie* from the navigation console while Daniel was on the hull. "Five minutes to extraction, sir!" the midshipman said when he saw Daniel come through the hatch. "Shall I relinquish command now?"

Daniel didn't snap at him. The lad was keen, after all. Unfortunately he wasn't overly bright, and he was far more concerned to avoid doing the wrong thing than he was to do the right one. Regardless, not a bad sort and an astrogator who was showing an unexpectedly good feel for the Matrix once Daniel started pointing out the subtleties to him.

"No, Mister Cory," he said, clumping onto the bridge. He didn't remove his rigging suit, though he unlatched and pulled off the gauntlets. He doubted he'd be going out again before landing, and this was the first time since they'd lifted from Pellegrino that he'd had the entire crew inside. "You can deal with the Ollarville authorities and take her down—but on automatic, I believe. I'll address the crew from the command console right now, though."

"Aye aye, sir!" chirped Cory. He'd really make a decent officer if he ever got his head around the fact that he *was* an officer, a person who might be expected to make life-and-death decisions on very little information. A good officer can get away with being wrong, but he can't be indecisive.

Daniel settled onto the console and gave it a moment to adjust to the added bulk of his suit. He manually set his output to General: the loudspeakers in every compartment as well as all commo helmets would project his words. It struck him as he made the adjustments that though this was a familiar task for most captains, he hadn't had to perform it since Signals Officer Mundy had joined the strength of the *Princess Cecile*.

"Ship, this is Six," he said, hearing his voice repeated from the compartments opening onto the A Level corridor. "I haven't explained my plans to you because I wanted you all to hear it from me at the same time. This is the first opportunity I've had to do that."

There was a way to project a real-time image of his face as he spoke, but also a way to hide it. The green bar behind the legend GENERAL on the bottom of his display meant one or the other, but damn him for a heathen if he could remember which.

He grinned, breaking his burst of frustration. If that was the worst thing he lost by not having Adele aboard, he was doing better than he'd feared might be the case.

"Our fellow Sissies under Lieutenant Vesey and Officer Mundy—"

Under Adele in reality, but even the most junior commissioned officer was superior to any warrant officer. Daniel would at least pay lip service to RCN protocol.

"—should by now have captured the *Rainha* in dock on Pellegrino and have lifted for Dunbar's World. When they land on Mandelfarne Island, they'll disable the missile battery emplaced there."

"And I ought to be with them!" Woetjans snarled. She wasn't using intercom or even looking at Daniel when she spoke from the lock foyer, but her voice, throbbing with emotion, carried.

"Lieutenant Vesey and I chose our crews on our best judgment of the needs of both ships," Daniel continued. "The choices weren't easy. We both could've used every one of you and more for the jobs we each need to do. I counted on every Sissie to work like three of any other spacer, and I'm glad to say you've performed. I'm confident that Vesey will tell me the same when we meet on Mandelfarne Island."

The choices *had* been tricky, though there'd been factors Daniel didn't intend to discuss with the crew he'd kept aboard the *Princess Cecile*. No spacer was likely to be a coward, but some weren't as ready to face gunshots and the possibility of knife work as others.

Even more to the point, some people couldn't easily—or simply couldn't—take the life of another human being. The assault on the Pellegrinian missile battery had to be handled swiftly, without the least flinching or hesitation. Daniel's stomach turned at the notion of commanding a crew of vipers like Adele's servant Tovera, but for the present task thirty Toveras would've been very useful.

Woetjans would've been handy for the assault party also, but Daniel had decided that her appearance was simply too identifiable to risk sending to the *Stoddard*. Adele had assured him that the Pellegrinian police weren't watching the crippled freighter, but the bosun's appearance was striking enough that a passing patrol might notice and comment.

Quite apart from that, eighteen of the thirty spacers in Vesey's crew were riggers, leaving the *Princess Cecile* herself very short-handed on the hull side. Woetjans' strength and skill—she had an instinct for where a line would kink or a block might freeze—had kept the *Sissie's* rig from descending into a complete shambles during the voyage back from Pellegrino.

Despite the good reasons for it, Daniel hadn't expected Woetjans to be happy with the decision. He'd been right.

"Now, you'll be wondering what this means for you and me," Daniel said. "It's pretty obvious that thirty spacers, even thirty Sissies, can't fight off a counterattack by a thousand Pellegrinian troops. As soon as the *Rainha* reaches orbit over Dunbar's World, Councilor Corius' mercenaries will load aboard one of his transports just like they did to come from his estates to Charlestown. This time they'll fly across the continent to Mandelfarne Island and finish what Officer Mundy's started."

Daniel licked his lips, wondering if the listening spacers understood how close the timing had to be. He supposed they did: his Sissies had more experience with firefights than most companies of the Land Forces.

Certainly Adele and Vesey understood. The transport couldn't come within missile range—say, three hundred miles—until the battery was captured, but it could be only a matter of minutes after the attack began before the Pellegrinians' overwhelming numbers blotted out the Sissies.

"I'll be at the controls," he continued, "and Mister Pasternak will run the gauges, because I don't trust any civilian to do the job fast and clean the way it has to be done. The RCN way!"

There were several cheers, but they seemed to rattle forlornly down the *Sissie's* corridors. There wasn't enough of a crew to make the ship ring properly, and those present clearly *did* know how chancy the business was for their friends and shipmates.

"So what does that leave for us, sir?" asked Rosinant, seated at the gunnery console because Sun was part of the assault force. "Do we come with you and the pongoes?"

"The rest of you," said Daniel, giving the answer as a full statement because most of the crew wouldn't have heard Rosinant's question, "stay aboard the *Sissie* under Midshipman Blantyre. You'll follow me in the transport to Mandelfarne Island. You'll pick me and Pasternak up and also our shipmates who arrived aboard the *Rainha*."

This time the cheers were real—sparse by necessity, but full-throated. Rosinant shouted louder than most, obviously looking forward to the chance to use plasma cannon on ground targets. It was quite obvious to everybody aboard that the battle for the base would still be going on when they landed on Mandelfarne Island.

"*Ship, thirty seconds to extraction from the Matrix*," Cory announced. He'd kept an eye on his duties during Daniel's confidence-building speech. *Definitely a lad with promise.*

The world around Daniel began to ripple and fold, causing alternate waves of nausea and vertigo to wash through him.

He hadn't lied to the crew, but he was very well aware that when he said they'd pick up "our shipmates from the *Rainha*," he'd really meant "our shipmates or their bodies."

Central Haven on Pellegrino

The diesel engine was rumbling, but the barge that'd brought the new High Drive motors was still tied up to the *Stoddard*'s outrigger. Though it wasn't time to set off, Vesey and the majority of the assault party were already concealed by the tarpaulin over the top of the barge's forward hold.

Tovera, Dasi, and Barnes stood with Adele as she talked for the last time with Captain Evans, at the head of the short boarding bridge between barge and starship. The other officers remained aboard the ship, avoiding the knowledge of what was going on. Adele didn't mind the riggers' presence—she had nothing to say to the *Stoddard*'s officers that the Sissies shouldn't hear—but the stocked impellers they insisted on holding might very well attract attention even at this hour of the night.

"Master Nordeen is seeing to it that more workmen will arrive in the morning, Captain," she said. "While I don't expect them to be of quality equal to those who're leaving tonight, they will at least be shipyard workers by profession. They should have you ready to lift within a matter of days."

"If I'd known what you were doing, I'd have told you not only no but *hell!* no," said Evans in a miserable voice. "Bloody hell, woman,

Chancellor Arruns doesn't fool around with treason. I'm for the high jump and so are all us other poor bastards!"

Dasi rapped him over the ear with his impeller's muzzle. It wasn't a heavy blow, but it was more than a tap for attention.

"She's Officer Mundy to you, boyo!" the rigger said. "Or you can call her sir, your choice."

"I didn't ask for your permission," Adele said calmly. "I told you your duty. If you keep your mouth shut, however, there won't be any repercussions before you've taken the *Stoddard* off Pellegrino."

She hadn't wanted or needed Dasi, her self-proclaimed escort, to deliver that etiquette lesson, but it'd more than a little pleased the part of her that was still Mundy of Chatsworth. Her father had been leader of the Popular Party and the people's friend, but he'd never forgotten he was Mundy of Chatsworth either.

The big freighter on the opposite side of the slip was being loaded under lights. A sharp *whack!* followed by a ringing *whang* and the crunch of a heavy weight hitting the ground sounded from it. The ship's masts were telescoped but not completely folded; in silhouette against the floodlights they looked like spikes of hoarfrost, enormously magnified.

"A cable parted," Barnes said with a chuckle. "We seed that happen often enough, right, Dasi?"

"They'll be lucky if somebody didn't get killed," his partner agreed. "Cut right in half. Remember Trent Johns?"

They laughed together.

"Look, I see the guns," Evans said, his whisper harsh. His head was bent away from Dasi and his left hand touched his scalp. "If you think you can use them on Pellegrino and the cops look the other way, you're bloody wrong!"

"You don't *know* what we're doing," Adele said, her voice so cold that the captain wilted away from it, for the moment forgetting Dasi's mere physical threat. "If you're not too stupid to live, you'll avoid speculating on the question. You'll tell anyone who asks that the work on your ship was carried out by Pellegrinian shipwrights and that you were glad to get off planet. Do you understand?"

"It's easy for you to say there won't be trouble," the captain said, "but—"

"Should I kill him, mistress?" Tovera said. "We can be sure he won't do anything foolish if he's dead."

"No," said Adele. "Well, only as a last resort. It'd cause more problems than it'd solve."

She looked at Evans again. The quiet discussion had frightened him in a fashion that Dasi's blow had not . . . which meant he *was* beginning to understand.

"You will not tell anyone that you ever saw us," Adele said. "You will finish the work on your ship and lift. *Do* you have further questions?"

"No ma'am," Evans mumbled to the toes of his boots. "Whatever you say. We didn't see anything, not a bloody thing."

"*Mistress?*" Vesey said over the intercom. She and Dorst had always called Adele "mistress" or "sir" even though midshipmen had general command authority and a signals officer did not.

"Yes, time to go," Adele said aloud. "Good night, Captain Evans. I suggest you forget us."

"You can be bloody sure I'll try," the civilian muttered as Adele climbed from the boarding bridge down into the barge.

"Cast off," ordered Casuaris, who'd been a fisherman before he became a spacer; a civilian at the bow and a Sissie at the stern freed hawsers from ringbolts on the outrigger. Master Nordeen had provided two crewmen with the barge, but they were simply carrying out RCN orders on this trip.

Casuaris had told Adele that he'd sold his catch for a good price in Xenos and awakened in the morning with a bad hangover as the destroyer he'd been carried aboard lifted. His experience with small boats came in handy now; and though he grumbled about the way he'd been pressed into service, he'd spent the past fifteen years in the RCN despite his many opportunities, formal and otherwise, to get out.

The civilian helmsman eased his throttle forward as he engaged the single prop. The diesel lugged for a moment, then built back to a burbling grumble as the barge backed into the pool.

Adele prepared to squat as she pulled out her personal data unit. "Here you go, ma'am," Sun said, guiding her against the bulkhead where to her surprise a seat—a metal tray with a cushion of coiled rope—stuck out from the sheer metal.

"I bolted it there for you, ma'am," the gunner said proudly. "We didn't want you sitting in the bilges again, you know."

"Thank you, Sun," Adele said as she sat as directed. They were really very good to her; they *cared*. They were her family.

The terminal in the *Rainha's* entry hold was being used to display a pornographic video involving a human female and three aliens of different species. Adele frowned for a moment, wondering if there was a way she could identify the aliens more quickly than calling up an anthropological database—which her little unit didn't have—and sorting by eye. Though of course it didn't matter, except to her desire to properly catalogue *everything* with which she came in contact.

What did matter was that the crewmen on entry watch weren't any more concerned than their fellows on the two previous nights had been. The *Rainha* had filled its manifest and would be lifting at midmorning, but the crew had a final night of liberty.

The anchor watch was six spacers under the second mate. The remaining twenty-one officers and crew were supposed to return at dawn but would, Vesey assured her with all the listening Sissies nodding agreement, dribble in over the course of the morning. That timing wasn't necessary for the success of Adele's plans, but it'd be helpful.

"Sir, we're nearing the *Rainha*," Vesey whispered. Her lips were close to Adele's ear so she could hear over the chugging of the diesel.

Adele looked up, shut off her display—she'd been checking the freighter's main computer for readiness estimates on the thrusters and High Drive—and put the little unit away. She hadn't been really concerned about the *Rainha* being able to lift as planned and she wasn't the person to determine that anyway, but it'd been something to do instead of stare at steel bulkheads and at spacers who were quivering with anticipation.

Standing, Adele said, "Barnes and Dasi with me, and nobody else. Lieutenant Vesey, see to it!" She climbed the ladder gracelessly but without difficulty and stood on the gunwale-level walkway with Tovera and the two riggers. The barge nosed toward the slip at which the *Rainha* was anchored.

They clanged against the concrete quay and glanced away. Adele swayed against the railing, but Dasi was holding her firmly by the shoulder. The diesel grunted unhappily as the helmsman did something to his controls.

"Get a bloody fender out, you clot-brains!" Casuaris shouted, springing forward and hurling out a bundle of coiled rope between the quay and the ship's side. They'd recoiled three feet and were swinging farther away.

"Ma'am, we're gonna pass you ashore!" Dasi said in an urgent voice. He seized Adele around the waist as Barnes vaulted the railing. They'd left their impellers in the hold as ordered, but each had a length of pipe under his belt.

Dasi tossed Adele over the railing to Barnes, who lowered her to the dock. She hadn't heard the riggers discuss this plan; perhaps they'd just instinctively come to the same conclusions by dint of long experience of working together. Tovera jumped also, holding the attaché case close to her body; she landed lightly.

"Come along," Adele muttered as she strode toward the *Rainha's* entry ramp, her boots clicking against the concrete. Behind them the barge was rumbling toward the dock again, but that had ceased to be her concern.

She was in civilian clothes, a suit of dark blue fabric. Thin diagonals of powder blue kept the garment from looking like a uniform in sunlight, but Adele had chosen it for the ambiguity it had at night. Tovera looked like a clerk as usual, and the riggers were in the dull, loose garments of working spacers anywhere. Utilities were formal wear for on-duty RCN personnel.

Both the crewmen on watch stepped to the top of the entry ramp to see what the noise was about. Adele continued to walk briskly toward them without waving or calling.

"We're not supposed to get cargo tonight," one of the watchmen called. "You've got the wrong ship, I guess!"

Adele reached the end of the ramp and started up it. "I'm from the Chancellor's office," she said. "We're here for Officer Luntz."

Luntz was the watch officer tonight. He was a Pellegrino native, like the captain and first mate. The crewmen, according to the ship's records, were mostly from various places in Ganpat's Reach. There were three Pellegrinians and three more spacers born on Alliance worlds.

"I'll get—" said the watchman who'd spoken before. He turned in to the compartment.

"Don't warn him," snapped Adele, "or you'll be guilty of treason yourself!"

"What?" said the watchman. He held his hands out to his sides in horror. "Look, I'm no traitor. Bloody hell, what'd Luntz do, anyway?"

"I *really* think you'd be wiser to avoid that question," Adele said tartly as she stepped between the spacers and walked toward the flat terminal on an internal bulkhead.

The woman and her three companions continued to caper on the display. Perhaps they were all computer simulations?

Adele locked the terminal and turned to watchmen. Both were staring at her with worried expressions. "Unless you're already involved, of course," she said. "Are you?"

"No!" said the nearer watchman. He had a ruddy face and was sweating profusely. "We—"

Barnes and Dasi swung their short clubs together. They were using lengths of the high-density plastic tubing intended for the hydraulic system that worked the *Sissie's* rig. The hollow *whop-p!* of the impacts echoed in the compartment.

The silent watchman crumpled in place as though he'd been shot. The speaker pitched forward—mouth open, arms windmilling, and blood spraying from the cut in his scalp. There was a bald patch on the peak of his skull. Adele stepped aside; the man hit first the bulkhead, then the deck.

Her nose wrinkled. She'd started to say, "Did you have to hit them so hard?" but swallowed the words. Yes, they *did* have to hit the watchmen that hard. There was a near certainty of concussion, a real chance of permanent brain damage, and the possibility of death from blows like that—

But if the watchmen hadn't been put down *certainly* from the first, Tovera or Adele herself would've shot them dead. There couldn't be any chance of them getting away or giving an alarm.

Barnes was strapping the watchmen's arms behind their backs with cargo tape while Dasi stood in the hatchway and signaled Vesey with his left hand. One man was snoring loudly; the other lay as slack as a half-filled bladder, his mouth and eyes open. His scalp wound should be bandaged, but perhaps the Sissies coming from the barge could take care of that when they arrived.

"To the bridge," Adele snapped as she stepped into the up companionway. "And Tovera, put that thing out of sight!"

Tovera had taken her little sub-machine gun from its case. If they'd been intending to assault the *Rainha*, killing everyone they met, that would be appropriate. It wasn't what Adele had in mind, however—as her servant well knew.

Tovera appeared bland on all but the closest contact, but she really did have a personality; she possibly even had a sense of humor. What she lacked was a conscience.

Adele trotted up the companionway past open hatches on three levels. The stacks in the old section of the Academic Collections on Bryce had grated floors and wrought-iron spiral staircases with brass finials. Adele wondered how many times she'd gone up and down those stairs in the years when she was a student of, then assistant curator to, Mistress Boilleau. Those were probably the happiest days of her life before she joined the RCN—and they were *very* good training for getting from one deck to another on a starship.

She reached the top of the companionway on A Level, traditionally not only the bridge but also the accommodations deck on a civilian vessel. A warship's larger crew usually required that the enlisted personnel be berthed lower down, but of course a warship's interior wasn't given over to cargo holds.

All the hatches along the A Level corridor were open. The sound of snoring came from one of the accommodation blocks toward the stern. Lights were on in the bridge forward; Adele already knew that the main console was live.

She paused, not indecisive but waiting for Barnes and Dasi to come out of the companionway. They were followed almost without pause by half a dozen Sissies who must've run from the barge as soon as they got the signal. Sun was at their head, holding a sub-machine gun at high port with the air of a man who knew how to use his tools.

Adele pointed to the accommodation block, then turned and with Tovera at her side walked silently onto the bridge. The man at the main console was slumped so that she couldn't see his head, but his worn boots were splayed out to either side. There were two flat-plate terminals—not all-purpose consoles—on the right side of the compartment, but their integral seats were empty.

Adele stepped toward the console, then leaned forward quickly and switched off the power. She brushed the man dozing on the couch. He woke up, muttering, "Whazzat?"

"Officer Luntz," said Adele, clearly but without shouting. "Wake up, please."

Luntz was very young. He had pale blond hair and he shouldn't have tried to grow a mustache; it simply made his upper lip look furry.

"What?" he said, straightening. He was fully awake, though he didn't seem particularly alert. "Say, who are you?"

"I'm Mundy from the Chancellor's Planning Office," Adele said calmly, giving the deliberately deceptive title of Arruns' secret police. "You and the entire crew are under arrest until we've gotten to the bottom of the smuggling. Zastrow—"

There must be a dozen Sissies in the accommodation block so Zastrow—a Power Room tech as broad as he was tall—had tramped into the bridge compartment instead. He wore a slung sub-machine gun, but the prybar in his right fist and knuckleduster over his left made clear the kind of fight he preferred.

"—tie him up now."

"I don't know anything about smuggling!" Luntz said. He got up but staggered against the console as his knees threatened to give way. His face was white. "Oh my God, look, I'll tell you everything, you don't have to torture me!"

Tovera giggled. She waggled the muzzle of her weapon toward Luntz as though it were a black finger.

Zastrow'd stuck his bar under his waistband. He grabbed Luntz's wrists with his left hand; the knuckleduster didn't seem to get in his way. He efficiently trussed the weeping Pellegrinian officer with cargo tape from the dispenser on his belt.

"We have four of them, sir!" said Vesey from the hatchway. "One was passed out drunk in the head."

"Officer Luntz, how many crewmen are aboard?" Adele said. "Luntz, answer me!"

"Six," Luntz gurgled through his sobs. "Look, Duval runs the smuggling, I don't get anything out of it. Hardly anything!"

"Put him with the rest of them in the room they sleep in," Adele said. She frowned at her sloppy terminology and said, "The accommodation block. Keep them tied at least for now."

She turned the console back on as two Sissies hustled the Pellegrinian out by the elbows. The crew would probably have to remain tied, taped that was, for the entire voyage. They couldn't be left on Pellegrino where they might be able to give the alarm soon enough for a courier ship to get to Dunbar's World before the *Rainha* and her escort, and there weren't enough Sissies in the assault party to provide more than an exiguous guard on the prisoners.

"Ma'am, I've sent the dock party out," Vesey said from the hatchway. "Barnes and Dasi are in the entrance compartment."

"Very good," said Adele without looking up from the console display. "I'll leave that to you, Lieutenant."

The console had an infuriating delay, presumably some software problem. She finally found the external optical pickups and focused them on the quay outside. The party of six under Sun sauntered toward Harbor Drive carrying the packing case which held their weapons.

Barnes and Dasi would deal with the crewmen as they returned to the ship, barring the lower end of the companionway while a large armed party waited at C Level, the next deck above the entrance hatch. Their story, that they'd just signed on to the crew, was flimsy, but it should be adequate for drunks who were doing well to stagger aboard. Sun's party was ready to deal with anybody who made it out of the ship and ran for the street.

"Sun, this is Mundy," Adele said. She used the *Rainha*'s FM intercom but passed the signal through an RCN scrambler to Sun's tiny plug earphone. "The man coming toward you is Wilkes, the chief engineer."

Sun didn't have a sending unit with which to reply, but he made a hand signal behind his back. The display was too blurry and distorted for Adele to see more than the fact of the signal—but that was enough.

She let out her breath slowly. So far, so good. Perhaps in eight or nine hours, they'd be off this wretched planet—and on their way to Dunbar's World, which was even more wretched and where she would kill an uncertain number of people.

Adele smiled wryly. *Family obligations often require a degree of personal discomfort.*

CHAPTER 20

Ollarville on Dunbar's World

"All right, Colonel," said Councilor Corius. "Begin loading *now*."

Colonel Quinn wore a fist-sized communicator clipped to his bandolier. He pulled it to his mouth on a coiled lanyard and said, "Red One, this is Rainbow. Execute Evolution Brick, over."

Daniel wondered if he'd get a better idea of how the loading was proceeding if he were on the *Greybudd*'s bridge instead of standing with Corius and Quinn in the cage of Port Eastern's only gantry. He'd have plenty of opportunity to try other locations, he supposed, since they were drilling only one of the four battalions at a time.

Officers below on the dock trilled whistles. Five hundred of Corius' Volunteers burst out of the warehouse where they were billeted, and double-timed down the dock toward the transport. They carried only their personal weapons and small packs with ammunition and a day's rations.

The *Greybudd*'s three boarding ramps were lowered, but the soldiers—the Second Battalion—were supposed to use only the one at the bow. The man on the left of the first rank started toward the stern ramp instead, taking twenty-odd of the nearby troops with him.

An officer ran up screaming—the tone was audible in the gantry though the words weren't—and batted at him with a swagger stick.

The misdirected men turned and rejoined the head of the main body just as they started up the correct ramp.

Hogg, leaning through a side window of the cage to get a good view, shook his head. Fallert was sitting on top of the cage; a burst of his clucking laughter rattled from there.

"Red One, don't let them bunch on the gangplank!" Quinn snarled into his communicator. "Bloody hell, Bancks, we don't want to drown them here in the harbor!"

He glanced sidelong, obviously worried about how Commander Leary was going to react to the confusion. Daniel leaned forward slightly. He kept his eyes on the loading and clasped his hands behind his back.

"They're accomplishing the business in quite good time, Colonel," he said cheerfully. "Lots of enthusiasm! It's not as though they've been selected for their skill in drill and ceremony, after all. And that's basically what this is."

"Thanks, Leary," Quinn said gruffly. "The opinion of a man like you counts."

Daniel's *opinion* was that the drill was less of a ratfuck than it might've been, but saying something so qualified wouldn't make the boarding process go more smoothly nor improve his working relationship with the colonel. Besides, Daniel preferred to give people the benefit of the doubt. Often that caused them to do better in the future, though he didn't suppose that really had much to do with why he behaved the way he did.

Daniel grinned. Adele's tart criticisms no doubt improved the performance of both victims and also people who didn't want to be similarly skewered. But that was Adele, not Adele's considered plan to make the universe more efficient.

"These aren't our best troops, you know," Corius said. He'd managed to smooth the frown off his forehead but his lips still pursed as he watched the loading process. "We've got our shock troops in the First Battalion, but they'll load last to be first out for the assault."

"Right," said Daniel in a tone of approval. The benefit of the doubt, after all. "A very sensible plan. Our safety and that of my friends on the *Rainha* depend on a quick victory by the Volunteers."

Corius' mercenaries were an assortment of men who'd lost their farms or their businesses, people wanted for crimes in one or more jurisdictions, and a leavening of veterans. Few if any were first-class soldiers—but neither were the Pellegrinians they'd be facing. An army like that of Chancellor Arruns got all of its experience in internal security activities: dragging dissidents out of their houses in the middle of the night and breaking heads if anybody dared demonstrate against the ruler.

The Volunteers would have surprise and numbers both on their side when Daniel landed them on Mandelfarne Island. He hoped that would be enough; the difference between victory and defeat was less a matter of what advantages you started with than how you used what you had.

Colonel Quinn made quite a decent training officer for the motley raw material Corius had hired. Quinn wasn't, however, the man Daniel would've picked to lead the Volunteers across an enemy base in a rush.

The smile never far from Daniel's lips spread again. Corius noticed it and said, "Yes, Commander? You have a criticism to offer, that you smile about?"

"What?" said Daniel, surprised by the sharpness of the Councilor's tone. "No, though I suggest that if you place officers at the base of the entry ramps, they can reduce the amount of bunching on the ramp itself. Officers with white batons, perhaps."

He cleared his throat. "I was smiling," he lied, "to think of how surprised the Pellegrinians are going to be to have your men land in their rear that way. If you keep your men moving, Quinn, you'll sweep through the base without anything like a battle. Though you'll need to keep moving, of course."

What Daniel'd really been thinking was that he himself was the best person available to lead the assault—and he wasn't available, even if Corius asked him. He knew his duty as a Leary and an RCN officer, but even if the Volunteers managed to hit the ground running, they were ill trained and as dangerous to their friends as they were to the enemy. Daniel was willing to risk his life in a good cause, but being shot in the back by a farmer who shuts his eyes when he jerks the trigger wasn't the way he'd choose to go.

Corius and his military commander nodded sagely in agreement. Perhaps the comment would even help Quinn execute the plan in the only survivable fashion.

"Right, they've got a lot of spirit," Quinn said with false enthusiasm. Well, maybe not false: say rather *exaggerated enthusiasm.* "And remember, they're not our best battalion by a long shot."

The troops were milling their way aboard the transport. It was a moderately difficult job, as the holds of an ordinary freighter had been fitted with temporary decking so the ship could carry the maximum number of human beings. Access from deck to deck was by vertical ladders. Climbing them was an awkward task for men carrying packs and slung weapons. Until the first to board had cleared the entry hold, the later ranks could only wait on the ramp and quay.

"And of course while we want to load promptly," Corius said, "the only thing that matters is that we reach Mandelfarne before Arruns' spies warn him that we've put the whole force on a single ship. That'll take hours, don't you think?"

"I think it'll be at least hours before the Pellegrinians understand the significance of what's happening," Daniel said; limited agreement, but agreement. "It's *very* important that we arrive as soon as possible after the *Rainha* touches down with our friends aboard, though. I want to make it clear—"

He heard the change in his voice. So did Corius and Quinn, turning from the mob scene below to meet Daniel's gaze with sudden wariness.

"—that we will lift off before the full complement of troops has boarded if I deem that necessary."

"Now, see here, Leary—" Corius began, his face a sudden cloud.

"Councilor!" said Daniel.

Fallert dropped like a scaly gray cat from the roof to the pierced-steel platform at the back of the cage. Hogg was already facing him, twirling a short length of his fishline across the doorway as if by chance.

"If we wait too long," Daniel continued, "the Pellegrinians will recapture the missile battery before we arrive. In that event, we'll *all* die when they destroy the ship as we approach. I don't mind taking risks—"

In all truth, he rather liked it. Otherwise he'd be in another line of work, or at any rate wouldn't have had so distinguished a career.

"—but I'm not going to commit suicide and throw away another two thousand lives besides. Yours among them, I should point out."

He smiled broadly, taking away the sting he knew was in his tone.

"Ah!" said Corius. He forced a smile which quickly softened into reality. "Yes, I see that. I perhaps hadn't considered all the risks when I agreed to the plan. If you think it's too dangerous . . .?"

"It's not," said Daniel. "It's perfectly workable. I just want everyone to realize that I'll do whatever is necessary to make it work, even if other parties haven't fully executed their own duties. Right, Colonel?"

"My men'll be aboard," Quinn said stiffly. "Never fear that. Look, they're loaded already."

That wasn't quite true—the last thirty or forty troops were still on the entry ramp, waiting for those ahead of them to move. On the day of the real operation, the First Battalion still would be waiting to load behind the other three so that they'd be first off the transport when it landed on Mandelfarne Island. The First Battalion might not deserve to be called shock troops, but they were at any rate the best men in the Volunteers.

Daniel wasn't really concerned about the time it took to load in Ollarville. The real worry was how quickly the troops would disembark under hostile fire. There was no way to practice that.

"Not bad!" Quinn said with the artificial verve he'd shown before. "And a first drill! Now we'll see if the Third and Fourth Battalions can better their time."

The troops had finally vanished into the ship, though Daniel was sure they'd still be packing the entry hold for another several minutes. Nonetheless, quickly enough.

"Well, I'm glad to hear you say you're still in favor of the plan, Commander," Corius said, patronizingly expansive again. "Because I don't mind telling you that I'd hate to cancel the operation and come up with another method of defeating Arruns. That wouldn't be an easy job, I'm afraid."

"I don't think you need worry about that, Councilor," Daniel said diplomatically. "So long as we continue to work on execution, we'll be fine when the time comes to do the job for real."

Colonel Quinn was talking to his battalion commander again. Daniel heard a tone of qualified approval in his voice, which the event scarcely justified.

We can't cancel the operation, Councilor, Daniel thought grimly, *because we can't get word to Adele and her detachment. I'm going to be taking a ship into the Pellegrinian base one way or another, even if it's the* Princess Cecile *with a skeleton crew.*

Central Haven on Pellegrino

"*Striker to Football,*" crackled the voice of the signals officer of the *Duilio,* already in orbit. "*Report your status, over.*"

"Striker, this is Football," Adele said. She'd listened repeatedly to the exchanges the *Rainha*'s signals officer, Clerk 7 Lena Hilbert of the Alliance Fleet, had with ground control on Mandelfarne Island, Central Haven, and with the cruiser. "Captain Cootzee says we're ready to lift. Over."

They'd been lucky that though none of the societies in and around Ganpat's Reach allowed women in their governments, militaries, or the crews of their ships, the signals units servicing the invasion of Dunbar's World were provided by the Alliance. Hilbert was fat and unkempt, but she was female and thereby made Adele's life easier. Adele was distorting her voice electronically, but making the transmissions completely sexless would raise questions.

"*Hilbert, is that you?*" said the *Duilio*'s officer—Clerk 7 Wang. "*What the hell's wrong with you, over?*"

Vesey was going over her checklist, exchanging comments with Boise in the Power Room. She had Adele's conversation running as a text feed at the bottom of her display, but she knew that if there were anything she as captain *needed* to know, Adele would bring it to her attention.

"Look, Wang," Adele said, the exasperation in her voice real. "*I've already got a hangover. I don't need a ration of shit from you too. Cootzee says, 'Are we cleared to lift?' over.*"

Adele's lip curled, but she knew what Hilbert would say and how she'd say it. If the woman had been a person of greater intelligence and breeding, she wouldn't have been a low-ranking clerk in a hardship posting . . . but it still distressed Adele to ape her manners. Lack of manners.

She smiled sadly. Most things distressed her if she let herself dwell on them. That was a good reason, if she'd needed one, to focus her intention on information and avoid considering the realities beyond the information. She'd ably mimicked Clerk 7 Hilbert's tone; that was all that mattered.

"*Football, this is Striker Command,*" said a different, heavier voice from the cruiser. It wasn't Captain ap Glynn but rather his executive officer, Commander Diehl. "*You may lift off, over.*"

"Roger," Adele said. "Captain Cootzee, Striker has cleared us to lift off. Over."

She pointed her finger at Sun, sitting tensely at the second bridge terminal. His voice naturally sounded quite a lot like that of the *Rainha's* captain, and Vesey'd written him a script. Sun, who'd enthusiastically led armed assaults in the past, was white-faced with fear of acting; even very modest acting, as this was.

Adele shut off her terminal's audio. "Sun," she said, "don't fail Commander Leary!"

"*Roger,*" Sun squeaked. "*Out.*"

Vesey lit all twelve thrusters together, following Captain Cootzee's practice as shown in the ship's electronic log. Adele smiled again. It wasn't the way Daniel or anybody Daniel had trained did things. This was probably as hard for Vesey as Hilbert's vulgarity was for Mundy of Chatsworth.

"*Signals, this is Command,*" Vesey said over a two-way link. "*Is the intercom, ah, secure, over?*"

Adele checked her terminal before she spoke. "Captain," she said, "no one will know what happens or is said aboard this ship unless I determine that they should. Over."

"*Ship, this is Command,*" Vesey resumed over the general push. "*We've carried out the first portion of our mission. Now comes the hard part: managing to look as sloppy on the way to Dunbar's World as the wogs we're pretending to be. We're all Sissies so I know it'll be a strain, but remember that it's worth it. If we pull this off, we'll get a chance to show ten thousand monkeys from the back of beyond what RCN spacers are like. Are you with me?*"

By heaven! thought Adele as the crew cheered. *By heaven, Vesey's voice wobbles a little but she's as much like Daniel as anyone could be! Out of sheer effort, she's mimicking what Daniel does by instinct.*

"Ship, prepare to lift," said Vesey as the enthusiasm faded to a happy expectancy. She slid her joined throttles forward; the ship began to shudder upward in a pillar of steam and fire.

Adele's hand fell unconsciously to the butt of her pistol. She'd have very little to do over the five-day voyage to Dunbar's World. When they reached orbit, she'd have to exchange communications with ground control and Wang aboard the *Duilio*, but Vesey could handle that by herself now that Adele'd cleared the Alliance encryption gear.

The real work would come when the *Rainha* landed and her hatches opened. At that point the Sissies' task would be to kill people; and with the possible exception of Tovera, nobody aboard was as skilled at that as Adele Mundy.

CHAPTER 21

Mandelfarne Island on Dunbar's World

The landing jounced Adele so hard against her terminal's simple lap belt that it broke her concentration on the message traffic swirling around the Pellegrinian base. She turned her head with a frown. Vesey was sitting rigidly at her console, hands poised over the controls.

Of course. Vesey had to follow Captain Cootzee's standard operating procedure, so she was letting the *Rainha*'s computer land them instead of easing the ship in manually the way Daniel'd taught her to do. With an ordinary water landing it didn't make a great deal of difference, but the reflected thrust made a ship coming in over land quiver like a ball on a vibrating table. A skilled pilot could land much more smoothly by matching thruster output to the terrain.

Of course an unskilled pilot could drop his ship sideways or even flip it onto its back. Cootzee preferred discomfort to a chance of disaster, and Vesey perforce had to use the techniques of the man she'd supplanted.

Was the capture of the Rainha *piracy or an act of war? Probably piracy, because we weren't in uniform . . . and for that matter, Pellegrino isn't at war with Cinnabar. Though that might change if Chancellor Arruns loses his temper as badly as he may when he learns whats happened on Dunbar's World.*

The *Rainha* touched hard, her stern slightly below her bow; Adele's torso swung to the right. The bow dipped and the stern rose with a second paired *Clang-g!* from the outriggers. Adele swung left, wondering if this was the way the ship always landed. Probably, probably; but how did they stand it?

Vesey—slight, pale, self-effacing Lieutenant Vesey—shouted, "Fuck this fucking piece of shit!"

The thrusters shut off while the *Rainha* was in the air. The ship fell—only a few inches, but three thousand tons hits bone-jarringly hard even in a short distance—with a ringing crash. Adele had enough experience with machinery to understand what'd happened: Vesey, conditioned to the razor-sharp controls of the *Princess Cecile,* had switched off the thrusters when the *Rainha* was down. The lag in the freighter's mushy circuits and feed pipes meant the vessel'd lifted again before the command took effect.

As the freighter hissed and pinged, cooling till it'd be safe to open the hatches, Adele unbuckled her lap belt. The strap appeared to have left bruises over her hip bones.

That didn't matter. As well as the little weapon in her tunic pocket, Adele was carrying a service pistol. She secured its holster flap in the open position, leaving the butt clear to be gripped. She found the big weapon heavy and awkward, but the tiny pellets from the pocket pistol weren't effective beyond fifty yards. She was likely to need greater range tonight.

Most of the crew was already in the entry hold, but Wheelus and Heska were poised at the dorsal airlock with stocked impellers. Under normal circumstances that hatch was used only by riggers coming and going from the hull. At present the two spacers were waiting to be told to take firing positions on the upper hull.

Sun rose from his console, looking in silent expectancy from Vesey to Adele. He slanted his sub-machine gun across his chest; he'd removed the sling. Adele got up also, feeling—

Not feeling much of anything, she supposed. She wondered with detachment whether she'd be killed in the next few minutes.

Tovera carried a full-sized sub-machine gun but wore the miniature weapon from her attaché case in a belt holster. She'd strapped a pack in front of her where she could reach the contents easily.

Tovera was smiling. Adele didn't know what that meant. It irritated her to think that despite her skill as an information specialist, she couldn't answer questions about those so close to her.

"Fellow Sissies!" Vesey said, using the public address system. Her voice buzzed out of the tinny speakers in each compartment. "You all have your instructions. The most important one is that you don't shoot, *none* of us shoot, until Officer Mundy orders or the wogs start shooting at us. We're going to go out there as quiet as mice. With luck we'll take the missile battery without a shot being fired."

Adele had to force herself not to fidget. Intellectually she knew that it would cause questions if they lowered the ramps too early. Plasma exhaust baked the ground as hot as fired porcelain. Even experienced spacers couldn't leave the ship for several minutes after landing unless they were wearing rigging suits.

Adele knew that, but she was keyed up and desperate to get on with what she knew was coming. It was half-possible that they'd capture the battery without shooting, but even if they did the night wouldn't be over.

"Remember, Sissies," Vesey went on. "No one on Cinnabar may know where we are or care, but Mister Leary's counting on us. Let's not fail him. Out!"

Vesey'd been rising as she finished her speech. She took the submachine gun hanging from the back of the console and turned toward the hatch. Sun, cued by the movement, started for the companionway. Tovera nodded the lieutenant ahead of her and Adele; Vesey hesitated an instant—but only an instant—and obeyed.

As the group from the bridge passed, Wheelus and Heska climbed into the airlock and cycled it shut. The inner and outer hatches were interlocked so they couldn't both be open at once.

Adele kept her right hand over the companionway railing as she followed, knowing how easily she could lose her footing on the wear-polished steel treads. She wasn't afraid of dying, but if she lived to be a hundred she'd never learn to shrug off embarrassment.

She grinned coldly. It didn't seem likely that she'd live to a hundred. Well, it'd never been a priority.

The *Rainha's* entry compartment was smaller than the *Princess Cecile's*, in keeping with the freighter's civilian crewing standard. Twelve spacers would've been comfortable in it; thirty carrying weapons and bandoliers of reloads were squeezed together like canned fish.

"Ten of you up the up companionway *now!*" Sun bellowed. The force included two bosun's mates, Schmidt and Quinsett, but they hadn't taken charge in this situation. Sun, the armorer and gunner's mate, was in his element.

There was an immediate undulation in the crowd, enough that Adele could worm her way to the front with only a modicum of pushing. Her skin felt hot and prickly as though she were about to faint. She'd be all right when she started down the ramp, but the packed hold was working on her agoraphobia. It crushed her with the weight of so many people who weren't moving and couldn't move.

"Remember, we wait for Officer Mundy!" Vesey said. She had to raise her voice, because shuffling and the sound of excited breathing created a susurrus like the incoming tide.

At Vesey's nod, Quinsett gave a 90 degree turn to the wheel controlling the hatch mechanism. The machinery groaned for a moment; then the heated seam broke free. The ramp dropped slowly with a peevish hydraulic whine. Hot, dry air swirled in, sharp with ozone and hints of cremated organic materials.

The ramp creaked to horizontal, paused minusculely, and continued winding down. Adele stood frozen in a cocoon of her own thoughts. Ordinary spacers would start across the ramp long before it was fully down; often they'd jump the last of the distance to the ground and saunter off, gay in their liberty rigs and their hope of a good time.

Adele wasn't a spacer; she was a librarian who lived and worked in space. But she was RCN and she was a Sissie, and those were all that mattered.

The words KNOW THYSELF had supposedly been written above an ancient oracle. Adele had that lesson down as well as anyone she knew. So long as she didn't have to like the person she knew she was, she was fine.

The ramp banged to the ground with a shudder that would've knocked her off her feet if she'd been on it at the time. She started down now, smiling to herself and at herself. Tovera was to her right side, half a step back.

They were dressed for the occasion in loose, dark blue clothing. The garments weren't a uniform, but in the darkness they looked a great deal like Alliance Fleet fatigues. Her RCN commo helmet was white, not dark gray like the Fleet equivalent, but that couldn't be helped. The Alliance communications unit with Arruns didn't use helmets anyway.

Tracked vehicles were rolling toward the *Rainha*, their rectangular headlights knifing through swirls of dust and fumes. Adele turned toward the battery's control unit, a hardened trailer a hundred yards from the supply ship's landing place near the eastern end of the island. Because of the danger of exhaust and missile backblast, the positions nearby had to have heavy overhead cover. There were bunkers on the shoreline, but the troops in them were concerned with an attack from across the channel rather than one that'd dropped straight down on the island.

Two men buzzed up on a wheeled scooter. If they wore insignia, Adele couldn't see it even with her visor's light enhancement. The man on the back called without dismounting, "Do you have the manifest?"

Adele thumbed toward the open hatch. "You'll have to talk to the captain about that," she said, trudging on nonchalantly. She didn't look back.

Powerful engines honked and hooted, moving equipment toward the *Rainha*. Adele walked faster. She'd seen during Daniel's reconnaissance that the Pellegrinians brought banks of floodlights on wheeled carriages up to the ship to illuminate it so that unloading could go on night and day.

To capture Port Dunbar would require great expenditures either of men or of shells, and the Chancellor *couldn't* provide more men. There were no permanent port facilities on Mandelfarne Island, so Arruns had to speed delivery of the necessary munitions in some other way.

The control trailer was the center of a web of leads to the array of vertical spike antennas thirty meters out from it. The edges of the narrow path to the door were taped so that those entering and leaving didn't trip over the lines. Adele thought of spiders. The corners of her mouth curled up: she and Tovera were the predators, not the technicians on watch inside.

A light stuck out above the lintel like a tiny shelf fungus, casting a fuzzy glow over the door and the ground in front of it. An optical pickup with a wide-angle lens was tacked to the panel at eye height in place of a vision block; beside it was a small grating, also an add-on, connected to the inside of the trailer by a hair-fine fiber.

The door was outward-opening; its latch plate doubled as a handle; Adele pulled it with her left hand in her pocket. The plate didn't give. She rapped on the door with her knuckles and called, "Open up! I'm Lieutenant Delacrois from the Signals Section."

"What are you doing here?" said a voice from the grating. It was so distorted Adele wasn't sure whether the speaker was a man or a woman. "We can't let anybody in without authorization from Group Captain Rousch."

"Look you bloody fool!" said Adele, glaring at the camera. "This isn't something I can shout through the door about. Field Marshal Arruns sent me. Open up!"

Adele saw her servant only from the corner of her eyes. Tovera had opened her pack. She patted the upper door hinge, then squatted and touched the lower one. She left a putty-like lump on each.

"Look, you can't come in, I don't care if you're the Chancellor himself!" the angry, sexless voice snarled. "Only authorized personnel are allowed into the antenna farm, and you're not authorized!"

"Step away, mistress," Tovera said. "To the side."

A siren on the roof of the trailer ran up to a piercing howl, and a strobe light on a short mast nearby began to pulse alternately red and white. Adele stepped around the corner of the trailer with Tovera, wondering how thick the armor was. After a moment's hesitation, she drew the heavy pistol from its holster, leaving her personal weapon in her pocket.

Tovera thumbed a remote control. The twin blasts sounded more like colliding anvils than explosions. The trailer shook like a wet dog. The siren choked off but the strobe continued to flash with painful intensity. The helmet's active sound cancellation saved Adele's hearing, but the concussion—even with the trailer between her and the source—felt like a ton of sand shoving her.

She was around the corner with Tovera. Gray gases swirled; the helmet filters dropped over Adele's nose. The door was askew, blown loose at the hinge side but still hanging from the latch; light from inside outlined it sharply.

Tovera seized the door's back edge with her left hand and pulled hard. She was ungodly strong, but the blast must've warped the bolt; it bound. Adele saw movement and fired through the crack. The pistol lifted on the recoil of the heavy pellet, but she lowered the muzzle to present as Tovera threw her weight into the door and tore it loose.

A dying man sprawled forward, spraying blood from his mouth and the bullet hole over the top of his breastbone. Another man was on his back on the floor, scrabbling to get up; he'd probably been at the door when Tovera's plastic explosive went off, knocking him down deafened.

Adele ignored both to shoot the third man swinging a bell-mouthed weapon toward her. Her bullet punched through his right eye socket and out the back of his skull. He triggered a blue-white blast into the trailer's ceiling.

Vaporized metal sprayed Adele, graying her visor and searing her bare skin. Her finger twitched again, blowing a hole in the control console before the slug ricocheted back from the armored wall beyond.

Tovera put a three-round burst into the face of the man on the floor. His spine arched, then bowed, and his heels drummed violently.

A snake of crackling light writhed across the pedestal of the control. A transformer in the cabinet to the right of the console exploded with a dull *whump*. Smoke the color of fresh asphalt poured through its cooling louvers, brightened by an occasional orange flame.

Adele turned, flipping her visor out of the way. She could see through the coating of redeposited armor plate, but not well. She supposed the visor had saved her eyesight, but now it was just in the way.

"There's manual controls on the battery itself," Adele snapped to Tovera. "We have to disable them too."

She started toward the entrance to the missile pit. Construction engineers had heaped and compacted the spoil into a berm, then topped it with a spool of razor ribbon. Though it was so close to the control trailer that several of the northeastern antennas were on the slope, the single opening was some distance around the circuit.

Adele was furious with herself. If she'd captured the trailer intact, they wouldn't have to worry about the battery controls: she could simply have locked them out. By using the heavy pistol—

She turned, caught the strobe in the weapon's holographic sight, and squeezed off. The light exploded in a shower of sparks. The pistol's barrel, already glowing from the previous shots, shimmered yellow.

—she'd destroyed the controls instead of just killing the gunman. An alert technician—it's never safe to assume your enemy isn't alert and skilled—in the cab of the launch unit could blast the *Greybudd* out of the sky as it approached Mandelfarne Island.

There was shooting from the direction of the *Rainha*. Adele didn't know what'd happened. Probably some of the Sissies had just killed a truck driver or someone equally innocent; out of nervousness or mistake or simply the desire to kill somebody now that there was a colorable excuse.

It didn't matter. This was war. This was what happened in war.

Lights went on, then very quickly off, on the other side of the berm. Adele could see the entrance at an angle. A soldier stood in front of the guardhouse. The gate, more razor ribbon on the frame of metal pipes, was partly open.

Three ground vehicles with sirens howling jounced east from the direction of Base Headquarters. At least the first two, painted by the headlights of those behind, were light trucks with pintle-mounted automatic impellers on the bed. The rudimentary road was choked with supply haulers, so the emergency vehicles had pulled around them onto terrain that didn't even pretend to have been improved.

The leading vehicle disintegrated in sparks and flashes, ripped at point blank range by a volley from stocked impellers and sub-machine guns. The members of the emergency response team, probably military police, were so focused on racing toward the alarm at the battery control trailer that they hadn't noticed the Sissies who'd poured from the *Rainha* until they were on top of them.

The truck flipped and rolled, flinging out equipment and the corpses of several men. The second vehicle braked screechingly. Its body lost definition in a sleet of shots, and it crashed into what was left of the first vehicle.

The third truck skidded left to avoid the wreckage and roared past spacers who were shooting enthusiastically without leading the fast-moving vehicle enough. *They need Hogg*, Adele thought, *or Daniel*. She lifted her pistol, aiming at where the driver's face would be when the truck was within seventy-five yards.

The gun's pintle sparkled and the windshield blew out. The driver slumped forward, the gunner who'd been trying to horse his heavy weapon around flew off the left side of the bed, and the officer in the back with him crumpled, dropping his handgun. Somebody with a sub-machine gun had made up for the twenty-odd Sissies who were wasting ammunition.

The truck bounced away in a slow curve, its headlight touching sea foam as it headed for the shore. The Pellegrinians hadn't fired a shot.

The man in front of the gate in the berm was staring at the carnage screaming, "Oh shit! Oh shit!" He caught movement in the corner of his eye and turned to face Adele, twenty feet away.

"Who're you?" he said, raising his impeller. Adele shot him through the forehead. The heavy pellet flung him back into the gate; the wire sang and the pipe framework made an ugly jangling. A man unseen till that moment shot from the guardhouse window. A bullet kicked Adele in the left side.

Tovera fired into the guardhouse; one pellet of her burst hit the Pellegrinian's weapon and ricocheted through the roof of the shack in a neon helix. She jumped to the window, leaned in, and fired again toward the floor.

Adele stumbled forward. The muzzle of her pistol was slowly sinking; it'd gotten too heavy for her to hold up. She licked her lips and gripped her left wrist with her right hand to raise the weapon. It slipped out of her fingers.

"Mistress?" said Tovera. She jerked Adele's tunic up and slapped something cold and astringent in the hollow of Adele's shoulder.

"Go on," Adele said. She was whispering. "Go on! We have to disable the missiles!"

Three men, blurry in the randomly lighted darkness, approached the gate from inside the enclosure. "Dauphine?" one called. "What the hell's—"

Tovera shot the speaker, then shot the man next to him as he started to present the weapon he'd held out nervously in front of him. Razor ribbon sprang apart, the ends of the strand white hot where a pellet had clipped it. The third soldier turned to run but sprawled headlong at the second step when Tovera shot him in the back.

Adele reached into her tunic pocket with her right hand and brought out her little pistol. She normally shot left-handed, but her right was her master hand and she practiced with both. Besides, it didn't matter. If she had to hold the gun with her toes, she would.

Tovera knelt, ejected the loading tube from her sub-machine gun, and slapped in a fresh one. Her barrel shroud glowed bright yellow, and the bore of synthetic diamond must be hot enough to have melted any lesser substance. Haze from vaporized driving bands twinkled in the air before her.

Soldiers inside the pit were firing long bursts toward the gate, emptying their impeller magazines and reloading to fire again. There were at least three of them, maybe four or five. The osmium pellets left glowing tracks as they snapped through the air and danced like miniature fireworks displays when they hit wire or the gate frame.

Adele walked to the gate. A pellet hit a stone in the soil and howled away, spraying chips of rock. Some bits cut her shins above her RCN ankle boots.

The operations and maintenance staff for the missile battery was quartered in six bunkers on the inner face of the berm to the right of the gateway. They were accommodation trailers which'd been sunk waist deep, covered with spoil from the battery pit, and sandbagged across the portion of the front that was still above ground. So long as those within were lying flat, they had sufficient protection even if the missiles were launched.

Now soldiers inside were kneeling to shoot out from the doorways. The nearest was twenty yards from Adele, the farthest some thirty-five.

"Mistress!" Tovera shouted.

Adele fired twice at the pale oval of the nearest face; it vanished. She shifted left, fired twice; shifted left—

Metal splashed from the gate and spattered her; a spark burned through her tunic just above her navel. The backs of her wrists were oozing blood from the burns she'd gotten in the control trailer.

She fired twice and shifted left.

Two faces appeared in the nearest doorway, replacing the first gunman Adele had killed. She ignored them—one thing at a time and she had very little time left—and fired twice at her fourth target, a Pellegrinian using a rifle whose chemical propellant made great red flashes and spat bits of jacket metal at every shot. The soldier slipped backward, leaving his weapon on the step of the bunker.

Tovera was at Adele's left side, raking the nearest bunker with two neat bursts instead of a single long one. Adele had no doubt that when the bodies were examined, those men would have patterns of three holes each in the middle of the forehead.

The last Pellegrinian vanished down into his bunker, leaving only an ionized haze to show where he'd been punching pointless holes in the air and gate. Tovera called, "Cover me!" and slipped like a wraith through the gap by which the gate was ajar.

The barrel shroud of Adele's pistol glowed yellow-white, blurring the sight picture. That was only a theoretical problem, though; she didn't think she'd missed a shot tonight.

Her head felt cold. Her scalp was sweating and she'd lost her commo helmet. Had she taken it off? She didn't remember that.

Just as Tovera reached the end bunker, the man inside raised his head. The sub-machine gun clacked like an angry woodpecker, flinging him back where he'd hidden.

Tovera had stuck a blue strobe into the berm, a signal to draw the rest of the assault force, but there wasn't time to wait for them. Adele eased through the gate. She'd memorized the battery's layout, but the terrain was rippling in her mind as though it'd been drawn in colored smoke. She moved deliberately down the curving ramp into the pit, aware that if she lost her balance she wouldn't be able to get up.

The missiles were mounted in trios on either side of an armored cab. They were forty-six feet long and fat in proportion. The battery was still in its horizontal travel position, and Adele didn't see a light on in the cab.

She reached the bottom of the ramp and took another step. The change made her dizzy; she closed her eyes briefly, then opened them and walked toward the steps. Her pistol had cooled to a red glow that was barely visible, but she still couldn't put it back in her pocket; besides, she might need it.

Adele reached the steps; they were already folded out. If she'd had to unlatch them and pull them down . . . well, she'd have managed somehow. She started up to the cab, unable to grip the railings. She couldn't feel her left arm at all, while her right throbbed as though she were gripping a burning coal instead of the butt of her pistol.

There was more shooting above her; it could've been either inside or outside the berm. It didn't really matter. She heard the snarling discharge of a plasma cannon and saw the sky brighten momentarily in her peripheral vision. If the Pellegrinians ever figured out what was happening, they could crush the assault in a matter of minutes with their APCs.

Adele pulled the cab door open and flopped across the bench seat inside. She'd memorized the layout of the controls, but she'd expected to have the use of her left hand. Now she had to reach across her body and switch on the interior lights with the muzzle of the pistol.

She laid her pistol on the seat beside her and brought live the control module in the center of the dashboard, then methodically locked each of the functions out with a separate eight-digit password. When she was done, she aimed the pistol at the module and fired three times. The casing was armored, but her pellets shattered the projection lenses for the display.

Adele rested her forehead on the dashboard, but the cab stank of burned insulation, ionized aluminum, and her own sweat and blood. She lurched upright, slid to the cab door, and managed to step out onto the pressed-metal landing.

Tovera was waiting there. She caught Adele around the waist and walked backwards down the six steps to the ground.

"I'm all right," Adele whispered. "I can stand."

The second part was true. Maybe the first was also; she was better than the many people she'd shot at tonight, anyway. She hadn't missed, not once.

Tovera released her carefully but watched her for a moment. Adele smiled. "I can stand," she repeated in a stronger voice.

A burst from an automatic impeller stitched the sky over the pit, the hypervelocity projectiles glowing with the heat of their passage. They'd splash into the sea miles away, harmlessly unless some fish picked the wrong moment to surface for a gulp of air. Adele giggled with the humor of the thought.

Tovera bent and picked up something from the ground with her free hand. It was Adele's commo helmet. A bullet had struck the peak, cracking the shell nearly into two pieces.

"I brought this to show you, mistress," Tovera said. "The next time you decide to shoot it out with five of them, they may not miss you."

"I didn't expect them to miss me tonight," Adele said softly. "I thought . . ."

I thought it would be over. I can't stop killing other people till I'm killed myself. I will not stop.

Another plasma cannon fired. To Adele's surprise, people were cheering from the edge of the pit. She heard Vesey among them.

They had to be the rest of the assault force, but why were they cheering?

The sky to the southeast brightened from the glaring exhaust of a starship three hundred feet in the air, thundering across the strait toward Mandelfarne Island. Daniel was bringing in the *Greybudd*.

Adele thought of the face of the man she'd shot inside the control trailer, his gaunt features swelling as her pellet ruptured his skull from the inside. *And it isn't over yet.*

Daniel wore a smile as he fought the transport's controls, but even he had to admit that it was rather a fixed one. Starships aren't meant to fly in an atmosphere, and the *Greybudd* was particularly a pig.

The valves in the lines feeding reaction mass—water—to thrusters Seven, Nine, and Eleven were sticking; if they weren't kept full on, they were likely to cut out unexpectedly. Daniel kept them flared at maximum flow but ran the other nine at normal apertures and lower throttle settings. If he'd mushed along with all twelve thrusters at full flow, he'd have emptied his reaction mass tanks before he got across the continent.

"I didn't realize it'd be so rough!" shouted Corius over the buzzing roar. He was sitting at the second console, the one meant for the navigation officer. "My God I didn't! Do you think the men will be in shape to fight?"

For your sake they'd better be, Daniel thought grimly. He didn't speak aloud, both because he was busy and because he didn't have anything useful to say. *I don't expect to be staying around very long myself.*

The *Greybudd* yawed but righted herself. Daniel kept his hands steady. If he'd acted as instinct urged him, he'd have overcorrected and very possibly lost the ship for good and all.

The left side of his display was a real-time strip map of the terrain over which the transport flew. The top was the limit of the land painted by the ship's mapping radar at this low altitude, somewhere between twenty and thirty miles ahead of them as the transport porpoised along.

Port Dunbar came in sight, its northern suburbs outlined by muzzle flashes and explosions in the optical feed on the upper right of the display. Daniel saw the channel, then seconds later the low bulk of Mandelfarne Island beyond.

Hogg was sitting on a flip-down seat against the starboard bulkhead, seemingly as placid as a mushroom on a tree stump. He held a stocked impeller between his legs.

Fallert had been on another of the three jumpseats, but he'd gotten up and begun pacing within minutes of liftoff from Ollarville. His long legs gave him a wide stance, and his balance was better than a cat's.

A corner of Daniel's display showed the bridge compartment. He'd been sure some of the lurches the *Greybudd* made when crosswinds conspired with vagaries in the thrusters would throw the snakeman to the deck, but he'd been wrong.

Crossing the shoreline into the relatively cool, dense air over the channel made them bob upward slightly. Daniel rebalanced his thrusters, portside aft and then the other nine. The ship wobbled, then wobbled back. It was a thoroughly unpleasant motion but he didn't dare take both hands off the attitude control to adjust both groups of controls at the same time.

Shots rang from the hull. From the flashes on the ground, both the Bennarian defenders and the Pellegrinians were shooting at the transport. Daniel smiled wryly. Chances were that none of them had the faintest idea what the ship was. They were simply shooting because it was moving and they had guns in their hands. He didn't despair about human beings the way Adele sometimes seemed to, but occasionally people's behavior, while predictable, was difficult to feel good about.

It took pretty good shooting to hit them, though. Sure, a starship is a big target, but they were moving fast and the sheer size was daunting.

Daniel would've liked to hug the ground all the way from Ollarville or alternatively to have stayed in the stratosphere until he dropped onto the Pellegrinian base. The *Greybudd* didn't control well enough to trust making the journey on the deck, though, while if they didn't stay fairly low they'd have been in sight—and range—of the missile battery long before Adele's crew could capture it. This was an awkward compromise, but it'd worked.

"*Six, this is Three!*" said Pasternak over the command channel. "*We'll start losing thrusters in ten minutes, maybe less. The jets aren't meant for runs this long, over!*"

"Three, we'll be down in less than that, over," Daniel said, scanning the optical display.

"*Six, we may* have *less than that!*" Pasternak said. "*You could shave on the edge of Two and Five, they're burned so thin, out.*"

The assault group was to mark its perimeter with Search and Rescue strobes. Every starship's computer was designed to caret that particular shade of blue. Daniel's display now did so, three narrow, pulsing spikes on the berm around the missile pit. Adele had captured the battery.

Of course. The *Greybudd* would be a fireball spewing scrap metal and burned meat if she hadn't.

"Ship, prepare for landing!" Daniel said. He wished he knew the *Greybudd* better, and he wished he had somebody trustworthy backing him up in the Battle Direction Center—

But a freighter doesn't have a BDC, and he wasn't being asked to do anything that the *Rainha's* civilian captain hadn't done a score of times: bring a clumsy, wallowing pig of a ship down on a mudpile safely. Laughing and aware of the Councilor's gaping amazement— which made him laugh louder—Daniel dilated the nozzles of Thrusters Three, Four, Five, and Six without changing their flow rate. Diffusing the exhaust reduced thrust, so the *Greybudd* began to sink perceptibly without losing her forward motion. Daniel nudged the attitude yoke half a point to starboard.

"Ship, coming down in five, four—" Daniel said, flaring all the nozzles but boosting flow. They were very low, now, bathed first in steam and then in the smoke of tents and supplies and men.

"—three, two—"

Daniel hit the virtual button on his display that cycled the three cargo hatches. The hydraulics barely started to groan, but that instant of anticipation broke the seals before the impact could twist hatches and coamings together immovably. The difference between life and death. . . .

The *Greybudd* hit with a horrible crash, her outriggers furrowing the ground as she skidded forward. Daniel chopped his throttles. Thruster Eleven *didn't* shut down, the bitch, but a gout of mud choked it into an explosion an instant later.

The tubular struts attaching the outriggers bent back, dropping the hull till the bow plates scraped the dirt also. The *Greybudd* ground to a halt. The forward starboard strut tore out of the shoulder socket; the hull sagged lower still, but the hatches were continuing to wind down.

The transport's nose was within twenty yards of the berm around the missile pit. By shutting off his thrusters and sliding to a halt, Daniel'd avoided baking the soil where the Volunteers had to jump out. It was hell on the ship—he'd probably turned the *Greybudd* to scrap despite his carefully optimistic comments when he broached the plan to Corius in Port Dunbar—but it was the only way to ensure that the troops could begin disembarking immediately instead of waiting for the ground to cool.

"Power Room, report," Daniel snapped over the command channel as he unlocked the web restraints that held him onto the console.

"*As soon as these pongoes give me a little space, I'll come out the aft inspection port, Six,*" Pasternak said. "*That wasn't half a hard landing, out.*"

Hard it was, but it hadn't been a bad one. Daniel'd executed his plan better than he'd hoped would be possible. He grinned in satisfaction as he got up.

"You can undog the bridge hatch," he said to those around him, though he didn't care whether someone did or didn't. He'd ordered it locked to keep out Volunteers who might panic at *just* the wrong time during the flight.

Daniel couldn't blame them; there'd been moments when he'd have jumped for the controls himself if he weren't already at them. On the other hand, it wasn't going to help to have a frightened sergeant grabbing him by the shoulder—to pick one of a half-dozen possibilities—as he angled the jets to compensate for the cold wind blowing down the channel of the Meherrin River.

"*Six, this is Victor One,*" said Vesey, her weak signal boosted into crackly audibility by the *Greybudd*'s antennas and amplifiers. "*We've secured the objective. All personnel are inside the berm, over.*"

Daniel undogged the exterior hatch—he had to hammer the left dog with the heel of his hand to start it—and began spinning the hand-crank to wind it up. Except for cargo and Power Room, the transport's hatches were manually worked. Fallert had opened the internal hatch so the babble of thousands of troops flooded the compartment.

"Roger, Victor One," Daniel said. His commo helmet was sending by the same route. He could only hope Vesey understood him through the static and distortion. "Hogg and I will be joining you ASAP. Are you in contact with Baker, over?"

Baker was the *Princess Cecile*, inbound under Blantyre with the remainder of the Sissies aboard. Daniel'd ordered her to make an ordinary liftoff to orbit, then drop onto Mandelfarne Island. He had a healthy appreciation of his own skill, but the low-level flight across the continent had been a strain. It wasn't something he was going to ask a midshipman to undertake.

Not just babble reached the bridge from the body of the ship. Judging by the stench, half the Volunteers must've puked their guts up during the flight and landing. On the other hand, the Pellegrinians here in what was supposed to be a rear area couldn't be in good shape either, watching a starship full of attackers land in their midst.

"*Roger, Six*," said Vesey. "*Baker One says five minutes, I repeat, five minutes. She'll home on our beacons, over*."

A slug whanged off the *Greybudd*'s hull, rather too close to the hatch Daniel had just locked open. It seemed that the Pellegrinians weren't all cowering in their dugouts.

"Six out," he said as Hogg threw a coiled line through the opening; the other end was tied around the base of the command console. Daniel drew on gauntlets from a rigging suit. Anything further he needed from Vesey could wait till they were face-to-face.

Hogg handed Daniel one of the impellers he'd brought; he'd already snubbed the sling of the other around his chest. "I'll lead," Hogg said. He grabbed the line—he was wearing the mesh gloves he used with his weighted fishline—and swung himself through the hatch.

Daniel took time to sling the impeller securely, then followed his servant into the night. It might be ten or fifteen minutes before enough Volunteers had disembarked for the bridge personnel to leave via the normal hatches, and he didn't have that much time.

Quite a lot of shooting was going on, though that didn't necessarily mean there was much fighting. Indeed, Daniel had noticed as he climbed out the hatch that the most enthusisastic firing came from the west end of the island. The Volunteers certainly hadn't gotten that far, and it was unlikely that the Bennarians had chosen this precise instant to launch a cross-channel raid.

Daniel started down, guiding the quarter-inch line with his boots but controlling his speed by the gauntlets. Slugs hit the hull and ricocheted, sometimes thrumming close enough to make his lips purse. There was a risk of being hit by a stray shot, but there was a risk to getting out of bed in the morning. You couldn't worry about such things.

When Daniel heard the drive fans approaching, he was still twenty feet in the air. He twisted to look over his shoulder. A Pellegrinian APC was driving in from the east, a black bulk silhouetted by lights and gunshots on the ground.

"Clear below!" Daniel shouted because he didn't have time to check where Hogg was. He kicked the hull to get clear and let go of the line. He was still falling when the vehicle's cannon ripped a bolt at the transport, biting the lip of the lighted hatch directly above.

Daniel hit the ground, taking the shock on his flexed knees. He'd stripped the gauntlet from his right hand as he dropped; now he released his impeller's sling because that was quicker than spreading the loop. Hogg was firing, his slugs red and purple and pastel green as they bounced from the APC's armor.

Not all bounced. Spurred by Hogg's example, scores—perhaps a hundred—of the Volunteers opened up as well.

The weight of armor a vehicle could carry and fly was limited. When some two hundred yards away the APC turned, presenting its left side to the rain of heavy-metal slugs. They'd occasionally penetrated the much thicker bow plating; now pieces flew off. The vehicle staggered, rolled to port, and drove into the ground, barely missing the *Greybudd's* stern on the way.

"Pasternak, are you all right?" Daniel said, sloughing proper protocol in the shock of the moment.

"*Aye, by the skin of my teeth!*" the engineer replied. "*Bugger, though! If I never come so close to dying again, it'll be too soon!*"

His voice was clearer but also weaker than before. The APC's bolt must've knocked the transport's commo system out of action. Had Corius gotten off the bridge before the jet of plasma gutted it?

"Head for the missile battery," Daniel ordered. "Can you make it by yourself, over?"

"*Aye, I see a pickup light,*" Pasternak said. "*I'm on my way.*"

There was a pause, then, "*Bugger that was close, out.*"

Daniel switched on the miniature strobe at the crown of his helmet and strode forward in a pulsing blue halo. Well, it'd have been blue if he weren't using his visor's monochrome light amplification. An irrational part of his mind told him that he was making himself a target for every Pellegrinian on the island, but realistically the risk of being shot by a mistaken Sissie was higher by an order of magnitude.

Hogg followed, half-turned so that he kept Daniel in the corner of his right eye while concentrating his attention on what might be happening behind them. His impeller was ready.

"Sir, is that you?" Vesey shouted from the gate fifty feet ahead. Daniel could see the lumps of four prone figures on the berm, nestled under the razor ribbon with impellers aimed.

"This is Six!" Daniel replied. "Hogg and I are coming in. We're coming in!"

"Let's go," he muttered to his servant, breaking into a trot. Then, raising his voice again—had Vesey's helmet intercom gone out? And where was Adele?—he added, "And watch out for Pasternak! He's coming from the stern so he's got a little farther."

Daniel heard Sissies begin dragging open the gate. His footing was tricky—light amplification doesn't give you relative distance—but he made the gap without a serious stumble and dodged to the side where the berm blurred his outline.

"Very good to see you, sir," said Vesey, emotion trembling under the careful formality of her words. Standing this close, Daniel felt heat radiating from the barrel of her sub-machine gun. "We haven't had a bad time yet, not as these things go, but it wouldn't have taken Arruns much longer to get things sorted out. And then to sort *us* out."

"*This is Three coming,*" Sun announced over the intercom. "*Let him by, everybody.*"

A moment later Daniel heard Pasternak pounding toward the gate, his boots and his wheezing both. He should've called ahead but he was an engineer who'd never been involved in ground fighting. And Daniel was sure that APC *had* come bloody close.

"What's the butcher's bill, Vesey?" Daniel asked bluntly. He looked upward; when slugs snapped through his field of vision, the visor overloaded and blacked out their glowing tracks. The *Princess Cecile*'s exhaust ought to be visible very shortly, but for now it was still lost in the star field.

"Hoskins and Bladel're dead," she said. Her voice was quiet, but there was a tremor beneath it. "We brought the bodies in. Three more bad but they're stabilized. Dorsey lost her foot; lost it, I mean, an impeller took it off and we couldn't find it afterwards."

"Vesey, where's Officer Mundy?" Daniel said, his mind watching himself and his lieutenant through thick glass. The *Sissie* was dropping toward them now, coming out of the west in a rapidly swelling flare. The deep bass pulse of her exhaust was building to thunder.

Vesey licked her lips. "Sir, she's resting," she said. "Her servant's looking after her. She's medicated now but she was walking."

"I see," said Daniel. "Not surprising, I suppose. That she'd have been hit."

He switched his visor to normal viewing. The *Sissie's* blazing plasma would've flooded the whole field of view otherwise, even with his head turned away from it. Blantyre had been coming in a little too fast, so now she had to use full thrust for braking.

"She cleaned out this enclosure," Hogg said, wonder in his voice. He'd gone off and now returned; having talked to Adele's servant, apparently. "*She* did it. Tovera said she just walked in and shot them all."

"How could . . .?" Vesey said, looking from Hogg to Daniel, then to the inside of the berm where Tovera's slight figure squatted beside an equally slight form lying on the ground.

"I never seen Tovera mad before," Hogg said in the same odd tone. "I didn't think her mind worked that way, getting angry or sad or, you know. She blames herself, but she says the mistress just walked straight in and killed them all."

The *Princess Cecile* landed between the *Greybudd* and the missile battery, her thrusters blasting gobbets of fused clay in all directions for the instant before Blantyre shut them down. The island's soil was largely silt from the sea bottom. Organic compounds in it burned, smelling like a fire in an abattoir.

The Volunteers had been warned to keep the area clear for the corvette. If any of them forgot or became confused, well—Sissies had died tonight. Daniel had no sympathy to waste on others, not now.

"Yes, Adele tends to be direct in her approach," Daniel said, so softly that even those nearest probably couldn't hear him over the sound of battle and the pings from the *Sissie's* hull and thrusters cooling. "Well, in three minutes we should be able to get her aboard and into the Medicomp. And then—"

He didn't get angry in a battle, but he heard the anger in his voice now.

"Then we'll see if Sun and our plasma cannon can't convince the wogs here on Mandelfarne Island that it's time to surrender!"

CHAPTER 22

Mandelfarne Island on Dunbar's World

Daniel settled into the *Sissie*'s command console with a sigh of relief. It was like putting on a pair of comfortable slippers after a day of marching in heavy boots. Blantyre had shifted to the navigation console and—

"Good anticipation, Blantyre," Daniel said as he went over a status diagram of the corvette's systems. It was such a reflexive action that he'd have probably run the checklist even if the ship were under immediate attack. "Lighting the thrusters when Woetjans closed the entry hatch."

The praise was reflexive with Daniel also. Both were a part of being an RCN officer and of training midshipmen like Blantyre to be officers also. She'd reasoned on hearing the corvette was being closed up that the whole assault force was aboard. Lighting the thrusters before Daniel reached the bridge might only save thirty seconds, but that could be time the *Sissie* and her crew needed.

Sun threw himself onto the gunnery console. "*Ship, I've got the guns, out!*" he said, breathless from excitement and from having run up the companionway to the bridge. Midshipman Cory in the Battle Direction Center had been manning the guns, but this was the sort of opportunity a gunner dreamed of. Sun had no intention of passing it up.

He'd simply dropped his sub-machine gun onto the deck beside him. *I hope it's on safe*, Daniel thought, but he had more pressing problems.

"Ship, prepare to lift," he said. He'd already balanced the corvette's eight thrusters; even before he spoke, he began easing them forward. The *Princess Cecile* hesitated, wobbled as she broke gravity, then rose slowly. For several seconds she danced like a ball on a water fountain, but when Daniel'd gotten ten feet of height between the thruster nozzles and the ground, the reflected thrust smoothed into a pillow rather than a series of sharp pulses.

Daniel was aware of the dorsal turret rotating—it changed the corvette's weight distribution slightly—but he was so absorbed in the delicacy of his liftoff that the implication didn't get below the mere sensory level. When Sun fired both four-inch guns, the paired shocks twisted the ship into the start of a roll. Reflex made Daniel's fingers twitch toward a correction; intellect snatched them back in time.

"Bloody *hell*, Sun!" he shouted, but the fireball in the eastern sky was the remains of an APC. The forward half of the vehicle'd vanished, but the stern spun end over end into the ground.

Daniel was running a real-time panorama using enhanced visuals across the top of his display. He relegated the *Sissie's* thruster performance to a narrow bar across the bottom—Pasternak'd warn him if there were a problem—and just above it two square terrain maps: to the left, Mandelfarne Island itself, and beside it a larger-scale one including Port Dunbar as well.

Red blinking lights marched down the right margin of the display, urgent communications demanding his response. *Adele's hooked up to the Medicomp, getting microsurgery while blood and antibiotics drip into her.* For the first time Daniel thought of that as a professional loss rather than a personal one.

"Blantyre, take over commo!" he said, gaining altitude as he slanted the corvette over the missile battery. The midshipman probably wasn't the right person for the job, but she'd have to do. The person who *was* right lay on her back in the Medicomp. "Handle it! Don't send anything to me unless I have to see it, over."

They were still low enough when they thundered over the battery that Daniel had an instant's fear that the *Sissie's* exhaust would cook off the missiles' solid fuel. He'd picked the direction so as not to endanger the Volunteers; Corius'd been warned not to advance east of where the *Greybudd* landed until Daniel gave the word. It hadn't struck Daniel as he did the planning that the missiles, even if their guidance was disabled, contained enough explosive to make one *hell* of a bang.

Sun fired again, this time at a gun pit on the east shore of the island. It erupted, leaving a smoking crater and a slowly fading mushroom of plasma trembling upward. Stored ammunition had added to the blast.

"*Sir, where's Officer Mundy?*" Blantyre bleated. "*Over?*"

"*Six, this is Five,*" announced Vesey from the BDC. The red lights vanished. "*I've got the commo, out.*"

Daniel felt the ventral turret, retracted for landing, begin to rumble into firing position. A little more vibration while the thrusters were at high output would've meant nothing to a stranger, but Daniel was part of the *Princess Cecile*.

Sun fired, still using the dorsal turret; another gun pit blew up. At maximum depression the dorsal cannon barely bore on the shoreline positions as the *Sissie* climbed and headed eastward toward the sea.

The gunner'd switched to single shots, quite as effective on these targets as the usual paired rounds. Daniel'd apologize for shouting at him, but that could wait till they were out of this. Sun knew perfectly well that plasma bolts were directed thermonuclear explosions, and he shouldn't've have had to be told that they bloody well affected the handling of a ship skittering in ground effect.

The *Princess Cecile* crossed the coastline at three hundred feet, still accelerating. Daniel expected half a dozen bolts from the Pellegrinian plasma cannon, but only one pit fired. The charge hit aft, making the hull ring and probably ruining a furled sail. Sun replied with both guns in the corvette's belly turret, scooping the enemy weapon out in a gush of steam and quivering ions.

"Blantyre, take the helm," Daniel ordered as he swung the *Sissie* to port, proceeding east to west a half mile out to sea from Mandelfarne Island. "Keep us parallel to the shore, thirty knots and a hundred feet up, got it? Over?"

"*Aye aye, sir,*" Blantyre squeaked. "*I have the conn! Out!*"

She immediately bobbled the attitude control yoke, sending the corvette into a sideways shimmy. Daniel remained poised, his hands spread above his controls. If Blantyre didn't—

But she *did* let the *Sissie* stabilize instead of compounding her mistake by overcorrecting. The surest way to learn is by falling on your face; so long as that's survivable, of course, and this time it had been.

Both turrets were firing, back to single shots now that Sun'd made sure of the gun which'd hit them. Sun and Rosinant—now in command of the ventral guns—raked the shore defenses. The Pellegrinian crews had almost certainly abandoned their positions in the face of the inevitable. So long as the corvette held this height and course, both turrets bore on the enemy positions—but they needed the proper targets.

Daniel expanded the map of the island to half his screen. Before she disembarked on Pellegrino, Adele had marked the base installations, using the signals she gathered the night the aircar probed Mandelfarne Island.

Working from her data, Daniel prodded the display with his index finger to caret targets: Arruns' headquarters, four trailers backed into the shape of a cross and surrounded with a berm like that of the missile battery; the communications center with its array of antennas for both surface and satellite signals; and the tents (with a few semi-permanent shelters) housing base staff and transients. The accommodations were probably empty, but they were the closest thing to home that the garrison had. Blasting them into fiery ruin was bound to hurt the defenders' morale.

"Guns, I'm transmitting a target list," Daniel ordered. He sent the data as he spoke, but he changed it from a terrain map into an overlay on the turrets' targeting displays. "Execute it, then cease fire unless somebody shoots at us. Six out."

The Pellegrinians mostly *weren't* shooting. They couldn't effectively engage the corvette this far out. The 50-mm plasma cannon—if any survived—didn't have the range.

Half a mile through an atmosphere considerably diffused the *Sissie*'s bolts, but that only increased their psychological effect. They hit as broad showers of ions, igniting square yards of their present unprotected targets. Tents became infernos, and the light-metal antennas of the communications center melted or burned.

At every ringing shot, the off-duty Sissies—most of the crew—cheered enthusiastically. Vesey was echoing the targeting displays on every screen in the ship. She'd learned the trick from Adele. *The memory of your friends is a kind of immortality. . . .*

The sandbagged trailers of the HQ got multiple bolts. The *Princess Cecile* was high enough that the berm was no protection.

Woven plastic sandbags vanished in smoky flames; their contents either burned or fused, depending on the ratio of loam to sand in each one. After the third or fourth round, one of the trailers collapsed; after half a dozen more the installation had fallen into mounds of earth with flames licking from within.

A red light flashed on the right of Daniel's display. "*Sir, I think you'd better listen to this,*" Vesey said on the intercom. "*Five out!*"

Daniel, his face suddenly still, opened the transmission by touching the light with his index finger. "*—ender at once!*" snarled a man. His anger and Pellegrinian accent made the words almost unintelligible, but Vesey remembered—*finally! She's doing a great job, but God I miss Adele!*—to run a text crawl across the bottom of Daniel's display: *CAIO DUILIO*.

Sun and Cory had run out of targets, but Daniel didn't have any more to offer them. By this point the Volunteers might be anywhere in the base. Without proper fire direction from the troops engaged, Daniel couldn't risk shooting at further targets that weren't shooting at the *Princess Cecile*.

"Blantyre," Daniel said, verbally keying the direct intercom link. "I'm taking the helm. Break. *Duilio*, this is Commander Daniel Leary, RCN. To whom do I have the honor of speaking, over?"

As he spoke, he flared the thruster nozzles and boosted flow. He carried out the two operations so smoothly that only the Power Room crew would've known what'd happened. Because of inertia, it took longer to increase the flow of reaction mass than it did to iris down the Stellite laminae of the jets. It seemed very likely that the *Princess Cecile* would have to accelerate shortly.

"*Listen you bloody pirate!*" the cruiser transmitted. "*This is Captain Owen ap Glynn! You'll surrender to me now, I mean* now, *or I'll blow you to Hell! Do you surrender, over?*"

"Ship, prepare for maneuvering," Daniel said. "Break. Captain ap Glynn, I'm an officer of the RCN and carrying out the orders of the Cinnabar Senate. I appreciate you—"

"Six, he's launching!" Blantyre said. Vesey had blocked the intercom link, but the midshipman's shout was audible over the thrusters.

Daniel didn't need the warning, but this was definitely a case where Blantyre was right not to take a chance. He slammed the jets tight as he swung the attitude yoke to starboard. Starships really didn't accelerate very quickly, even a warship without her usual load of missiles. Nonetheless the *Sissie* accelerated as quickly as she could.

The *Duilio*'d been holding in a powered orbit above Dunbar's World while waiting for the *Rainha* to unload—as ap Glynn had thought. Now, just as the cruiser moved into the planet's shadow, she'd launched two missiles toward the ground. That was a waste of expensive hardware, Daniel thought, but he wasn't going to chance ap Glynn getting lucky. He was taking the *Princess Cecile* as far out of the possible impact zone as the thrusters could move her.

"Ship, action stations," he ordered, suddenly cheerful and a little surprised to realize it. This wasn't a good situation, but nothing—not even sex—made Daniel feel more alive than needing to function at ten-tenths capacity. "Woetjans, get your people ready to set sail ASAP when I give the order. You may have to work under full acceleration, out."

The riggers'd started pulling themselves into their hard suits as soon as Daniel'd warned that he was about to maneuver. The *Princess Cecile*'s crew was not only veteran, they were razor sharp.

The corvette was low enough that at maximum output and minimum aperture her thruster exhaust dimpled the sea. Columns of steam drifted north on the sea breeze as the *Sissie* roared east at nearly three gravities' acceleration. *Distance is our friend. . . .*

"*Listen, you Cinnabar dogturds!*" ap Glynn continued. So far as Daniel was concerned there was no longer any point in talking, but the Pellegrinian captain obviously had a different opinion. "*If you think you can come here and make a fool out of me, think again! I'm not going back home and have the Chancellor hang me, no bloody way!*"

Daniel didn't know for sure what the *Duilio*'s missiles were aimed at, but it didn't really matter: a ship launching into an atmosphere had only a random statistical chance of hitting any particular target. Not even the planetary surface was a complete certainty.

The missiles screamed out of the eastern sky, tracing dazzling streaks on the optical display. The first of the pair suddenly began to corkscrew in increasing circles.

Missiles were powered by High Drive motors like those which starships used when they were above the atmosphere. They ejected a certain amount of antimatter into the exhaust—and if it was in an atmosphere, the atom-by-atom explosions ate away at first the motor, then the vessel itself.

That was happening to both Pellegrinian missiles. The first was obviously destroying itself but the other's motor was certainly degrading also. Despite that it drove into the sea almost precisely between where the corvette had been and the shore of Mandelfarne.

The first spun in an expanding helix until, three miles above the surface, it broke apart and sprayed down like the heart of a comet. Perhaps half the fragments hit the island. Smoke and a single orange fireball shot skyward. Daniel had no better idea of who or what they'd hit than Captain ap Glynn could.

Ap Glynn didn't care. Ap Glynn was so angry and frightened—Daniel was sure he'd been right to fear hanging if he returned to Pellegrino—that he'd committed an act of war against direct orders. Chancellor Arruns might be very angry that his invasion of Dunbar's World had failed, very possibly with the death of his son, but he certainly knew that declaring war on Cinnabar meant his reign on Pellegrino was finished also.

"*Land your bloody ship, Leary!*" ap Glynn said. "*You surrender and you tell the other dog-turds from Bennaria to surrender, and then the bloody dogturd farmers on Dunbar's World can surrender also! All of you give up, or I won't leave one stone on another in Port Dunbar. And I'll land on Mandelfarne and blast it till it bloody glows, I will!*"

There was movement in the compartment. Daniel's whole attention was focused on the Plot-Position Indicator with which he'd replaced the terrain maps, but from the corner of his eye he saw Sun's head jerk to the right. Somebody'd sat down at the Signals console; at Adele's console.

"*Cinnabar Six, this is Rainbow One,*" said a voice. Daniel knew it was Adele's only because it *had* to be Adele's; she quavered like an octogenarian speaking around an oxygen tube. "*We have the captured battery operational again. Do not, I repeat do not, attempt to approach within thirty kilometers of Mandelfarne Island. The targeting and launch are automatic. Acknowledge, please. Rainbow One over.*"

"Rainbow One, this is Cinnabar Six," Daniel said. He set the astrogational computer to plotting a course to orbit, taking into account the position of the *Duilio. This is going to be very tricky....* "Acknowledged. Be very careful, because the wogs had Alliance advisors. They dispersed two missiles to the west end of the island to avoid commando strikes. Six out."

So much for the risk of ap Glynn bringing the cruiser down on Mandelfarne and blasting the Volunteers out with 15-cm guns. Adele had thought fast and then done the impossible.

The computer assembled five alternative courses in red, orange, yellow, green, and blue. The Pellegrinian cruiser was a bead on a white oval; a predicted course only, and one that would probably change when the *Princess Cecile* began to climb out of the gravity well.

Daniel chose Option Red and pressed Execute. "Ship, this is Six," he said. "We're rising to orbit but the maneuvers are likely to be severe. *Don't* leave your stations, out. Break, Signals, how the hell did you do that, over?"

He'd chosen Red because it involved full thrust. He wouldn't normally have lifted at such high acceleration, but the *Sissie* couldn't afford not to react instantly if the *Duilio* launched more missiles.

A starship isn't streamlined. The *Sissie's* increasing speed through the atmosphere made her shudder fiercely. A *bang!* and fluttering followed by a series of crackles from the hull meant a furled sail had carried away and been shredded in the airstream. They'd be lucky if they didn't lose at least one antenna before they got out of the thicker layers of air.

The riggers waiting to go onto the hull gripped the railing around the foyer; they didn't have seats and restraint webs to keep them from flying around. The rigging suits, heavy at the best of times, must be crushing now. For Daniel, simply moving his fingers on the virtual keyboard was a strain.

"*Six*," said Adele and paused. Daniel inset a tiny image of her face at the top of the PPI display which now filled his display. She looked as worn as the blade of an old kitchen knife; her eyes closed briefly. "*I sent the message to the* Rainha *on tight-beam microwave; it doesn't have laser. And retransmitted on short wave as though it were originating there. I don't think the* Duilio's *direction finding apparatus is good enough to be sure it isn't coming from the missile control trailer. Over.*"

"Out," Daniel said. There was a great deal more he'd have liked to say, but this wasn't the time for it . . . and anyway, there was no need. The way she'd come out of the Medicomp when violent acceleration warned her that something was going on showed she understood how much he and the *Princess Cecile* depended on her.

"*Cruiser launching,*" Blantyre announced. Her voice came over the intercom; Adele was handling commo again, taking a less Draconian approach than Vesey had done. "*Two missi—no, four missiles, over.*"

Again Daniel didn't need the warning, but he was pleased to see that Blantyre was keeping an eye out. He adjusted his yoke a point to port but didn't change the rate of climb. The corvette was rising through ten thousand feet, still low enough that missiles from the *Duilio* would pass through too much atmosphere to hit a moving target.

He'd plotted the *Sissie's* course at 90 degrees to the cruiser's. They'd still intersect in plane, though at considerable differences in altitude. The high deflection made the job of the *Duilio's* missileer more difficult and gave Daniel more options to evade.

In the event, this salvo too plunged down at Mandelfarne Island. By accident or design one hit the *Greybudd*. There was a bright red flash, then an iridescent flare of the fusion bottle ruptured.

The other missiles cratered the island, though Daniel couldn't tell the extent of the damage without going to more effort than he had time or reason to expend. Ap Glynn must be in an insane rage to ignore the thousand or so Pellegrinian troops in the impact zone, either as prisoners or still resisting.

"*Captain, Councilor Corius is contacting the* Duilio *through a satellite link,*" Adele said. "*I'm cutting you into the conversation.*" Noticeably later, "*Out!*"

"*—isten you Bennarian dogturd!*" ap Glynn said. His vocabulary seemed limited, though his stress was some excuse. "*There's a state of war, all right, between you and me, screw Bennaria! You're not on Bennaria, you're here, and you're going to surrender or starve, do you get me? No ship lands on Dunbar's World, anywhere on Dunbar's World, until you surrender and Port Dunbar surrenders. Screw the rest of this bloody planet, but you and the port turn yourself over to Field Marshal Arruns. Over.*"

"Power Room, prepare to switch to High Drive in one minute, out," Daniel warned. That'd be cutting it close; he'd probably wait eighty seconds so that erosion of the motors wouldn't require their replacement before a voyage of any length.

He was wearing the thrusters badly as it was, and the *Sissie's* reaction mass tanks were edging toward fifty percent capacity. There hadn't been time to refill them after the corvette's hop from

Ollarville, and the plasma drive was inefficient compared with antimatter conversion.

"*Captain ap Glynn,*" said Corius' voice. It was definitely the Councilor speaking, not Colonel Quinn. "*You have no authority to blockade a free and independent world. This is piracy, and you'll be hanged by your own government if you attempt it.*"

"Ship, lighting the High Drive," Daniel said, executing with the words. For a moment the sharper, smoother note of the antimatter annihilation increased the acceleration, but Daniel shut down his thrusters as soon as he was sure the High Drive was running properly. He'd have liked to hold the higher rate, but he simply didn't have the reaction mass to dare.

"*Cruiser launching,*" Blantyre announced. "*One missile only. Out.*"

Though the *Princess Cecile* had reached the troposphere by now, occasional pings indicated damage from air molecules. They weren't frequent enough to make Daniel regret his judgment.

He echoed the gunnery screen. Sun had resumed control of both turrets, slewing them to follow the Pellegrinian cruiser. Missiles followed a ballistic course after they'd burned their reaction mass in achieving the fraction of light speed that made them so devastating on impact. Their tracks were as predictable as those of their targets.

A ship which found itself on an intersecting course with a missile could fight its own inertia by trying to accelerate or decelerate out of the target zone, and it could attempt to deflect the missile. Plasma bolts blasted away the missile's own structure as reaction mass and skewed its direction. At the present short range, Sun's little four-inch weapons weren't going to do much good, but he intended to die trying.

Daniel grinned. That was a spacer's joke

The missile streaked downward rather than toward the *Princess Cecile.* Ap Glynn hadn't replied verbally, but he'd sent a missile into the center of Port Dunbar to show what he thought of Councilor Corius' statement.

The *Princess Cecile* was out of the gravity well and heading away. At no point would their course be precisely in line with that of the orbiting cruiser—there was no reason to tempt fate—but apart from that consideration, Daniel only wanted to put distance between them and Dunbar's World as quickly as he could.

"*Captain,*" said Adele, "*Field Marshal Arruns has ordered the* Duilio *to remain above Dunbar's World and carry out a complete blockade, as Captain ap Glynn proposed. They do not intend to pursue us.*" A pause. "*Over.*"

"Adele, they'd left their antennas up and sails spread while they were in orbit," Daniel said, a friend speaking to a friend instead of captain to signals officer. "They can't match our acceleration—they'd tear their rigging off if they did. Once we got out of the atmosphere with the planet between us and them for the next ten minutes, we were free."

He stretched his arms, first overhead and then out to his sides. He chuckled.

"Ship, this is Six," he said, his voice echoing itself from the public address speakers in each compartment. "We can't fight a cruiser, even a sorry-ass Pellegrinian cruiser, without missiles, so we're returning to Bennaria to get some. And then, my fellow Sissies, we're coming back. Six out!"

En Route to Bennaria

Adele opened her eyes. She'd returned to the Medicomp when the *Princess Cecile* entered the Matrix, but she had *no* idea how long ago that'd been.

"You've been out for seven hours," Daniel said as she looked around. "We're about to extract into sidereal space, and I thought I'd see how you're feeling."

As a general matter the Medicomp, the ship's medical facility—doctor and surgeon in one electronic package—was a B Level compartment the size of a narrow closet. It handled one patient at a time from anything from sunburn to stroke. Now it'd been rotated—as it was designed to be—to face onto the corridor. Arms extended from it to the four cots end to end along the bulkhead. Warships weren't built on a spacious scale, so there was barely enough room to get by.

Adele's cot was the farthest aft. Vesey, Cory, Pasternak, Woetjans and Daniel stood beside it. The bosun wore her rigging suit, obviously ready to return to the hull as soon as this command meeting concluded. They all looked worried to a greater or lesser degree; it took Adele a moment to realize they were worried about *her*.

"I feel detached," she said with a deadpan expression. "Completely normal, in other words."

She quirked what for her was a smile and—because they were friends as well as colleagues—added, "Possibly a little more detached than usual, but I'm functional."

Adele sat up and rotated her legs off the cot. The Medicomp retracted its arm, leaving a faint tingle where it'd rested on her throat.

She squeezed her left hand into a fist and opened it again. "I think for the next while I'll continue shooting with my right hand," she said. "That works well enough."

"So I heard," Daniel said. His tone and the glance he flashed toward Tovera, standing politely at the foot of the cot, made Adele wonder exactly what he *had* heard. She remembered only shards of the action: the way a slug sounded as it ricocheted from a rock . . . the flash of her pellet hitting an impeller's receiver when the soldier holding it spasmed from her previous shot . . . the swelling face of the missile tech. She'd see that last face every night till she died.

"Ah," Daniel continued. "I don't think there's any more chance the Council will give us missiles now than they would to begin with. I plan to, ah, remove the missiles we need from Bennarian control to accomplish the mission I've been assigned."

"Daniel, do you think that being shot has made me stupid?" Adele said, perhaps a little more sharply that she would've done if she hadn't so recently been on drips containing God-knew-what-all drugs. "We're going to steal missiles from the Bennarian navy. I'm going to assist you in whatever fashion is required."

She paused as she looked at him. "Do you want me to kill everyone in the Fleet Pool?" she added. "I'm getting quite good at that sort of thing."

As the words formed on Adele's lips, the analytical part of her mind knew that she was speaking out of disgust for what she'd done at the missile battery and out of anger at Daniel for being the cause of it. The anger was unjustified and perhaps the disgust was also, but she'd let them spill from her anyway. It must be the drugs. . . .

"Oh, I don't think that's the way we'll want to proceed, Mundy," Daniel said with an easy smile. "With the trouble in Charlestown, I suspect most of the squadron personnel have brought their familes into the base for safety. They'll be on high alert. What I'm hoping you can counterfeit some authority that directs them to help us."

Only the tightness around Daniel's eyes showed that he understood what'd been going on in Adele's mind—and was politely concealing it from the others, because they'd be shocked and dismayed to learn that Officer Mundy paid a cost for the people she killed. The rest thought, if they thought about it at all, that she must enjoy something she was so good at. . . .

"And it's not precisely a matter of stealing missiles," Daniel continued, his smile spreading and softening with real humor. "I don't think we dare land directly in the Squadron Pool, and we don't have time to off-load the *Sibyl*'s missiles, lighter them down the river, and then take them aboard the *Sissie* in Charlestown Harbor."

Adele touched her thigh pocket. Her personal data unit was there. She brought it out, giving herself time to think as the familiar surfaces soothed her.

"Sir, I don't see what the alternative is," Vesey said. She'd waited for Adele to speak, but Adele was holding her tongue. "Are there missiles stored somewhere else on the planet than at their naval base?"

"I propose to borrow the *Sibyl* herself," Daniel said, grateful for the opportunity that Adele's silence had denied him. "Fly her to a quiet place—we might even use Corius' estate, don't you think? And transfer the missiles to the *Princess Cecile* there. I've been on the *Sibyl*'s bridge and checked her readiness. I'm sure we can lift off within a few minutes of boarding her, so long as we're allowed to. What we *can't* do—"

He nodded to Adele.

"—is fight our way aboard and expect to be able to get clear. Squadron Pool has point defense batteries that could certainly bring us down."

Adele nodded as she brought up files on her personal unit. Her face was expressionless, but she was angry with herself for having refused to set up Daniel's chance to crow at his cleverness. He *was* very clever, and his wish to shine was understandable and proper in an enthusiastic young man.

"I'll bet none of 'em at the base have the balls to blast their own destroyer outa the sky, sir," Woetjans growled. "Even if we've taken it away from 'em."

"I rather suspect you're right, Woetjans," Daniel said coolly. "But I'm not going to take the chance with our lives and the operation."

"Sorry, sir," Woetjans muttered. She ground her toe against the deck, staring at it.

"Daniel?" Adele said, lost in the universe of her holographic display. The others were presences hovering around her. "Why are you planning to transfer the missiles? Wouldn't it be easier to . . . that is, you're familiar with the *Princess Cecile*, we all are, but it would be much quicker to return to Dunbar's World with the *Sibyl*, wouldn't it?"

"Ah . . .," said Daniel. The words blurred in her head and his figure faded to gray monochrome through the quiver of her display. "We don't have the crew to handle a destroyer in combat, Adele. We can lift and land her, and we could sail her back to Cinnabar. But not fight."

Pasternak was muttering about the chance that the *Sibyl*'s thrusters would be *buggered, buggered for good'n all*; Cory was asking Daniel . . . or Vesey? or perhaps just talking? about action stations on a destroyer.

Adele stared at crew lists, laying them out in her mind; matching, noting gaps and duplications. The complement of the *Princess Cecile*, the table of organization for an Alliance destroyer of the Moewe class like the *Sibyl*, and the—

"Daniel?"

She shouldn't be addressing him as Daniel, but she couldn't remember his rank through the buzzing sharpness at the edges of her mind. She was concentrating on the one thought that mattered.

"Landholder Krychek has one hundred and eighty-one Infantans, his retainers," she said aloud. She wasn't sure if the others were speaking or not. She heard voices, but she thought they might be echoes of her own words. "And himself. They're soldiers and experienced spacers both. Couldn't they help you man the *Sibyl*?"

"Good God, Adele," Daniel said. "Would they?"

"Will you let me negotiate with the Landholder?" Adele said, gripping present reality with her whole consciousness. A layer of white fire was rising under her skin and the buzzing was closing in. "Will you back any deal that I make?"

"Yes," said Daniel. "On my honor as a Leary."

"Then arrange with Master Luff to transport the Infantans to where you want them," Adele said. "I'll get Landholder Krychek's agreement—on my honor as a Mundy."

She felt laughter rising to her lips and bubbling over them. She almost never laughed.

"Or die trying," Adele said, and felt Tovera's cool hand on hers, sliding the little data unit into its pocket as the cot rose up and met her.

CHAPTER 23

Charlestown on Bennaria

Daniel, wearing utilities like the rest of the detachment and cradling a stocked impeller, stood on the tractor's right fender with his buttocks braced on the roll cage. Sun with a sub-machine gun was on the left side.

"*'She was poor but she was honest!'*" bellowed Hogg from the driver's seat. He had a good bass voice, though roughened by the carloads of doubtful liquor he'd put down over the years.

"*'Victim of a rich man's whim!'*" the Sissies on the flatbed sang, a few at first but all twenty by the end of the verse. On the way from the harbor on their commandeered vehicle, Hogg had started off "The Bastard King of Georgia," "Seven Old Maids" and "A Gentleman of Leisure." Woetjans had alternated with him to lead the detachment in a series of chanteys.

Locals stared in amazement from buildings, around corners, or out of door alcoves. Daniel hadn't noticed any group of more than three—a woman holding two young children by the hand as she sprinted down an alley—but evidence of large mobs was everywhere. Ground-floor windows were either shuttered or smashed, bullets had pocked building fronts, and on the two-mile route to Manco House the Sissies had passed at least a score of wrecked vehicles.

"*First he fucked her,*" the Sissies sang, "*then he left her!*"

Each verse ended in a full stop. This wasn't—Daniel smiled—a trained chorus, but the singers' enthusiasm drowned out the jangle of track pins and cleats on the pavement. They were chewing up the street, no mistake, by driving cargo-shifing apparatus at top speed through the middle of the city.

Two men, each carrying a length of pipe and a bottle, stood on the steps leading into an apartment block. Sissies waved and called cheerfully. They were in good humor, but everybody in the detachment had an impeller or a sub-machine gun. The locals backed up the stairs, not running exactly but not wanting to have that many gunmen watching them either.

Manco House came in sight to the left, a brown stone column. "Here," Daniel said, then realized Hogg might not be able to hear him. He banged on the woven wire side of the driver's cage, then pointed to the tall structure. Hogg nodded.

Manco House didn't have windows on the ground floor, only a steel door wide enough to pass a large truck; the second-floor windows were narrow slots. One of the latter and two of the larger—barred—windows on the third floor had been broken out, but it didn't look like there'd been a serious attack. No reason there should've been, of course; but then, mobs don't need much reason.

"Shall I take us in, master?" Hogg shouted as they jangled toward the vehicular entrance.

"No, just turn around and I'll go in through the wicket," Daniel said. The pedestrian door, also steel, was in a separate alcove instead of being inset in the larger valves. "I don't expect to be long."

Hogg pulled the tractor and lowboy in a sweeping curve, then shut down the big ceramic diesel. As Daniel hopped down, Hogg slid out of the cage and faced the Sissies on the trailer.

"Me and the master's going in!" Hogg said. Daniel pressed the call plate, a flush crystal disk in the wall. "You can keep the wogs from stealing the truck while we're gone, I guess."

"I'm coming!" said Woetjans, and pretty much all the others shouted the same thing. It sounded rather like a frog pond after an evening rain.

"None of you are coming!" Daniel said. Holding his impeller at the balance, Daniel tossed it to Hogg with a straight-armed motion. "I don't need you tramping around while I talk to my colleague."

"You hope you don't, you mean," Hogg muttered, but he wasn't seriously objecting.

Daniel grinned as he turned again to the door, still shut. They might even have agreed with him, but they understood from his tone that there wasn't going to be more discussion.

"Yes?" said the plate in a clipped, sexless voice. "Who's there?"

"Open up, Luff," Daniel said, his anger suddenly rising. "You don't have to worry about a mob breaking in if you open the door while my crew's down here, but you bloody well *do* have to worry if you don't open it!"

It was probably only a few seconds before the latch clicked and the door swung inward, but it was a little longer than Daniel was happy with. He grinned and shook his head as he stepped through. He supposed he was feeling the strain himself; he ought to be used to this sort of thing.

Luff stood in the entrance corridor. He wore a long beige robe with soft slippers, and his hair was disordered.

"I don't have a soul left here!" he blurted as he turned to the lift shaft. "Not one! My employees all left me to whatever the mob decides to do. And none of the Councilors will talk to me either!"

"I don't think there's much danger at present," Daniel said as the lift rose. Luff seemed to be taking him up to his sixth-floor office, probably the best choice from Daniel's viewpoint. That's where the communications gear would be. "Though if you'd like, we can carry you back with us to the *Princess Cecile.*"

Which'd be a great deal less safe than anything likely to happen in Charlestown, but it wasn't the time to say that.

"I can't do that!" the agent snapped. "There's critical trading information here, matters of the greatest import! If I should abandon my post, why, I'd be ruined!"

If you really think the locals are going to lynch you from a lamppost, thought Daniel, *then I'd say there were other jobs than being a flunky in Ganpat's Reach.*

The lift stopped. Luff bowed him forward, then pursed his lips in sudden irritation. He'd treated his guest with the courtesy due a superior, then remembered that Daniel was an officer in the RCN rather than a Bennarian Councilor.

Concealing his flash of anger, Daniel said, "As I say, things have quieted down a good deal." Shrugging he added, "And this is quite a strong building, a fortress. If you've got a few gas bombs or—"

"Oh, nothing like that," Luff said, a sneer in his voice. They entered his office. He'd drawn the drapes, and the only light was from a small fixture on the desk. "I'm a gentleman, you know."

"Ah," said Daniel, nodding sagely. There were various ways to take the agent's comment, but he found viewing it as humor the best and most natural response for him. Daniel very much doubted that his father'd killed anyone personally, but he was quite sure that in similar circumstances Corder Leary would've been standing in the doorway with a gun and the complete determination to use it on the first prole who came at him.

The agent sat at his desk and hunched forward. "They'll be back as soon as it gets dark," he muttered into his hands. "They burned Layard House the first night, you know? He'd taken all his guards out of the city with him. They attacked Waddell House first, but Waddell left most of his guards here and they drove the mob off with gunfire."

Luff shivered. "I can't shoot. I'm alone and I can't do anything," he whispered.

"On the contrary, Master Luff," Daniel said heartily, "you're in a position to aid Cinnabar greatly. I need the use of one of the barges belonging to Manco Trading to transport cargo upriver."

"What?" said Luff, raising his head. "Give you a barge for personal use? And at a time like this! Why, I moved them north of the city for safety sake, you know."

Instead of responding immediately, Daniel stepped to the outside wall; Luff twisted to watch him. In place of curtains, a polarizing screen darkened the window. He threw the switch in the corner to turn the wall into a single clear panel looking out over Charlestown. A haze of smoke hung over a complex of buildings to the northwest, perhaps Layard House.

Daniel walked back to face the Manco agent across the desk; he remained standing. "Master Luff," he said, crossing his hands behind his back, "I'm not asking you to do anything for me personally. I need the use of the barge to carry out an RCN mission."

"To help Corius, you mean!" Luff said like a dog snapping in fear.

"To prevent Port Dunbar from becoming an Alliance base, sir!" said Daniel, not shouting but certainly intending to be heard. "Because the Alliance personnel attached to the Pellegrinian forces have already started preparations for that. The Manco family may not be enthusiastic about Councilor Corius gaining greater influence on Bennaria, but I'm quite sure that they'll be even less happy about an Alliance squadron across their trade routes."

"What?" Luff said. He jerked against the back of his chair, not straightening so much as putting another few inches between himself and Daniel. "That can't be true! The war's purely a matter between Pellegrino and Dunbar's World."

"It most certainly is true," said Daniel. "We've captured Alliance personnel and stored data which lay out the Alliance plan in great detail."

That was technically correct, but the information had to be pieced together from bits and pieces; even then it required a great deal of interpretation. The conclusion required absolute confidence in the analysis Adele had done while the *Rainha* was en route to Dunbar's World. Daniel—all the Sissies—had that confidence, and so presumably did Adele's other employer. People who didn't know her well might question it, however.

"Oh my God," Luff said. All the bluster'd gone out of him, but he continued to stare at Daniel instead of lowering his head again. His mouth dropped slightly open and his lower lip trembled. "Oh God."

"I'm not here to threaten that you'll be executed for treason, Luff," Daniel said, deliberately softening his tone. "You'll have no problem with your employers or with the Senate, so long as you act in line with your duties as a Cinnabar citizen."

This whole business was a calculated performance, the sort of thing he'd seen his father do many times. Daniel hadn't understood the nuances when he watched it, but the knowledge was there nonetheless for when Corder Leary's son needed to bully someone into action without raising a hand.

"I'm quite confident we can thwart the Alliance designs," Daniel continued. "So confident that I'm staking my life and my ship on it. But I need you to order a barge to the *Princess Cecile* in Charlestown Harbor ASAP."

"You realize I'm ruined, ruined or dead, if I do that, don't you?" Luff said bitterly. "Whatever you or Senator Manco do to me, Waddell will see to that!"

Daniel pursed his lips. "Come here, Luff," he said, walking around the desk again. He gestured. "Come here to the window, man."

He stretched out his hand, thinking for a moment that he'd have to grab the fellow by the shoulder and lift him. Luff rose of his own accord before they touched, though with a grudging expression.

"What is it then, Commander?" Luff said. He sounded tired and disgusted, nothing more. "Is it my salvation, do you think?"

"No sir, the reverse," Daniel said. "Look out there. Do you see Councilor Waddell? Do you see any sign of the power you believe he has?"

"He'll be back!" Luff said.

"Will he?" Daniel demanded. "And even if he is, Luff, he's a fat foreigner and you're a Cinnabar gentleman! What do you care what Waddell thinks? He didn't have the balls to stay in his own city with a fortress to live in and three hundred men to defend him! He went scuttling off!"

"If Corius wins, that won't help either," Luff said. It was a statement, not a protest. "I've had it regardless."

"Buck up, man," Daniel said, hearty again. He put his arm around the Manco agent's shoulders. "The RCN is going to put a spoke in the Alliance's wheel, and when we've done that it won't matter who's in power in Charlestown. Whoever it is'll have a healthy respect for Cinnabar citizens, because they know the RCN'll hand 'em their heads if they don't."

He patted Luff on the back and stepped away. "I'd say it was your best choice, my good fellow," Daniel said with a broad grin. "But the truth is, it's the only choice you have that won't result in you being condemned as a traitor. What do you say?"

Luff shuddered. He closed his eyes, then turned away and wiped them fiercely with the back of his right hand.

"What do you want, then?" he whispered. He seated himself back at his desk, already reaching for the integral phone pad. "A barge? All right."

"Just that," Daniel agreed. His face remained impassive, but in fact what he'd just done made him queasy. It'd been necessary; but it made him aware that many of the things he despised his father for might've been necessary also.

"Dorlitus, I need you to bring *A79* back to the harbor," Luff said, his face intent. Daniel had heard the voice on the other end of the line only as a narrow crackle; the agent was using an in-ear plug. "It'll take you less than an hour, won't it?"

The air crackled again.

"No, I don't think it *is* too dangerous," Luff said, sounding brusque and professional. "I think it will be tonight, though. That's why I want to get the contents of the strong room in Warehouse 12 aboard the freighter *Pomponio* immediately. There's three million florins in jewels and furs, all of it easily disposed of if the rioters get their hands on it. We can't take the chance."

Crackle.

"All right, I'll expect you inside the hour at the company pier," Luff said. "Till then."

He thumbed off the phone switch and glared at Daniel. "There," he said harshly. "Are you happy? Just take your gang to Manco Pier and wait for the barge to arrive."

"What did you mean about the strong room?" Daniel said in puzzlement. "We might be able to carry some cargo, but—"

"There's no cargo!" Luff said. "There's nothing, just you and your men waiting on the pier. Dorlitus wouldn't have returned to the harbor simply because I told him to; but he'll come to steal three million florins in goods. Which will be blamed on the mob, of course. And besides, what does he care?"

Luff shrugged. "You'll have to persuade him to do what you say when you get aboard," he added. "I assume you can manage that, can't you? You've assured me how resourceful the RCN is, after all."

"We can persuade him, yes," Daniel agreed quietly. "Thank you, Master Luff."

"Oh, don't thank me," Luff said. He gave a brittle laugh. "I have it on good authority that it's no more than my duty as a Cinnabar citizen. Now you'd better get out of here, Commander. You have work to do, I'm sure."

Daniel opened the office door but paused. "Luff," he said. "Come with us. I won't tell you it's going to be safe, but you'll be with friends."

"Thank you, Commander," Luff said with surprising dignity. "But I believe I'll stay here. It's my post of duty, after all . . . and I'm not a Bennarian to abandon it."

Daniel waited for a further moment, then threw the Manco agent a salute before striding for the lift. It wasn't according to protocol: the fellow was a civilian and therefore not authorized to receive the salute of an RCN officer.

But it felt right anyway.

Hogg's water taxi had remained at the *Mazeppa*. The Infantan who'd just ferried Adele and Tovera between ships knocked on the library door and said, "Lady Mundy to see you, lord."

"Send her in, Pyotr!" the Landholder called. "My dear Mundy, a great pleasure to see you again."

The servant opened the door and stepped back. Adele made a tiny gesture with her left index finger. Having her bodyguard present would set the wrong tone for the interview with the Landholder.

Even so slight a motion had sent a dull ache all the way up to Adele's left shoulder. The Medicomp had repaired the physical damage; even the bruising was nearly gone. Some nerve pathways had been rerouted, though, and for the moment they were registering neutral inputs as pain.

That would pass in time, the Medicomp had assured Adele. All it meant for now was that the pistol had moved from her left to her right tunic pocket.

Tovera shrugged; Adele started down into library. Before the door closed behind her, she heard Tovera say, "Is there a place a girl could get a drink around here, spacer?"

While still aboard the *Princess Cecile* Adele'd seen Tovera take a Drytab which would metabolize alcohol in her stomach. She didn't know whether her servant ever drank for pleasure, but she was very definitely at work now.

Landholder Krychek waited at the bottom of the stairs. To Adele's surprise, he had a striking blond woman on his arm. Both beamed at her.

Adele almost missed the last step. "Master Elemere?" she said.

"Just Elemere, milady," the blonde said, dipping in a graceful curtsey. Her—well, his—dress was gold with shimmers of green and purple as the light changed. "You and Commander Leary gave me not only life but a reason to keep on living."

"Here, sit," said Krychek, ushering Adele to the chair where she'd sat before. "I set out the Vaclos. You liked the vintage, I believe?"

Adele remained standing. She nodded to Elemere to make it clear she wasn't snubbing him, but she returned her eyes to Krychek. "This isn't a social call, I'm afraid, Landholder," she said. "I'm here to negotiate with you. And with . . . Elemere, that is, as a matter of fact."

"So, we negotiate," Krychek said calmly, offering her the long-stemmed glass he'd just filled with wine. "But we negotiate as friends, do we not? And we can sit as we negotiate, surely?"

Adele seated herself, feeling uncomfortable. She smiled—mentally, at least, because she didn't feel the humor touch her lips—at herself. She knew that this business would involve some stressful passages. She'd have preferred that the Infantan treat her with professional courtesy rather than the kindness of a friend, given that they might not be friends at the end of it.

Krychek sat opposite her with a glass of brandy. He raised an eyebrow. Elemere remained standing, his fingertips resting on the Landholder's shoulder.

Setting her wine untasted on the adjacent table, Adele said, "Master Leary intends to steal a Bennarian destroyer and with it drive a Pellegrinian cruiser off Dunbar's World."

Krychek laughed, though the sound was initially muffled because he'd clamped his lips over a swallow of brandy. "Ho!" he said when he got the liquor down. "He doesn't half have dreams does he? I'd say you meant steal a cruiser to fight a destroyer, but the Bennarians don't have any cruisers."

"Is that possible?" said Elemere, frowning. "It doesn't sound possible."

"Well, dear one," the Landholder said as he patted the hand on his shoulder, "let's say that it's an ambitious aim, even for the redoubtable Commander Leary."

His face sobered as he returned his gaze to Adele. "I do not mean that in mockery, Lady Mundy," he said. "I have the highest regard for your captain's abilities. What you outline is, however, a daunting task indeed."

"Daniel is well aware of that," Adele said, using the given name deliberately. "Nevertheless, his mission requires it, so there's no choice."

She touched her thigh pocket but left the data unit where it was. She'd have liked to have the wands between her fingers, but that too would send the wrong signal.

"He wishes to hire you and your retainers, Landholder," she went on. "To have any chance at all. It will, of course, be very dangerous. Your reward, if we succeed, will be in keeping with the risk."

Krychek had been raising his glass for another drink. He paused and put it down very carefully on the table.

"Mundy...," he said, and paused to clear his throat. "Lady Mundy, I regret, I very much regret to refuse you. Yet I must."

"But Miroslav, it's the commander who—" Elemere said.

"Not now, dear one!" said Krychek. "This is men's business!"

He stood up, desperate to move rather than gaining a height advantage over Adele. Understanding that, she remained seated. It struck her—without either amusement or anger—that the Landholder was implicitly classing her as a man and Elemere as a woman. Though if it was worth distinguishing by gender—this *did* almost cause her to smile—that was probably an accurate assessment.

"I suggested this course to Master Leary," she continued, "because I recalled you saying you wished to enter service with Headman Ferguson. It's my hope that you'll be willing to follow a better man in a better cause."

"Lady Mundy!" Krychek said, forcefully enough to sound threatening to someone easier to threaten than Adele. Besides, she didn't think that was his intent. "I owe you and I owe Commander Leary a debt of honor, a very great debt. But I am a man of honor, milady! I am Landholder of Infanta and cannot join the Cinnabar navy, whatever I think of the worm Porra who rules from Pleasaunce today. I am not a traitor!"

"If you were not a man of honor, milord," Adele said, "Master Leary wouldn't have made this offer. We depend on it, because only a man of honor can recognize honor in another."

For effect she took her glass from the table and sipped the wine. She found it easy to keep her voice calm and her words clipped; indeed, it was hard to do anything else.

"Of course you wouldn't serve the RCN, Landholder," Adele said. "But will you serve a Leary of Bantry?"

"What?" said Krychek, startled out of his anger. "What? But that's the same thing, surely? Leary of Bantry *is* Commander Leary."

"Not in this instance," Adele said firmly. "The *Princess Cecile* is a private yacht, her crew are spacers hired by Bergen and Associates—a firm owned by the Learys privately. And the *Sibyl*, when we've stolen her, will certainly not be an RCN ship."

Krychek's brow furrowed. From his expression he might be furious, but Adele suspected he was thinking about what she'd just said.

"You may be a pirate, of course," she added, "subject to hanging if captured by any civilized power. But you won't be an RCN officer."

Krychek guffawed and turned to the tantalus. He lifted the decanter and drank from it.

"The Pellegrinians call me a pirate already," he said, lowering the square crystal bottle, "and who knows? It may be that they are right. Faugh, I spit on them!"

He did spit, a long, accurate pitch into the presumably false fireplace across the compartment.

"But even if I were willing, how would this happen?" he said. He looked at the decanter, scowled, and set it back on the secretary. "My ship cannot lift, even to orbit, until the thrusters are replaced. That will take time, and there's no chance of the work being started until the riots subside."

"I'm afraid the *Mazeppa* will have to be abandoned," Adele said. "As you note, it can't be moved in its present condition. Perhaps it'll be possible to salvage it later, but that can't be expected."

She shrugged. "Of course if you die, as seems likely," she said, "that won't matter anyway."

The Landholder looked at her in delighted amazement, then burst out laughing again. "Oh!" he said. "So Leary thinks I'm one of those death or glory boys he can trick into following him by saying how dangerous it is, yes?"

"Yes, that's correct," Adele said, sipping more wine. She looked over the top of her glass. "You are, of course. And so is Master Leary, as I'm sure you realized since you've looked into his record."

Krychek began laughing so hard that he had to bend over. The decanter in his right hand tapped the floor twice; Elemere bent gracefully and swept it away from him before it shattered.

"Ho, you're clever devils, you Cinnabars!" the Landholder said when he'd gotten his breath. "Crooked as corkscrews, every one of you. So crooked you're straight! So!"

He hugged Elemere, then seated himself and eyed Adele. "The *Mazeppa* is a clapped-out old whore, no loss," he said, shrugging. "My collection of tobacco pipes, *that* I will regret. Still, I have lost much in the past and at my present age I must look to the future. Your Daniel Leary will make us whole, you say?"

"Daniel will do very much better than that," Adele said. "If he survives, of course."

"Of course," said Krychek. "Of course. . . ."

Then in a thoughtful tone he repeated, "So. We accept. What are we new Leary retainers to do, milady?"

"A few of you will join the crew of the *Princess Cecile*," Adele said. She put down her glass empty. "Most of you'll be taken to the Squadron Pool, by barge because there's no proper ground transportation system here."

"You have numbers?" Krychek said, becoming businesslike. "How many the corvette, how many to Squadron Pool, I mean?"

"I don't, no," Adele said. Elemere'd filled her glass. She'd almost waved him off, but her mouth was still dry and she found the wine pleasantly astringent. "You'll have to discuss that with Daniel when he returns from arranging the transportation."

"And the Bennarians will give us a destroyer?" Krychek said, raising an eyebrow. "Or we will have to fight our way in, which? Either is acceptable."

Adele's lips suddenly felt parched. Nonetheless she set down the glass and crossed her hands in her lap as she met the Landholder's eyes squarely.

"That brings me to my other request," she said. "Daniel has determined that it wouldn't be practical to fight our way into the base—not if we intend to fly out in a destroyer, that is. Entry will require very specific authorization by Councilor Waddell, and to gain that I need the help of Elemere."

She looked up at the entertainer. "I want you to visit Waddell's estate in company with me and my servant Tovera," she went on. "The business will be *extremely* dangerous, but while it entails risk I can assure you that there will be no dishonor."

She smiled coldly. *Almost the only way I do smile, I suppose*, she thought. Aloud she said, "On my honor as a Mundy."

Elemere stood transfixed. Krychek looked up at him and said, "I don't think—"

Elemere silenced the Landholder with a curt gesture; his eyes were locked with Adele's. "You say there will be no dishonor," Elemere said. "How will you ensure that?"

"If things go wrong," Adele said calmly, "Tovera or I will kill you. Even if that means we're captured ourselves."

"Lady Mundy, I can't allow—" Krychek began.

"Be quiet, Miroslav," Elemere said as a mother might speak to a child. He continued to look at Adele. "I didn't object to the danger. This is my business. Lonnie is my business."

A slow smile spread across Elemere's face. He was really quite attractive, though the matter was of no greater importance to Adele than the color of his dress. "What do you need from me?" he asked.

Adele shrugged. She'd finished the second glass of wine also, she found. "Only your presence," she said. "And—"

She transferred her eyes back to Krychek.

"—from you, Landholder, the aircar in Hold Three. It's the only way we'll be able to get to Waddell's estate in time to make this work."

"How do you know about the aircar?" Krychek said, his face again a glowering mass of furrows. "I've never let anyone on Bennaria see it!"

Probably because you were planning an illegal last-ditch measure which required an aircar, Adele thought. This man wasn't the sort who'd quietly starve with his retainers because the local power structure resented him.

Rather than describe the extent to which she'd penetrated the Infantans' systems, she said, "Well, it's time for them to see it now. We'll return with Elemere to the *Princess Cecile*. Just us—Tovera can drive the aircar."

She rose from her chair. "We won't actually leave the *Sissie* until it's fully dark, but I have a great deal to prepare."

Krychek got up. Elemere kissed him but slipped out of his grasp before his arms could close. To Adele, Elemere said, "Should I change clothes?"

"I'd rather have the extra time aboard the *Sissie,*" Adele said. "We'll have clothing there for you."

Elemere offered Adele his hand. "All right," he said. "We can go now."

He looked over his shoulder. Krychek stood as though waiting to be shot. "Don't worry, dearest," he said to the Landholder.

As Elemere and Adele started up the stairs he said, "I thanked you for what you and the commander did for me, Lady Mundy. Now I'd like to thank you on behalf of Lonnie also."

CHAPTER 24

Bennaria

"*Unidentified vehicle,*" said the a guard in the gatehouse a quarter mile from Waddell's mansion, "*halt in the air so we can examine you. Or else!*"

"*I'm halting as directed,*" Tovera replied with cool courtesy as she brought the aircar to a hover. They were speaking on a two-meter hailing frequency, though the ground unit was transmitting with enough power to come in on light bulbs. "*We're unarmed as we said we'd be, and we have the package with us. Over.*"

Adele, seated beside Tovera, was using her data unit to identify the sensors tracking them. The house proper was in the middle of a twenty-acre compound including a terraced formal garden. The stone perimeter wall had projecting towers at the northeast and southwest corners. Each mounted an automatic impeller which was now aimed at the aircar.

The slave lines were a half mile north of the compound. Rice paddies stretched into the night in three directions.

From the roof of the mansion the aircar was being followed by a basket of twelve six-inch rockets, free-flight weapons which pirates salvoed to strip the rigging of their prey. Their high-explosive warheads wouldn't penetrate a starship's hull or damage the cargo, but any one of the dozen could blast an aircar into bits too small to identify. That wouldn't have concerned Adele even if she'd been thinking of the matter in personal terms rather than as data on her display

"*All right, you can come in slowly,*" the guard ordered. He was trying to be forceful but sounded nervous instead. Waddell had retained only a dozen or so troops here; the remainder were defending his town house from the mob. "*Land on the roof where you see Hesketh with the light. Slowly, mind!*"

"Mistress?" asked Tovera, speaking over the sound of the fans. The car's top was retracted to make it easier for Waddell's guards to examine them, and the intake rush was very loud even when the vehicle wasn't moving forward.

Adele rechecked her preparations; she had the necessary codes and two alternative means of access to Waddell's security system. "Yes," she said, setting the data unit on the floor without shutting it down. "You can go in, now."

Tovera nudged the yoke forward. The aircar staggered, then wobbled badly for the first twenty feet before she adjusted the fan tilt to smooth their descent.

Tovera treated driving as a technical problem to be solved by intellect rather than through any emotional understanding of the process. She wasn't a good driver, but she was good enough.

Adele smiled. Tovera'd learned to act as though she had a conscience in much the same way, come to think.

There was a grunt from the back seat; Adele looked over her shoulder. Elemere'd slid against the locked door. He met her eyes but didn't speak.

The entertainer wore the gold dress, but his makeup was smudged and he'd lost his wig. His wrists were tied in front of him. A cable anchored on the supports for the running boards ran between his elbows and back; the bights at either end were padlocked. Elemere could neither brace himself with his hands nor cushion the impact when the car threw him from side to side.

A man waving a glowing yellow wand stood on the roof of the mansion. The small lights on the coping showed he had a sub-machine gun in the other hand. A second guard waited with his back to the penthouse over the stairhead; he was covering the oncoming aircar with a carbine.

The tower-mounted impellers continued to follow the vehicle as it settled toward the roof. Electronic lockouts would prevent the guns from firing in this direction—otherwise they'd riddle the mansion they were supposed to protect—but the guards either didn't know that or were bluffing.

The car bobbed violently as it crossed the coping. Tovera's mouth was set in a hard line. When the vehicle was completely over the roof, reflected thrust bounced it higher. Instead of easing the throttles back, she cut them completely. The car dropped what was probably only a few inches but felt to Adele like a foot. Elemere jolted forward, crying out as the cable bit the inside of his elbows.

Adele rose carefully, keeping her face blank. She didn't want to show any expression that Tovera could take as disapproval. She stepped out of the car, raising her hands as she did.

"Hold it right there!" said the guard who'd dropped his yellow wand in order to grip the sub-machine gun with both hands. The other guard continued to point his carbine, though his aim wavered from Adele to Tovera and back again. "Sir! Sir! They're here!"

The penthouse door flew open; the landing beyond was brightly lighted. Four guards came out, three holding carbines and the fourth with a slung sub-machine gun and a resonance scanner.

The last was older than the others and had three vertical gold bars on his sleeves. He ran the scanner over Tovera—who watched with a bemused expression—and then Adele.

"Councilor?" he said, cocking his head—unnecessarily—toward the microphone on his epaulet. He'd closed the armored door behind him. "They're not armed."

"I told you we wouldn't be," Adele said, letting waspishness color her tone. "I'm here to make peace, I told you that too. And we brought him."

She nodded toward Elemere, bolt upright but silent. He followed the guards with his eyes, but his head barely moved.

"Put a light on him!" rasped a speaker over the door. Adele recognized Waddell's voice. She moved to the side while a guard obediently shifted his carbine to his left hand to shine a powerful belt light on the entertainer.

"That's him!" said Waddell. There was a video pickup in the frame of the speaker. "By *God* that's him."

"Of course it's . . .," Adele said, but she let her voice trail off when the door opened again. Waddell stepped out, followed by half a dozen guards including an officer with a sub-machine gun.

"So!" sneered the Councilor to Adele. "You brave Cinnabars have had to climb down a peg, have you not?"

"Look," she said quietly. "Commander Leary's neck is stiffer than mine. *I* just want to get home, and without repairs here in Charlestown we'll be six months doing that. If we even can."

She made a curt gesture toward the entertainer. "I don't doubt that Leary'll fume when he learns what I've done," she said, "but I'll bet he'll be just as glad it happened. He was drunk when he took the fellow in, and when he sobered up he was too much a Leary to get himself out of the mess. So I'm getting us *all* out."

Instead of responding, Waddell leaned into the car. He chucked Elemere under the chin with his index finger. Several of the guards stiffened and aimed at the entertainer's head. Elemere jerked away and screwed his eyes shut. He didn't speak.

Waddell straightened, laughing like oil gurgling from a punctured drum. "Bring him in," he said to the guard officer. "Into . . . we'll start in my bedroom, I think."

"You two," the officer said to a pair of guards. They handed their carbines to the men next to them and fumbled with the cable.

"Here, we have to unlock it," said Adele. Then, when the guards now standing between her and the car didn't move quickly enough, "Out of the way, you fools!"

She bent over and released one end of the cable; Tovera was on the other side of the car. The padlocks were programmed to open to either's right thumbprint. Straightening together, Adele and her servant slid their hands down the front of Elemere's low-cut dress and withdrew the pistols hidden in the false bosom.

Adele fired across the car, hitting the guard holding two carbines just below the left eye socket. The officer dropped his scanner but he didn't have his hands on his sub-machine gun before she'd shot him in the middle of the forehead. He'd ducked. She'd aimed for the bridge of his nose, but it didn't matter because her pellet punched through the bone at this short range.

Tovera's shots were sharp as whiplashes. Something tugged Adele's right sleeve, the hand of a spasming guard or possibly the pellet itself. It didn't matter.

A guard clubbed his carbine at Tovera. Adele shot him through the neck, missing his spine. Blood sprayed from entrance and exit wounds, then from the victim's mouth. He lost his grip on the weapon but fell into Tovera before slumping to the ground. She continued to shoot with the regularity of a metronome.

Adele had three targets in a clump, trying to raise their weapons. Hesketh still held the light wand. She shot out his right eye, shot the man to his left through the chin and throat, then snapped a shot at the third as he tried to duck behind the car. She thought she broke his spine with a raking shot, but Tovera glanced down and fired twice more to be sure.

Everyone on Adele's side of the car was down; across from her, only Waddell and Tovera were standing. The Councilor's mouth was working but no sounds came out. Ozone, ionized aluminum from the driving bands—a thick, hot smell that both bit and coated Adele's throat—and the stench of blood filled the air.

The barrel of Tovera's pistol shimmered bright yellow. She jerked the sub-machine gun from the hands of a dead officer, then slapped Waddell with the pocket pistol. He screamed and staggered backward, pressing both hands to the welt on his cheek. Tovera giggled, then tossed the pistol onto the floor of the aircar.

"That's enough!" Adele said sharply. She reloaded her own weapon, ignoring the barrel's searing glow. The skin on the back of her wrist throbbed and the fine hairs had shriveled, but she didn't think she'd have blisters.

Adele didn't know how many of the twenty rounds in the magazine she'd used, but experience had taught her it was probably more than she'd have guessed. She had a lot of experience at this. . . .

A carbine bullet whacked the coping and howled into the night. The automatic impellers in the towers wouldn't fire, but the guard to the southwest was using his personal weapon. Waddell wouldn't have thanked him, if Waddell's mind'd had room at the moment for anything but sheer terror.

Tovera dropped the knife from a guard's belt with which she'd just freed Elemere's wrists. She raised her sub-machine gun. The tower was out of effective range, and neither she nor Adele were particularly skilled with long arms. Besides, there was a better way. . . .

"No!" said Adele, dropping the pistol into her pocket. It'd probably char the lining but that was one more thing that couldn't be helped. She bent into the car and grabbed her personal data unit. "Get Waddell inside. And you too, Elemere, now!"

The tower guard emptied his carbine in full auto. At least one bullet hit the masonry—Adele heard the *spang-ng-ng* of the ricochet—but most of the burst punctured empty sky. Tovera waited beside the doorway while Elemere pulled Waddell inside, gripping him by the crotch of his loose, silken pantaloons. In the entertainer's free hand was the knife Tovera'd used to cut him free.

Bent over and clutching the data unit to her chest, Adele ducked into the penthouse. She sat cross-legged on the landing, ignoring the others for a moment except to snap, "Close and bolt the door. Now!"

A console in the mansion's basement controlled the basket of rockets. Rather than go to its physical location, Adele slaved it to her data unit. She'd prepared for the contingency, though if asked she'd have said it was unlikely she'd need it. Preparation was never wasted effort.

The guard had reloaded. This time he aimed. A shot rang from the armored door, and Adele thought she heard another slap the wall. The fellow was wasting his time at present, but he had to be silenced before it'd be safe to fly out again.

Waddell screamed from the room at the base of the stairs. "Don't harm him till I'm there!" Adele said, moving the orange dot across the targeting display in a series of jerks. *Daniel would do a much better job. . . .* She felt the building shiver as the basket gimbaled to follow the display.

The pipper lay in the middle of the gun tower. Adele sent a firing signal. Two rockets blasted out, jolting the landing enough to lift Adele. She hadn't expected two at the same time. Red flashes and balls of dirty black smoke concealed the target a heartbeat before the doubled explosions shook the mansion. Windows shattered, maybe all the windows on the mansion's façade.

The smoke and dust cleared. A ten-foot section of wall had collapsed—the rockets obviously weren't very accurate—but the other warhead had destroyed the impeller and the fool who'd been standing beside it to shoot.

Adele began swinging the basket toward the other tower. The panoramic view at the top of the targeting display showed the surviving guard leaping off the back of the wall and presumably running in the direction of the slave lines. Just in case he decided to come back, she loosed three pairs of the remaining rockets, shattering that corner of the compound into smoking rubble.

She rose and put away her data unit as the echoes rumbled to silence. Waddell was spread-eagled faceup on the floor below. His wrists and ankles were tied to the legs of a couch and two heavy chairs; he could move his limbs, but not easily and not far. Elemere squatted near the Councilor's head; Tovera stood at his feet. All three watched in silence as Adele descended the stairs; Tovera was smiling.

"Councilor Waddell," Adele said with polite formality. The man had fouled himself; feces were oozing through his thin pantaloons. "I want you to call Commandant Brast at the Squadron Pool and order him to offer Commander Leary and his companions every facility. If you do that in a sufficiently convincing fashion, I will leave you unharmed when we go."

Waddell's left cheek was swollen to angry red except for the long white blister in the middle of it. "Well, without further harm," Adele corrected herself primly.

"I hope he refuses," Elemere whispered. "I really hope you refuse, Councilor."

He jabbed before Adele could stop him. Waddell screamed again, but the knife point merely slit the blister. It began to drain toward Waddell's ear.

"I'll do it!" Waddell wailed. His eyes were shut but tears squeezed from beneath the lids. "I'll do anything you say!"

Tovera giggled again. "Don't worry, Elemere," she said. "Perhaps we'll have better luck the next time we need something from him."

"Good evening, Commandant Brast!" Daniel called cheerfully as he approached the gate in the perimeter of the Squadron Pool. It stood out like a tunnel through the vines and small trees interweaving the remainder of the chain-link fence. "I'm glad you came to meet me yourself."

Two Sissies and a pair of Infantans were tying *Manco A79* to trees on the shore just below the Pool. Yellow warning lights were spaced across the top of the dam; area lights on poles threw a white glare on the ground before the gate and the lock building. The administration building brightened the sky in the near distance, but intervening trees hid the structure itself.

Except for Daniel, the barge's two hundred passengers remained aboard. Even Hogg and Landholder Krychek stayed, though only after loud protest. Daniel *couldn't* take any chance of something going violently wrong, and ultimately both men were intelligent enough to accept a decision they knew was correct.

"Look, Commander," Brast said miserably through the gate. A junior officer'd been pointing a carbine at Daniel from the gatehouse; now he pulled the weapon back and concealed it behind him. "I've got the highest respect for you and the Cinnabar navy, but I can't let you in. I've got orders, you know."

The lock on this side of the dam was big enough to pass the barge, but a dozen Bennarian spacers were hunched around the control building, pointing automatic weapons. *A79* wasn't carrying any cargo except spacers, so it'd be faster to march them in by the wicket than to lock the barge into the Pool. Once the formalities had been taken care of, that is.

"Of course, Commandant," Daniel said, continuing to approach with a friendly smile. "It's about your orders that I came, as a matter of fact. I hope that you'll let me—alone and unarmed, I assure you— through the gate to discuss matters, but I can fully understand if you're afraid to."

He was wearing utilities and a commo helmet, but he'd left his equipment belt in the barge instead of simply detaching the holster from it. He wanted to look professional but not threatening.

The junior officer standing beside Brast whispered in his ear. *The fellow's name is Tenris. . . .* Brast gripped the gate with both hands and rested his forehead against the steel wire with his eyes closed. The pose emphasized his missing little finger.

Brast straightened. "All right," he said harshly, sliding the bar clear; it hadn't been locked. "Come in, then."

He glanced toward the bargeload of spacers. Daniel had told them to keep their weapons out of sight, but he wasn't sure any of the Infantans had obeyed. "Just you alone though!" Brast added.

"Of course," Daniel said. He carefully swung the gate shut after he entered. He gestured toward the gatehouse. "You have a commo terminal here, don't you? There should be a call from Councilor Waddell any time now—"

He prayed there'd be a call and *bloody* soon.

"—to explain the change in circumstances. I'd sooner stay near my crew, but if you like we can go back to your admin building."

"Why would Waddell be calling here?" Tenris said. The overhead light distorted his puzzled expression into a counterfeit of fury. "Especially the way things are now, I—"

"Commandant!" called the officer in the gatehouse. "They're relaying this from HQ. They say it's Councilor Waddell for you! What do you think it means?"

"Bloody hell," Brast whispered as he stepped into the gatehouse, a shack of 5-mm plastic sheeting on four vertical posts. *If Tenris follows him, there won't be room for me.* Daniel gripped the Bennarian by the shoulder and moved him back, then squeezed in behind the commandant.

The terminal's flat-plate display was unexpectedly sharp, except for the three-inch band across the middle in which squares danced like the facets of a kaleidoscope. Despite the flaw, nobody who'd seen Councilor Waddell could doubt it was him on the other end of the connection. He was flushed and agitated, and he held his right hand to his cheek.

"Councilor?" Brast said. He tried to salute but his elbow bumped the junior officer beside him. Now flustered, he continued, "Sir, this is Commandant Brast. You wanted me?"

"There'll be a Cinnabar officer coming to see you, Leary his name is," Waddell said in a hoarse voice. "Give him whatever he wants."

"Sir, he's here now," said Brast. "Ah—"

"Then give him what he wants!" Waddell shouted. He glanced to his side as someone off-screen spoke; the voice was only a murmur on this end of the connection. When he lowered his hand, Daniel saw the angry welt on his face.

Waddell glared back at the display. "He'll want a destroyer," he said. "Give it to him. Give him whatever he wants!"

"A destroyer?" blurted Tenris, listening from outside the gatehouse.

"But sir!" said Brast, too startled to be deferential. "The only destroyer we could give him is the *Sibyl*, unless you mean—"

"Yes, the *Sibyl*!" said Waddell. "Damn your soul, man, why are you arguing? It's necessary that Leary get everything he wants. Now! Now!"

"Sir, I understand you," Brast said. Daniel doubted whether that was true or anything close to being true, but it was the right thing to say. "But as you know, Admiral Wrenn has directed that—"

Waddell shook his fist at the display. "*Damn* you, man!" he cried, spraying spittle with the words. Droplets clung to the pickup, blurring the image slightly. "I'll have Wrenn shot if you like! Will that satisfy you? Now get on with it, do you hear me?"

"Aye aye, sir!" Brast said, saluting again. This time his subordinate edged back enough to allow the gesture. "I'll see to it at once!"

Adele's arm reached across the display area and broke the connection.

Brast turned, wiping his face with a kerchief he'd taken out of his sleeve. Daniel backed out of the shack and said, "May I direct my personnel to enter the compound, Commandant? Time's very short, you see."

"I don't understand this at all," Brast said in wonder. "Yes, yes, bring your people in."

He looked at Daniel sharply and said, "It's about the riots in Charlestown, I suppose? That the Councilor is so . . . forceful?"

"I can't go into the details now, sir," Daniel said politely. He nodded to the armed Bennarians standing close by, then opened the gate. Raising his voice he called, "Landholder Krychek, you may bring the crew in. Smartly now, if you will!"

"I don't know what Wrenn's going to say," Brast muttered. He sounded more puzzled than concerned. "I suppose it doesn't matter. He's gone off to his estate."

The spacers from the barge trotted toward the gate. They were singing "Rosy Dawn." Daniel heard Woetjans bellowing along with the Infantans, adding to the volume if not precisely to the music.

"Yeah, but he'll be back after things settle down," said Tenris, shaking his head in wonderment.

"One step at a time, gentlemen," Daniel said, beaming with pleasure. "We'll deal with that when we need to. After all—"

He smiled even more broadly at Brast and his subordinates.

"—we've dealt with everything that's come up thus far, haven't we?"

That wasn't really true for the Bennarian officers, but by God! it was for the *Princess Cecile* and her crew.

CHAPTER 25

Bennaria

"*Six, this's Woetjans,*" the bosun said, using the command channel because Daniel hadn't figured out how to set two-way links on the *Sibyl*'s Alliance-standard commo system. "*We've got that day-room hatch fixed. I guess she'll hold as good as any other seal on this dozy cow, though that's not much to say. Didn't the Bennarians do any maintenance after they took possession? Over.*"

Strictly speaking, Pasternak as Chief of Ship should've been in charge of repairing hatch seals, but the engineer had his hands full and more in the Power Room. Damage control parties were largely formed of riggers, since they were rarely on the hull while the ship fought in sidereal space. Woetjans and her personnel had plenty of experience in the basic hull repairs that Daniel'd set them to in the emergency.

He suspected the answer to the bosun's question was "No, the Bennarians *didn't* do any maintenance," but that was a historical puzzle which didn't matter on the eve of combat. Aloud he said, "Check the rig, then, as much as you can before we lift. That'll be at least ten minutes; maybe more, I'm afraid. Six out."

He glanced at the Power Room schematics again. Pasternak was methodically examining the pumps, the lines, and the antimatter converters. Daniel'd have liked the job to go more quickly. Personally, he'd have cut more corners than the engineer, but Pasternak knew what he was doing: operating without part of the propulsion system merely degraded performance, but having part of the system fail under load was potentially catastrophic.

But bloody *hell*! the man was slow.

If Adele were aboard to configure the commo system, Daniel would've been able to ask Woetjans how the Infantans were working out. He couldn't do that—or anyway, he wasn't willing to—with Krychek on the same channel. He *needed* Adele.

The Landholder was at the gunnery console, putting the equipment through its paces in a thoroughly competent fashion. He'd rotated the two dorsal turrets, then elevated and depressed the paired 10-cm plasma cannon. The ventral positions would have to wait until the *Sibyl* lifted off—at present they were recessed into the hull and under water—but Krychek had done full software checks on them as well.

The Landholder had made his appointment as Gunnery Officer a condition of him signing on with Leary of Bantry. Neither he nor Daniel had used words quite that blunt, but they'd both understood the nub of the negotiation. Sun'd been furious—he'd stayed with Vesey on the *Princess Cecile* instead of transferring to the *Sibyl* as a result—and Daniel himself had been doubtful, but it turned out that Krychek had the necessary instinct and experience both.

Daniel sorted through the three course projections he'd set. That was excessive: he didn't imagine that there'd be ten minutes' difference among the options over the short voyage back to Dunbar's World. It was the way Uncle Stacey had taught him, though. In a situation like the present one, Daniel acted by rote.

Returning to Dunbar's World would be quick and easy. What happened there, when they faced a cruiser in an unfamiliar destroyer, wouldn't be easy at all. Daniel gave the display a quick, hard grin: it certainly might be quick, though.

The top of his display was a real-time panorama. Daniel glanced at it, as much as anything to take his mind off his Pasternak's glacial caution, and saw hundreds of Bennarians watching from the administration building and the roughly mown grounds. The naval personnel had their families with them, as he'd expected: a good third were women and children. But there was quite a number of spacers, too. . . .

Making up his mind abruptly, Daniel said to the midshipman beside him at the navigation console, "Officer Blantyre, take charge for a moment. I'm going to talk to the crowd."

"Sir?" said Blantyre in surprise, but Daniel was already on his feet and striding to the dorsal hatch. He could adjust the hull lights so that the spectators without night vision equipment could see him.

It wasn't till he was halfway up the ladder that Daniel remembered this wasn't the *Sissie*. He wasn't certain the *Sibyl* had public address speakers built into the outer hull, and he certainly didn't know how to activate them if they existed.

"Blantyre, this is Six," he said. "Can you tell if this ship has an external PA system? If it does, I want it slaved to my commo helmet. Over."

He supposed he could bellow through his cupped hands. *And look like a fool, probably an inaudible fool. Damn, he should've thought it through before he started!*

Daniel grinned. Maybe Pasternak was right.

"*Six?*" replied not Blantyre but Cory. He was in the Battle Direction Center with the dour, bearded Infantan second-in-command. "*I've done what you want with the PA speakers, sir. I've watched Officer Mundy do it and I think I know how. Over.*"

Well, I'll be damned! thought Daniel as he stepped onto the hull. The antennas, telescoped and folded, were nearly waist high. Daniel jumped onto Dorsal 2 so that the motion itself would call the attention of those watching to him.

"Good work, Cory!" he said—and almost fell, startled by the boom of his own voice. Cory'd done good work, true, but he wasn't quite at Adele's level yet. She'd have made sure that intercom messages didn't key the external speakers. Of course since Daniel himself didn't know how to do that, he wasn't going to complain about the midshipman's performance.

Daniel ran through ways to start his speech. He stood higher than the Bennarians, even those on top of the admin building. *All the more reason to address them as equals. . . .*

"Fellow spacers!" Daniel thundered. It was a mixed crowd, but the men he cared about *were* all spacers. "For the first time in her career, the *Sibyl*'s going off to battle the enemies of Bennaria. She'll be fighting for you, for your families, for your world against a powerful enemy."

He struck a pose, hands on hips and jaw jutting outward. "Now, you can let your ship lift without you," he continued, feeling the echoes roll back to him from the wall of the building. "You can let strangers, Cinnabars and Infantans and spacers from a dozen other planets, fight for you and protect you from the Pellegrinian warlord who expects to enslave you. You *could* do that—but you won't, not if you're men! Not if you ever expect to look your wives in the face, not if you ever hope your children will look up to you!"

Daniel eyed the spectators. There was more a puddle of them than a sea, but even a handful of men with experience of the destroyer's systems could be the difference between life and death in the coming hours. Every ship had quirks, and the *Sibyl*'s new crew wasn't going to have a shakedown cruise to determine hers.

"You have one chance, men!" Daniel said. "We'll be lifting shortly. Come join us to drive away the enemies of your planet and to save your women from the lust of a warlord's mercenaries! Join us and know that if we succeed, you'll come back rich as well as honored by all who know you. I'm Daniel Leary, the luckiest captain in the RCN, and I swear it to you!"

"Hip hip!" a chorus of spacers shouted, their powerful voices reverberating from the *Sibyl*'s open entrance hold.

"*Urra/Hooray!*" they and at least a few of the Bennarians replied. Most of the leaders must be Infantans, but Woetjans was there also.

"Hip hip!"

"*Hooray/Urra!*" This time the Infantans were clearly in the minority. The locals had joined in with a will, and by God! a few of them were starting for the *Sibyl*'s boarding ramp.

"Officer Blantyre," Daniel boomed, "get down the entry hatch at once and see to it that these brave men are assigned to their proper places aboard their ship! And now—"

Daniel thrust out his right arm, his hand clenched, in a Bennarian salute.

"Hip hip—"

"*Hooray!*"

"Will Miroslav be on the *Princess Cecile* when she picks us up, Lady Mundy?" Elemere asked.

Adele was cross-legged on the roof of the mansion with her data unit on her lap. She looked up from the display in which she'd immersed herself. She'd been reexamining electronic emissions from the *Duilio* with the aid of the *Rainha*'s decryption algorithms, copied into her personal data unit during the voyage from Pellegrino to Dunbar's World.

For a moment Adele didn't speak. She was unreasonably—irrationally—angry at being drawn out of her task. When she had control of her temper she said equably, "I don't believe so. The Landholder told us both he expected to accompany Master Leary on the destroyer. Plans may have changed since we left Charlestown, of course."

Plans hadn't changed—of course. Elemere knew that. He'd only spoken because he didn't want to sit in silence with his fears.

"Yes, I see," Elemere muttered. He looked at his hands; he'd washed them several times, going down into the building each time to do so. "I guess it really doesn't matter."

Adele smiled wryly, at human beings generally and particularly at herself. It wasn't surprising that Elemere didn't want to dwell on his present surroundings: the bodies of Waddell's guards lay all about them in pools of congealing blood. The night was cool enough that the corpses hadn't begun to rot, but there was the stench of feces some of the men had voided when they spasmed into death.

Adele Mundy too wanted to escape the present, though she'd chosen to leave through the display of her data unit. Elemere hadn't been responsible for creating the slaughterhouse, after all.

"When are you going to let me loose?" Councilor Waddell said. He'd tried to make the words commanding, but there was a quaver in his voice.

They glanced at him. They'd left the Councilor seated on the roof and tied to the hinge of the stairwell door.

Tovera giggled. Though she'd slung a captured sub-machine gun, she was holding a carbine as she prowled about the roof looking for signs of trouble.

There wasn't likely to be any, of course. The slaves might not've heard the shooting, since the small electromotive pistols which Tovera and Adele'd used didn't make much noise. Everyone for miles around must've noticed when multiple rockets blew down the gun towers and chunks of the nearby wall, but that wasn't the sort of thing that made sensible people want to come rushing closer in the night.

"You promised you'd let me go!" Waddell said, his voice rising. "Does your honor mean nothing?"

Elemere picked up the knife he'd dropped on the roof. He stepped toward Waddell. His face was stiff.

"No!" Adele said.

Elemere glanced over his shoulder at her; he didn't put the knife down. "No," Adele repeated, bringing the pistol out of her pocket. She had to jerk it free. The lining of her tunic was a synthetic of some sort; it'd melted to the barrel shroud.

Elemere turned and walked toward the edge of the roof. He stood facing in the direction of Charlestown, though that might've been coincidence. He didn't speak.

"Councilor," Adele said with the cold anger of a judge sentencing a particularly despicable criminal, "I told you that if you cooperated, we'd do you no further harm. If you misstate me again, I will consider you to have breached our agreement."

"I'm sorry," Waddell said, licking his lips. "Look, I'm sorry. But you can untie me now. I'm no danger to you, I just want to move my arms and legs."

Adele went back to her display. The commo module on the *Rainha* was Fleet standard. If the *Duilio* was using an identical model—and why shouldn't it be?—then if Adele gained access to the cruiser's systems she'd be able to read the scrambled operating data.

"Please!" Waddell said.

Adele looked at him again. Elemere turned to watch, though he remained silent.

"Councilor," Adele said very distinctly, "be silent. I can't risk you communicating with anyone until we've left Bennaria. You'll remain where you are until someone arrives to release you, which I suspect won't be too long after daybreak."

"If you leave me like this, they'll kill me!" Waddell said. His eyes were open but they'd gone blank. "You've killed all my guards. If the field hands find me like this they'll, they'll. . . . I don't know what they'll do! I have to get away from the house and hide!"

"Would you prefer that I kill you instead?" Elemere said. "I'd like that, you know."

"Mistress, there's a ship coming," Tovera said. "To the southeast, just above the horizon."

Adele looked in the direction indicated. She saw a hint of plasma like a glowing horsetail cloud. The trembling of the thrusters could be felt through the building though not as yet heard.

"Councilor," she said, rising carefully to her feet, "I'm not responsible for the way you've treated your slaves. I didn't have that in mind when I made my offer. But I won't pretend I'll regret it if your concerns prove well-founded."

She slipped the data unit into its pocket. Waddell began by shouting abuse, but his voice quickly choked into a terrified stammer. The *Princess Cecile*, dropping even closer to the ground as it approached the mansion, drowned him out.

"*Victor One to Ship Six-three,*" Vesey called, giving Adele's formal call sign. Daniel never used it, addressing Adele as "Signals" or "Officer Mundy" whenever he chose to be formal. "*We'll land just outside the compound and I'll shut down the thrusters. I'd appreciate it if you boarded as soon as the ground has cooled enough for you to cross it, over.*"

Adele noted approvingly that Vesey'd used the laser communicator instead of one of the radio options. At low altitude in an atmosphere, the thrusters' exhaust billowed around the antennas. When the ions snatched electrons to change state, they created deafening static across the whole RF spectrum.

"Victor One, this is Signals," Adele said. "If you'll open the entry hatch as soon as it's convenient, we'll fly our aircar aboard immediately. Over."

Krychek wouldn't be getting his aircar back; they'd have to pitch it off the ramp rather than block the *Sissie*'s entry hold. That was the sort of waste one got used to in war. Adele had melted a hole in her tunic pocket, and a dozen of Councilor Waddell's guards were cooling to air temperature. . . .

The corvette settled to the ground just outside the compound, spewing steam from the boggy soil and chunks of dirt baked to stone. Adele could see the *Sissie*'s hull through the barred gate and the hole she'd blown in the masonry. A final bubble of plasma rose and dissipated into rainbow twinklings.

"*Wonderful!*" Vesey said, startled out of her careful formality. "*Six's already lifted for Dunbar's World, and I want to get to the rendezvous point ASAP. Though without missiles, I don't suppose there's much we can do to help him. Victor One out.*"

I want to get there too, Lieutenant, Adele thought. Tovera was already at the controls of the aircar and Elemere was getting in. *And I believe we just might be able to do more than you think.*

CHAPTER 26

En Route to Dunbar's World

Daniel cycled the four attack plans through his console, just letting them flash across his display in order to catch the sort of obvious error that sometimes escapes a person who's been poring over details. Nothing struck him, beyond the awareness that there were more variables in what he was attempting than there'd be in trying to handicap the Five Systems Unlimited.

The *Sibyl's* Alliance electronics were at least as good as the Kostroman units aboard the *Princess Cecile*, but they weren't quite what Daniel had grown used to. Simply the fact that images formed from the edges in rather than the other way about caused him barely perceptible discomfort every time the display changed.

The destroyer trembled as she slipped from one universe to another, each shift increasing the rate at which she sped toward Dunbar's World. Daniel would've loved to be out on the hull, eyeing the flaring Matrix and directing the riggers with hand signals to get the absolutely best performance out of his new command. You could cut days off a long run—*if* you'd been trained by Stacey Bergen, the finest astrogator of his age, and *if* you shared the natural talent that made Uncle Stacey the subject of amazed stories wherever RCN officers gathered.

Both those things were true of Daniel Leary, but he was on the bridge while Midshipman Blantyre was outside on the hull. It *wasn't* a long voyage: half an hour was the most the Gods in Assembly could've shaved from the time.

There was nobody else aboard the destroyer whom Daniel would trust to set up a missile attack, and if there had been he'd have still believed in his heart of hearts that Commander Daniel Leary could have done it better. No few of the Alliance officers who'd been on the receiving end of his missiles would've agreed with that assessment.

"Command, this is Six," Daniel said. "I'm going to run the plan of operation by you first. When we've got the bugs out, I'll explain to the whole company. Over."

He'd always felt better about knowing what he was getting into. That was true even when he didn't feel good about it at all.

Daniel expected a series of *Rogers* or whatever the Infantans used in its place. Instead he got from Cory, "*Sir! Sir, wait, you're broadcasting to everybody! Give me a moment and I'll . . .*"

Daniel was too startled to object. Which was the correct response, because he saw immediately that there wasn't anything to object to: Cory'd violated protocol a trifle, but only in order to keep his commander from screwing up due to unfamiliarity with his new ship's commo system.

Bloody hell! but he needed Adele. Midshipman Cory was taking up more of the slack than anybody would've expected, though.

"*There you go, Channel Twelve, sir!*" Cory said proudly. "*Five-three out!*"

A series of miniature images at the top of Daniel's display indicated that he, Pasternak, Krychek, Victor—the Infantan navigator seated in the next console—and Cory were connected, and that Blantyre and Woetjans had access to the channel but were out of range. It'd taken all this to get to where they'd have been when Daniel spoke the word "Command" if they'd been aboard the *Sissie* . . . but the *Sissie* didn't have missiles.

"Right," he said aloud. "We'll be reentering sidereal space five light minutes out from Dunbar's World, just a quick in-and-out. That'll give us a real-time, or anyway an almost real-time, location for the *Duilio*. We'll extract again at ten thousand miles from the cruiser, salvo missiles from all four tubes, and then slip back into the Matrix. Comments? Over."

"*Commander, this cannot be,*" Victor said heavily. His image scowled in what could as easily've been fury as consternation. "*You talk of light-minutes when we have not taken a star sight since we entered the Matrix off Bennaria. This is real war, not some test for an award! You cannot cut things so close.*"

"*Commander Leary doesn't need some pansy to teach him his—*"

"Mister Cory, shut up!" Daniel roared, knowing it was too late.

"*—business!*" Cory said. Then he added, "*Oh my God.*"

"Mister Cory," Daniel said austerely, "pray replace Blantyre on the hull at once. Break. Officer Victor, you may take it as read that all members of the *Princess Cecile*'s crew, myself included, know what war is. My plans have been made on the basis of what I believe we can accomplish in action, so please limit your corrections to matters of which I may not be cognizant, over."

Listening to himself, Daniel began to grin through his pique. *I'm just as angry as Cory was, and I've just been even more insulting than he was . . . though I used words which weren't in themselves impolite.*

Krychek bellowed with laughter, calming the situation as soon as Daniel was sure it really *was* laughter. "Vasiley, you shut up too. Leary is a nobleman, not some numbskull a peasant fathered on a nanny goat like you are."

"*Yes, Landholder,*" the navigator said with a degree of humility which surprised Daniel, albeit pleasantly. "*My pardon, Lord Daniel.*"

"*Then I will ask you, Leary,*" Krychek said, carefully polite. "*I do not know missiles, this is true, but I know plasma cannon very well. If we are so close to the cruiser when you launch your missiles, will she not be shooting at us with her guns? And these guns are fifteen-centimeter, so I recall.*"

"They are indeed," Daniel agreed, "and we'll be coming in close enough to the muzzles to make them a real danger."

He took a deep breath, nodding as he reviewed the situation before laying it out. This was a very acute question, as was to be expected given the number of years Krychek had survived as a pirate trader.

"First," Daniel said, "I hope that the *Duilio* is keeping a bad lookout or at any rate is concentrating on the surface of the planet below. Second, if they do spot us extracting from the Matrix—"

The process of returning from the Matrix into sidereal space took anything from thirty seconds to a minute. The process created distortions in the optical and RF spectra, though catching them at early stages required either sensitive equipment or a great deal of attention.

"—I hope that they'll be too concerned with deflecting our missiles to waste bolts on us. I say 'hope,' but if they don't make the missiles their priority, I would expect part of our salvo to get home."

Krychek wouldn't take that as boasting the way an experienced missileer might. Daniel's statement implied that, launching within seconds of returning to sidereal space, he'd be able to target the Pellegrinian cruiser precisely. He *did* feel confident that one of his preset attack plans would be too accurate for the *Duilio* to safely ignore, but a missileer who didn't know Daniel well would question the assumption.

"Finally," Daniel said, "we'll extract wearing a full suit of sails. I'll adjust our angle so that the *Duilio* has only fabric to shoot at. We may lose many of our sails and some of our spars, but at least for the first time we go in I don't believe the hull is at risk. Now—"

He took another deep breath. He'd come to the risk that they couldn't avoid if the *Sibyl* were to have a real chance of damaging the cruiser.

"If the *Duilio*'s crew is very alert, and if they launch at us while we're still in the process of extracting, we'll inevitably be destroyed. They won't have any idea who we are until we're fully in sidereal space—we could be a friendly vessel, even another Pellegrinian warship—but at the point we left the system previously, Captain ap Glynn was already skirting the edges of what I consider rational behavior."

Daniel grinned brightly. "I offer you this comfort," he said. "We literally won't know what hit us. Are there any questions or suggestions, over?"

"*If the sails are spread, then they will block my guns too, will they not?*" Krychek asked.

"Yes," said Daniel. "If we can shoot, the Pellegrinians can hit our hull. Their bolts are very much heavier than ours, besides their plating being thicker. Over."

The Landholder's tiny image shrugged. "*Another time, perhaps,*" he said. "*Or perhaps as you say, Leary—we won't know what hit us.*"

"More questions?" Daniel said. "We'll be extracting very shortly. Over."

No one spoke. He heard the light hammerblows of the outer airlock dogs disengaging: Woetjans was bringing her riggers inside. It was *very* close to time.

"Ship, this is Six," Daniel continued, hoping that the verbal "Ship" did what he meant it to even if "Command" did not. "We're about to make a hit-and-run attack on a cruiser. We'll extract, launch, and reinsert into the Matrix again as quickly as we can. If we hit her on the first run, well and good."

He paused, grinning. If Adele were handling commo, his face would've expanded to fill every display. He'd been spoiled during the past two years.

"Chances are we won't end the business so easily, though," Daniel continued. "Those of you who've served with me before know what that means: we go in again, and we keep going in. We attack till they're either destroyed or they follow us into the Matrix. Either way, we'll have broken the blockade of Dunbar's World and achieved our objective."

Krychek and his navigator had turned at their consoles to look at Daniel directly; he continued to watch them on his display. The Landholder was grinning.

"Yesterday some of us were Sissies and others were Infantans," Daniel said, letting his voice rise. "Now we're all Sibyls, and we'll be Sibyls till we've chased these wogs back to Pellegrino. Or blown them to hell!"

The inner airlock opened; Woetjans, unmistakable because of her height, led a party of hard-suited riggers back aboard. The destroyer had a second lock in the stern ventral position; a faint clanging and an icon on Daniel's display indicated that the rest of the outside crew was returning there. There was no advantage to leaving the riggers on the hull during this attack, and the risk was suicidal.

"Are you with me, Sibyls?" Daniel said.

"Urra!" Krychek shouted, grinning like a bearded fiend. "*Urra!*"

Spacers, Sissies and Infantans both, cheered enthusiastically. Their voices rattled in the big hull. If Adele'd been aboard, she'd have cut the crew's voices into the PA system, but this was good enough.

"*Extracting into sidereal space in thirty, that is three-zero, seconds,*" Midshipman Blantyre announced from the Battle Direction Center.

As the familiar queasy feeling came over Daniel, indicating the ship was about to shift out of the Matrix, Landholder Krychek said over a two-way link, "*You are a crazy man, Leary. Almost as crazy as me, I think.*"

His laughter boomed in Daniel's ears as the *Sibyl* dropped into normal space to fight a ship four times her size at knife range.

Above spread glowing beads and clouds of light so subtle that Adele always suspected that she was seeing colors that didn't exist in the sidereal universe. The Matrix touched her with stimuli which an irrational part of her mind insisted didn't come through her eyes.

Adele had intended to use a simple air suit. The Infantan officer who acted as bosun of the *Princess Cecile* during Woetjans' absence had insisted with scatological determination that if Lady Mundy *must* go on the hull, she would wear a rigging suit. Tovera quietly explained that the Sissies who'd gone off aboard the destroyer had made it very clear to the Infantans that Adele Mundy was as valuable and delicate as a masterpiece in spun glass.

Disgruntled but with no way to do anything about it—Tovera merely smiled at her mistress' protest—Adele had let crew members lock her into a hard suit. The limbs and panels were stiffened, and shields overlay the joints to prevent catastrophic decompression in case of a fall. Riggers got used to their suits, but a layman like Adele would be bruised and scraped on the suit's interior by the time she took it off.

Nobody seemed to mind about that except Adele herself. Likewise, she was the only one who didn't care if she died in an accident.

The *Sissie* wore a partial suit of sails, midcourses on the dorsal and ventral antennas and midcourses with topsails to port and starboard. They had a precise, balanced look, more regimented than Adele was used to on a ship of Daniel Leary's. But Daniel wasn't the *Sissie*'s captain now.

A rigger twenty feet away—one of the original Sissies; the Infantan rigging suits were ribbed with battens—gestured toward Adele, then brought his—her?—right arm down three times sharply as if chopping wood. Riggers used a complex semaphore code to communicate while ships were in the Matrix; even the tiny output of an intercom was enough to throw an astrogator's calculations wildly off. Adele didn't know the hand signals, however, and it was a moment before she realized that the spacer was simply telling her to look behind her.

When she did, she saw Vesey walking toward her from the stern. The acting captain had her own rigging suit; its helmet was painted white to identify her to the crew when she was on the hull. Her magnetic boots clamped and released like strokes of a metronome.

Adele was standing on a relatively open section of hull. Thinking that she might be in Vesey's way, she sidled toward the base of the nearest antenna, Dorsal A. Vesey made a circular sweep with her left hand and adjusted her own course.

She's coming to me, Adele realized, and crossed her arms in front of her. She felt mildly uncomfortable, uncertain about what Vesey wanted and more than a little embarrassed to be where she was. She'd never before come out on the hull of a starship unless Daniel was present.

Vesey bent sideways toward Adele so that their helmets touched. "Mistress Mundy?" she asked. "Is there something wrong?"

"It's just a whim on my part, Captain," Adele said. "I've done all the preparation I can, and I decided to come out here. If that's all right?"

They were standing side by side, shoulders and helmets touching but both of them looking out over the corvette's bow. The lights glittered more brightly there. They weren't stars, as Adele knew now, but rather universes in themselves. Every one was as real as the worlds in which she and other humans had been born, but their realities were as inimical to life as the hearts of suns.

"Of course, Mistress," Vesey said, as if shocked by the question. "I was—"

She paused. Vesey—and the late Midshipman Dorst, who'd had everything an RCN officer needed, except the luck to stay alive in the places Daniel Leary led him—always treated Adele with the greatest deference. That pattern continued even now that Lieutenant, Acting Captain, Vesey was in formal rank far the superior of a junior warrant officer aboard her ship.

"I'm concerned about this . . .," Vesey continued. "About my duties, about the situation. I'm afraid—"

She turned to look at Adele, breaking the contact between their helmets that was the only means they had to communicate. Grimacing, she laid her head beside Adele's and said, "I'm afraid that I'll fail Mister Leary. We're to join the *Sibyl* at the rendezvous point he set a light-hour from Dunbar's World. We'll wait there, of course, but if they don't arrive within an hour as Mister Leary specified . . . It's then I worry about."

Adele almost jerked her head around to stare at Vesey. The Infantans in the mixed crew would almost certainly mutiny if the acting captain didn't make every attempt to rescue their Landholder, but that was nothing to the reaction of the Sissies. Signals Officer Mundy would be leading them, of course.

Restraining herself but in a very cool voice, Adele said, "In that case we jump to Dunbar's World ourselves and view the situation from close at hand, surely?"

Vesey stepped aside and gestured with both hands to the bosun's mate standing at the control panel offset between Mast Rings 3 and 4. He immediately punched his keyboard. The hydro-mechanical semaphore near him swung into life; another on the opposite side of the hull would repeat the signal. Adele saw the topsails begin to shift. Starboard 3 must've stuck, because an Infantan rigger started briskly up the antenna.

Vesey's wry smile was visible through her visor in the instant before she touched helmets with Adele again. "Yes, we sail to Dunbar's World," she said. "That's what the RCN expects, that's what Mister Leary showed me to do by his example. But mistress—"

Her helmet moved, then instantly clicked against Adele's again.

"—if Mister Leary were in command, he'd know what to do *then*. He'd save the *Sibyl* if she could be saved, defeat the Pellegrinians if they could be defeated, he'd *know*. I'm afraid I'll fail him because I *don't* know, It's like staring at a bulkhead, mistress, and trying to imagine what's on the other side. I can't see anything but gray!"

Adele smiled. "I came onto the hull," she said, "because this is where Daniel would be if he were in command. So long as I stand here, I can imagine that he's beside me. Inside I tend to imagine him having been torn to atoms in a battle that's already concluded."

She smiled still wider, though she knew it wasn't an expression that'd suggest humor to anyone watching her.

"Unlike Daniel," she went on, "I find the Matrix a very unpleasant environment. That's useful also, because the lesser discomfort takes my mind away from a possible future I would find very bleak."

Adele hadn't been thinking of Dorst until the words came out of her mouth. She froze, though of course no one could see her expression anyway.

"Yes," said Vesey. Her voice was tinny because it was transmitted helmet to helmet but perhaps it'd beome a little thinner, a little colder than before. "That would be a tragedy, for all of us and for Cinnabar."

"Captain," Adele said in the silence, "I came out here to pretend Daniel was present. I found you doing exactly what he'd have done, adjusting the *Sissie*'s course by eye to bring the best out of her. He *is* present, in you and in me and in everyone aboard who's served with him in the past. If the *Princess Cecile* has to make the run to Dunbar's World alone, we'll do everything humanly possible to bring the best result for Cinnabar. That's what Daniel taught us."

Vesey's laugh was shaky, but it was still a laugh. "Yes, of course," she said. "Now, let's go below. We'll be extracting in a few minutes and our sensors will tell me more than my naked eyes. Especially since I have the best signals officer in the RCN."

Adele remembered to take up her safety line as they started toward the forward airlock. Her left arm twinged as she moved it.

All around her the Matrix blazed, but it no longer felt quite as hostile as it usually did.

As the *Sibyl* shuddered into normal space, Daniel felt a curtain of ice slide through them bow to stern. The bulkheads and furniture whitened in a broad line, then returned to normal, leaving him uncertain as to whether he'd really glimpsed it or if instead it was a hallucination caused when his mind attempted to grasp the simultaneous realities of mutually exclusive universes.

It didn't matter now: Daniel had a battle to plan.

An image of the volume of space centered on Dunbar's World filled his display. Initially it ranged 100,000 miles out from the surface, but the AI quickly adjusted the scale to the minimum needed to contain the *Duilio*'s elliptical orbit, some 49,000 miles across the long axis.

The observed track was purple; its expected continuation showed light blue. A dark blue bead marked the cruiser's predicted location at the moment the *Sibyl* extracted from the Matrix to attack.

Imagery gave the plan solidity, but Daniel knew how many variables, how many assumptions, were in the equation. His plans were as insubstantial as hoarfrost or that memory of ice.

He had the plot of the cruiser five light-seconds away. Adjusting his planned course minusculely, he nodded to himself and said, "Ship, prepare to insert into the Matrix *now.*"

Instead of a caged rectangle with the word EXECUTE printed on it like that of the *Princess Cecile*, the *Sibyl's* button was oblate and bright red. Daniel twisted it clockwise to free it, then thumbed it down.

As the electrical tension built, Daniel pressed himself against the back of his seat and stretched. He was wearing his hard suit. Looking about, he realized that despite his orders some of the Infantans were in utilities. One of the riggers just in from the hull had started to strip off his gear also, but Woetjans had that under control.

"Ship, this is Six!" he ordered. "All personnel suit up immediately! There won't be time after we take hull damage, and there's a bloody good chance we *will* take hull damage! Over."

Daniel switched his display into two separate screens: on top, a Plot-Position Indicator, now blank—in the Matrix, a ship *has* no position. Beneath it was an attack board on which pastel spheres overlay one another, waiting for the targets and vectors which would appear when they returned to the sidereal universe.

Cobwebs dragged the surface of his mind. For a moment, he saw the bridge inverted. That was a common delusion when slipping between universes, but when Daniel blinked in reflex he was in the center of jagged fluorescent lines which twisted into infinity without losing color or sharpness.

He opened his eyes instantly, shocked speechless. There was nothing overtly threatening in what he'd seen, but he knew beyond question that the environment he'd glimpsed was inimical to anything a human would recognize as life.

Daniel licked his lips. Sometimes people went irretrievably mad during travel through the Matrix. That was an unavoidable risk for a spacer, but it'd seemed slight as risks went. The moment just past, though, made it seem a lot more real.

"*Extracting into normal space in thirty, that is three-zero, seconds,*" Blantyre warned. Under normal circumstances the bridge controlled insertion, but the BDC kept watch on the timing of extractions.

Daniel grinned. His glimpse of madness had the benefit of proving there were worse things than being smashed by a missile or vaporized by a plasma bolt. It was good to remember that, especially when you were about to go up against a cruiser in a destroyer you'd never commanded before.

Daniel's surroundings flickered silently from purple to orange and back a dozen times or more; then the light was normal, sound was normal, and the PPI showed the *Sibyl*, an orange bead traveling at .04, only 12,000 miles from the blue bead of the vessel orbiting Dunbar's World. An instant later both the PPI and the attack board threw the legend DUI up beside the other vessel. If Daniel'd wanted he could've highlighted the legend and read the full particulars of the Pellegrinian cruiser *Caio Duilio*, but he hadn't had the least doubt about its identity from the moment they extracted.

"—*unknown vessel*," said a voice on the 20-meter hailing frequency, "*brake and lie to or we'll destroy you!*"

Bloody hell, they're waiting for us! Daniel thought as his fingers moved swiftly. The *Sibyl's* virtual keyboard had a slightly wider stance than he was used to. He didn't make mistakes, but each stroke required serious concentration. *Preset 3 will work, but I need to adjust for relative motion. . . .*

"*Our guns are trained on you!*" said the voice from the *Duilio*; ap Glynn himself, Daniel thought. "*No vessels are allowed to land on Dunbar's World until the pirates there have surrendered to the forces of Nataniel Arruns!*"

Of course! The Pellegrinians didn't expect an attack, but they were keeping a close watch to prevent anyone from reinforcing Councilor Corius. They probably hadn't identified the *Sibyl* as a warship yet—Daniel had learned tricks from Adele to cloak a ship's electronic identity—but they were prepared to rake a freighter with 15-cm bolts if it didn't halt as ordered.

"Prepare to launch!" Daniel said. His right hand twisted the EXECUTE button free. Before he could press it, the *Duilio's* dorsal turret fired.

The single round was probably aimed across the destroyer's bow as a warning, but the Pellegrinian gunnery officer hadn't properly factored in the target's high velocity. The powerful bolt didn't spread very much at all in the millisecond between leaving the muzzle and blasting into the topsail yard of the *Sibyl's* Dorsal 1 antenna.

Thirty linear feet of the tubular steel yard and antenna exploded in a rainbow fireball. The shock wave stripped the sails from all but the ventral antennas in Rings 1 and 2 and slammed the destroyer's hull like a load of gravel. The blow pushed the *Sibyl* away like a hydroplane leaping from a deceptively high wave.

Everything happened at once. A loud clang amidships signaled the flash of steam trying to expel the first of the four queued-up missiles. Daniel hadn't finished executing the launch order—he didn't think he had—but the impact or the momentary bath of ions was enough to trip the control.

Missiles didn't cut in their High Drives until they were well clear of the ship launching them. Otherwise antimatter in their exhaust would eat away the rigging and possibly the hull. This time a grinding shriek still louder than the hammerblow of steam indicated something had gone wrong.

Daniel didn't have time to look at the damage control schematics, but he had a pretty good notion of where the trouble was: the destroyer's slender hull had torqued enough to collapse the launching tube, binding the missile inside it. If the High Drive lit now, it'd dissolve enough of the vessel's interior to hold Adele's town house. He couldn't do a bloody thing about that for the moment, so he focused on the one action that might save his ship and crew.

Shunting his display from fire control back to astrogation with his left hand, he slammed the EXECUTE button home. "Inserting immediately!" he said. Shouted in all truth, though the intercom software would take care of the volume.

A charge built across the exposed surfaces of the destroyer's hull, easing her from normal space into the interstices between other universes. The *Sibyl* was tumbling on her long axis like a thrown knife, though the motion was too slow to be worse than uncomfortable.

If the *Duilio* fired again, the bolts would tear the destroyer apart in the seconds before she left sidereal space. Ap Glynn didn't fire. Daniel grinned wryly. Hitting the *Sibyl* was almost certainly an accident; the Pellegrinian, for all his fury, was probably concerned about what he'd done by mistake.

A rapid *clang-clang-clang-clang* from above and below the bridge shocked Daniel. It wasn't enemy action: Landholder Krychek, his forward turrets cleared by the Pellegrinian bolt, was shooting back in the instant his guns bore on the *Duilio*.

Daniel grinned even wider. As the destroyer slipped into the Matrix, Krychek and the other Infantans were singing, "Should I meet my death, I'll perish as a bold trooper!"

CHAPTER 27

Above Dunbar's World

The sun of Dunbar's World was a moderately bright star forty light-minutes from where Daniel stood on the *Sibyl's* bow. The sun of Bennaria was a less bright star above the *Princess Cecile*, which hung a quarter mile away, parallel to the destroyer. Starlight gave the hulls a ghostly presence, as if they were mirrored in polished ice.

He and Woetjans were working on the stump of Antenna Dorsal 1. He held a safety line belayed around the bitt at his feet. Its tension braced the bosun on the other end as she leaned into a prybar longer than she was tall.

The base joint, welded by the sleet of ions, released with a *clang!* Everything close by on the hull quivered. The bosun's boots flew up when the strain came off her bar, but Daniel's firm grip on the line allowed her to right herself easily.

Woetjans had recovered from more dangerous situations than the present one without needing either help or a safety line, though. Worst case she could've thrown the heavy bar as reaction mass, but that probably wouldn't have been required. Daniel'd seen the bosun's long arms snag lines that an arboreal monkey couldn't have reached.

With her magnetic boots firmly on the hull again, Woetjans bent forward slightly to ease her breathing. Freeing the mast had been a strain even for her, but it'd speeded the process of clearing the *Sibyl* for action by hours. The tangle of lines and melted sail tacked to the stub could be dumped into space as a single mass instead of having to be cut loose individually.

Normally crews would use a hydraulic jack on that sort of problem, but the *Sibyl's* tools had gone the way of every other fitment that could be removed from the destroyer and sold. If the jack wasn't in the maintenance shops on a Councilor's estate, it was lifting vehicles in a service garage run by some spacer's cousin. Daniel knew too much about government to believe that any social class had a monopoly on corruption.

As soon as Vesey'd maneuvered the *Sissie* alongside the destroyer, she'd sent across riggers and equipment to help clear the damage. Getting the jacks and power clamps across took time, though, and that was in short supply. Woetjans wasn't the sort to wait for somebody else to help with a job she thought her own brute strength could handle, which was most things. In Daniel's experience, her judgment was generally correct.

Quite a lot had been accomplished; already a mixed party was heaving the clot of top-hamper off at an angle from the destroyer where it wouldn't be a danger when they got under way again. The Sissies and Infantans worked well together, if only because neither group wanted to anger Woetjans.

Nonetheless Daniel shook his head minuscuelly as he viewed the damage, careful not to rap his brow or nose on the interior of his rigid helmet. It was such a *bloody* mess.

Going into action with all sails set—most of them aligned to cancel one another in the Matrix—had been the correct tactical decision: the 15-cm bolt would almost certainly've penetrated the hull otherwise, and heaven only knew what internal damage the plasma-lighted fireball would've done in the ship's interior. As it was, the plates were pitted and icicles of steel hung down from the bitt Daniel'd used to belay the line. They'd melted from the bitt itself as well as being redeposited from the mast and yards.

So of course it'd been the right decision, but the ruin the bolt'd smeared across the *Sibyl's* bow was enough to make any spacer weep. Four antennas and their yards were completely destroyed; two more were usable for the time being but would certainly be replaced when the ship reached a repair dock. The steel exploding from Dorsal 1 had damaged sails all the way back to Dorsal 6, though to port and starboard the hull had protected all but the topgallants, and the ventral rig was unharmed.

It wasn't really that bad: with a good crew and himself plotting the course, Daniel'd venture to better the time over any distance that the Bennarians could've accomplished when the *Sibyl* was new. It *looked* terrible, though, and besides what was visible, the hull's torquing might've done worse than collapse one missile tube.

The other three tubes were clear, though. For the time being, the destroyer's ability to fight was more important than the possibility she'd taken structural damage.

Woetjans had straightened, but she was surveying the work in general rather than diving directly into another specific job. She was Chief of Rig, so the damage was hers to correct. Though technically she was acting under the captain's direction, Daniel knew he had nothing to teach his bosun about the task in hand. He'd joined her as a moderately skilled helper, not to oversee her work.

Wrist-thick hawsers of braided monocrystal held the ships together at bow and stern. That way the vessels damped one another's slight moment, and the cables kept all strain off the thin transit line amidships.

Three figures were crossing from the *Princess Cecile*. The two on the ends carried the third between them in a basket of safety lines. Adele was the only person who was so valuable—and so frequently clumsy in free fall—that Vesey would've provided such an escort from the few spacers still aboard the corvette.

Daniel signaled to Woetjans, then started for where the line was clamped to a stanchion on the *Sibyl's* hull. He moved in a rigger's long, loping stride, closer to skating than walking. It kept the lifted boot near the hull, the experienced spacer's alternative to a safety line.

There were times that you simply leaped for a cable because speed was more important than anything else; people who sailed the Matrix for a living didn't put a high premium on personal safety. That was true in spades of riggers and of successful RCN officers.

Butterick, a Sissie from the Power Room, was the first of those crossing; she unhooked a line from her belt and clipped it to Daniel's. Adele was on the other end. Between them, Butterick and the Infantan at the end of the procession slapped the soles of Adele's boots down firmly.

Daniel dismissed the spacers with a wave; they started back to the corvette. The Infantan would've given Daniel the second safety line also, but that was simply absurd. If not precisely humorless the Landholder's people were at least a deeply serious lot, so the offer probably hadn't been meant as a joke.

Daniel leaned to touch helmets with Adele. To his surprise, she backed a step and held out a half-watt radio intercom. His face blanked, but he locked the unit into the slot on his helmet.

"*I know one doesn't normally use radio on the hull, Daniel*," Adele said calmly. "*I have things to discuss that I can't do where the Infantans might overhear, and I'm too awkward out here to do so while contorting myself to speak.*"

Daniel chuckled. "Intercoms can be issued for suit use only by order of the captain and the signals officer both," he said. "This is perfectly proper."

He still didn't like it: no rigger would. It'd take an unlikely series of things going wrong before one of these radios was used catastrophically in the Matrix, but things *did* go wrong. A smart spacer—a spacer who survived—avoided situations where he *might* screw up, because sure as hell he was going to screw up sooner or later if he had the opportunity.

But Adele wasn't out here on the hull without a bloody good reason.

"*According to Vesey*," Adele said, "*you'll probably attack the Pellegrinians next time with both ships in company. Is that correct?*"

Daniel shrugged invisibly. He hadn't had time to discuss the plan in detail, but Vesey'd served with him long enough to be able to figure it out on her own. It was the best use of his slight available resources.

"Yes," he said, "though at longer range than I'd expected to engage before I saw how alert the *Duilio*'s gun crews are."

He licked his lips, then added, "That means the *Sissie* will simply be distracting the Pellegrinians. It's possible that she'll be sacrificed without any chance of doing actual harm to them."

"*Daniel*," Adele said, "*I think I can convince the Pellegrinians that the* Princess Cecile *is actually the* Sibyl. *If we—if the* Sissie—*insert alone and at some distance from the* Duilio, *we'll draw her whole attention, won't we? And then you can attack with the* Sibyl *while they're not expecting you.*"

Daniel touched his lips again. "They'll be expecting two ships," he said.

"*Will they?*" said Adele. "*Daniel, do you think a Pellegrinian officer would fake an attack in a ship which doesn't have missiles? And they know the* Sissie *doesn't have missiles.*"

So they did, from the inspection when the *Sissie* landed at Central Haven as well as from the fact that Daniel hadn't replied to the salvoes ap Glynn launched when the corvette escaped from Dunbar's World. But there was a basic flaw with the plan nonetheless.

"Adele, if we're close enough to threaten the *Duilio*, they'll have us in sight," Daniel said. "Sure, her optics are monkey models, not first-line gear built to Fleet specs, but nothing comes out of the Pleasaunce Arsenal that can't tell the difference between a corvette and a damaged destroyer within five light-minutes."

He grinned, wondering if Adele could see him through the faceplates of their helmets. "The *Sibyl*'s optics are the same quality, you know," he said. Regardless, she knew him well enough to hear the smile in his voice. "They're not the first thing I'd upgrade if I had the choice."

Another mare's nest of tubes and rigging spun slowly away from the destroyer, this time most of Starboard 2. Woetjans and her crew would have the damage cleared in another hour. Handling a ship with a badly unbalanced rig could be tricky, but Daniel'd sailed a jury-rigged heavy cruiser to Cinnabar in seventeen days. He wasn't worried about that aspect of the coming action.

"*Yes, but Vesey says that if we remain end-on to the Pellegrinians and four or five light-seconds away,*" Adele said, "*they'll have to depend on their computer to complete the identification. They won't have anybody skilled enough to be certain without the software.*"

Daniel pursed his lips, wondering why Adele was discussing this. Aloud he said, "I suppose that's true. But in fairness to our Pellegrinian friends, Adele, I don't know that I could tell a destroyer from a corvette under those conditions. In any case, they certainly do have the software to complete the identification."

"*Yes,*" said Adele, "*but I have all the communications codes from the* Rainha. *That gives me access to the* Duilio's *computer. If I'm quick enough, I believe I can enter a different—a corrected, if I may call it that—result.*"

"Oh!" said Daniel. The stars were a cold scatter in all directions; nowhere especially dense, but nowhere completely absent. To Daniel sidereal space seemed static and cold compared with the roiling excitement of the Matrix, a cut-glass vase instead of a cat quivering as it makes up its mind whether to pounce.

He looked at his friend again. His heart was leaden after its sudden thrill of hope. "I'm afraid that won't work, Adele," he said. "You have their commo, but that'll be completely separate from the battle computer which they use for identification."

"*My mother would have hated the term 'monkey model,'*" Adele said with apparent irrelevance. "*She was strongly against the practice of demeaning less technologically sophisticated peoples. Still, I don't suppose her views on the matter are controlling anymore.*"

"Pardon?" Daniel said. It was Adele speaking, so the words meant something.

"*Daniel, any ship built for us or the Alliance Fleet would handle communications, astrogation, and attack in physically separate computers,*" she said. "*But the* Duilio *was built for export. All her functions are in a single unit, and I'll have access to it as soon as I'm close enough to the Pellegrinians to feed a signal through their secure network. Let us go in first and only follow when we've gotten their full attention.*"

"This is going to be very dangerous," Daniel said, thinking aloud rather than objecting. "The timing will be critical."

He understood why Adele hadn't wanted the Infantans to overhear. The plan was only possible because the Alliance had commo teams on all the ships supporting the Pellegrinian operation.

He clapped Adele on the shoulder, his gauntlet clacking against the glass-filled plate covering the joint of her suit. "By God, Adele, this doesn't do much for our chances of survival, but it certainly does make it more likely that we'll be able to put paid to that wog cruiser! By *God* it does!"

"My mother particularly disliked the term 'wog,'" said Adele austerely. "But as I said, I don't suppose her views are controlling."

"*Counting down to extraction!*" announced Pleshkov, the Infantan executive officer now in the *Sissie's* BDC. "*Ten seconds, nine seconds—*"

Adele grimaced and blocked her input from the general channel for the next eight seconds. The Infantans had their own procedures, and there hadn't been time to harmonize them with those of the RCN.

To correct them to RCN standard, *she* thought. She didn't need somebody yammering while she concentrated on a problem.

Adele sank back into the silence of her familiar display, a simulation of what she expected when they extracted from the Matrix: Dunbar's World, the *Duilio* in close orbit, and the *Princess Cecile* herself appearing 600,000 miles out, twenty seconds before the cruiser passed into the planetary shadow. The image gave the events a specious reality, but Adele knew they were as evanescent as the light beams interfering to create the holograms.

The *Princess Cecile* shifted out of the Matrix. For an instant Adele's bones were replaced by simulacra of frozen steel; they seared and shrank her muscles from the inside. The pain would've been disabling if—

Well, if she'd been a different person and not completely focused on the task in hand.

The *Princess Cecile* completed its transition back into the sidereal universe. Adele's body returned to normal, her flesh trembling slightly with remembered pain. The High Drive pushed her hard against her couch.

The enemy was in sight.

An icon on the top of the display informed Adele that the *Sissie's* antennas were adjusting automatically, as they were programmed to do. She'd chosen the laser communicator to enter the cruiser, since ap Glynn wasn't using it himself and also because the corvette's sending unit was of low mass and could be quickly slewed.

The latter turned out to be important, because the *Duilio* would cross behind the planet in seven seconds, not twenty. It'd take over three seconds for Adele's impulse to reach the cruiser.

She had the commands preset. When her laser communicator locked on to the destroyer, the queued data fed in a burst to a suspense file aboard the cruiser. The steps had to be executed in sequence, and she wasn't confident that the Pellegrinian computer would respond promptly enough to cycle through the instructions before the planetary shadow broke the transmission.

"—*known vessel, lie to immediately or*—" the *Duilio* ordered, the same demand it'd directed at the *Sibyl* when Daniel'd attempted his abortive attack. This time there was a difference, not in the formal hail which dissolved in static as Dunbar's World intervened but instead in the cruiser's general RF signature.

"Captain, both of the cruiser's turrets are rotating," Adele said, half stumbling over the first word. She'd almost said Six. That would've keyed Vesey as intended, but it would've made both of them uncomfortable. "One was tracking us from the moment we extracted. Over!"

The last word sharply, because she'd almost forgotten it. Again.

Vesey didn't reply; there was no need for her to and she doubtless had other business. Adele felt the direction of *down* change, the result of the thrusters gimbaling to adjust the *Sissie*'s course. The approximation Daniel and Vesey had created was remarkably close to what the corvette actually found when it returned to normal space, a comment on the high quality of planning and execution. Vesey had extracted within a few hundred miles of the intended point.

There was also a great deal of luck in the business. The *Duilio* had lifted into a marginally higher orbit since the Cinnabar officers made their calculations on the basis of data that was an hour old. That increased the orbital period, so only chance made the cruiser's location so nearly coincide with the prediction.

Adele wasn't sure what Vesey was trying to accomplish now. Accelerating a 1,300-ton vessel was a slow process even with the High Drive operating at maximum output. The ship groaned under the strain, though, and Pleshkov shouted on the general channel, "*Back off, you fool! The rig is set and—*"

Adele disabled the Infantan's ability to transmit. That was no doubt very wrong: it was insubordinate, it was potentially dangerous since Pleshkov might have something useful to say at some later point, and it carried the risk of a serious incident as soon as the fellow realized what'd happened. Besides which, Adele's mother would've objected strongly to the discourtesy.

It's what Daniel would've wanted her to do. If Vesey felt otherwise, that was only because she put a higher value on protocol than Daniel or Adele either one.

If Pleshkov challenged Adele to a duel because of the insult, he wouldn't be the first person she'd shot; if he simply came storming onto the bridge to complain, Tovera would kill him without bothering about a challenge. And Evadne Rolfe Mundy had been dead for seventeen years. Some of her opinions still existed within her surviving daughter, but not to the degree that they'd affect

Adele's willingness to do what Commander Leary would expect of her.

The *Duilio* swung back into sight; she'd stopped transmitting the challenge. Adele assumed that meant she'd decided the *Princess Cecile* was the destroyer returned to the attack. When the cruiser fired her plasma cannon, both guns from the dorsal turret but only one from the ventral, the assumption became a certainty.

"*Hoo, that's right, laddies!*" Sun crowed on the general channel. "*Burn your bloody barrels out for nothing, why don't you! You couldn't raise a sunburn at this range!*"

The gunner shouldn't have been chattering that way, but Adele didn't cut him off because what he was saying was good for morale. Adele's morale included, since Sun had expert knowledge of the bolt's potential effectiveness.

The cruiser fired the same three guns again. One of the tubes must not be working. Had it failed recently, or could Adele have learned about it previously if she'd done a better job of sifting data gleaned from Pellegrinian files?

The *Princess Cecile* continued to brake hard. Her rigging creaked and muttered as thrust bent the antennas and their full array of sails. The hull twisted also, enough that Adele heard the keen of air leaking through spreading seams. She even thought she felt the internal pressure drop, but she knew that might be imagination.

It didn't matter. Adele wore a flexible atmosphere suit, as did all the other crew members save for those who'd chosen the even greater safety of rigging suits.

A slash of ions arrived simultaneously with the instrument readings indicating the *Duilio* had fired another salvo. Adele's display blurred and every light in the ceiling of the A Level corridor went out; a circuit breaker tripping from an overload, she supposed.

The damage wasn't serious: her display came back as sharp as a knife edge a moment later, and in seconds somebody reset the lighting circuit as well. *Sun was stretching the point when he explained how harmless 15-cm bolts were at this range. . . .*

Adele lifted against her seat restraints; loose gear flew about the compartment as though gravity had been abolished. In effect it had: the High Drive motors had shut down. Her first thought was that the bolt had crippled them, but after an instant's reflection she realized that Vesey was trying to throw off the cruiser's gunnery officer by the cutting the *Sissie's* acceleration. They could hope it'd work, at least for long enough.

Given that the corvette's mission was to draw the attention of the Pellegrinians, the question of how much damage the cruiser did to them wasn't significant. Adele smiled. For the sake of the friends she'd made in the *Sissie's* crew, though, she'd regret it if they were all killed. Most of them took a more serious view of oblivion than she did.

A new signal spiked on her display; the software matched it against a standard template.

"Captain, the *Duilio's* launched a missile," Adele said. "It's an Alliance Type 12A3, a single-converter type."

She was aware as she spoke that her voice sounded dry. That didn't change the content of the message, of course, but Adele'd learned the hard way that people were more likely to listen to tone than they were to words. So far as she was concerned, that was utterly wrong; but the analytical part of her mind realized that it was *her* job to communicate. She should work harder at sounding excited.

The cruiser's three operational cannon fired again, this time without hitting the corvette. The High Drive kicked in again, though the renewed acceleration appeared to be the 1 g that starships maintained to counterfeit gravity. On Adele's display—

"Captain, the *Duilio* has fired two more missiles," she announced. "And five more missiles, a total of eight. Over."

That was a full salvo for the cruiser. Adele wondered how long it'd take the Pellegrinians to reload their tubes. She recalled forty-five seconds to a minute being normal on the warships she'd sailed on, but she'd never been aboard a cruiser in action.

"*I'm tracking!*" announced Sun. The upper four-inch turret fired half a dozen rounds, rattling loose fittings. The lower turret joined in for another three or four, then both fell silent.

"*Bloody sails!*" the gunner said. "*Cap'n, rotate us fifteen degrees clockwise so I have a clear shot, on my bloody soul!*"

"*Bridge, we must reenter the Matrix!*" Officer Pleshkov said over the command channel. "*There is time, please, but not much time. We must!*"

Adele's wands twitched, but she didn't cut the Infantan out of the command loop after all. He was no doubt correct in his assessment of the danger, and it was his job to inform the captain in case she hadn't noticed it herself.

Which of course Vesey had, but Pleshkov wasn't speaking out of turn until Vesey told him to shut up. In which case Adele would instantly silence him. It didn't matter what happened to the *Princess Cecile* so long as they held the Pellegrinians' attention until—

Sudden activity lighted up the radio frequency band. It was as meaningful to Adele as close-range optical images would be to most RCN officers.

"The *Sibyl*'s arrived!" Adele said. "The *Sibyl*'s launching missiles, three missiles! Daniel's here!"

Apparently I'm capable of enthusiasm under the correct stimulus.

"*Ship, we're inserting into the Matrix in fifteen seconds,*" Vesey said. "*Gunner, cease fire to avoid disturbing our surface charge.*"

She paused there. Adele expected her to sign out—Vesey was punctilious about that—but instead she continued, "*I think we have enough time, spacers. Commander Leary will be proud of us. Captain out.*"

Perhaps Vesey was putting a positive gloss on reality the way Sun had. Adele didn't have the equipment or the expertise either one to determine whether the *Sissie* could leave normal space before the Pellegrinian missiles intersected with their computed course.

Regardless, "Commander Leary was proud of them" wouldn't make a bad epitaph.

At the instant the destroyer inserted into the Matrix, the bridge rippled like a scene projected on a windblown curtain. Daniel barely noticed it. Generally short insertions didn't have the gut-wrenching effects you could face when you extracted after a long voyage without a break, and this'd been just a quick dip.

Many astrogators made touch-and-gos to get star sights to check their location. Not only did Daniel pride himself on his dead reckoning in the Matrix, the most cack-handed officer the RCN had ever commissioned could manage a hop of fifty-five light-minutes without missing his extraction by a significant degree.

What *Daniel* needed was a recent fix on the Pellegrinian cruiser. Five light-minutes out from Dunbar's World was the compromise he'd decided on, reasonably current imagery of the *Duilio* without putting the *Sibyl* so close in that the Pellegrinians might become aware of her before she arrived.

By making two insertion/extraction sequences while the *Sissie* covered the same short distance in one, Daniel also built in the delay he needed for the plan to work. He couldn't launch his attack on the *Duilio* too quickly this way—

And being too quick meant failure. If the choice were purely Daniel's to make, he knew full well that he'd shave thirty seconds or even a minute off the calculated interval. The *Princess Cecile* was his ship, many of her crewmen had been his shipmates throughout the past two years; and of course Adele had become even more important as a friend than as a colleague.

But the *Sissie* had to be alone long enough in the vicinity of Dunbar's World to completely concentrate the attention of the *Duilio*'s crew. Otherwise they all might as well've stayed in Charlestown and partied the way Councilor Waddell had suggested in the beginning.

"*We will extract in thirty, that is three-zero, seconds,*" Cory announced from the BDC with careful formality. Daniel's display was as it'd been on the previous attack: Plot-Position Indicator above, attack board beneath.

He hadn't carried a Chief Missileer on this mission, since it would've been a wasted slot when the *Sissie* had no missiles. Besides, it was a task for which Daniel himself had both a flair and experience. His fingers poised.

The emptiness which Daniel's screens maintained in the Matrix now filled with data. The PPI showed the *Duilio* orbiting forty-six miles above Dunbar's World and over four thousand miles—4,173 and closing—from where the *Sibyl* had returned to normal space.

The real-time optical image inset in the upper right-hand corner of the display showed the cruiser as it emerged from the planetary shadow. Ap Glynn had taken in his rig since the destroyer's previous attack. The sails were furled and the yards rotated parallel to the masts before the masts themselves were folded against the hull. That gave the heavy guns full traverse and elevation.

The two ships were on nearly parallel courses for the moment, but the *Sibyl* viewed the cruiser from thirty degrees below the center of her long axis. Both 15-cm turrets were rotated to track the *Princess Cecile* at a nearly reciprocal angle to the destroyer.

Landholder Krychek had been waiting for this chance. He adjusted the *Sibyl*'s four turrets with a momentary squeal; then the 10-cm guns began to hammer.

Either Krychek or the destroyer's gunnery program blocked a weapon's discharge if anything was within 100 meters of the muzzle. The *Sibyl*'s sails, those which remained after the previous attack, were set, so initially only six and after a few seconds four guns fired.

Flashes lit the *Duilio*'s hull, patches of plating subliming under the lash of deuterium ions. The destroyer's weapons didn't deliver nearly the impact of 15-cm guns—the relation of bore to charge was logarithmic, not linear—and the cruiser's hull was much thicker besides, but the light weapons cycled much quicker also. Krychek was at least as accurate as Sun would've been at this short range, and Daniel knew from experience that the bolts would do serious if not incapacitating damage.

But that was the gunner's business; Daniel was picking the first of his new preset attack orders. The calculated spread of his salvo—only three missiles this time, but that was still one more than the *Sissie* herself could've managed—showed in green lines which flared as each missile separated after burnout. That didn't spread the footprint significantly in the present instance because the target was so close; without adjustment none of the missiles would pass within ten miles of the *Duilio* on her predicted course.

It felt like an unconscionable length of time before Daniel got the corrections entered into his attack board, but in all truth it was a matter of seconds. It would've taken a minute or more if he'd had to plan the attack from scratch instead of tweaking a preset order.

He was pretty sure they didn't have a minute. Until the moment Daniel twisted and depressed the EXECUTE key, it was a toss-up in his mind as to whether they had the seconds the present reality had required.

Whang!

"Ship, launching three!" he shouted over the general push. He wasn't so much reporting to the crew—they'd already heard the first missile launching, followed at five-second intervals by the *whang! whang!* of the other two—as he was crowing with pride at having executed a difficult operation in a timely fashion.

The *Princess Cecile* was a speck on the PPI, driving slowly off at a tangent from Dunbar's World. The salvo of missiles the cruiser'd launched were closing at .07 C. They'd divided at burnout and were now a spreading straggle of chunks, each weighing a tonne or more.

"May the God of Battles aid you!" Daniel muttered under his breath, but his present duties were to the *Sibyl* and her crew. Blantyre had the conn, but he'd ordered her to hold course at 1 g acceleration unless the bridge took a direct hit; in that case she could use her discretion. Daniel's concern was his attack board.

Missiles rumbled on their tracks, shaking the destroyer like freight cars shifting in her belly. The fore and aft tubes had separate magazines to keep the feed run short; jerks and clanking indicated to Daniel's experienced ear that the launchers were reloaded even before green ready lights flashed along the side of his display.

An iridescent cloud blurred the *Duilio's* real-time image. On the sidebar of the attack board, a legend under the cruiser's icon indicated she was braking hard. Captain ap Glynn had reacted to the oncoming missiles by lighting both High Drive and plasma thrusters. He must be running them up to overload output.

Plasma flared with molecules of antimatter which hadn't combined in the High Drive. Though ionized, the thrusters' exhaust was nonetheless ordinary matter. It converted completely to energy along with antimatter when they mixed.

If the *Duilio's* antennas had been stepped, the strain of deceleration would've sheared them at the base hinges. Even as it was, the cruiser's hull must've been flexing like a rubber toy. Daniel'd commanded ships in similar straits. He knew how terrifying the groans of plates against the ribs and the squeal of escaping air would be to the crew, particularly those who didn't have immediate duties.

Daniel *knew*, but he had no sympathy at all. The Pellegrinians were The Enemy, the people who'd chosen to fight the RCN. He'd grind them into the dust, by *God* he would!

The *Duilio* had been firing at the *Sissie* when Daniel's display locked into sidereal space; the bolts of heavy hydrogen, detonated by laser arrays in the breaches of the cannon, showed as tracks on his attack board. The cruiser's turrets began slewing as soon as the Pellegrinian gunnery officer realized he had a much more pressing target, but her heavy acceleration made both aiming and traverse more difficult.

Daniel recalculated for his second salvo. Ap Glynn was fighting the inertia that carried his ship into the *Sibyl's* initial spread of missiles. Allowing for that—

Whang!

"Launching three!" Daniel said as the crew cheered over the continued hammering of Krychek's guns.

Whang! Whang!

The attack board covered too small a region to show the fleeing *Princess Cecile*, but on the PPI the missiles were red beads nearing the blue dot of the corvette. God of Battles, aid them!

Daniel saw almost as soon as his missiles released that he'd misjudged. Though the board predicted that the yellow tracks of his second salvo would cross the orange bead of the cruiser, Daniel—and the battle computer, but a computer can't feel embarrassment when it screws up—had failed to factor in the gravity of Dunbar's World. This salvo would miss ahead of the *Duilio* just as the first had. The cruiser, wrapped in a cloud of fire-shot radiance, was slipping into the planet's shadow as it continued to plunge toward the surface.

Ap Glynn wasn't as certain as Daniel that the *Sibyl's* salvo was misaimed, or at any rate he'd decided not to take chances. The single working tube in the cruiser's ventral turret fired, catching a missile just before it separated. Half a tonne of solid metal swelled into a fireball, thrusting the remainder of the projectile away at an angle that increased the *Duilio's* margin of safety.

The next trio of missiles shook the destroyer on their way to the launching tubes. Daniel had to hope that they'd continue to feed smoothly, because he didn't have trained missile crewmen aboard to correct problems. That was why he was holding a straight course at 1 g acceleration, ideal conditions for the conveyors. There was always a chance of something breaking on a ship that'd sat idle for several years, however, and the missile-handling equipment provided more opportunities for failure than most installations.

As the remaining missiles of the salvo slanted into the atmosphere, they corkscrewed before breaking up in a tumbling light show. Daniel regretted the danger to people on the ground, but even a civilian can slip getting out of the bathtub. . . .

For a moment Landholder Krychek had all four turrets clear. The simultaneous rapid fire of his 10-cm guns made the destroyer shake like a dog come in from the wet. Daniel clenched as his fingers computed the next salvo, knowing that if Krychek could shoot then there were at least four points at which the *Sibyl's* spreading sails didn't protect the hull from the cruiser's bolts.

The *Princess Cecile* vanished from the PPI as the swarm of Pellegrinian missiles crossed her computed track. At this range, the *Sibyl's* electronics couldn't determine whether the corvette had slipped into the Matrix or had been reduced to a cloud of gas and debris.

The cruiser'd been maneuvering too hard to launch missiles at the destroyer, a *bloody* good thing. From the evidence of her first salvo, her Chief Missileer knew his business.

The *Duilio's* dorsal turret fired at the destroyer. Red telltales on the command display quickly switched back to green. A circuit breaker astern had tripped, but neither bolt struck squarely.

The shroud of plasma and pure energy bathing the *Duilio* suddenly streamed a sparkling curlicue. That stream pinched off, but two more—one bow and one stern—blazed out in the wake as the cruiser continued to descend.

Daniel was poised on the EXECUTE button and his mouth was open to shout, "Launching three!" Instead he jerked his hand up, allowing the button to twist back into its safety position.

"Cease fire!" he said. "All personnel, cease fire!"

The *Sibyl's* guns were still firing; only four of them now, but that was a result of the angle rather than because Krychek was taking a gradual approach to obeying orders. Daniel'd expected that. It took him a moment longer to find the gunnery lockout on this command console than it would've done on the *Sissie's* familiar display, but only a moment.

The guns fell silent. At the gunnery console, the Landholder shouted curses as he furiously fault-checked his equipment. Eventually he'd figure out what'd happened, at which point he and Daniel would discuss the matter in whatever fashion he chose.

Or Hogg chose, if Daniel didn't watch his servant carefully. Still, that was a problem for a later time.

The cruiser's guns had missed because three of her High Drive motors had destroyed themselves violently. Captain ap Glynn's complete focus on the oncoming missiles had dropped his ship too deep into the atmosphere for the High Drive to operate safely. When the motors began to fail, they shook the *Duilio* like a rat in a terrier's jaws.

"Ship, we've done it!" Daniel said. He made what would've been the correct series of keystrokes on the *Princess Cecile* but he got a TRANSACTION FAILED legend. "Break, Cory, damn this bloody thing to hell! Can you echo the cruiser's image on all the ship's displays, over?"

The *Duilio* continued to fall toward the surface, braked by plasma thrusters alone. She'd stopped being a threat. Indeed, given the sort of damage chronic High Drive failure did to the ship mounting the motors, ap Glynn'd be lucky if he managed a controlled crash rather than simply augering in. Acute failure—lighting the High Drive with the throat of the motor full of normal matter—destroyed the unit itself in a shattering explosion, but antimatter leaked into a thin atmosphere was a cancer. It ate the external hull until the converter finally managed to destroy itself and stop the process.

"Ship," Daniel said, "we've crippled the Pellegrinian cruiser and—"

An image of the *Duilio* filled his display. Cory'd found the instruction set that'd eluded Daniel a moment previously, but he'd applied it a touch too generally.

Daniel opened his mouth to bellow a protest, but the midshipman caught himself before the words came out. The cruiser shrank back to a small inset on the command display, but the gunnery and navigation consoles still showed a full-screen image.

"Right!" said Daniel. "Crippled them, knocked them right out of the fight, Sibyls! We hold the space around Dunbar's World in the name of the Federal Republic, and our allies on the ground hold what'd been the invaders' base."

He hoped that was still true; he didn't actually know what'd happened on Mandelfarne Island since the *Sissie*'d lifted under fire. Still, ap Glynn wouldn't have been enforcing his blockade so fiercely if the Bennarian Volunteers had surrendered to Nataniel Arruns.

"As soon as we see what happens to Pellegrinian cruiser—"

The *Duilio* curved onto the hidden side of the planet in a cometary blaze. Daniel knew it was possible to import satellite imagery, but he didn't care that much. The cruiser was certainly out of the fight. Adele would've had the pictures for him, though, without him needing to ask.

"—we'll make further plans. At present I expect to contact our allies and provide support from orbit while Councilor Corius arranges the surrender of the invading forces. Fellow Sibyls, we've shown everybody what it means to fight the finest professionals in the galaxy!"

It'd been on the tip of his tongue to say, "fight the RCN." That would've been a bad mistake when most of his crew claimed allegiance to the Alliance.

The image of the *Duilio* reappeared, blurred because the optics weren't really up to the corrections necessary to look deeply through the atmosphere. It was details like that which reminded Daniel he was in a ship built on the cheap for the export market. Though she'd done the job, you couldn't argue with that.

"*Sir?*" said Midshipman Cory.

Daniel's face blanked. *How's Cory gotten into a channel that should've allowed only me to speak?* Then, *Because he's my signals officer, that's how!*

"*What's happened to the* Princess Cecile, *sir? Are they all right?*"

"I don't—" Daniel said. If he'd had Cory in front of him, he'd have throttled the boy, put his hands around his throat and squeezed till his eyes popped out.

"—know at this moment—"

Because Daniel was always watching his display, no matter what was on his mind or how angry he might be, he saw the blue bead wink onto the PPI screen. Even before the icon with the legend PRI appeared beside it, he knew what it was.

"Fellow spacers," Daniel said, "I was incorrect. The *Princess Cecile* has just extracted from the Matrix at a distance of 41,000 miles from Dunbar's World. I expect her signals officer will be contacting us very—"

And as he spoke, a familiar voice on his helmet earphones said, "*Daniel, are you all right?*"

"Yes, Adele," Daniel said. It wasn't proper protocol, but protocol be hanged. "Now everything is all right."

CHAPTER 28

Mandelfarne Island on Dunbar's World

"Gentlemen and ladies," said Daniel, pulling out his own chair. "Please be seated."

The plural "ladies" was stretching the point. Adele was at his side, while Elemere sat with Krychek across the square table. Between them were Corius and Colonel Quinn to Daniel's left, and to the right a pair of Federal Republic officials—Field Marshal, formerly General, Mahler and a civilian named Bartolomeo, the Finance Minister, who'd just arrived from Sinclos.

There wasn't a suitable conference room on Mandelfarne Island, but the weather was sunny with a brisk wind that kept the summer heat from being incapacitating, so Daniel'd ordered a sailcloth marquee spread over the *Duilio*'s dorsal turret. The covered area was fifteen feet by twenty-five, quite sufficient for eight people around a table.

They could've cleared the cruiser's Great Cabin for the meeting, but Daniel preferred the outdoor location for a number of reasons. It was the highest flat surface on the island, so the gathered leaders could both see and be seen by everyone else. It gave them a close view of the damage done to the cruiser by the *Sibyl*'s guns, which demonstrated to the local officials just how effective plasma cannon could be.

Perhaps the most important reason was the fact that Daniel found the setting congenial but he suspected that the others did not. If they were uncomfortable, they were less likely to bluster and force him to demonstrate that the real power was in the hands of the RCN representative. Bartolomeo had initially spoken as though he were in charge.

Daniel'd learned from his father's example that in the long term you were better off leaving your opponents with their dignity. If you robbed them of that, you had to destroy them utterly so that they couldn't come back and stab you at a later moment. Speaker Leary had understood the latter rule also, as the sole surviving Mundy could've testified.

Spacers were using a diamond saw to replace the cruiser's High Drive motors. The keening was audible, but it wasn't the overwhelming shriek it'd have been if the conference hadn't been seventy feet above with the depth of the hull between. The replacement units had been unbolted from the wreckage of the *Greybudd* in normal fashion, but flaring antimatter had welded the remains of the *Duilio's* motors into the remains of their mountings.

"I'm not clear on the purpose of this meeting, Leary," Bartolomeo said, mopping his forehead with a checked kerchief. He was a florid man whose quick, darting eyes had never quite made contact with Daniel's. "And I don't mind saying that I don't like heights!"

And I don't mind hearing it, Daniel thought. With a bland smile he said, "You can think of this as a logistical conference, Minister. As the ranking representative of the Republic of Cinnabar, it falls to me to suggest some dispositions."

"I don't see that you have any right whatever!" Bartolomeo said. "Dunbar's World is an independent—"

Corius rapped the table sharply with the tips of his right index and middle fingers. Marshal Mahler touched the minister's shoulder and, when the latter glanced up angrily, gave a quick shake of his head. Fallert was on the Dorsal 2 mainyard, watching the meeting from thirty feet away; Hogg and Tovera were on Dorsal 3, a similar distance aft of the turret. Bartolomeo hadn't noticed them or hadn't understood the implications, but Mahler certainly had.

"Commander Leary's skill and intelligence gave me my victory," Corius said calmly. "I'm more than ready to endorse any suggestions which such a benefactor chooses to make. Given that Dunbar's World owes her very liberty to him, I should think that in simple courtesy you'd grant him the same precedence, Minister Bartolomeo."

"Well, of course I'll listen to what he has to say," Bartolomeo said, licking his lips. "I . . ."

His voice trailed off; he'd finally noticed Fallert's grin. He jerked his eyes down to the table in front of him.

"To begin with, there's the problem of the Pellegrinian prisoners," Daniel said. "I suppose under the laws of war they're the responsibility of the Federal Republic, but—"

"We don't have the facilities to feed and house eight thousand men," said Marshal Mahler. "Thus far they've been eating their own supplies and the weather's been temperate enough to keep them in the open here on Mandelfarne Island, but neither of those things will last long."

"We're not responsible!" Bartolomeo said quickly, though he kept his face lowered. "And they *certainly* can't be allowed back onto the mainland. Why, they're just pirates, you know. We should shoot them all!"

"Do you have any idea how long it would take to shoot eight thousand people?" asked Adele. She'd been sitting primly with her personal data unit on the table in front of her. Now she eyed Bartolomeo like a hawk over a vole. When the minister didn't look up, she tapped his earlobe with the wand in her right hand.

"*Do* you, Minister Bartolomeo?" she repeated in a tone as thin as a razor. "Or are you proposing that we of the RCN handle the task with plasma cannon? Is that your plan?"

"I don't—" the civilian said. He leaned away from her, his eyes wide. "I didn't—"

Mahler put his hand firmly on Bartolomeo's shoulder and said, "Commander Leary, what solution do you propose?"

The fellow's showing himself to better advantage than he did as a rabbit being dug out of his hole, Daniel thought. Aloud he said, "I've discussed the matter informally with Councilor Corius. As I understand it, he's prepared to supply the prisoners and transport them off-planet."

Corius nodded. He was a handsome man and had a very pleasant smile, if you didn't look up at his eyes.

"I've already started making the arrangements," he said. "I've held discussions with the surviving Pellegrinian officers, and I'm pleased to say they're in enthusiastic agreement."

"They agree, you say?" said Landholder Krychek in a tone of surprise.

"I believe they were expecting alternatives of the sort Minister Bartolomeo proposed," Corius said. He chuckled. "Gathering sufficient shipping may take as long as ten days. I trust I can expect the help and forbearance of the Federal Republic during the delay?"

He raised an eyebrow toward the minister. "Well, I . . .," Bartolomeo said, then looked down at his hands again.

"Given that ten thousand trained troops are in favor of your plan, Councilor," Daniel said with a cheery smile to lay a swatch of velvet over the iron reality of his words, "it'd seem extremely dangerous, not to mention inhumane, for the Republic not to support it fully. Wouldn't you agree, Marshal Mahler?"

"My troops'll do all they can to make sure supplies get to the camps and to generally keep a lid on it while you're hiring transports, you bet," Mahler said. "But the sooner the better, Councilor."

"And to that end," Daniel said, "I've arranged the sale of the *Rainha*, an RCN prize, to Councilor Corius."

Referring to the *Rainha* as a prize was shading reality a trifle. Strictly speaking, Adele was the only active-service RCN officer involved in the taking, which otherwise bore many similarities to piracy carried out by Cinnabar citizens. Daniel was quite willing to pay the normal quarter share to Navy House when he returned to Xenos in order to beg that question.

He cleared his throat, then continued, "The prisoners are taken care of, then. The next—"

"One moment!" Bartolomeo said. "One thing I must know: where is Nataniel Arruns himself? We cannot compromise on this!"

"My servant Tovera," said Adele, looking at the minister but speaking with less emotion than a voice synthesizer would inject, "informs me that Arruns and his personal staff refused to surrender. They were killed in the fighting."

"Rather a fortunate result, frankly," said Corius with his usual smile. "His presence would've complicated my negotiations with the other Pellegrinian officers."

"Is that true?" said Marshal Mahler, looking past Bartolomeo to Adele. "I would've have expected . . ."

"I'm quite sure that Arruns is dead if Tovera says he is," Adele said in the same flat tone. "If you believe it's necessary to look into the circumstances of his death, you have my permission to question my servant."

Mahler looked over his shoulder. Hogg grinned and waved with his left hand. The marshal faced around quickly and said, "I misspoke. My apologies."

"Next," Daniel continued in the pause, "is the matter of captured equipment. I propose that the small arms be delivered to Councilor Corius in consideration of Bennarian help in resisting the invaders. Marshal?"

Mahler grimaced. "I'd been hoping—" he said, then angrily shook his head. "No, I'm not going to get in your way, Leary."

He snorted. In a more cheerful tone he added, "I've seen what happens to people who do."

"Your society is already unsettled by the invasion," Adele said. Though dry, her voice was as harsh as a saw blade. "The availability of that number of automatic rifles would have even more serious consequences for the social order. I can give you examples after the meeting, if you'd like."

She smiled without humor. "I've *seen* examples."

"There remains the captured gear other than weapons," Daniel said, "including vehicles and heavy equipment. I believe these will be of value to your army, Marshal."

Bartolomeo looked from Daniel to Marshal Mahler. "The disposition of spoils is a matter for the finance ministry, not the army," he said sharply.

Daniel shrugged and smiled. "That's an internal matter for you gentlemen to discuss at leisure," he said. "I'm sure you'll be able to find a satisfactory solution."

Really he was sure that a number of local officials, including Mahler and Bartolomeo, were going to make a very good thing out of the loot, while little or none would go to either the army or the treasury. That didn't even begin to be a concern of Daniel Leary or the Republic of Cinnabar.

Krychek had been sitting with his hand over Elemere's. Now he removed it and thumped both palms on the tabletop. Leaning forward slightly, he said in a tone of challenge, "You haven't mentioned this *Duilio*, Leary, this cruiser. You are repairing it as we all hear. You plan to give it to Cinnabar, that is so?"

"It most certainly is *not* so, Landholder Krychek," said Daniel. He straightened in his seat and tried to give the words a properly upper-class nasal twang. *Adele could've done it much better....* "I would regard any such action as a violation of my agreement with you—a despicable violation! In fact, I intend to transfer the *Duilio* to the Bennarian naval forces in exchange for the destroyer *Sibyl*. Which in turn—"

Krychek's face had flushed, then gone pale. Elemere laid her palm on the Landholder's bearded cheek. She smiled at Daniel as she spoke reassuringly in an undertone.

"—I propose to make over to you, milord," Daniel continued. "I hope you'll consider the *Sibyl* fair recompense for the *Mazeppa* and your valuable services to Leary of Bantry in my personal activities on Bennaria and here."

"By God, Leary," Krychek said.

He stood and reached over the table. Bartolomeo jumped back to avoid a brawl, but the Landholder merely gripped Daniel's hand and pumped it enthusiastically. "By *God*, you're a man!" he said.

Daniel rose and clasped the Landholder with both hands, then disengaged by stepping back. He looked to either side, largely to break eye contact as a hint to Krychek that it was time to sit down again.

"I realize that it may seem I'm being cavalier with other people's property," he said, "but I'm able to be the honest broker in this case since I have no share of the proceeds."

"The starship *Rainha*, you said," Bartolomeo noted with a fierce glance. "That's surely something, is it not?"

"The *Rainha* was captured on Pellegrino by persons under my command," Adele said, her voice rising. "In no respect does that affair become the business of yourself or Dunbar's World, sirrah!"

Daniel couldn't see his friend's face from his present angle, but Mahler flinched back as she focused her gaze on him. "Marshal," Adele said, enunciating with unusual precision even for her, "I suggest you muzzle your dog or I'll have him whipped into the sea. On my oath as a Mundy!"

Adele wouldn't ordinarily do that, Daniel thought. The shoulder wound, or perhaps what she'd been doing when she was wounded, was affecting her.

Loudly he said, "Remember your place, Mundy! I'm the ranking officer here."

He paused, then went on, "*I* will have him whipped into the sea."

Bartolomeo's mouth opened and closed twice. His expression wobbled between fear and anger as he tried to determine whether he was being threatened or mocked. *Both, I suppose*, Daniel decided.

"Commander, mistress," Mahler said. "We beg your pardon." He sounded sincere.

Adele visibly relaxed. She turned, looking up to Daniel, and nodded. "Sorry, sir," she said quietly.

"Quite all right, Mundy," Daniel said as he settled back onto his chair. "You were provoked. Now, getting back to business—"

He smiled brightly at the assembled group. Colonel Quinn looked extremely uncomfortable. Daniel wondered if it'd been a misstep at a meeting with Headman Ferguson and his magnates which'd cost Quinn his nose, ears, and position. That wasn't going to happen here, but Quinn was correct in feeling out of place.

"—there's the matter of crew for the *Duilio*. Many of her spacers aren't Pellegrinians, of course. They should be as willing to work for Bennaria as they were for Chancellor Arruns. Nonetheless, a prudent commander—"

He nodded to Corius and grinned; Corius grinned in reply. Quinn edged his chair a little further back from the table.

"—would want his officers to be men—"

Daniel would've said "persons" if he'd been speaking to a Cinnabar audience, but "men" was precisely the correct usage here.

"—of unquestioned courage, skill, and loyalty. With that in mind, Councilor Corius, I suggest you discuss the matter with Landholder Krychek. And Krychek?"

He cocked an eyebrow at the Landholder. Elemere was gripping his right hand in both of hers, looking happily excited.

"Aye, by God!" Krychek said. From the words and expression alone he might've been furious, but Daniel thought he knew the fellow well enough to be sure that wasn't the case.

"You were considering entering service with Headman Ferguson," Daniel continued. "I suggest—"

"Bloody *hell*, you don't want to do that!" blurted Quinn, shocked out of his worried silence. He tapped his nose. Though the shape was natural, the pale pink of the tip ended in a sharp line where the rest of the face was reddened and wind-burned from the weather here on Mandelfarne Island. "He's a right psycho, that one, and I'm the man to tell you!"

"Yes, I'm sure you can, Colonel," Daniel said. "On a more positive note, Councilor Corius has proved to be a colleague whom I could trust and respect. Given that he led the assault on Mandelfarne himself instead of waiting in safety on the mainland, he may even—"

Daniel let his grin spread into a broad, completely honest smile.

"—be crazy enough to command a man of your demonstrated courage, Landholder."

Krychek guffawed and turned to Corius. "So?" he said. "We talk, yes? But after the commander has finished."

He gave Daniel a look that was certainly well-meaning but would've seemed normal at feeding time in a carnivore's cage.

"The commander, he is bloody worth listening to, by *God!*" he said.

Daniel gave the Landholder a nod of appreciation, but when he shifted back to Corius he let the smile fade to neutrality. "Though my last subject isn't really a matter for group as a whole," he said, "I'd like to say it, so to speak, in public. Councilor, your planet has seen a good deal of disruption recently. I'd expect that to continue for a time after you've returned to take up your responsibilities."

"Go on, Commander," Corius said politely. A less intelligent politician would've bragged about his intentions. Corius was no more the man to make that mistake than Speaker Leary had been when he planned the Proscriptions.

"The Government of Bennaria is no business of mine nor of the Republic I represent," Daniel said quietly. "But the safety of Cinnabar citizens is a proper concern both of the Senate and of the RCN. The Cinnabar consular agent on Bennaria, Master Luff—"

"The Manco factor," Corius said; not loudly nor in a hostile tone, but with great clarity.

"I'm not talking about Manco House or its employees," Daniel said, just a touch more harshly. "I'm talking about the *Cinnabar* representative, Master Luff. A man whose courage in a difficult situation made this victory possible. I might describe him as a friend."

Daniel gestured generally toward the scene around them. Ap Glynn had been skilled as well as lucky to land on the east end of the island, near the *Rainha* and the wreckage of the *Greybudd*. The landing beacon still worked, if only because the Bennarian Volunteers hadn't thought to disable it.

The prison enclosure was in the muddy high ground of the island's center. The cruiser's dorsal cannon and those of the *Sibyl* and *Princess Cecile* on the shore to the west supplemented the razor ribbon and quickly built guard towers.

Corius laughed. Someone who knew what to look for—and Daniel did—could notice Fallert, Hogg and Tovera all relax minusculely.

"I'll need officials whom I can trust in difficult situations," Corius said. "Since the slave trade on Bennaria will be ending shortly, Master Luff's present employers will have no further use for his services. I'll contact him on my return."

He smiled. Unlike the laughter a moment before, the smile was cold as a glass knife.

"I don't need to be taught that Daniel Leary is a bad enemy," Corius said, indicating their surroundings with a sweep of his chin. "Rather, I'll make it a policy to convince him that I'm a good friend."

Krychek banged the table with the flat of his hand. "Done, then?" he demanded.

"Done, I believe," Daniel agreed.

"Then time for a drink," said Krychek. "Many drinks, by God!"

Daniel, wrung out but completely relaxed, could only nod. His tongue was too dry from adrenaline to speak another word.

The sound of knuckles ringing on metal outside the missile command trailer brought Adele to her feet. She reached into her pocket by reflex, but there was no need for that now.

She smiled wryly as she stepped to the doorway: it was the wrong reflex besides. She'd reached into her left tunic pocket, but the little pistol was still in her right.

Daniel stood ten feet away. When she appeared in the ragged opening from which Tovera had blown the door, he threw away the steel cartridge box he'd knocked on to signal and gave her a cautious smile.

"I won't intrude if you're busy," he said. "I just thought I'd come see, ah, how you were getting along."

Adele transferred the pistol to its usual location. Her left arm still twinged, but not enough to pose a problem. Not a problem as great as having the wrong reflex in a crisis, anyway.

"Well enough," she said, amused to notice that she'd weighed the question before answering it. That in its way proved she was all right. "Come in, if you like. Or—"

When she turned back into the command trailer, she realized what a shambles it was. A stinking shambles. The corpses of the Alliance missile controllers had been buried with the Pellegrinian dead in a trench dug by a captured backhoe, but nobody'd tried to mop up blood and fluids flung about by the bullets. The splatters had quickly ripened in the heat.

One of the operators had fallen into his arcing console. The odor of his burned flesh remained as the only monument the man would ever have.

"Here, let me get my data unit," Adele said, slipping the wands into their slots as she spoke. "We'll find a place outside to sit. I suppose we could go back to the ship. The *Sissie.*"

"No need," said Daniel, gesturing to a short line of sandbags interlaid with boards from packing cases. The bunker it'd been part of had collapsed, but this knee-high section of wall remained. "I've been in one ship or another for the past two days, and I don't mind being out in the open."

He grinned. The expression was real, but Adele knew her friend well enough to see the caution still in his eyes.

"I'm a country boy at heart, remember," he said as they sat down together. He cleared his throat and added, "I've been overseeing the installation of the new motors on the *Duilio*. It's the *Duilio* for now; I suppose Corius will change the name."

He chuckled. "Hogg's, ah, befriended the widow of one of Arruns' officers. They've gone off on a picnic, Hogg said."

"I'd heard," said Adele. She let her mind follow the direction the statement led her, then shied away with a grimace. Of course it was just information, rather like the process of decomposition. . . .

"Heard?" said Daniel. "That is, ah . . ."

"I'm not spying on Hogg's private life, Daniel," Adele said in mild reproof. "Fallert and Tovera have gone with them. Fallert borrowed the Councilor's aircar for the purpose, as a matter of fact."

"Good God," said Daniel, blinking. "Good *God*. Fallert and Tovera and . . ."

He stopped and licked his lips. "Well, that's a good thing," he said, though the cheeriness of his tone didn't ring quite true. "I was afraid that Hogg was driving the car. Whatever he thinks, I know very well that he'd not safe at the controls."

"Yes," said Adele, agreeing with both what Daniel'd said and what he determinedly wasn't saying. *It's not our business, after all.* "And we also don't have to worry about them being set upon by bandits while they're—"

She grimaced. "Concentrating on other matters," she said, sounding even to herself as though she had something unpleasant in her mouth.

A pair of earthmovers, part of the Pellegrinian siege equipment, were crawling from the cruiser to the *Princess Cecile* with a missile slung between them. Spacers whom Adele didn't recognize were withdrawing another missile from *Duilio's* loading hatch while a bulldozer and a backhoe maneuvered into position to take it.

Daniel followed the line of Adele's eyes. "Some of the Pellegrinians decided they'd rather be Sissies than see how Chancellor Arruns felt about the way things worked out here," he said. "We've got proper missile handlers now."

He smiled and gestured toward the equipment squealing past loudly. "Strictly speaking, we haven't handed the *Duilio* over to the Bennarian navy yet," he added. "It seemed to me simple prudence to equip the *Sissie* to fight if we have to on the way home."

Adele smiled faintly. *Fight if we have a chance to,* she thought. *As we well might, with Commander Leary in command.*

"The *Duilio'll* have forty-three missiles left after we've filled our magazines," Daniel said. "Bennarian ships haven't launched that many in the past generation. Of course that might change. A great deal's likely to change when Councilor Corius takes power, I'm afraid."

Adele noted the concern underlying the words. She shrugged and said, "The people of Bennaria deserve a better government than they have now. Perhaps Corius will give it to them. Not that it's a proper concern of mine, so long as he remains a friend to Cinnabar."

Mistress Sand would care about that; therefore Adele cared also. From the beginning of Adele's activities as a Cinnabar spy, Mistress Sand had been as much of a friend as a superior officer.

"One thing that puzzles me about the Councilor's plans . . .," Daniel said. His voice trailed off as he watched spacers walk hooks dangling from the *Sissie's* crane into eyebolts on the missile they were about to take aboard.

Catching himself, he grinned apologetically at Adele and continued, "Saying he was going to end slavery on Bennaria, I mean. Now, I'm in favor of that, of course, but frankly, Corius hadn't struck me as moral reformer himself."

"I don't think he is," Adele said. "That was my suggestion—and before you ask, no, I'm not a reformer either, merely an observer. I pointed out to him that the abolition of slavery would destroy the basis of his fellow Councilors' wealth. That'd make it much more difficult for them to attempt a counter-revolution."

"Ah!" said Daniel. "I see. Yes indeed, I see."

Adele saw his eyes flick toward the trailer. It was a tiny motion, there and back, but nonetheless it showed her that he really *did* understand. That shouldn't have been a surprise; it was Daniel, after all. It surprised her nonetheless.

Aloud and more harshly than she'd intended, she said, "I'm quite sure Corius will have quite a number of people executed out of hand also, Daniel. But that's none of my business either, because *I* won't be the one shooting them."

Adele paused, playing back in her mind the words, the tone, of what she'd just said. She pressed her fingertips to her brow and her thumbs to her jawbone, covering her down-turned face for a moment but not closing her eyes. The last thing she wanted just now was to close her eyes to the present, leaving only memories to fill her mind.

"I'm sorry, Daniel," she said, looking at him as she crossed her hands primly in her lap. She nodded toward the trailer. "I wasn't inside to remind me, you know. I was just punishing myself. I didn't need reminders."

"You don't need punishment either, Adele," Daniel said quietly. "But I don't suppose I can convince you of that."

"Not emotionally, no," Adele said, smiling wryly. "Intellectually I prefer a universe in which I killed another... a number, I'm honestly not sure. In which I killed another dozen or so soldiers to a universe in which I failed, so that you and two thousand Bennarian Volunteers were killed instead. But emotionally, what I see in the gunsight stays with me."

The sounds of heavy equipment quieted to a grumble of idling diesels. For the time being the chain hoists were still and the diamond saws silent.

"*Then oh then, the loved ones gone . . .,*" came a clear, rich voice.

Adele turned; Elemere stood on the cruiser's turret, singing without a microphone. Krychek, Vesey, and a number of others sat on chairs behind him, but on the ground below hundreds of off-duty spacers listened.

"*Wake the pure celestial song...,*" Elemere sang. He was in full costume, the blond wig and a dress that seemed a shimmer of sunlight.

"Woetjans asked if it'd be all right," Daniel murmured. "She'd heard about the show at the Diamond Palace but she'd missed it in Charlestown."

"*Angel voices greet us there....*"

"I said of course, if Elemere was willing."

"*In the music, in the air,*" Elemere sang, concluding the piece.

As the crowd of spacers cheered, Adele felt her lips spread in an unintended smile. "I have difficulty imagining my mother and father as part of a chorus of angels," she said, looking at Daniel again. "My sister Agatha, perhaps. But that's an intellectual difficulty. The song—"

The song by a decent, caring human being who is alive because I was willing to kill people who were neither decent nor caring... but those words didn't reach her lips.

"—helps emotionally despite that. I don't understand emotion, Daniel."

He rose. "I don't think anyone does, Adele," he said. "Let's move closer, shall we? I'd like to hear—"

"*Little white snowdrop...,*" Elemere sang, beginning her next number.

The innocent delight of Daniel's smile shone brighter than sunstruck gold. And for the time being, it washed away the last of the memories that'd returned Adele to the bullet-scarred trailer.